Sign up for our newsletter to hear
about new and upcoming releases.

www.ylva-publishing.com

Other Books by Wendy Hudson

Mine to Keep
Four Steps

Meant
TO BE Me

Wendy Hudson

Acknowledgements

Thanks to the Ylva Publishing team for their hard work and continued support.

To Andrea Bramhall, much love and thanks to you as my friend and editor. You got me through another one and somehow we still kind of like each other.

My fellow writer pals have been invaluable and are always there for random ramblings and to cheer me up when every word is a load of crap. Huge love and thanks to G Benson, who always just gets it. To Clare Ashton, for her two-hundred or so title suggestions (I'm only exaggerating a little). To A.L. Brooks, who I can rely on for an honest opinion. And to Clare Lydon, who is never too busy to buy me a pint.

To L.A. Hill, friend and beta reader extraordinaire, for our conversation that never ends and her world class GIF skills.

Thanks to my colleagues on the day job, who have always been a fantastic source of support and encouragement. In particular, Susan Burns, who listens to me talk books on an almost daily basis and never complains. Also, Kay Sillars, Fiona Montgomery, Stephen Low, Danny Phillips, and Trisha Hamilton—thank you all for reading, for the kind words and humour, kicks up the arse, and boosts of confidence whenever I need them.

Thanks to Shona Moir, for her endless and infectious enthusiasm—now hurry up and get that book finished!

Love and thanks to all my family and friends, who continue to cheer me on and tell anyone who'll listen about my books. If you ever meet my Mum in a pub, I guarantee you'll leave with a copy of my book ordered.

Special thanks to Tree Middlemiss, for her support and insight into the world of policing.

So much love to Lynsey Duguid, for picking up the slack and never complaining (much). Thanks for making the best tea, and for bringing biscuits and hugs with it. I couldn't do it without you.

A heartfelt thanks to all the readers, book groups, reviewers, and champions of this genre—those who protect it fiercely and keep us writers going.

Finally, thanks to Graeme Coutts, for that line in *Mine to Keep*, because I forgot last time and he won't let me hear the end of it…

To Susan—the real Work Wife

Chapter 1

THE BRIDGE WAS SO CLOSE.

Eilidh huffed a breath and swore aloud. "Fuck." The word came out in a prolonged wheeze. "C'mon, Grey. Nearly there. You're. Nearly. Bloody. There." It was a straight stretch now, less than fifty metres. She screwed her face up and focused on every step that pounded the pavement.

"Yes!" She touched the middle lamppost, threw her arms in the air, and then bent double and concentrated on taking long, slow breaths rather than the ragged ones causing stars in her vision. Finally, able to stand upright again, she leaned her thighs against the cold brick of the bridge wall and braced her arms on top of it, taking a moment to admire the view.

The River Ness wove its slow path below her. At this time of year, meandering blocks of ice jostled one another on their journey, destined to melt before they reached the great Loch Ness. Streetlights lining its banks still projected their yellow orbs; the sun hadn't yet appeared to snuff them out. The castle on the hill glowed white under blinding floodlight, creating a ghostly effect that was surreal yet friendly, unimposing despite its fortress status.

Her gaze flitted from one landmark to the next, but always returned to the shadow of Ben Wyvis almost thirty miles in the distance. She scanned its shadowy outline as her breathing slowed and her heartrate returned to normal.

An impatient voice snapped her out of the reverie, and she turned to see a harried-looking woman headed her way, muttering obscenities into her phone. It was held in place with her shoulder, while one hand balanced a tray of four coffees and the other rooted in a huge handbag slung over the opposite shoulder.

Eilidh knew she should have called out; she saw it coming. One bag strap slipped from the stranger's shoulder, followed in slow motion by the other. As she came level with Eilidh, the weight of the bag yanked the crook of her arm and the tray toppled. In her vain attempt to save the cups of coffee, the phone dropped with a clatter alongside one unlucky cup.

"Oh shit." Eilidh reached to catch the underside of the bag in order to relieve the weight. "Are you okay?"

The woman flinched at first, then looked embarrassed. She glanced from the precarious tray to her phone on the ground and then the bag Eilidh was holding. "Aye, aye. I'm fine. Thank you. Would you mind?" She held the tray in Eilidh's direction, and Eilidh dutifully took it.

The woman bent to retrieve her phone, and Eilidh winced when she saw the cracked blank screen. "Not a great start to the day, eh?"

The woman shook her head. "At least it was only the boss's coffee I dropped." She retrieved the now-empty cup from its brown puddle on the pavement and jammed it back in to the tray. "She never returns the favour anyway."

Eilidh chuckled. "I'd call that karma, then."

Knackered phone in bag, bag back on shoulder, with spots of coffee wiped from her sleeve, the woman was set. She reached for the tray. "Thanks again…" She drew the last word out, waiting for a name.

"Eilidh. And it was no problem…"

"Darcy." The woman returned her name and held Eilidh's gaze for a moment. She gestured around them with her free hand. "It's rare I see anyone about the town this time of the morning. Especially on a Saturday. What on earth forces you out of bed to run before the sun comes up? In minus temperatures, no less?"

Eilidh patted a gloved hand to her tummy. "Christmas belly. It's my resolution to finally get rid of it."

"Finally? It's only the eighth of January."

"Ah, but this band of chub has been hanging around since at least Christmas 2011."

Darcy laughed. "Oh, I know how that goes. Good intentions in January, then suddenly you're scoffing chocolate eggs the entire Easter weekend."

"Exactly," Eilidh agreed. "Then it's summer barbecues and beer gardens, followed by an autumn of eating half a loaf with every bowl of broth."

"And then we're back to Christmas." Darcy nodded her resignation. "I feel your struggle. It's a vicious circle."

"Indeed. Hence the six a.m. self-inflicted-pain regime. What's your excuse for being up at this ungodly hour on a weekend?"

"Conference call to Hong Kong. They're seven hours ahead and, apparently, it's urgent. So…" Darcy took a cup from the tray and offered it Eilidh's way. "I can only offer black, no sugar, I'm afraid. I'll never survive if I don't get my fix, and my work pal will be raging if she doesn't get hers either. The other guy. Meh. He'll live."

Eilidh waved her away. "Not for me, thanks, and also not necessary. Honest. I need to get moving again and get home before I start seizing up in this cold anyway."

"Okay, well, thanks again for your help." Darcy glanced at her watch. "Crap, I better get a move on too. It was really nice to meet you." She held Eilidh's gaze for a moment longer and seemed about to say something more before changing her mind. Her head dropped. "Your shoelace is undone."

Eilidh looked down. Oh, hell, this meant she had to squat. "Cheers for that. I hope the call goes okay."

Darcy smiled and turned to go. Eilidh watched her a moment, making sure she didn't turn back and catch the grimace that would accompany her squat to tie her lace.

As was her luck, midway down to the ground, Darcy turned and headed back her way. Eilidh pasted a smile on her face despite the burning in her thighs. "Hey again."

"Hey. Erm…" Darcy shifted nervously, and Eilidh wished she'd spit it out. Her hamstrings were screaming. "I know this is random. It's six-thirty in the morning, and we've only just met but…well, maybe I could buy you a coffee you might actually enjoy? To say thanks for being so kind."

Dammit. Eilidh was pretty sure she was stuck down there now. She held up a finger. "Give me one sec." Her gloved fingers fumbled impatiently before the lace was finally tied. Then she held up an arm. "You could return the kindness right now and help me up if you like?"

Darcy chuckled and reached a hand down for support. "I guess the seizing has already started."

Eilidh struggled to her feet with a groan. "Yup. I'm going to pay big time for this later." She leaned back against the bridge wall. "Thanks."

"You're welcome." Darcy tugged at the thick green woollen scarf wrapped around her neck. "Does this mean we're even and you don't fancy that coffee?"

It finally clicked in Eilidh's mind that Darcy wasn't asking to say thank you. She was asking her out. Holy crap. It had been a long time. "Sure I do." Her mouth engaged before her brain, and Darcy's smile stopped Eilidh from backtracking. "You got a pen in that shoulder suitcase you call a bag?"

After much rummaging, Darcy produced a pen and a crumpled receipt, and Eilidh dutifully recited her number onto it. Her real number. She was doing this. She was inviting Darcy, another woman, to get in touch. To take her for coffee.

Darcy held up her broken phone as if to remind Eilidh. "As this has failed me, I'm going to be one of those people and give you a business card." She seemed a little tentative when offering it over. "And now you know where I work."

"*Infinite Energy Renewables. Darcy Harris. Senior Engineer.* Wow. That sounds cool."

Darcy shrugged self-consciously. "Not really. It's mostly dealing with tedious amounts of data." She glanced at her watch again. "Okay, now I definitely have to go. It really was lovely to meet you, Eilidh. I'll text you once my phone is fixed. Yeah?"

"Sure." Eilidh raised a hand as Darcy headed toward the high street. "I'll look forward to it."

Chapter 2

Darcy managed to make it the rest of the way to the office with the three remaining coffees intact.

"It's six forty-five on a Saturday morning and you're smiling." Anja popped her head above their desk divider. "There's something wrong with you."

"Moi?" Darcy held a hand to her chest. "I'm perfectly fine."

"Which is why there's something wrong with you." Anja skirted around her desk and nabbed a coffee from the tray. She popped the top and sniffed. "Ah. Chai latte. Have I told you today that I love you?"

"You talking to me or the coffee?"

Anja took a sip and sighed with pleasure. "Both."

Darcy relieved the tray of her own drink before turning and leaving the last one on Joe's desk. It was guaranteed he'd arrive with a minute to spare before their seven o'clock conference call.

"So why are you so perfectly fine this morning?" Anja perched on her desk and raised an inquisitive eyebrow.

Darcy craned her neck toward their boss's office. The door was shut, and being Saturday, no one else was around. "I think I may have got myself a date."

"A date? Really?" Anja seemed surprised, which irked Darcy a little. "I thought you were done with that given the last disaster."

She waved her hand dismissively. "Who hasn't said that after a break-up? Or a no-show, as the case was last time. And the time before that."

"And the one before that," Anja added with a wry smile.

"Whatever." Darcy wasn't deterred. "We all know it really means: done with it until the next one comes along. Or jogs along like this morning."

"You were jogging?" Now Anja's eyebrows had shot to her hairline. "Seriously, what's wrong with you?"

"Cheeky bitch. She was jogging, I was on my way to work. She helped me out when I dropped the boss's coffee, and my bloody phone, so to say thanks I asked if I could buy her a cup sometime."

"Smooth."

"It wasn't really. But she said yes, so that's all that matters."

"Who said yes to what?" Joe breezed out of the lift ruffling snow from his hair. "Snow's on again."

"None of your business." Darcy glared at Anja with her 'keep your mouth shut' eyes. "And no shit." She pointed at the floor-to-ceiling windows that made up the entire front of their building. It made her almost dizzy to look out. The snow was falling thick and fast.

"Aw, don't be like that. You two never let me in on the gossip. You're so sexist."

Darcy nearly choked on her first sip of coffee. "Sexist? Are you kidding? More like because you're the boss's pet. You can't be trusted."

"Pftt, that's bollocks and you know it. She'd let you away with bloody murder, Darcy."

On cue, the boss's door swung open and she gestured towards them. "Joe. I need you a minute first. You two"—she pointed between Anja and Darcy—"go get the video link set up."

"Run along, pet," Anja muttered under her breath in Joe's direction.

He gave her the finger but obediently went on his way. When the door closed behind him, they both burst in to laughter. "Do you think they're shagging?" It was Anja who asked what they were both thinking.

"Nah." Darcy picked up some files and started heading in the direction of the conference room. "But I think he wishes they were."

"I don't know. I always thought he had a little soft spot for you, Darcy."

"So you keep saying, but there's no way. I'm definitely not his type. Besides, he's certainly not mine, so what does it matter?"

"True." Anja hit some buttons on a remote and prepared them for the call to Hong Kong. "Tell me about this mystery date, then?"

Darcy shrugged. "Nothing much else to tell. We had a bit of a laugh at my clumsiness, and despite all the sweating and red face, there was something about her that got my attention. She had a kind face, and I thought what the hell. You know I'm a sucker for the sporty kind."

Anja rolled her eyes. "Maybe that's where you're going wrong? All that obsessing over miles run and calories burned—where's the time to be someone who's actually fun?"

"Whatever. I dropped my bloody phone, though, so I had to be all cheesy and give her a business card. Then I said I'd text her and went on my way. The end."

"You gave her your card?" Anja stopped midway to reaching for one of the files. "She knows where you work then?"

Darcy braced herself for the telling off. "Erm…yeah."

"For fuck's sake, Darcy. You do remember what the police said, right? About being careful around strangers? About not handing over any personal info to someone you don't know?"

"I know, I know." She put on her whiny 'please don't be mad' voice. "It was a moment of weakness, and by the time I thought of that I was already handing it over. I would have looked a right weirdo suddenly grabbing it back."

"Did you not think looking like a weirdo might be better than the alternative?"

"Woah. Harsh. What happened to not thinking about worst-case stalker scenarios?"

Anja sighed. "Well, that was before you started handing out your business card to strangers you randomly meet in the city at the crack of dawn. I worry. That's all."

"I know." Darcy moved to drape her arms around Anja's shoulders. She resisted for a moment, then allowed the hug. "But if you think about it, stalker person already knows where I work. I have a dozen bouquets of flowers, chocolates, champagne, and gig tickets to prove it."

Anja stepped away and busied herself sorting through the reports she'd need for the call. "True. Still, I'm not sure going on a date with someone you just met in the street is a good idea."

Darcy grinned. "Why? You jealous?"

It was a running joke, as if she'd ever have a chance with someone like Anja Olsen. Beautiful, smart, fiercely loyal, and wonderfully funny Anja. With her long blonde hair that always sat perfectly over her shoulders, and her cute-as-anything Norwegian accent. Inflected with enough of a Scottish twang here and there to make it even more perfect.

Anja—who was also married, and according to her, to the perfect guy. Weren't they all? She'd had a bit of a thing for Anja in the beginning and had even thought it was reciprocated. They had worked in separate teams, but Anja had always seemed to go out of her way to speak: in the lift, the kitchen, passing in a corridor. But a workplace romance had burnt Darcy in the past, so she had quickly talked herself out of the idea and hadn't allowed herself to be anything but polite. She loved and needed her job too much to jeopardise it.

Then Anja had become her team's Lead Engineer, and Darcy had spotted the framed photo of a smiling husband on her desk. Before long, a strong friendship had replaced any potential fantasy that had simmered within Darcy, but she didn't mind. Anja had become one of her closest friends, which were as rare to her as girlfriends.

"You wish." Anja winked. "And you're taking me to that gig, by the way."

"Do you still think that's a good idea? Shouldn't I hand them over to the police to go with the other stuff?"

"Nonsense. Who knows how many people will have handled them before they got posted to you? I doubt the person they're after even touched them. They're useless as evidence."

"But what about how they were paid for? If they were bought online, there might be an account to trace. A card payment?"

Anja shook her head wearily. "As if. I think we know better by now. That gig was sold out months ago. My guess is they bought some extortionately priced tour tickets off a private seller."

Darcy's shoulders sagged. She remained hopeful her mystery torturer would slip up at some point, but the signs so far showed it was unlikely. The police kept talking about escalation and complacency. That one of those would occur and that would be their opening. Darcy knew which scenario she preferred.

"Wow, you really want to go to that gig, don't you?"

Anja smirked. "And you don't?"

"Well…" Darcy couldn't deny she had been dying to see the band for ages. "Maybe a little. Although why you would think I'm taking you…"

Before Darcy could attempt to wind Anja up and pretend she had someone else she'd rather take, Boss Woman Bridget sailed through the conference room door, with Joe close on her heels. "When you're quite finished, ladies. Can we get on with this?"

"Aye." Both women nodded.

"Then let's get it done." She sat down and hit the call button. "I've far more interesting people I'd rather be spending my Saturday with."

Darcy strolled the high street without a care in the world. That's why it was so easy to watch her. It had become second nature to slip from doorway to doorway, use the crowds and traffic as cover, never allowing Darcy's image to get too far away.

Part of the thrill of the follow was that Darcy had no idea who watched her and when. Who hunted and haunted every part of her life. She was oblivious to the fact that she was unwittingly sharing every secret and sacred moment.

This close to the anniversary was always the hardest as the thoughts of the past ran riot and the question of what might have been mercilessly nagged. Meanwhile, Darcy continued on with her life completely unaware.

The familiar lump lodged in their throat and grew day by day. It showed no sign of diminishing, along with the anger and the memories.

Darcy approached the bridge, the same one she'd met that girl on early in the morning. Was she smiling? Remembering the moment? Every ounce of happiness that Darcy experienced gnawed and irritated. Why did she get to be so happy? Why had she deserved it more? Why was it fair that other people should suffer while she was so blissfully ignorant? Decent parents were a precious gift to be cherished. Why should some people have that and others get nothing?

In the beginning, it had all been so innocent.

The voice had been merely a faint murmur.

But it had been a long road to this point and things had changed. Years of research and sacrifice to track Darcy down. Then more years of calculating and plotting, as the objective had become clear.

As the voice had grown louder.

Torture her with uncertainty until she couldn't stand it anymore. Darcy had never witnessed someone she loved torn down, had never had her spirit broken by others. Her sunny outlook had never been challenged. She needed to experience and understand what the real world felt like. What a childhood of scorn and pain could cause.

For a long time, that had always been the plan, but lately some things had changed. It was becoming harder each time to witness the disappointment on her face. To execute each scheme knowing its ultimate effect. An unexpected and unwanted struggle had begun to materialise.

The voice stirred inside. A reminder of why it couldn't be stopped, despite the inkling of new doubt.

He thought they were better than us. He loved them more. He chose her over you.

She needs to know the truth. Someone must pay for what was done to us.

For what we became.

And she is all that remains.

Chapter 3

IT WASN'T ONLY THE CHRISTMAS belly that had Eilidh running the morning she'd met Darcy. She'd awoken too early with a weight on her chest. In her nightmare she was suffocating, as something nameless, faceless, and bodiless pressed down on her and sucked the air from her lungs. It was no better after she'd gasped a few panicked breaths. The room had been stuffy, the central heating up too high, and the walls had pressed in from every side.

After pulling on her joggers, a cosy hat, and gloves, she'd crept downstairs in an attempt not to wake her girlfriend, Claire, who was sleeping in the spare room. But it turned out she hadn't even made it to the spare room. Eilidh had found her asleep on the sofa, the TV on low, an empty bottle of wine on the table. She'd thought about stirring her, putting on some, coffee and finally having "the talk", but a glance at the clock changed her mind. Six in the morning probably wasn't the time to be breaking up with someone.

The early morning frost had bitten at first, until her legs stretched and the blood began to pump and only her nose felt the chill. She'd wanted distance, so she'd cut back around their street, taking the long way through the park, until eventually the road to town had opened up before her. Normally she'd avoid Inverness and head in the opposite direction out along the back lanes towards Loch Ness, but so early on a weekend morning, there'd be few souls about.

The bridge was to have been her halfway mark, but instead it had become her final destination. For her run, at least. After watching Darcy walk away, she knew her muscles would protest if she tried to get going again, and another injury would do her no good if she wanted to get back to work any time soon. So, she found a café and grabbed a cup of coffee and a newspaper before walking along the river bank towards Ness Island.

The paper wasn't for reading. She found a bench and used it as a buffer between her arse and the snow. Around her, the city began to come to life, and she watched for a while, focusing on nothing in particular but sipping her coffee and the heavy flakes as they hit the water. Eventually, though, Claire found her way back into Eilidh's thoughts, and she sighed.

This was not going to be pretty.

They both knew it was over, had known for a long time. Eilidh couldn't even remember the last time they'd shared a meal or a laugh, never mind shared a bed. She'd known that night for certain, the night of the incident; they'd finally voiced the words they both were thinking. Finally had that difficult conversation. But then the world had come crashing down, and now guilt kept Claire from leaving. Eilidh knew it was going to be up to her.

She thought of Darcy. What had she been thinking giving Darcy her number? Agreeing to coffee? She might have already started to move on from Claire in her mind, but until it was official, this wasn't the way to do things. If Darcy texted, she would explain and hope she understood. She seemed so lovely; Eilidh hated to let her down.

She had to admit the excitement that had flushed through her when Darcy asked her for coffee was something she hadn't felt in a long time. But Claire still came first, no matter their state of affairs. After nine years together, they both deserved to move on, and Eilidh knew only she could release Claire from the guilt. It had been almost six months since the incident. It was time to set them both free.

Chapter 4

It had been three long, phoneless days, but Darcy finally had the device fixed and back in her possession. She'd collected it that morning and was gutted they'd had to reset it. All her photos were lost forever and, not for the first time, she cursed herself for not backing them up.

She held Eilidh's number in her hand and tentatively typed it in to her contacts, saying each number out loud so as not to get it wrong.

"What are you up to over there, rain woman?" Anja appeared above her monitor. Glasses perched on the end of her nose, and she peered over them curiously at Darcy.

"My phone's finally fixed. I'm making sure I get Eilidh's number right." She turned her attention back to the screen.

"Ah, that's this mystery woman's name, is it? How do you even spell that?" Anja stood and stretched her fingertips up to the ceiling. "Cup of tea?"

"Sounds good." Darcy got up to follow her to the kitchen, keeping her focus on the phone. "It's pronounced A-lee but spelt E. I. L. I. D. H."

Anja frowned. "You Scots and your weird language."

"Aye, like you can talk. With all your Ks and letters not even in our alphabet."

"Touché. Are you really going to text her, then?" Anja was busying herself getting the tea started, and Darcy heard the hint of accusation in her voice. She was clearly trying to avoid eye contact, which meant a lecture was probably on its way.

"Yes. Why wouldn't I? And don't give me all the chat about the stalker. If it wasn't for my clumsiness, I would have never stopped, and we would never have spoken. I'm sure she's perfectly innocent of any crimes you're about to charge her with."

"It's not only about her and you know it. You can act tough all you want around other folk, but I know you, remember? I see it in your face every time a call comes to say something has arrived at reception for you. Even when it turns out to be something you've ordered yourself."

"I know, but…"

"But what? I've seen the tears and I've seen the fear. Remember the disaster when that last girl legitimately sent you flowers and you freaked out on the phone to her and screamed for her never to do it again? Have you heard from her since? No. Aren't you better sticking with folk you know for now? Until the police catch up to this freak?"

"And what if they never do?" Darcy couldn't help her own harsh tone. She was angry and frustrated by the whole situation and didn't need this from someone who was meant to be her best friend. "I mean, do you ever *really* know anyone?"

Anja stopped stirring the tea and stared in to space a moment. "I guess not," she whispered. Then she was crying.

"Oh my God, Anja. What is it? What did I say?" Darcy moved towards her and tried to pull her in to a hug, but Anja waved her away.

"I'm okay. Sorry. It's fine." She propped her glasses on her head before yanking a piece of kitchen towel from the roll and swiping it briskly under her eyes. "Honest. It's nothing."

Darcy frowned. "Clearly it's not nothing. You can talk to me, you know?"

"I know." She smiled, but it was obviously forced. "Really, I'm all right. Time of the month, that's all."

Darcy didn't believe her but didn't push. She finished making the tea, passed Anja a mug, and they wandered back to their desks in silence. She heard Anja rummage for a minute in her desk drawer before producing a half-eaten pack of biscuits. "Fancy helping me finish these?" She smiled as she extended the peace offering.

"Sure." She took the pack and relieved it of a biscuit. Darcy considered prodding again about the sudden tears, but after over two years sharing a cubicle, she'd learned Anja would speak when ready and not a second sooner. She settled for a safer topic. "How's Jason, by the way? When does he get home?"

Jason.

Anja's perfect husband.

He worked offshore on the oil rigs and ships and could be gone for anywhere between two weeks and two months, depending on what the job was and where he was sent.

"Tomorrow. Apparently, I'm being treated to a special culinary feast, and he has something to tell me."

"Sounds perfect and intriguing. Maybe he's finally got that onshore job?" For Anja's happiness, Darcy hoped so. She couldn't help but feel a little jealous; despite Jason's long absences, Anja still had someone. By the way she talked, it sounded as if she was his whole world when he was home and more than made up for their lost time.

"Aye, maybe."

Darcy glanced towards the phone on her desk. She hit unlock, and Eilidh's name shone out at her. "You know what? Sod it. I'm definitely going to text Eilidh later."

"Fine. Fine." Anja waved a biscuit her way dismissively. "Don't come running to me when it all goes tits up."

Darcy laughed. "Your confidence is inspiring. But you know I will, right?"

Anja nodded her head resignedly. "Oh, I know."

The day he left had been filled with tears, confusion, and futile screams. With repetitive calls after him down the driveway of, "Daddy, don't leave."

Pathetic.

It hadn't changed anything.

He'd still ruined two lives that day.

Most mothers would have found strength for the sake of a child. Instead, she'd withered and spewed bitterness, pining for a man who had deserted his family without a backwards glance. She might as well have left that day too, rather than torturing those left behind. For years.

She'd been a simple woman, yet full of adventure. Whole days spent exploring the woods behind the house were common: building forts, playing hide-and-seek, camping, fishing, toasting marshmallows on the fire. Idyllic, wonderful days.

After he'd left, adventures for her began with booze, then upgraded to pills. Every day she had demanded, then begged, the universe to know why she hadn't been enough. Every. Single. Day. People had tried to intervene. They'd tried and failed, and gradually she had wasted away, piece by piece. Then one day, she'd disappeared altogether.

He had destroyed her. Destroyed one family for the sake of another.

Yes, this—all of this—was for the right reasons. Any doubts needed to be put aside. Discarded. Only an awful person wouldn't feel some empathy, and a fondness for Darcy was natural. It was human. But Darcy had to know what that day had cost those left behind. She had to know what heartache felt like or she would never understand.

The next gift was sure to get her attention. Darcy would pretend it meant nothing, say she wished it would all stop. But intrigue would still manage to sneak in to her eyes. She'd hate the feeling and try to hide it. Despite the obvious anxiety and second guessing, there would still be thoughtful glances when she sat in a coffee shop or walked in the park. Yes, Darcy would always wonder if someone was watching, her curiosity eager to get a glimpse of something out of the ordinary.

Was she secretly enjoying the attention? At least in some small way?

It was attention that had lured him away, after all.

Chapter 5

I<small>T HAD BEEN FIVE MONTHS</small> and eighteen days since that night, and eleven weeks since Eilidh had come home from the hospital. If home was what she could call the four walls she restlessly roamed within. The doctors and physios, colleagues of hers, were wary of discharging her home earlier than they would have liked. According to her friend Sam, her girlfriend had rarely visited and seemed to give up entirely during the coma stage. So she understood their reluctance.

They worried about the support she would get, knew about her lack of close contact with family, but Eilidh had reassured them. Her mum would stop by regularly; medication would be taken; and exercises would be done. She would eat, sleep, drink, and wash as required. She knew the drill, and they could trust her to do things right.

The doctors didn't know that the night of the incident was the night Eilidh and Claire had decided to end their nine-year relationship. It had been civil, if a little nippy. Neither had wanted to blame the other, but both were incapable of admitting their own failures. They'd talked, drank, picked at a meal, and, in hushed tones across the table, divided up the furniture and the contents of joint bank accounts.

Kids, pets, mortgages—the trinity of reasons for an amicable breakup to turn sour, as well as why many people who shouldn't be together inevitably stayed together. They had none of those things, so three hours later they'd left the restaurant hand in hand with an agreement to begin the process of separation the very next day. Eilidh couldn't remember if either of them had cried. She didn't think so.

She wondered if Claire had held her hand in hospital. Had stroked her hair or her cheek? Had she pleaded for Eilidh to come back to her? Willed her to live? In the months since her return home, Eilidh had been unable to remember a single touch. They were simply strangers now who shared the same space. Biding their time and wondering when it was polite to leave. She knew it was guilt that kept Claire in the spare room, despite the boxes stacked in the hallway.

It was time to have that difficult conversation again. It wouldn't take another three hours, but maybe they could share one last meal.

Eilidh pushed the living room door open and leaned against its frame. Claire sat on the sofa with her back to Eilidh, wine glass in hand. Some shite reality TV show had her attention, and if she felt Eilidh's presence, she didn't acknowledge it.

"Fancy a bite to eat?" Eilidh spoke to the back of her head. "Thought I'd do that chicken pad thai you love."

Claire jerked her head round a little in Eilidh's direction but didn't catch her eye. "Not bothered really. I had a late lunch."

"I don't mind waiting until a bit later." Eilidh tried again, entering the room fully and perching on the arm at the other end of the sofa.

Claire did look at her then. Her lids drooped a little with the effect of the wine, and her gaze held nothing Eilidh recognised. No warmth or friendship. No residual kindness for a woman she'd shared her life with. All Eilidh saw was regret and resentment.

"Don't bother." Claire waved the wine glass in Eilidh's direction. "I've got my dinner sorted." She reached for the remote and pointedly turned up the volume.

The obvious snub, clearly meant to provoke, had its desired effect. Eilidh's despondency quickly sparked and flared to annoyance. How could someone she had once loved become so maddening? She reached and snatched the remote from the coffee table, punching the red off button with purpose.

"You can leave."

"Excuse me?" She had Claire's full attention now.

"I said you can leave." It wasn't how Eilidh had planned it, how she had imagined the conversation in her head, but it was clear their relationship was more than over now. They'd lost each other a long time ago, and there were no feelings left to be spared. "Fill the rest of your boxes and go. You're free. Absolved. You've served your time. I don't need you here anymore."

Claire kept her gaze fixed on Eilidh's as she knocked back the last mouthful of wine. Her eyes were glassy, but no tears fell. Eilidh couldn't tell if it was relief, sadness, or the alcohol. She'd stopped being able to read Claire a long time ago. "I'll be gone by the time you get home from work tomorrow."

Eilidh hung her head. "If you need more time. There's no rush." She said it half-heartedly, hoping Claire wouldn't take her up on the offer.

"Yes, there is." Claire's tone was clipped. She turned away from Eilidh and reached for the remote again. That was it. Conversation over. Eilidh had agonised for weeks, and it had been done with three simple words.

She stood and headed towards the door. "I'm sorry, Claire." Despite everything, Eilidh knew some fault lay at her feet.

"Don't be." Claire didn't turn; instead, she reached to top up her glass. "I'm not."

Eilidh bit her lip. Every vile word and accusation she had wanted to throw Claire's way over the past weeks sat dangerously on the tip of her tongue. She couldn't say them. She wouldn't. For her own sanity, she merely needed Claire gone, and with her all the negativity that had sucked the life from Eilidh.

Without another word, she left the room, swiped a bottle of wine from the fridge, and climbed the stairs towards a hot bubble bath in the hope it might calm her, help her get some sleep. As she stripped off and ran the water, her phone beeped on the windowsill. She couldn't help but smile when Darcy's name showed on her screen.

> *How's it going? Saved any other inept women from their clumsiness lately? Darcy*

Eilidh tentatively climbed in to the piping-hot water and reached for the phone again. After what had occurred downstairs with Claire, she wasn't sure if Darcy's timing was perfect or impossible. She tapped back a reply.

> *Only you. I try not to make a habit of it. Did the boss forgive you?*

A few seconds passed before Darcy replied.

> *I don't think she even noticed. Pretty sure she's fuelled by acid anyway.*

Eilidh laughed out loud at that, and the anger she had felt towards Claire began to simmer as the hot water worked its magic and the easy chat with Darcy offered light relief.

> *Ah, one of those. Bitchy robot bosses are the worst. How do you cope?*

> *By eating a shitload of biscuits at work and drinking a shitload of wine at home.*

Eilidh smiled and reached for her own glass of chilled wine. She took a satisfying sip before replying.

> *Seems a well-balanced diet and strategy.*

> *It's got me this far. Speaking of wine…are you free for that coffee or do you fancy upgrading to an alcoholic thank you?*

Eilidh sank down further in the bath. Bubbles brushed her ears, and she could hear her heart beat faster in them. She thought about sitting across a table from someone who actually had a smile to offer her, and a beautiful smile at that. It had been so long since she'd felt the thrill of butterflies, and they tickled her now. This was it. Decision time.

Perfect or impossible?

It was something they had in common—cooking for one—and Darcy hated it.

Back pressed against the usual tree, a reoccurring thought surfaced as Darcy moved around the kitchen oblivious to her audience.

What would her reaction be if she knew?

That day it would have been so easy to grab hold of her. To step out from the shadows and shake her and say, *"Here I am. I'm the person you've been wondering about. Do you know who I am?"*

It was a fantasy that played out regularly. The moment Darcy found out the truth and discovered her real family history. How it had ended another. Would she believe it? Would she cry? Did she already know some of it?

But it wasn't the right time, and the reserves of willpower that were tapped into daily provided strength yet again. For now, it was still about watching, waiting, listening to the voice that insisted Darcy had to go through this. The anguish, the uncertainty—every emotion suffered by those left behind. So Darcy could genuinely understand when she learned the truth.

Darcy was a romantic; she longed for the fairy tale. She dreamed about finding the one, falling in love, and living happily ever after. Endearing as it was, it was her weakness and the obvious angle to attack. The best way to teach her what she needed to understand and to show her the pain she had no idea existed. To wear her down until she knew life wasn't all roses. To make her question a concept so dear to her…then tear it apart. To destroy that concept, that virtue Darcy had, the one they'd lost so long ago: Hope.

Until now, manipulating her various love interests had been simple. People were fickle, easily scared away. But dammit, Darcy was resilient, and she bounced back every time. It was hard not to admire that. Not to smile every time she picked herself up and dusted herself off. It also made the goal that much more difficult to attain. To a degree, the plan was working, but not enough. Resilience was a sign that hope lived strongly inside Darcy. The plan needed something more.

This was no time to soften. There had been too many years of hate, of building walls, to let her seep in and tug at any conscience reaching for the surface. It would undo too much.

No. It was impossible to even consider an alternative.

The alternative needed to be stomped out of existence.

Chapter 6

I𝐭 𝐡𝐚𝐝 𝐛𝐞𝐞𝐧 𝐭𝐰𝐨 𝐝𝐚𝐲𝐬, and Eilidh still hadn't replied to Darcy's text inviting her for a drink. Deflated was an understatement as to how she felt. She flopped on the sofa and reached for her hot chocolate, scooping out a mini marshmallow and popping it in her mouth before taking a sip. It wasn't doing much to cheer her up, but when was chocolate ever a bad idea?

Her phone pinged with a notification from the latest dating app she was trying. It was Amy. A recent match and someone Darcy had chatted with on and off for a month or so. She was attractive in a polished way, a nurse who enjoyed mountain biking and hiking, and on paper sounded ideal. Every now and then she had the ability to say something that tickled Darcy with excitement or made her swoon with the loveliness of it.

But Amy's unsociable hours made keeping the conversation flowing difficult, and so no sooner would the chat take an interesting turn before Amy would go quiet and the conversation quickly fizzled out. That and every attempt to meet seemed to get side-tracked, and so it had never happened.

Maybe now was the time to try again. Eilidh clearly wasn't interested but was obviously too polite to say so. Darcy needed to face facts and move on.

Amy's message was cute as always and brought a welcome smile to Darcy's lips.

> *I'm sorry, I know. I've been utterly crap. But even after four consecutive night shifts, I had to log on and see your face before crumpling in to an exhausted heap. Write me with your news. I want to make this happen. X*

The fire had begun to settle, but the orange glow was still fierce and warmed Darcy's toes as she pointed them towards it.

Amy wanted to make this happen.

In that moment, so did Darcy. Why the hell not? She wasn't tied to anyone and couldn't let her mystery torturer rule her life or force her to miss out on something potentially wonderful because of fear. It wasn't how she was prepared to live her life.

She tapped a message back to Amy.

You're right, you have been crap. But I'll forgive you. So long as I finally get to see your face in person. Lunch next Sunday? D x

Pleased with herself for taking the plunge, Darcy cast her gaze around the small space she called home and consoled herself that if it all went tits up as Anja had put it, at least she had somewhere awesome to live. And hide.

It was hardly grand, but the cabin was cosy and quiet, and best of all it was hers. She had lucked out while sailing solo on Loch Ness on a rare sunny day, when she'd stopped for lunch in the Dores Inn and met a local farmer at the bar. He had a woodland plot he was willing to part with and had assured her planning would be granted for a single-story cabin, given he already had three that he let to holidaymakers and folk looking for some isolation.

They'd agreed a price for the land that she could pay off in installments, and the work to extend the gravel track beyond his cabins to hers, as well as hooking her up to his small wind turbine. All that was left had been to find the cabin, clear the trees, and have it built.

Set high in to the hills on the south side of Loch Ness, it afforded her solitude without a crazy commute. In twenty minutes, she was at the local supermarket; in thirty she was in town and walking distance from work. The farmer kept her in firewood and helped her shovel her car out when the snow fell heavily. His farmhouse was only a ten-minute walk down the track, which gave her a small measure of comfort when things went bump in the night or a storm was brewing.

She stretched out to the end of the sofa and groaned in the satisfaction of a yawn. After working the previous weekend and a run of early mornings, her bed would be calling soon.

A sharp crack broke through the quiet, making her start, and she immediately tensed. "What the…" The curtains were drawn, but she was sure something had just hit the window. A bat, maybe? A bird wasn't likely at that time of night.

The sound came again, and she pinpointed it to the long window that looked out across the front porch. She glanced at the clock: eight-fifteen. There were no guests that she was aware of in the lower three cabins, but the farmer should be home. Her heart hammered. Should she go to the window? To the door? She reached for her phone as the sound of something faintly clattering against wood reached her ears. Was someone throwing stones? It sounded as if they'd missed the window and the rock had bounced on to her porch.

Her dining table sat under the offending window, making access difficult. She skirted around it to the tall lamp in the corner and clicked it off. Only the fire provided any light now, but if she peered out, she didn't want to be seen. Slowly she drew the curtain from the side an inch and brought one eye to the gap.

Darkness.

No movement, no light, no person that she could see. Had she imagined it? Was she hearing things that weren't there? The security light hadn't come on, so if anything was out there, it wasn't close. A shadow deep in the woods caught her eye, or was it a trick of the moon? She stared at the spot but saw no further movement and heard no recurrence of the noise.

She kept her eye on the woodland as she raised a hand towards the porch-light switch and flipped the button. Its brightness made her lean back a moment, then she pulled back the curtain fully and looked from one end of the porch to the other. Coldness ran through her when she saw it.

A box.

It sat perfectly aligned on her doormat.

"Are you fucking kidding me? No. No. No." She could feel it. Knew who it was from. "You do not come to my house. Oh no you don't." She snatched the super-sized Maglite from its clip next to the front door, stuck her feet in to snow boots, and unlocked the door with purpose.

The box stared up at her, taunting her with its presence. She flicked the torch on and scanned back and forth into the darkness. "Where the fuck are you?" she shouted out into the emptiness. "Who are you? Eh?" The fat beam of light didn't pick anything up. "Why don't you come tell me to my face what you want? Otherwise stop it. Just stop it…"

The fight was gone, the rush of adrenaline already passed and morphed into frustration. Her tears came then, hot and fast. She shouted into the night one last time before slamming the door on the box. "Fucking, fucking arsehole."

She swiped at the tears, angry at allowing them to happen. Teeth gritted, she kicked off her boots and reached for the phone.

Now for the process.

Call the police, drag them all the way out there to record the incident, and take away the box. Be asked inane questions that she still didn't know how to answer. Then listen to them say there's nothing they can do.

Then she'd call Anja and sob down the phone for an hour.

Fuck it. She decided on the reverse order for a change. "Fuck!" she cursed when Anja's phone went to voicemail. The panicky flutter in her chest increased in speed. Thankfully, Anja picked up on the second attempt. "Hey, sorry, I was driving. What's up?"

"There's a fucking box on my doorstep, and the arsehole that left it informed me of its presence by throwing stones at my window."

"Holy crap. Are you okay?"

"Understatement. And no. No, I'm not. Can you come? Please? Where are you anyway that you're driving?"

"I'm in the supermarket carpark. Jason's big meal, remember? He forgot the wine."

"Ah, shit." Darcy headed back towards her bedroom. She systematically checked windows as she went, putting lights on and off, illuminating every dark corner until she was satisfied she was alone in the cabin. "I totally forgot. Don't worry about it, love. Go enjoy your meal, and I'll get on to the police."

"You haven't called them yet?" Anja sounded exasperated, and Darcy understood why. It's not as if this was her first time.

"No. I kind of hoped you'd be here with me. I know they think I'm overreacting, and I wanted someone else here while they're patronising me. But honestly, don't worry. I'll be fine."

"Don't be daft. If smell was anything to go by, dinner was about to be a disaster anyway. Let me give him a call and I'll be there in twenty."

"You sure? I thought he had something to tell you."

"It can wait, Darcy. He'll understand. He knows how important you are to me."

"Aw...you big softie, you." But Darcy was smiling. It wasn't often she got anything more than teasing or sarcasm out of Anja.

"Shut up and tell me where you are?"

"In the cabin, duh."

"You know what I bloody mean, Darcy. Remember what we talked about if this happened. Are you locked in the bedroom? Have you got the bat I bought you?"

"Yes, and yes. I've checked all the windows. The doors are locked, and the bat is in my hand. I'll call the police as soon as we hang up."

"Okay, well, go do it now. I can't get there if I'm on the phone to you."

"Yes, ma'am." Darcy nodded curtly, as if Anja could see her. "See you soon."

Anja rang off and Darcy brought up her call log. Ten days. That's how long it had been since she last rang the police. The gaps were getting shorter: at first it was monthly, then every few weeks, to less than a fortnight apart. She tapped in 1-0-1 instead of 9-9-9. It didn't feel like an emergency anymore.

Chapter 7

Darcy closed the door on the two police officers and sighed with relief.

"You okay, **kjære**?" Anja came through from the kitchen with fresh hot chocolate for them both.

The Norwegian term of endearment brought a momentary smile to Darcy's lips. Anja rarely slipped into her native language with anyone but Darcy. "I guess. A lot of good that did though." She took a mug and headed for the sofa. Pulling a comforting blanket with her, she curled up at one end.

"Aye, I know." Anja joined her. "But you need to keep reporting it, even if they haven't a clue. It's best to have it all on file just in case."

Darcy's eyes widened. "In case of what?"

"Sorry, sorry. That came out wrong." Anja rubbed Darcy's knee reassuringly. "I didn't mean…"

"It's fine." Darcy waved her away. She knew exactly what Anja meant by "just in case" but didn't want to entertain for a second that her stalker might escalate their attentions. The possibilities were too flipping scary. Especially now they'd shown they knew where she lived.

"I only meant, well, you never know. Put all these little pieces together and they might come up with something." Anja drew part of the blanket towards herself, tucking it under both their feet.

"Aye, right. If we know anything, we know they're bloody sneaky and clearly not daft. Short of catching them on the doorstep, I don't think we're figuring this out any time soon."

"So, the police have no idea at all who it is?"

"Nope. Apparently, the calls have all been traced to unregistered mobiles, with no way of tracking down who bought them. There's not even CCTV along these back roads that might pick up a car. As if they're going to waste time doing that anyway."

"Have you thought about setting up a camera here? On the porch or on the track?"

Darcy blew on her chocolate and thought on that a moment. "You know, that might be an idea. At least at work I felt a little secure in the fact there's always other folk around me. Key cards and security on reception, and the deliveries have always arrived direct from the companies or royal mail. But here...out there..." She waved her arm in the direction of the window. "Unless there're folks staying in any of the other cabins, I'm ten minutes on foot down the track to the farm."

For the first time since she had moved in, thinking about the wild woodland wrapped around her tiny cabin frightened her. Before, it had made her calm. Given her peace. It was her little patch of solitude in a mixed-up, crazy world. Now it felt vast. A never-ending darkness where the unknown lurked waiting to pounce. This time it had felt more personal, not only because they had come to her home, but because it was obviously a personal delivery. Not some unknowing postie.

That was a first.

"Well, let me know if you do. I'll help. Anything to make you feel safe again." Anja smiled, and Darcy thanked her lucky stars for her friend. She had dropped her dinner plans at a moment's notice and rushed straight to her side, never complaining once.

"Thanks, sweetheart. I really don't know what I'd do without you. You've gone above and beyond work-wife duties." They both chuckled at the term. It was Joe who had inadvertently started it, referring to Anja as her wife one day, jealous he hadn't been invited to lunch with them.

"I like to think we're long past the merely 'work friends' stage. I've seen your sloth pyjamas, don't forget."

The tightness in Darcy's stomach released a little as she laughed along with her friend. "This is true. You're never going to let me live those down, are you?"

"Never." Anja winked. "They were way too cute to forget."

Darcy kicked her under the blanket. "Bugger off."

They both sipped their chocolate and stared in to the fire. Relief seeped into Darcy's bones with the warmth of the flames, and Anja nestled in close.

"What was in it?" Anja broke the quiet.

"Hmm?"

"What was in the box?"

"Oh." Darcy flashed back to the police officer transferring the box into a clear plastic evidence sack. From the initial moments of fear, to her panicked call to Anja, and then the procedure of dealing with the police, it was the first time Darcy had actually thought about the so-called gift. "Fuck, Anja. It was a bottle of my favourite perfume. How the hell do they know what my favourite perfume is? In fact…" Darcy was on her feet then and heading for her bedroom.

"What are you doing?" Anja followed her into the cosy room.

"Look." She pointed to her dressing table and the bottle that sat among an array of cosmetics. "And then look at the window."

Anja did as instructed and looked between the two. "I don't understand?"

"My bedroom window is at least twelve feet off the ground with the way the front of the cabin is on stilts and the back cuts into the hill. There's no way someone could peek through the window and see the perfume all the way over there."

"Okay, I see that."

"So how the hell did they know what my favourite was?" The panic was rising again as possibilities flew through Darcy's imagination. "Are they following me? Did they see me buy it in a shop? Or what… Have they been close enough to smell it on me? To recognise it? Shit, Anja, I'm really freaking out now. This was too far. Too fricking far. Have they been in here when I wasn't at home? When I was asleep?"

The tears came, then she was pulled into Anja's strong grasp.

"Shush, Darcy. Calm down. It'll be okay."

Anja rubbed her back and held her tight, and Darcy let the tears flow, sobbing in to her shoulder. "But how, Anja? And why? Why me?"

Anja held her at arm's length and wiped some tears away, then tucked errant strands of damp hair behind her ear. "Because you look so flipping cute in sloth pyjamas?"

Darcy laughed despite herself. "You're an arsehole. You know that, right?"

"Yeah, I know." Anja pulled her in for one last squeeze. "But I also know how to make you feel better."

"Will you stay the night? Will Jason mind?"

Anja released her and smiled as if it wasn't even a question. "Of course. I'm here as long as you need me."

Chapter 8

JOE SAUNTERED BACK FROM THE kitchen, pausing as he passed Darcy's desk. "Nice flowers. Did you send them to yourself?"

"Piss off," she growled. Sat with arms crossed on her desk, chin on forearm, she stared at the flowers and willed them to tell her who had sent them.

"Now, now." Joe sat back at his desk with a mug of soup. "I'm only trying to lighten your mood."

"Well, don't." She got a waft of the soup, and her stomach grumbled. "Although if you've got more of that broth it might help?"

He chuckled. "Sure. I can play wife while Anja's away. There's another batch in the fridge."

When he didn't move, she turned towards him, raising her eyebrows expectantly. "So…"

He looked toward the kitchen, then down at his soup, before looking her way again with a hard-done-by expression. "But I've just heated this, I didn't mean I'd actually get you it…"

Darcy slowly shook her head until his words stalled. "If you want to play wife, you'll get the soup."

"Fine." He roughly pushed his chair back like a petulant teenager. "Here. Bloody take this." He handed her the fresh mug, grabbed a plastic spoon from a pot on his desk, and chucked it into her lap. "But when she gets back"—he pointed at Anja's desk—"you will acknowledge that I took care of you in your hour of need and be nice to me for at least the rest of the day."

"Done." Darcy dropped her chin back on to her arm. "If you can scavenge a bit of bread, I'll even let Bridget know you make a decent broth. Might increase your chances."

"Bridget? My chances of what?" He feigned ignorance. "What are you talking about?"

"Oh, come on, Joe. You can tell me. You've got a thing for her, haven't you? Or are you two already secretly doing it?"

"Me and Bridget?" Joe hissed, careful not to draw half the office in to the conversation. "You've got it all wrong. I'm not interested in her."

"Yeah, yeah, mate. Whatever you say." She waved, shooing him towards the kitchen. "Bread. Now."

She watched him go and chuckled. It was one of her favourite sources of workplace amusement, winding up Joe. It didn't help that one, he was gullible as anything, and two, he was, actually, a pretty easy-going and good-natured guy, who she knew secretly enjoyed the banter.

She reached once again for the card that came with the flowers. Same lilac envelope, same plain ivory card inside that clearly wasn't from the florist's own collection. She couldn't help but smile at the baby sloth adorning the front cover—her favourite animal. Which made it creepier— whoever sent this knew it.

Although it didn't do much to pin things down. Aside from the pyjamas Anja had spied, it was known across the office that a baby sloth YouTube video had the ability to reduce her to tears. Her Secret Santa the year before had paid to adopt one for her which came with a mini toy version that hung off one of her dividing desk walls. There was a sloth on her keychain, the printed scarf Anja had bought her, and the novelty socks she had found cheap in Primark.

Yip, her love of the sloth was common knowledge.

It still always provoked a smirk from Anja when she showed her the picture, and inside the message was always the same.

One day you'll see me. One day you'll know the truth.

Darcy hoped that day would never come.

She sighed and sat up straight again. Tossing the card aside, she picked up the mug of steaming goodness. She glanced past the flowers at the empty space where Anja normally sat. Darcy hadn't heard from her in two days: no texts, no calls, not even a silly snapchat. She'd left numerous messages, and all Bridget would disclose was she had taken a few personal days.

Darcy knew Jason was still home, so it felt strange when she considered going to Anja's house. Despite the two years they had known each other, between his odd shift pattern, their propensity to spend every minute together when he was home, and Darcy's generally erratic love life, somehow Darcy had never managed to meet him. He felt separate to their friendship, something in the background that wasn't part of what Anja and Darcy had. It didn't seem to bother Anja, and if Darcy was honest, it didn't really bother her either. The thought of being a third wheel to them made her feel weird, and for reasons she wasn't sure she wanted to think about, Darcy knew she would be happy to never have to meet Jason or see him and Anja together.

Besides, maybe the issue was with Jason, and the two of them wouldn't appreciate Darcy turning up unannounced. That would be a very awkward first meeting. As always, Anja would come to her when she was ready. In the meantime, Darcy was left with two things to ponder. Who had sent the bloody flowers, and why was she so unlucky with women?

Amy still hadn't replied to her message asking about lunch that Sunday. Sure, it sometimes took her a few days, and wasn't it Amy who had started the conversation again? Had been all sweet and insistent that she wanted to make it happen. Unfortunately, the irrational side of Darcy wasn't listening to reason and the silence stung.

Then there was Eilidh. After their fun text exchange, she'd put herself out there and asked Eilidh out, then tortured herself for days when no reply had been forthcoming. The telling blue ticks on WhatsApp had taunted her. Eilidh had definitely seen the message.

After a glass of wine, or maybe two, the night before, Darcy had taken the plunge and sent a follow-up message to both women. She'd told Amy she was flexible if Sunday was no good and asked if Eilidh was free that Friday night.

Two blue ticks, but still no reply.

By the time Darcy had crawled into bed half drunk, she was convinced she was clearly un-dateable, and both women's silence was because they were thinking about the best way to let her down. As if not replying wasn't enough to let her know they weren't interested.

A text had arrived that morning, confirming her fears. When Eilidh's name had popped up, for a brief moment, Darcy had allowed herself to believe and felt a flutter of anticipation and excitement. Her joy was quickly quashed with the few short words Eilidh had sent.

I'm sorry, Darcy. I thought I had replied already? A drink probably isn't a good idea right now. The timing is all wrong for me and it wouldn't be fair to you. I hope you understand. E x

Now she felt hopelessly desperate. It wasn't as if she wasn't happy on her own. She was. She had a great life, but still missed the fun of dating, the thrill of the unknown. Okay, the sex as well. She definitely missed that.

Maybe she was trying too hard? Wanted too badly to meet someone. Perhaps her focus was better placed elsewhere, and if it was meant to happen, it would.

Darcy blew on a spoonful of the broth and savoured the warming comfort of the first mouthful. It was Eilidh's loss. That's what Anja would say. And there was still a little hope where Amy was concerned. No news was good news, right?

"I take it they're not the romantic gesture you were hoping for?" Joe reappeared with more soup and laid a piece of bread wrapped in a napkin on her desk before heading back to his own.

She swivelled in her chair to face him. "What gave it away?"

"We sit six feet apart. I know you don't include me in your little chats, but my hearing works."

She sighed and looked back at the flowers. "Whatever you've heard, it's only the half of it. So, no, this isn't my idea of romance."

"I thought girls liked the idea of a secret admirer. Would find it intriguing and exciting."

"Well, you'd be wrong. Unless you think late-night silent calls, gifts left on your doorstep, and attempts to hack your Facebook are exciting."

"Oh." Joe looked sorry he'd been so flippant. "I didn't realise it had gone that far. Sorry, Darcy."

She waved away his apology. "Unless you're behind it, don't be sorry."

"Still, that's pretty creepy. And you've no idea who it is? No ex that didn't want to be an ex? No one that's shown you unusual attention?"

34

"No, no, and no. Trust me, Joe, I've been through everyone I can think of. It's got to the point where I'm suspicious of the guy that serves me coffee in the morning."

Joe raised his eyebrows. "Shit. That bad, then."

"Aye, that bad. I've practically got Police Scotland on speed dial. But anyway…" She nodded in the direction of Anja's desk. "Don't suppose Bridget's let anything slip to you about why Anja is off work? You know, a little office pillow talk."

He scowled at her. "For the last time, Darcy, I'm not interested in, nor am I sleeping with, the boss. So leave it alone." He turned back to his computer screen, abruptly ending the conversation. All sympathy over her situation was gone.

Darcy was a little taken aback. It was rare Joe took the bait and got in a grump so easily.

"Okay, Joe. Whatever you say." When he didn't look her way, she spun around and checked her phone yet again for any reply from Anja. Nothing.

Fine. She was going to have to respond to Eilidh without any advice from her friend. Keep it brief, she thought, same as Eilidh's. But breezy too. Maybe the timing would be right at some point; Darcy didn't want to burn bridges, particularly not with a woman that had drawn her in as quickly as Eilidh had.

I'm disappointed, but I understand. You have my number if you change your mind. Take care, Darcy x

There. It was honest and didn't put any pressure on her, but it let her know she cared that Eilidh had cancelled. Anja would approve, she was sure.

It buzzed back almost immediately, and expecting Eilidh, she was surprised to see Anja's name on the incoming call.

"Hey! I've been worried about you. What's happening?"

It was immediately clear Anja was crying. Her sniffles came through the line before her choked response. "Jason. Cheated. Gone." Then she was sobbing with abandon while Darcy tried to find a response in her shock.

"Hey, shush. Take a breath and tell me what's going on. Did you say Jason's cheated on you?" The wail got louder, and Darcy held the phone away from her ear a moment. "Okay, okay. I think I get the picture. Where are you? I can leave work and come see you."

She heard the sound of a nose being blown in the background, then Anja was back on the line, a little more in control of herself. "I'm at home, but I don't want to see anyone."

"Well, I'm not having you sitting alone sobbing your heart out. Why don't you take an hour or so, have a bath, try to calm down some? I'll head over as soon as I can with a bottle of something and some food to wash it down."

"You don't have to do that. I'll be fine. I needed to say the words to someone, that's all."

"He really cheated?" Darcy whispered, conscious of Joe behind her. "And left?"

Anja snorted. "Left? No. I kicked the fucker out. I've no idea where he is now. Probably with her."

Darcy couldn't help but smile at the angry fizz that cut through Anja's obvious grief over the situation. She was strong, she'd get through this— of that Darcy had no doubt. But it would be a teary, wine-filled, angry journey, she was sure.

"Good for you, love. What an arsehole." She glanced up as Bridget stormed from her office. "Uh-oh. Boss on the warpath by the looks of it, so I better get off my phone. I'll be there in an hour."

"Seriously, Darcy, you don't have…"

"I said I'll be there in an hour. Sit tight." She hung up without another word as Bridget passed her desk on route to the kitchen.

"I've told you about personal calls, Darcy. That better have been important."

Darcy bowed her head meekly, unprepared for battle, her head still swimming with Anja's news. "It was, Bridget. Sorry though. It won't happen again."

The older woman's eyebrows knitted, clearly unaccustomed to anything less than a thinly veiled cheeky response from Darcy. "Are you okay?"

"Erm…aye." Darcy attempted to hide her surprise. She couldn't recall another time when Bridget had asked that question of any of her staff. "But Anja, that was her, she's had some upsetting news. Any chance I can nip out early today? She really needs me."

Bridget looked between Darcy and the flowers. "Is that another bouquet for the bin?"

"What?" Darcy was confused a moment. "Oh, these. Yeah, probably."

"Still not found out who the creep is, then?"

Darcy's eyebrows shot up. "Seriously, does everybody know?" She scanned around the room.

"Relax, Darcy. I'm the boss. I make it my business to know what's going on around here, that's all. You can leave early, but put those in my office first. Seems a shame to waste them."

She continued on her way to the kitchen, and Darcy sat momentarily stunned. She had been all set to fake a stomachache to get out early, but it seemed Bridget was only a bitch 99 per cent of the time.

She hurried to Bridget's office with the flowers and hastily gathered her stuff before she could change her mind. Joe surreptitiously looked her way. "Sure it's not you who's shagging her?"

Darcy shrugged on her coat and gave him the two-finger salute, unable to resist a parting jab. "Only in your dreams, little boy. Only in your dreams."

Chapter 9

A THICK TOMATO SAUCE, SPIKED with chilli, bubbled on the gas stove. Darcy dipped the wooden spoon in it and raised it to her lips. She blew gently before tasting her handiwork. "Perfect."

"Of course it is," Anja agreed. "When it's about all you can make, I'd hope you'd have it perfected by now."

"Cheeky bugger." Darcy topped up their glasses with the same red wine she'd used in the sauce and slid one across the breakfast bar to where Anja sat. Her eyes were red rimmed and still a little puffy, but the tears had subsided at least. "How're you feeling?"

Anja shrugged and took a gulp of the ruby liquid. "I'm not really sure."

"Well, that's okay," Darcy reassured her. "It's a lot to process right now. You're bound to be all mixed up and uncertain."

"I guess." Anja reached for a fresh tissue and brushed it under her nose. "I think at this point I mostly feel let down. When he walked out that door…" She covered her mouth with her hand and choked on a small sob.

Darcy moved around beside her and lay an arm across her shoulder, pulling Anja in to her side. "Hey, there. C'mon. You don't have to explain for my benefit. Talk when you're ready."

Anja blew in to the tissue and looked up at her gratefully. "Thank you. It's just…it's too hard right now. I don't think it's sunk in, to be honest."

She took another gulp of wine, and Darcy pushed against the sensible part of her that wanted to tell Anja to slow down. Instead, she touched her glass lightly to Anja's and matched her. After the flower delivery that morning, a hazy wine buzz was damn appealing.

"Of course it hasn't." Darcy squeezed her hand before moving back around to the stove. She gave the sauce a stir, then pulled a packet of spaghetti from a cupboard. She dropped a healthy batch into the boiling water before turning her attention to a basil plant. "Here." She plucked a few sprigs and pushed them Anja's way on a chopping board. "Chop that."

Anja offered a weak smile. She clearly knew what Darcy was trying to do—distract her in any small way possible from thinking about the fucking tragedy her marriage had become.

"You're a good friend, Darcy."

"Oh, I know. Although it doesn't feel that long since I was calling you in a blubbering mess, so we work both ways, I reckon." She laid a peck on Anja's cheek as she passed, heading for the dining table. She laid out plates and cutlery and opened a fresh bottle of wine. Then Darcy strained the pasta and sprinkled basil into the sauce with a final flourish before combining them both to create a steaming bowl of comfort.

She carried it to the table, pulled out a chair, and gestured to Anja. "Come sit over here."

Anja did as instructed and refilled her glass to the brim. Darcy again said nothing. If blind drunk was what she needed, who was Darcy to argue? She'd never made it past the year mark with previous girlfriends, and still those break-ups had hurt. She couldn't begin to comprehend the pain Anja was in right now.

"I can't make this better, so I'm not going to try." Darcy heaped spaghetti and sauce on Anja's plate. "All I'm here for is hugs and to keep you alive."

Anja's head shot up, eyes wide. "Alive? What the hell, Darcy? Do you really think I'm going to hurt myself because of him?"

"What? No." Darcy held her hands up in supplication. "I was meaning by making sure you're fed and watered. It was a joke."

Anja continued to hold her gaze, but her expression gradually changed from shock and anger to dismay. She scrubbed at her face before dropping her gaze in to her lap. "Sorry. I didn't mean to fly off on one then. I… Of course you didn't mean what I thought you did."

Darcy studied the top of her head. She could count on one hand the number of times Anja had ever raised her voice or taken that tone with her, and Darcy normally deserved it.

"Hey, it's fine. You're all over the place, I get it." She reached a hand across the table as Anja looked back up at her. "Let's just eat, drink, and then go watch something shite on the telly, eh?"

Anja seemed to hesitate a moment before reaching across and gripping Darcy's hand. "Sounds like a plan."

"Great." Darcy picked up her fork and pointed towards Anja's plate. "Eat."

The second bottle of wine was gone, which probably wasn't a great idea, considering how little spaghetti Anja had managed to eat. But now she lay with her head on Darcy's lap, her breathing heavy as she dozed.

A flutter of affection passed through Darcy as she studied Anja's face, whilst continuing to gently run her fingers through silky blonde hair. She knew Anja enjoyed her hair being played with, and sure enough, it had soothed her to sleep. Her lashes twitched lightly, and Darcy could see her eyes moving behind their lids. She wondered where her dreams had taken her. Was she dreaming of Jason?

Jason.

What a bloody idiot he was. How could anyone even contemplate cheating on Anja? She'd never met anyone so loyal and true to the relationships she formed. Whether wife or best friend, you were never in doubt how she felt about you. Even if she didn't say it, her actions spoke for her.

She gently removed Anja's glasses, then reached across her for a cushion before replacing her legs under Anja's head with it. She unfurled the blanket from the back of the sofa and laid it over her friend, careful not to wake her.

Darcy tiptoed in the direction of the stairs and the spare room. She settled under the duvet and clicked off the light, and for the first time in a long while, wondered if she and Anja could have been more than friends.

She remembered back to the early days, when she was sure Anja was flirting: The little looks and the shy words over the coffee machine in the staff kitchen. The times she would stand a little too close in the lift, or how she always made a point to sit next to Darcy in multi-team meetings.

You're being ridiculous, Darcy. She mentally shook herself. How many times had she told herself back then that it had merely been her imagination and wishful thinking? Anja was married and simply being friendly. She'd been the new girl in the office trying to make friends, that was all.

Darcy chastised herself for even allowing the thoughts to cross her mind. Here was her friend, broken and bereft, relying on Darcy for support. It was not the time to be remembering an aimless crush she'd moved past long ago.

The latch on the door clicked open, and a sleepy Anja appeared in the crack of light from the hallway. "I didn't want to be alone," she whispered.

As Anja climbed under the covers, Darcy reached an arm out and waited for Anja to tuck herself into the crook of it. She resumed her earlier rhythm of fingers through hair. "It'll be okay, darling. I'm sure of it." She planted a firm kiss on the crown of Anja's head. "I love you."

"Love you too," she mumbled into Darcy's neck.

It was only a few moments before Anja's breathing changed as she fell asleep, but Darcy lay awake a long time after. Between her stalker and now Jason, she couldn't help but wonder if it really would be okay.

Chapter 10

THE TEXT HADN'T CHANGED IN the hundred times Eilidh had read it. Darcy was disappointed but had left the way open if Eilidh changed her mind. She sighed, set the phone aside, and tried to focus on the notes she'd been typing up.

After a week working back in the hospital physiotherapy department, she'd settled back into the routine well enough. Her previous patient was seventeen, recovering from a broken arm after a nasty fall from her horse. Eilidh hoped to have her back in the saddle in a couple of weeks, and when she had told her that, the girl had beamed as if Eilidh had offered her the world.

Patients like those made other, more regrettable situations easier to deal with. Her next patient was an example of that. Eighty-seven years old, he was on stroke number three, and the best they could both hope for was to progress from a wheelchair to walking short distances with an aid. Still, it was a goal, and one she would push and support him to achieve.

She clicked save on Horse Girl's notes, and her hand automatically reached for her phone again. What was stopping her meeting Darcy? Claire was gone, along with every last trace of her from the house. Eilidh was free to do as she pleased, see who she pleased, so what was holding her back?

She tucked the phone in a drawer and headed back to the gymnasium where Mr Davies would be waiting.

"Oi, Grey," Sam Thompson hollered across the large space. "How's that shoulder holding up?"

She smiled and sauntered towards her best friend and personal physio champion, as he coaxed a middle-aged woman across the walking bars.

"It's got me through the week, so we must be doing something right."

"Glad to hear it. Mrs Superhero Smith and I still have twenty minutes to go, but can I get a word afterwards?"

"A word" in Sam language meant, *"Fancy a pint when we finish up?"*

She laughed. "Sure, let's get a word. I've got Mr Davies first, but catch you out front at five-thirty?"

He grinned and fist pumped a meaty arm. "Perfect. Catch you later, Grey."

And it was perfect. If anyone could give her some straight-up advice on Darcy, it was Sam. The guy who, despite the fact he wasn't her actual physio, had still bullied her through hours of additional exercises. She'd cursed and slapped and bullied him right back when the pain became unbearable, but it had paid off in the end and she was grateful. He'd been her own personal cheerleader, solid and willing to take any grumbling shite she threw when it all got too much. In fact, during the aftermath of the incident, he'd been her entire support network outside of the medical professionals and the odd visit from her parents. It had cemented an already pretty great friendship.

The Castle Tavern was a favourite of Eilidh's in the winter, for the roaring log fire, cosy atmosphere, and epic selection of craft beers. It was Sam's because whether a live match or a repeat, there was always rugby on the telly.

They jammed themselves into their favourite corner, picked for its equal distance to the bar and the toilets, with a view of the door and one of the larger flat screens. The last two were on Sam's insistence because when his eye wasn't on the game, it wanted to be the first to see when someone attractive walked in.

"She's easily a seven."

Eilidh rolled her eyes. "You're a pig. You know I'm not going to play that game with you."

He shrugged. "I know. The real fun is winding you up over it."

She slapped his arm and threw him a dirty look. "It might be more interesting if you actually went and spoke to one of them."

He looked at her as if she'd spontaneously sprouted a beard. "Don't be ridiculous. You know my biggest fear is rejection. I'm all about the certainty and safety of dating apps. I let them come to me."

"But what if she didn't reject you?" She looked him up and down. "I mean, if I were to put you on that scale, I think you could scrape a six-and-a-half. Seven if I've had a few. That's not so bad."

It was his turn to slap her, and he flicked a stingy backhand at her thigh. "Like you can bloody talk. You stayed with Claire five years too long because you were too scared to find out what else might be out there."

Eilidh leaned back in surprise. She was used to the straight talk, but it wasn't normally quite so blunt, however insightful it might be. "I think five years is a bit of an exaggeration."

"Whatever." He waved her impending defensive argument away. "It might as well have been, but at least you've finally seen sense."

Eilidh took a long gulp of her beer. Five years was an exaggeration; it had only really been the last two when things had soured, but that was still long enough to have wasted. So he was right...to a degree. Not that she was ever going to admit that to him. After nine years with someone, it was scary as hell even contemplating starting all over again. It was also terrifying the thought that it might not even be starting again with only one person—there could be many.

Oh God, how many first dates might she have to go on before it clicked? How many stilted conversations over dinner and awkward first times in bed? How many mornings after with shy smiles and bad breath? Not to mention the uncertainty of who should call who and when. Fuck, she'd hated dating before Claire, and after nine years of not having to think about it, she hated it even more now.

She thought of Darcy. The thick, green wool scarf that seemed to be wrapped half a dozen times around a neck she imagined to be as pale as the fair skin of her face. Her cheeks had been pinched pink by winter's icy fingertips, and her blue eyes had shone in the dawn light. As she remembered the shy smile as Darcy had handed over her business card, Eilidh realised there were two sides to dating. Darcy could be as scared as her.

"I met someone."

Sam's head jerked instantly from the telly to Eilidh. "Seriously?"

"Well, we met on a bridge, and we exchanged numbers and have texted a little. But that's it. We haven't been out or anything, so when I say met, I mean, I think she's a ten and I really want to take her out."

Sam laughed and nudged her shoulder. "Claire's out the door five minutes and here's you picking up women on the street. I didn't think you had it in you."

"I didn't pick her up. It wasn't like that. We sort of bumped into each other, and she was being polite because I helped her. But I think there was an inkling of a spark."

"So go for it. Ask her out."

"Says the man who quivers at the mere thought of talking to a potential date in person."

"Aye, but that's me and this is you. Let's stick to you for now."

Eilidh chuckled. "Fine. Well we made plans for a drink, but I cancelled because Claire was in the process of moving out. Since then I haven't called or texted, and now I think I've maybe left it too long."

Sam spun on his stool to fully face her. "Listen, this happened because you were open to it happening. I know it's all raw and quite soon after Claire, but this doesn't have to be your next great love. Maybe you have coffee, or a beer, share some food, have sex, and then never see each other again? Maybe it lasts a week, a month, or ten years. Who knows? You never will if you don't give it a chance."

He was right. Eilidh took a few sips and wondered at the scenarios. First step, text Darcy. Maybe she wouldn't reply, and then at least Eilidh would know. Or she would reply, and all the things Sam had reeled off were possibilities.

"Okay, Tommo. I'll make you a deal." She slipped her phone from her coat pocket. "The second I press send on a text to Darcy, you go and talk to your *seven*. Deal?"

His eyes narrowed, flicking between the phone and the woman now chatting with friends at the bar. "You're sneaky and I hate you."

Eilidh began typing. "Nah, you don't."

It was the anniversary tomorrow, and the vile taste of nausea and dread seemed to have settled in permanently. The tears came fast and hard, without preamble, choking every breath.

The smallest irritation was enough to cause hands to ball into fists as the rage built almost to boiling. Someone would utter the words, "Are you okay?" and it took every ounce of resolve left not to scream, "No. I'm not fucking okay. I will never be okay." Then let the fists fly.

But that wouldn't help anything and would do no one any good.

The relief would be temporary and the consequences lasting.

There was calmness to be found in watching Darcy, being close to her. Despite the turmoil it brought and as difficult as it was to admit, it was becoming more of a challenge to transfer the loathing and hate from father onto daughter. Well, step-daughter; Darcy had never truly been his.

Darcy was someone folk enjoyed being around, someone they wanted as a friend. That much had become clear quite quickly. The friendly smiles, her tactile nature, the open laugh that drew people in.

Her single status surprised a few people, but not those who knew her well. Darcy was looking for the dream. She wanted a love that was invincible, that could withstand time as well as trouble.

Her idealism made many people scoff. The ones who had never dared to risk ending up alone in the quest to find what most people deemed unobtainable. Maybe even ridiculous. But Darcy refused to believe that it didn't exist out there for everyone.

Well, reality would crash down on her one day.

No matter how unbearable it was becoming to witness Darcy's anguish, whether by fate or design, devastating her dream was inevitable.

Chapter 11

DARCY DROPPED AN OVERNIGHT BAG on the bed of the spare room and sighed. She didn't mind staying with Anja but would have been happier if she'd been able to get her to leave the house. Even to come to Darcy's for the night, to do a food shop, to go to work. But in the five days since she'd kicked Jason to the curb, the curtains hadn't been open.

That was going to change today.

She scanned the room and noticed small things missing. Bike-maintenance books that normally sat on a shelf, a baseball cap that hung on the back of the door, and a picture of Anja and Jason's feet in the surf with "Barbados" scrawled nearby in the sand. They were no doubt bundled into the half-dozen black bags that cluttered the hallway. From his toothbrush and shower gel, to the contents of his wardrobe, Anja had been quick to rid the house of every trace of him.

The only photo that remained on the bedroom shelf was one of Anja and Darcy smiling from the bow of the small sailboat that Darcy was part owner of. She remembered when the photo had been taken. It had been a gloriously sunny day, and Darcy had ended up with a sunburnt nose that had glowed pink for days. She couldn't wait to get out on it again and knew Anja would be right there with her.

She headed back towards the kitchen where Anja nursed what she suspected was cold coffee. She stared in to space, not even acknowledging Darcy's presence.

"Right, that's it."

Anja's head snapped up. "What?"

"We're going out."

"No, Darcy. I'm not up to it. Please."

"I don't care. Unless you want spaghetti again…"

Anja let out a small groan.

"Exactly." Darcy stood hands on hips. "You need food, you need sunlight, but first of all, you need to shower."

Anja looked down at the pyjama, hoodie, and woolly sock ensemble she had going on. "I've washed." She was defensive.

"On Tuesday morning you washed. Now it's Friday. Tea-time. That's a whole lot of non-washing between then and now." She softened her voice a little. "You'll not be welcome to creep into my bed again tonight if you haven't had a shower."

Anja huffed out a breath and took a gulp of the coffee. Her nose turned up in disgust, and the swallow was audible as she forced the cold swill down. "Fine."

"Okay, good." Darcy watched her shuffle towards the stairs. "And I want real clothes on you," she called after her. "We're going to the supermarket whether you're happy about it or not."

Anja flicked two fingers Darcy's way as she disappeared in to the hallway. Darcy smiled. They'd reached the tough-love stage, and despite the grumbling, she knew Anja appreciated it.

Darcy took stock of the cupboards and fridge and made a list before systematically drawing back curtains, opening windows, shaking out throws, and fluffing pillows. She loaded the dishwasher and set it going, then wiped down the countertops.

"Better," she muttered to herself.

"It's bloody freezing down here." Anja appeared in the doorway, hair still damp and cheeks scrubbed raw. She wore jeans and a light blue sweater, and despite a bit of residual puffiness around her eyes, she looked like a new person.

Darcy moved to shut the windows again. "The place needed a quick blast of freshness."

Her phone beeped from the coffee table, and she picked it up along with her list and keys. Eilidh's name caught her eye, and her heart thumped a little faster in excitement. "Holy crap, Eilidh's texted me."

"Who?" Anja moved into the room and dropped onto the arm of the sofa.

"That girl, remember? I met her on the bridge when I dropped the coffees that morning."

"Oh, right, her. I thought she cancelled on you, and you'd decided to finally set up a date with Amy?"

"She did, but it was more of a 'I can't do it now, maybe later' kind of message. Seems women are like buses. I'm meant to get lunch with Amy Sunday afternoon."

"They both sound flaky to me." Anja moved back towards the hallway, where she plucked a coat from the hook and jammed a woolly hat over her head. "And I didn't have you down as the type to string two along."

Darcy wasn't really listening; she was reading Eilidh's message.

Hey, I know it's been a while, but do you still fancy that drink? Tomorrow night? E x

Tomorrow. As in Saturday. As in the very next day. Darcy's couldn't help the ball of nervous anticipation that bounced in her stomach because she was going to say yes—of course she was. In the weeks since they'd last spoken, Darcy had caught herself thinking about those big brown eyes and wind-whipped freckled face more than a few times.

"Hello, Darcy. Are we going or what?"

The tone of annoyance in Anja's voice cut through her daydreaming, and she couldn't help the smile that beamed in her friend's direction. "She wants to go for a drink tomorrow night."

"Oh, right. That's great."

Anja's happiness was clearly forced, and Darcy couldn't help but call her on it.

"It doesn't sound as if you think it's great."

"I do. Honestly. Go out with her. Go out with Amy. Have a great time. Have all the sex. One of us should be." Anja pulled off the hat and dropped her coat on the stairs. "I think I'm going to go have a nap. Don't worry about the shopping."

"Hey." Darcy crossed the room and grabbed her arm. "What's going on? Why are you being this way?"

"Being what way? It's fine, Darcy. If you don't want to be here with me, then leave. Go drink wine with your runner girl instead."

"What? It's not about one or the other, Anja. I don't understand why you're getting so upset with me."

"I'm not getting like anything. I'm tired, that's all. Seriously, tell her yes and have a great time. You can regale me on Monday about your weekend full of women."

Anja's tone was anything but enthusiastic or fine. Darcy was a little surprised at how she was being, but given the situation, it was also understandable. Anja's marriage was falling apart, and she hadn't seen her husband in nearly a week and had no idea where he was. And here was Darcy talking about going on not just one date, but two. *Christ, I can be an insensitive idiot sometimes.*

"Hey, wait." Darcy caught her hand as she started up the stairs. "I'll tell her another time and I'll cancel with Amy as well. It's no big deal. You're my priority right now."

"You don't have to do that, Darcy. I'm okay, honest."

"I want to." She pulled Anja back down the stairs and into a hug. After a quick squeeze, she held her at arm's length.

"C'mon, let's go restock the wine and buy something that isn't spaghetti for dinner."

"Seriously, I'll be fine. You're obviously excited, and I'm not exactly stellar company. Go on your dates."

"I am serious. They've made me wait; it won't hurt them to wait for me a little. Besides, we can't waste the fact that you're finally smelling fresh again and ready for the outdoors."

That got a smile, and Darcy returned it. She picked up the discarded hat and tugged it down lopsided onto Anja's head. "I didn't mean to be insensitive, talking about dating. What with Jason and everything."

Anja straightened the hat and gave her a shove towards the front door. "You've done nothing wrong. You've been perfect."

Darcy grinned and gave her a shove back. "Perfect, eh?"

Anja unhooked her keys and threw them to Darcy. "Shut up and drive."

Chapter 12

EILIDH HAD ACTUALLY PUMPED THE air when the reply came back from Darcy. Despite her initial disappointment that she wasn't available on the Saturday, it held the promise of a definite future date.

It was now Monday morning, and Eilidh had been hanging in anticipation all weekend waiting for Darcy to get in touch again. That told her a lot and gave her a lift of positivity. She was not only doing this, she was ready for it. The thought of all those firsts she'd been dreading suddenly didn't seem so bad. Still a little scary, but surmountable.

She jogged along the corridor to the gym and caught Sam before his first patient.

"Darcy said yes." She couldn't keep the grin from her face, and he grinned right back at her and raised his hand for a high five.

"When're you going out?"

"Friday night. She's in Amsterdam working until Thursday."

"Oh, fancy. I wish our work took us to places as cool as Amsterdam."

"I know, right. But hey, we have a swimming pool." Eilidh gestured towards the hydrotherapy room and they both laughed.

"What about you? Any word from Miss Seven?"

"Excuse you, her name is Emma, and yes. We are also going out Friday night."

"Oh God, we better check each other's plans. Inverness is a small place, I'm not sure I could cope bumping into you on a first date."

Sam's hand shot into the air. "I bagsy the Castle."

"What? No fair! You know that's my favourite."

"Tough shit. It's mine too, and I've no clue where else to go. You know how primitive I am. Plus I think it might help with the nerves to be somewhere I know.

"Oh, so screw my nerves? Cheers, pal."

"You're welcome. Besides, you don't want to take her to the tavern. Pick somewhere a bit fancy. She sounds like a fancy lady, working in Amsterdam and all."

Eilidh thought about that for a moment. Shite. Was Darcy all sophisticated cocktails and European travel? Would she hate somewhere as traditional as the Castle? Eilidh realised how little she knew about her, and panic began to set in.

"Fuck, Tommo. What if she is? Then I can't exactly rock up in jeans and a sweater for a pint at the Castle. Where do people go on dates these days? What do they do?"

Sam was laughing, and Eilidh wanted to punch him. "It's not bloody funny."

"Aye, it is." He kept laughing. "Honestly, the look on your face right now is priceless."

"Well, a lot of frigging help you've been." She made to stalk away, but he grabbed her hand.

"All right. Hang on. How about you text her and suggest she picks the place? That way you get an idea of the kind of thing she's into and you can dress and act accordingly."

Eilidh mulled it over. "Good thinking. Okay, you've redeemed yourself a little."

He saluted. "Glad to be of help."

She gave him a half hug and wished him a good day before heading towards the waiting room. She was excited about Friday and didn't want something awkward like picking a crap place to screw it up. Whether it ended up a rebound, a disaster, or whatever, it felt good to be finally moving forward, because she sure was sick of standing still.

Had Darcy ever lost anyone precious? Apart from him?

His demise had been an accident, a turn of fate that eventually could be reconciled. There was no choice involved in his death, unlike his desertion.

Darcy's years in Australia remained mostly a mystery; social media hadn't existed then, and she was only a child. Had there been other losses? Any other tragedies that she kept hidden from the rest of the world?

It didn't seem so.

Darcy moved through the world so freely, with a lightness in her eyes and step. It wasn't the demeanour of someone downtrodden with grief or etched with scars. Or maybe that was her defence? Face the world with a smile and hope it smiled back.

How would Darcy have coped if the roles had been reversed? If she'd been the one abandoned? If she'd suffered through the slow and torturous demise of her own mother?

It'd been the same as any other Friday. Money had been left on the kitchen table for lunch, books were packed, and the school bus had pulled up at its regular time. Nothing of note had happened all day: there were the usual teachers, subjects, bullies to avoid, and friends to meet.

It'd been mundane and typical. The hours counting down until the dreaded moment when it was time to bundle back on the bus home, fearing the long weekend ahead. A two-day prison sentence that no child should be forced to endure. It wasn't a home any longer; it was simply somewhere to sleep and store things, and occasionally eat. Where time moved slowly towards the anticipated day of eventual escape.

As the front door swung open, something had felt different. The TV had been off and an unusual quiet had permeated the air.

"Mum? Where are you?" The words had echoed in the hallway, and despite straining for any small sound, no response was forthcoming. After checking the kitchen, the living room, and the garden where she sometimes idled the hours away, drinking and staring at the sky, the only place left was the next floor up. The stairs had loomed high as any mountain.

The bathroom door at the end of the landing had been closed, offering momentary relief. She had regularly steeped for hours in the bath, until either the hot water or the bourbon ran out. But that had been fine; at least she was in the house. There wouldn't be another call to the police, or another search to track her down.

The relief had only lasted a moment.

Where was the music? The usual murmur of the radio and tuneless singing. Where was the familiar waft of smoke seeping from under the door? When no response had halted the persistent knocking on the door, a number of deep breaths were required to push past the fear before the handle was turned and the door pushed open.

In dreams since that moment, the door had never been opened; the horror behind it stayed locked away. It waited for someone else to find it.

Because she had finally done it.

Her empty gaze had stared up from beneath the water, the last shred of her soul extinguished. It was a memory that would never fade. It would haunt and taunt forever in nightmares.

No one should have to see the eyes of their dead.

Chapter 13

MONDAY WASN'T EXACTLY AN IDEAL night for a date, but with a work trip looming the following day and Amy's shift pattern, it was all Darcy could offer her. Eilidh was going to have to wait a little longer, but something told her it would be worth the wait.

In the meantime, Amy deserved a chance. Darcy had taken extra care with her wardrobe that day. Not so over the top that folk might comment at work, but enough that she wouldn't feel so official when she met Amy straight from it.

The bar Amy had chosen was relatively classy, although a little dead given it was five-thirty on a Monday and outside the snow fell in droves. She glanced down at the profile picture again and then back up at the door; her stomach jumped a little every time it opened, only for her shoulders to drop when Amy didn't appear.

She was twenty minutes late, but Darcy wouldn't panic quite yet. This wasn't new for her. In fact, it was becoming annoyingly regular. Amy could simply be caught up at work, or in traffic. Twenty minutes was nothing to worry about.

After thirty minutes, she tapped out a quick message.

Hey, I'm at the bar, are you held up at work? D x

It was diplomatic and light, in case Amy had a genuine excuse. Although Darcy was beginning to wonder if there even was an Amy. There had to be. Surely, she couldn't have fallen for it again.

After forty-five minutes, Darcy gave up. She paid the tab on her unfinished, lonely glass of wine, and resigned to her date's fate, left the bar.

Don't look around.
Keep your eyes forward, head held high, neutral expression.
You are not annoyed.
There is no one watching you right now.
It's all simply been a misunderstanding.
They haven't got to you.
You. Are. Not. Fucking. Raging.

Back in the sanctity of her cabin, Darcy paced. How the fuck had she allowed this to happen?

Again.

The first one, Michelle, had been a mild inconvenience. She had shrugged it off as cold feet and taken the plenty-more-fish approach. It wasn't her, it was them.

The second one, Trisha, had been a little harder to swallow. Had she turned up, saw Darcy, and walked away? What was wrong with her? Stood up twice in as many months—was she completely undateable? What was it about Darcy that made these women think they could not show up without even an explanation?

But now she was wise to it. Or was meant to be.

Amy had seemed so genuine, the real deal. There had been pictures that a reverse-image check on Google hadn't shown to be stock photos. There was a Facebook page, locked down but with at least half a dozen profile pictures available with likes and comments. A LinkedIn account that didn't have a photo but did confirm all the career details Amy had told her. Darcy thought she'd been so careful and had found enough evidence to be sure Amy actually did exist.

Fucking, fucking, bastarding stalker. They'd won again. Toyed with her again. Given her hope then chewed her up and spat her out twisted.

She gulped back the last of a second glass of wine and grabbed her laptop. She knew what she would find, or wouldn't as the case might be, but had to be sure.

As suspected, the dating profile was gone.

She clicked and searched and checked more than once, but it was pointless. Amy's profile had been deleted along with her Facebook account, although the one on LinkedIn remained. Had they stolen it? Used it as inspiration for "Amy's" character, knowing it didn't have a picture and couldn't prove them a liar? It was risky but feasible.

Her mind strayed to Eilidh as Anja's words of warning echoed. Should she be questioning Eilidh's sudden appearance in her life, or had it truly been a magical coincidence that brought them together on that bridge?

At least she knew Eilidh existed. Or did she? The person existed, yes, but was that her real name? Was she who she professed to be? Their meeting had been oddly random, but how would Eilidh have known Darcy would be there that early on a Saturday morning? It had been a last-minute urgent meeting; only her colleagues knew about it.

She thought of the perfume, the gig tickets, wine, flowers, and chocolates. How had they known about any of it?

Darcy shuddered. She glanced towards the porch window, its curtains still open. Were they watching her right now? Was it Eilidh out there?

She shook the thought loose.

No.

She wouldn't do this. This is what they wanted, or so she thought.

Every move they made seemed conflicted, from a beautiful framed print by her favourite artist, that showed care and attention, despite the utter creepiness it left within Darcy's core, to fake profiles and dates, and the crushing emotions of being seemingly rejected.

Did they hate her or love her? Was it something in between? Would they physically hurt her? Would they one day reveal themselves, and what would happen if they did?

She moved to the window and yanked the curtains closed before checking the locks on the front door again. The worst aspect of the situation was definitely not knowing, who, when, why…if. The questions were driving her crazy.

And Darcy was convinced that was exactly what they wanted.

Darcy was livid. From the way she stalked around the cabin and knocked back the wine, it was obvious she was rattled.

A brisk wind blew and swirled the fresh powdery snow, creating small drifts and peaks against anything immobile. To get this close to the cabin was a risk rarely taken, but Darcy was distracted; she wouldn't be looking for shadows in the night.

The urge to comfort her would dissipate, but it was still disconcerting how often that feeling vied for attention and action. Each deception sat heavier on shoulders that refused to shrug it off. The prickle of different feelings for the woman angrily roaming the cabin refused to be dismissed. They continued to squeeze, demanding heart and head space.

The loss of control was infuriating. The mission had always been clear.

Darcy's pain and demise were the mission. No question. Yet there had to be constant personal reminders that no sort of relationship could develop with Darcy. It could never be a consideration, even for a second.

Still, the voice that guided every action fought to be heard in Darcy's presence. The one that reassured this was the only way, the one that knew peace would come at the end of the journey with Darcy.

Fight fire with fire; that's what Mother had said.

Fire wasn't the only weapon. There was betrayal, manipulation, and deceit, and all would cause Darcy the same pounding sorrow. Until Darcy felt that crushing grief, everlasting and relentless, it couldn't be over.

It was ridiculous to entertain that it could be anything different.

The curtains were wrenched closed, and the lights were dimmed. Darcy would find no trace of Amy—not the Amy she thought she knew, anyway. This one had been so easy. Darcy's unflappable faith in people had been her downfall. Again. Her constant ability to forgive and find renewed hope in any challenge, along with the whimsical and trusting way she approached the world, was as maddening as it was endearing.

Was that why he had favoured Darcy? Was she an easier child to be with? Was she easier to love? It wasn't the first time that thought had occurred, and the questions continued to churn as snow crunched underfoot.

Had Darcy been special to him? Had they spent a lot of time together? Had he loved her more than the child he had given life to? And what was so appealing about Darcy's mum that he would leave his family behind and sacrifice them to a life of misery?

Maybe one day soon Darcy could finally answer those questions.

Chapter 14

JOE FINALLY RELEASED HIS GRIP on Darcy's knee as the plane rolled to a stop at the terminal. She rubbed at it and threw him a dirty look. "You really should have had that vodka."

He smiled apologetically. "Sorry, I bloody hate flying, but not sure I could stomach vodka at seven-thirty in the morning."

"Wuss. It might have saved me some pain."

"I promise to down at least two on the way home, but we've got work to do today." He rubbed his hands together as if he was almost relishing the meetings ahead of them.

"Are you actually excited about this trip?"

"What?" He held his hands up. "I'm excited to be out of the flipping office that's for sure. And you can't complain about a free trip to Amsterdam."

"I suppose," she reluctantly agreed. "Although I doubt we're going to see much."

"Ah, c'mon. At least try to be excited. Couple of meetings, then we've got the night to ourselves. I promise you a good time."

Darcy glanced across the aisle to where Bridget was already flouting the mobile phone rule, and Anja stared out of the window. "I'll hold you to that promise because I'm not sure how much fun it's going to be with those two."

He shrugged. "We don't need them to have a good laugh. You might even find you enjoy spending time with me."

Darcy laughed. "Don't bet on it."

The seatbelt sign switched off, and they bustled in the small space, collecting coats and laptops from the overhead storage. Darcy laid a hand on Anja's arm as she squeezed into the aisle beside her. "You okay?"

Anja nodded and shrugged on her coat. "I will be once this is over with."

"If it helps, Joe is promising us a good time tonight."

Anja glanced his way and snorted. "Oh, I bet he is. But more likely he means you than me. Or Bridget," she whispered conspiratorially into Darcy's ear.

They both laughed out loud, and Darcy winked his way.

"What?" He looked between the two of them confusedly.

"Nothing," they chimed, and Anja laughed sincerely for the first time in weeks. It warmed Darcy's heart, and she thought the trip away and change of scenery might be a good thing after all.

After the most boring three meetings of Darcy's life, and an awkward dinner with some company seniors, they were finally propping up a bar sans Bridget and her fellow bosses.

"I want something Belgian and fruity," Anja declared.

"Is that a beer or a man?" the barman joked.

"Just give me a raspberry Bacchus," Anja snapped. She clearly didn't find him funny.

He pulled a face and moved on to Joe and Darcy. "And for you?"

"Two IPAs, please. Your pick."

As the barman set to serve them, Darcy looked around the bar Joe had insisted was one of the best in Amsterdam. Chalkboards covered most of the wall space, listing the hundreds of European and American beers in stock. They were interspersed with kitschy pictures and slogans proclaiming the positives of drinking beer, all of which Darcy was happy to believe.

The long wooden bar shone, despite being marred with knots and scratches. She hung her coat on to a tall stool and plonked herself down between Anja and Joe. It seemed safest to keep them separated given Anja's mood and Joe's excited chat.

"Told you it was a good one, didn't I?" He took a swig of beer and smacked his lips with a self-satisfied sigh.

"You've done well, Joey, I love it."

"Hey, less of the Joey. It makes me sound like a twelve-year-old boy."

"Aren't you?" Anja's tone was droll, and fortunately he didn't bite; he merely stuck his tongue out at her in the way a twelve-year-old boy might.

"So, Darcy." He spun his stool and turned towards her. "How's the love life?"

Darcy ignored Anja's contemptuous snort. The thought of her failed date with the nonexistent Amy and the frustratingly slow progress with Eilidh overrode her mild annoyance at her friend. She figured it might be nice to talk about Eilidh with someone vaguely interested, who might share her resolve to remain positive.

"Well, for your information, it might be on the up."

"Oh really?" He leaned in conspiratorially. "Do tell."

She took a sip of her own beer and thought back to their brief meeting and subsequent text conversations. "There's not much to tell to be honest. I bumped into her in the street, we exchanged numbers, and we're finally going out this Friday."

"Oh...so it's all lovely and new still."

"As if you know anything about that," Anja chimed in.

"Hey! I get dates, you know. Dude, are you even meaner than normal today?"

Darcy shoved Anja with an elbow and leaned close to her ear. "Quit it, you. It isn't Joe's fault, and this isn't like you. Play nice."

Anja's eyebrows furrowed, and she held Darcy's gaze for a moment before looking down into her beer. "Aye. Sorry."

Satisfied, Darcy turned her attention back to Joe. "Yeah, it's very new. But I think it might have promise."

"Seriously?" The sceptical tone was back in Anja's voice. "How can you tell that from what? Two minutes of chat and a half dozen texts?"

"What did I just say?" Darcy's patience was waning.

"Okay, okay." Anja held up her hands in acquiescence. "I'm sure you'll have a wonderful time and live happily ever after." She slid off her stool. "I'm away to the toilets."

Darcy watched her go and sighed. In the last few days, Anja had become distant and more than offhand in her negativity about Eilidh. Darcy knew she shouldn't exactly expect bubbling excitement about the upcoming date, but she had hoped Anja might find a way to put her own troubles aside even for a minute to be happy for her friend. Especially after the Amy disaster.

When she had told Anja about that, she had practically felt the "I told you so" vibrate from her, although she'd never actually said the words. There had been no reassuring hug or offer of wine and chocolate until they were sick. Only a shrug and a "stalker strikes again, don't worry about it".

It wasn't the Anja she knew. There felt more to her reticence, and Darcy worried about how hard the break-up was actually affecting her.

"I think she's jealous."

Darcy spun back around to face Joe. "Eh?"

He smirked and took a sip of beer. "Anja. I think she's jealous you've got a date."

"Don't be ridiculous."

"Ridiculous or right?"

"You don't know what you're talking about. She's recently split up from her husband, remember? The one who cheated on her after six years of marriage? She's heartbroken and down on love, not jealous."

"Yeah, yeah. Heartbroken and all that. But I'm telling you, she's jealous of your new bird, Darcy."

"Firstly." Darcy swotted his arm. "Don't call her that. And secondly, repeat that again anywhere near Anja and it won't be your arm getting a slap."

"Whatever you say." He looked smug, and she wanted to follow through on her slap threat. "You know her best."

A small part of Darcy wondered if what Joe was saying could be true. Then she shook herself; now she was being ridiculous. "Exactly. I know her best. She's simply feeling a bit lost and alone after Jason. She needs to know I'm here for her, that's all, and maybe she sees Eilidh as some kind of threat to that."

"Or she wants you all to herself."

"Joe, seriously. Shut the fuck up, okay?"

Anja appeared back at her side. "What's the boy saying now? He hitting on you?"

"Erm, I am here, you know."

Anja waved him away and pulled Darcy off her stool into a corner a few feet from Joe. "Can we go somewhere else after here, just the two of us?"

Darcy looked back at Joe for a moment, torn between feeling bad for him and also wanting to give her friend whatever she needed. "Naw, c'mon,

An. We can't ditch him in a foreign city on his own. Who the hell knows where he'll end up?"

Anja's shoulders deflated as she glared over Darcy's to Joe. "I can't cope with him right now. With his innuendo and silly banter. It's exhausting."

"Maybe you could just try a little bit? Eh? Let it go for a few hours and enjoy a bit of silliness. He's not that bad, you know. Please. For me?"

At that, Anja's face softened. "That's unfair. You know I can't say no to that face."

Darcy laughed and reached out to squeeze her hand. "C'mon, have a beer and a laugh, and I promise no more chat about women or men or relationships."

"Sorry. I'm being a total killjoy, aren't I?"

"I think given the circumstances it can be forgiven, but after the past couple of weeks of moping, how about we try something new tonight?"

"Fine. But you should know I'm not happy about it."

"That's the point."

Anja laughed and tugged her back towards the bar and an abandoned-looking Joe. Darcy watched her paste a smile on her face as she signalled the barman and asked what he would recommend next in her politest voice.

"Everything okay?" Joe murmured.

Darcy nodded, still thinking a little on what Joe had said. She knew he was being ridiculous; it was merely insecurity on Anja's part and worry because of the stalker situation. There was no way it was any more than that. Besides, of all people, what the hell did Joe know anyway?

Chapter 15

THEIR SECOND DAY IN AMSTERDAM was as uneventful as the first. They drank cheap prosecco at an exhibition on the evolution of wind turbines and sat through yet another presentation on future developments.

Darcy enjoyed her job, and Joe was right about getting out of the office for a few days, but holy crap it could be dull. PowerPoints had always had the ability to induce a nap in her. She longed for the moment they could escape and check out more of the city.

After freshening up, she met Anja and Joe in the bar. They looked to be having a heated discussion, and she sighed, fed up with playing referee.

"What's going on?" she interrupted them.

"This one"—Anja hooked a thumb in Joe's direction—"wants to invite Bridget to dinner."

Darcy pulled a face and looked at him as if he had two heads. "Why on earth would we do that?"

"I feel bad. We ditched her last night as well. It wouldn't be so terrible, would it?"

"Yes," Darcy and Anja replied in unison.

"Tell you what, Joey." Anja wrapped an arm around his shoulder. "If you're so worried, you have dinner with her. We're out of here."

She grabbed Darcy's hand before she could protest and headed for the lobby. Darcy glanced back and caught Joe's forlorn face, but he didn't follow. "Maybe he's got a thing for Bridget after all."

Safely out on the street, Anja let go of her hand. "Nah. I think he's kissing ass, that's all." She looked left and right then back at Darcy. "Where to?"

It was dark already and crisp with frost, and Darcy wanted to explore. "How about a walk to Museumplein? We can't leave without a photo at the *I Amsterdam* sign."

"Then you promise dinner and wine?"

"Promise." Darcy hooked her arm through Anja's. "What's the rule on expenses and alcohol again?"

They fooled around for a while at the *I Amsterdam* sign, climbing in and out of letters and taking selfies. The Rijks museum was beautifully lit, and Darcy caught a stunning picture of Anja sat on the letter 'D', staring up at its imposing form.

Her stomach growled at the wonderful smells wafting from food trucks, and she talked Anja into having dessert before they headed for dinner. She carried a large plate of Dutch pancakes smothered in butter, chocolate sauce, and icing sugar to where Anja sat by the pond.

Anja returned the grin plastered on her face. "You look flipping delighted with yourself."

Darcy sat close with the pancakes on her lap and offered Anja a fork. "Who wouldn't be? These look bloody awesome."

Simultaneous groans escaped them as the first few mini-pancakes were devoured. Light and rich with sticky, warm chocolate, they blissfully melted on her tongue.

Anja popped another pancake in her mouth, and Darcy joined her as she scanned the atmosphere around them. Teenagers stood around in large groups, speakers blaring music she and Anja were too old to get, as skateboards, backpacks, and large cups from the latest fast food trend sat amongst them. They jostled each other, flirted and laughed, as older tourists weaved between them, searching for the perfect picture angle. The unmistakable scent of weed drifted their way, and both inhaled deeply before laughing at each other.

"Oh, to be young again." Darcy chuckled.

"I came here once when I was young." Anja folded up the now-empty paper plate and tossed it in a nearby bin.

"Really? When?"

"I was seven or eight I think. My mother had family here, and we spent Christmas and New Year with them. My dad brought me here for *De kerstboomverbranding,* which means Christmas tree burning."

"Burning Christmas trees?" Darcy didn't understand. "Sounds traumatising."

Anja laughed. "It strangely wasn't. All these people turned up with their dead trees, tied to bikes or pulled in carts. They queued up in their hundreds to add them to a bonfire that the fire brigade had set. I remember standing there mesmerised as the flames roared. The embers were falling all around us, little smouldering flakes that landed like snow on our winter coats."

She had a wistful look on her face that made Darcy smile. "You don't really talk about your family, but that sounds like a cool thing for your dad to take you to."

Anja came back from the memory and shrugged. "Not a lot to tell. But yeah, it was pretty cool and has always stuck with me."

She stood and stuffed her hands in her pockets. "I'm absolutely freezing. Can we go eat some proper food?"

Darcy took one last look around. "Don't pretend it's food you're after when I know it's the wine."

Chapter 16

ANJA HAD BEEN BACK ON form, and Darcy hadn't laughed so much with her friend in a long time. A snug of a bar had happily welcomed them after dinner, where the woman serving had shamelessly flirted with them both and succeeded in getting them tipsy.

It had felt almost as if they were in someone's living room, where small tables folded down from the walls and people crammed themselves into the nooks and crannies and mismatched chairs. From the ceiling hung a forest of multicoloured ties amongst fringed light shades and walls covered in portraits, news clippings, and trinkets. High shelves were loaded with so many confusing objects that every time Darcy scanned them, she spotted something new.

Then there were the creepy dolls. Their eyes tracked Darcy's movements and made her shudder. She had never been one for dolls.

Two hot wines down, they had finally asked about the history of the place and discovered they were in none other than Amsterdam's first ever lesbian bar, Café 't Mandje, opened in 1927.

The stress and boredom of the day had long left Darcy, and she mused over how easy it was with Anja, when it was only the two of them. With the wine in her veins, she allowed her mind to wonder if it would be different if they were more than friends. Would anything change? Apart from the sex.

Oh God, she was thinking about sex with Anja! Where the hell had that come from?

She watched as her friend flirted right back with the bar woman. Darcy knew it was in the name of more free drinks, but she felt a small pang of jealousy twinge in her stomach.

Anja looked her way and winked, then leaned in close and whispered, "Don't worry, you're the only girl for me."

It wasn't possible that she'd read Darcy's mind, yet there was a prickle of satisfaction and reassurance in her words Darcy appreciated in that moment. Had she been too quick to dismiss Joe? Was that why Anja had been so contemptuous and uninterested in her dating plans? It didn't seem realistic given how recently Jason had left and Anja's reaction to his deception.

But what if she was simply angling for a rebound and thought Darcy was an easily accessible target? No. Anja would never play with their friendship like that.

Darcy signalled it was time for home with a tap of her watch in Anja's direction. The way Darcy's mind was running from her, it was clearly for the best.

As they stumbled back into the hotel, Darcy caught sight of Bridget sat alone at the bar, with a tumbler in one hand and her phone in the other. She cut a solitary figure, and Darcy felt a little guilty that they had ditched her and Joe earlier in the evening.

She tugged on Anja's sleeve and pointed in Bridget's direction. "Let's go have one for the stairs with her."

Anja groaned. "Really. You're too damn nice, Darcy. You know that, right?"

"Aye, whatever. C'mon, we can't leave her drinking with only her phone for company."

"Maybe she prefers it that way. Maybe she's chatting with someone hot on her phone. Actually, is she with anyone? I've never heard her mention a spouse or partner."

Darcy was thoughtful a second, wracking her brains. "Me neither. Let's go find out. I'm drunk enough to be brave. Who knows, we might even find out if she is actually sleeping with Joe."

They approached with caution, but Bridget afforded them an uncharacteristic smile. Darcy guessed the whisky in her hand had not been her first.

"Here's trouble. Have you been out causing havoc?" Bridget signalled for a member of bar staff and ordered a round of single malts. "That okay with you two?"

They both nodded, neither willing to turn down the boss's generosity or question her choice. "Thanks."

She laughed and gestured to a table away from the bar. "At ease, soldiers, we're off duty."

"Oh good." Darcy chuckled and threw an arm around Anja. "Because we're pretty bloody pissed."

"No. I'd never have guessed." For once, Bridget's sarcasm came with humour rather than loathing. "What have you been up to, then?"

They'd had a brilliant night, and Darcy was excited to regale it. She pulled out her phone and flashed pictures in Bridget's direction. "We went to the park and clambered all over the big Amsterdam sign trying to get a perfect selfie. Aw, look, An, that's a cute one." She showed Anja one of the two of them perched on top of the "M".

"Very cute. Don't forget the pancakes," Anja piped up.

"Aye, the pancakes were awesome. Then dinner, wine, the oldest lesbian bar in the city where Anja chatted up the bar girl and the creepy dolls watched you."

Anja scoffed. "The dolls were creepy, but the chat was for free drinks and you know it."

"Still happened," Darcy interjected. "What else? Oh yeah, we shared a space cake, smoked a joint..." She watched Bridget's eyebrows raise and maintained her seriousness for a few seconds before cracking up. "As if. We're too old for that malarkey. Although I might have been tempted at Joe's age."

"What happened to Joe anyway?" Anja asked. "We thought he was having dinner with you."

"Joe?" Bridget shook her head, clearly confused. "I haven't seen him all night. No doubt he did find his way to a coffee shop to sample the local delicacy."

The guilt Darcy had felt earlier tripled instantly, and she deflated a little. "Ah, sorry about that, Bridget. If we'd known you could have joined us..." She trailed away knowing the sentiment was half-hearted and Bridget wasn't daft.

"And be a third wheel to you pair?" She smirked. "No thanks. Besides, I had other plans."

This piqued both their interests. "Oh yeah?" Anja failed at casualness and got straight to the point. "Hot date?"

Bridget took a sip of amber perfection and quirked an eyebrow. "Wouldn't you like to know?"

"I thought you were married?" Darcy embraced her alcohol-induced bravery—who knew when she would get another opportunity to grill Bridget on her private life? They were off duty, after all.

She watched Bridget stare into the glass a moment and swirl the whisky around. She looked between them both as if considering how much to tell them. If anything at all. "No. I decided it wasn't for me. I've lost too many people to commit to that kind of dependency."

Anja side-eyed Darcy, clearly as shocked as Darcy was by the blunt honesty. All three women were quiet, and Darcy suddenly couldn't think of a single other thing to say to change the subject. Instead, she knocked back half her whisky in one.

Then Bridget continued, and Darcy sat still, afraid to break the moment. "I know you might think that's sad, but I'm happy. My career has always been important; it allows me to travel and explore. I'm not like you, Darcy, I don't believe in happy ever after. One day it might find me, but I'm not wasting energy chasing it."

Anja remained quiet, and Darcy attempted a subtle kick under the table. She needed help with this one. "Are you open to it at least? You won't find it if you're not."

Bridget smiled softly at her. Darcy couldn't be sure if it was in pity at her idealism or appreciation of her efforts. "You'll not change my mind on this, so don't bother trying."

"But wouldn't you want to share all those travel adventures with someone? What do you think, Anja?" She said her name firmly, inviting her to jump in at any time with a contribution. Instead, Anja shrugged and sipped her whisky, avoiding Darcy's stare.

"Nope. I'm an only child and I was never good at sharing," Bridget said. "Plus, I don't think you need a partner to be fulfilled in life. There are plenty of people like me out there, whether by design or coincidence, who are living perfectly happy lives on their own."

"Here, here." It was Anja's first contribution, and she reached to clink her glass to Bridget's.

Now Darcy felt awkward. She hadn't meant to intimate that Bridget was some sad and lonely case, or that she couldn't be content with her life as it was. Or that Anja couldn't continue to be a kick ass happy person without Jason in her life. "Of course. I didn't mean it in that way... I..."

"I know you didn't. It's okay, Darcy." Bridget laid a reassuring hand on Darcy's arm. "You never know, I might meet someone down the road that will bring something else to my life. I hear love is funny like that; it gets you when you least expect it. And yes, I'm open to it." She smiled. "But I also am, and will be, quite fine on my own."

Bridget looked at the clock on her phone. "Speaking of which, you pair of chancers have got enough out of me for one night. Bugger off and leave me be with my whisky."

Anja knocked back the last of hers. "Good idea. I'm knackered." She stood and plucked both hers and Darcy's coats from the back of their chairs. "You heard the boss. Let's go."

They wished Bridget goodnight and headed for the lifts.

Darcy bumped Anja's shoulder. "You could have helped me out there," she hissed. "Talk about awkward."

"You started it. And you're the one that believes in all that true-love stuff. I'm hardly in the position to be talking to Bridget about the benefits of finding happy ever after."

That put Darcy in her place. She didn't argue, and they rode the lift in silence.

At Darcy's door, Anja smiled. "That doesn't mean I don't hope you find it, by the way."

"What?"

"Your true love."

Darcy scoffed. "Aye, chance would be a fine thing."

"You never know. It might happen where you least expect it."

She held Darcy's gaze, and there was a moment of something. Darcy wasn't sure what it was, but soberness suddenly hit her and the air between them thickened. Then Anja was moving towards her, and she swore her heart stuttered. Her eyes closed. Why was she closing her eyes?

Then warm lips were on her cheek, and Anja squeezed her briefly in a hug. "Thanks for tonight, Darcy. I really needed it."

She watched Anja stroll along the corridor to her own room, as if she hadn't just given Darcy a minor heart attack. Darcy fumbled with her key card, shoved the door opened, and then slammed it closed with her back against it.

What the fuck? Why on earth did I think she was going to kiss me? We've said good-bye and goodnight a thousand times before. Why was tonight any different?

She flopped on the bed and buried her head in a pillow, hoping to quash her imagination from any other wild thoughts it might be conjuring. It didn't work, and she shot back upright.

Did I want her to kiss me?

No.

Don't be ridiculous, Darcy. It's been a long time since you last had sex. That's all.

Yet she couldn't help but wonder what she would have done if Anja had kissed her. Would she have kissed her back? Would it have been that easy? She could almost guarantee Anja would be a great kisser.

She tried the pillow method again, groaned loudly into it. *Stop it, you sex-starved idiot. Or you'll never be able to look her in the eye again.*

Lately Darcy's easy smile was more often tinged with worry and apprehension, but tonight it was back, and it had been missed. That truth should have been difficult to acknowledge, when in fact it came easy at the sight of her usual beaming grin. The one that shone like a beacon and attracted even the chilliest of characters to her.

More than one person peered Darcy's way as she entered the bar, openly as well as furtively over their partner's shoulder. She always drew a second glance. Even the bar person was enamoured; he'd shine a hole in that glass soon if he didn't tear his eyes away from her.

Her eyes were glassy and bright with alcohol, and her mouth moved animatedly. Occasionally a tooth nipped the edge of her lip, the effect matching the cheeky lilt in her voice. A blanket of contentment wrapped around those who were near her, and as she spoke, she would lay a hand on an arm, a shoulder, a knee. So expressive were those hands that if someone grabbed and held them still, Darcy would surely stutter.

Only one person was responsible for the dampening of Darcy's smile, and that thought couldn't help but tug and tear everything apart. Every plan had so far come to pass, had achieved its goal, but the rest might as well be tossed aside. It would be impossible now to undertake.

This hadn't been part of the plot. It was an unexpected and ugly truth after everything that had happened, and despite the feeling's Darcy's glorious smile brought, it had still choked for a long time. Now after months of trying to swallow it down, it demanded to be recognised. Accepted.

To finally admit it brought some relief, but it also meant deciding whether to walk away or do something about it. The tide was turning, but that didn't mean the current had to dictate their destination.

Because that's what love did.

It swept you along, and you became powerless to control it.

It was nerve-wracking.

No, more than that.

Terrifying.

It went against everything that had been ingrained internally over the years. Darcy had been one of the reasons for all the heartache. She had lived a stolen childhood that rightly belonged to someone else.

If it weren't for Darcy and her mother, death would never have come knocking.

Up until this point, every moment had been measured, the discipline admirable and the execution flawless. The voice that laid the plans had remained strong and reassuring throughout.

Now it faded.

It picked at every new weakness and berated each subsequent failing because the unthinkable had transpired. The one thing planning hadn't accounted for or could change.

And no one had the answers for what might come next.

Chapter 17

Bridget stalked from her office and nodded at Anja's desk. "Where's the wife?"

"How should I know?" Darcy snapped. "And we're just friends, you know."

Eyebrows raised, Bridget held up her hands in defence. "No need to be that way, I was only kidding. Can you send her into my office when she gets in?"

Darcy hung her head a little, unsure why she was being so defensive. "Sure."

Bridget nodded and headed for the kitchen. Darcy rounded on Joe.

"First, she knows about the stalker, and now she's calling Anja my wife? You are bloody sleeping with her, you little shitebag, aren't you? Admit it."

"Are you serious? You have met Bridget, right? Scary-as-hell, boss-lady Bridget?"

"Yes, although I hear some folk find that attractive. Do you, Joe? Tell me the truth."

"I swear, I'm not. And I never speak about you guys with her. It's like she said last week, she's the boss and loads of other folk talk about you and Anja. Half the guys in here have indulged in that fantasy, trust me."

"Well, fucking don't, okay? We're friends. That's it, all right? Are people not allowed to only be friends anymore? I might be a lesbian, but it doesn't mean I fancy every woman I know. Do your gender a favour and stop being so gross."

At the look on Joe's face, Darcy knew she'd gone too far.

"Okay, Darcy. Calm yourself. It was only a joke."

Without another word, Darcy stormed to the bathroom. She was angry at Bridget and Joe, but mostly with herself. Why was she getting so upset about a throwaway jokey comment that she'd made about herself and Anja a million times before? And anyway, what the feck did Joe know? He didn't know Anja beyond how she took her tea.

His words in the bar in Amsterdam still rang in her ears. She couldn't shake them after the corridor moment, no matter how many times she told herself the idea of her and Anja was absurd.

Anja wasn't jealous. She was purely upset because Darcy had a date lined up that meant she would be left home alone. They'd spent almost every evening together the past few weeks since she had kicked Jason out; it was no wonder she was feeling perturbed that someone else was taking away Darcy's attention. It was Darcy's fault for allowing her to become so dependent.

All that seemed logical, but still her mind wandered. What if Anja did like her? What would that mean for them? Darcy shook her head and glared at herself in the mirror.

"Impossible," she stated firmly to her reflection.

But what if?

A panicky feeling started to take hold. Apart from the first few months bumping in to Anja around the office, when she couldn't help but admire her classic Nordic good looks, she'd never considered they could be anything more than friends. Yes, they were close now, closer than she'd ever been to a woman who wasn't her girlfriend. So what? Wasn't that friendship in its best form? Was she simply freaking out because it was the kind of friendship she'd never experienced before?

Darcy ran her hands under the tap and patted her cheeks and forehead with cool fingertips. What was she thinking? Bloody Joe and his damn fantasies, driving her crazy and making her read more in to Anja's every look and action that would otherwise not even blip on her radar.

She straightened her suit jacket and smoothed down some errant curls. Took a few breaths and eyed herself again in the mirror. Joe had got to her. He was winding her up, nothing more. There was no reason or indication to think that anything he said had a grain of truth. Anja was her friend and had done nothing that should make Darcy think she wanted it any other way.

The end.

She returned to her desk, and there was still no sign of Anja, but there were three missed calls from her on Darcy's personal phone. Bridget seemed preoccupied on her own phone, so Darcy slouched down surreptitiously and called her back.

"Hey, what's up? Bridget's asking for you."

"Fuck Bridget."

Darcy held the phone from her ear. This wasn't good. "Okay, fuck her. What's happened and where are you?"

"I'm at home and I'm a mess. I've been trying to psych myself up to come in, but I don't think it's going to happen. That bastard."

"Bastard? Who's a bastard? Oh wait, Jason. Have you seen him?"

"Oh yeah, I've seen him. He showed up here last night, flowers, chocolates, perfume…the whole shebang. He was on his knees begging me to take him back."

"Shit. How did that go?"

"How the fuck do you think? I told him where he could stick his gifts. Didn't even let him past the front door. We ended up in a screaming match in the driveway. Gave the neighbours a real show."

"Aw, sweetheart. I'm sorry. What can I do?"

"I don't know, Darcy. I'm a frigging mess. I feel sick. I look a state. I didn't sleep a wink without you here."

Darcy was quiet a moment. This wasn't good. She'd headed home last night, despite Anja's pouting, but she had frankly been exhausted herself and needed a night in her own bed. It had been mostly fine hanging out at Anja's and the Amsterdam trip had been a happy break for them both, but the pull of a bath on her own turf and a bit of quiet had been too strong.

"Sorry, love. I needed a bit of time to myself, that's all."

"Hey, don't apologise." Anja's voice was starting to calm. "I didn't mean it that way. I guess I've got used to having you close, that's all. You've been amazing. You know that, right? I wasn't trying to make you feel guilty."

Darcy smiled to herself. "What did you say to him, anyway? When he asked if you'd take him back."

"What do you think?" A derisive snort came down the line. "Told him to go fuck himself. I can't believe he thought it would be that easy."

That made Darcy pause for thought. It had never occurred to her that at some point Anja might actually consider taking him back. She wouldn't be the first person to do it. "Do you think you might one day? Take him back, I mean."

She heard a long sigh, and Darcy found herself holding her breath before a quiet "no" allayed a fear she didn't realise she had. *What the hell was going on?*

"I feel on the brink, Darcy. I'm not sure what of, but I don't know how much more crying I can do. I'm exhausted."

"Get some rest, then. I'll tell Bridget you won't be in, and I'll head over as soon as I can get out of here. Until then, try to sleep and be good to yourself. Take a bath, eat some fruit, and drink some tea."

"No, Darcy. You've got your big date tonight. I'll be fine. Honest."

Darcy heard the crack in Anja's voice and knew she couldn't leave her alone in this state. She thought of Eilidh and wondered if she would be as understanding if Darcy were to cancel. She was sure she would be, and Anja was the most important person right now.

"It's not up for discussion. I'm sure Eilidh will understand, and if she doesn't, well, then she's not worth my time anyway."

"Are you sure?" Anja's voice was tinged with hope, and Darcy knew she was doing the right thing.

"I'm sure. In fact, you know what? Pack an overnight bag and head over to mine. I think a change of scenery will be good for you, and there's no chance of Jason turning up there."

"Have I told you how amazing you are today?"

Darcy laughed. "Only the once. But don't be shy about telling me again."

"You're amazing."

"I know. And I'm about to promote myself to super amazing. Make sure you pack a swimsuit."

"Hot tub in February?"

"You got it. I've been dying to try it out in winter. We can drink wine and eat cheese until we're either sick or pass out."

Anja chuckled. "Sounds like a plan. I'll see you later."

Darcy hung up and found herself smiling. Then she remembered the text she now needed to send to Eilidh. A stress ball bounced on her desk, and she looked up to find Joe and his smug grin looking at her.

"What?"

"Oh, nothing." He feigned innocence.

"Stop looking at me like that, then."

He clearly couldn't contain the reason for the smugness. "Cancelling your hot date for Anja? Maybe I had it the wrong way around."

She threw the stress ball at him, and it bounced harmlessly off his chest. "I'm serious, Joey, one more word about me and Anja…" She let the threat hang in the air, and he held up his hands before turning back to his screen without another word.

Little shitebag, trying to stir things up.

She returned to her phone and tapped out a text to Eilidh, still hoping she would understand.

> *Eilidh, I'm so sorry to do this at the last minute. But can we re-arrange tonight? Friend in need and I don't think she should be alone. Do you mind? D x*

The response was quick, and Darcy breathed a sigh of relief.

> *Of course. I understand. Why don't you text me a time and place when you're next free? I have a feeling you'll be worth the wait. E x*

Darcy glanced up at Joe to see if he'd noticed the grin she found herself unable to stifle. He was so wrong. Eilidh's few simple words stirred so many emotions, so different from how she felt spending time with Anja. Eilidh thought she would be worth the wait, and Darcy had a feeling she would be worth it too.

Chapter 18

DINNER HAD BEEN A TAPAS of all their favourite junk foods, washed down with a bottle of cheap white wine.

Darcy flopped on the sofa and rubbed her tummy. "I'm so stuffed."

Anja joined her and did the same. "Me too. Do I really have to put a bikini on now? I'm not sure my stomach is going to be happy about it." She puffed it out. "I look six months pregnant."

Darcy laughed. "Well, it's not as if you need to be strutting your stuff to impress me. I've held your hair for a drunken vomit, don't forget. Nothing will ever be worse than that."

"Ugh. You're never going to let me forget that one, are you?"

"Nope." Darcy groaned as she rose to her feet. "C'mon, the fire should have it hot enough by now, and it's an excuse to open another bottle."

"As if we need an excuse." Anja allowed herself to be pulled to her feet and dutifully traipsed behind Darcy to the bedrooms.

"True. But at least we can say we were simply following hot-tub law when we're hungover tomorrow. I'm pretty sure it's illegal to sit in one without alcohol."

Both changed, and despite being wrapped in thick robes, they squealed as the biting cold hit them as they scurried around to the back of the cabin. Snow fell in light wisps, and a good few inches still lay on the ground.

Fairy lights twinkled under the canopy hung over the wooden tub, and Darcy lit a few lanterns before reviving the wood-burning fire that heated the water. She stirred it with an old canoe paddle and dipped an elbow in. "Toasty."

Anja needed no further invitation; she hung her robe and immersed herself in the steaming water before Darcy had even opened the wine. "Here you go." She handed Anja a glass, propped her own on the side, and followed her friend in to the water, sighing in satisfaction as the warmth enveloped her.

"This is awesome." Anja lay her head back and sipped from her glass tipped at a precarious angle. "It's a shame we can't see the stars though."

"I know. The canopy can come down in summer, but for now, it keeps the rain and snow off our heads."

They closed their eyes and sat in silence for a while. The only sounds were the gentle lap of water against the sides and the crackle of the fire. Occasionally, something would scurry nearby in the woods, drawing their attention, but otherwise the forest slept around them.

A contented sigh from Anja made Darcy open her eyes. She studied her friend, the ends of her hair splayed in the water, her fringe damp from the steam. She looked serene, calmer and more relaxed than Darcy had seen her in weeks—which was something, given the circumstances. Darcy was pleased she could provide a place that made Anja feel that way. To return her friendship, be there in the same way Anja had been through the whole stalker ordeal.

The candlelight glowed and flickered upon Anja's face, highlighting the pinkness in her cheeks. Darcy marvelled at her skin, forever tanned and smooth; she'd bet money Anja never suffered with spots as a teenager.

Before she realised where her gaze was heading, it landed on the swell of Anja's breasts, semi-submerged and glistening. Darcy watched a droplet of water trickle from her collarbone, then trail to her cleavage…

What the…

Darcy shook herself. Literally. Wine slopped over the edge of her glass in to the water, and she sat upright abruptly.

Anja's eyes were open and looking at her. "You okay?"

"Yeah. Fine. Thought I heard something, that's all."

She pretended to scan the woods, and Anja followed suit. Only darkness and shadows met their search, and Darcy forced herself to sit back again. Relax. Joe had been talking nonsense, and she was being bloody stupid. She could slap him for playing with her head. So she checked out her friend's breasts. It didn't mean anything. They were right there, two feet away; no one would be able to stop themselves from noticing.

Besides, she'd already had this conversation with herself after Eilidh's last text. It was Eilidh she should be thinking about, excited about, because Eilidh was interested in her and wanted to date her. This right now with Anja was not a date. It was two friends enjoying each other's company, and one of those friends simply happened to enjoy boobs.

"Does it worry you?"

Anja's question snapped Darcy out of her internal ramblings. "What?"

"Being out here alone all the time. What with everything that's happened."

Darcy shrugged. "A little, I guess. I try not to think about it."

"Easier said than done, I imagine." Anja swallowed back her last mouthful of wine and scanned the woodland again. "I think I'd be scared. I'm not sure I'd be able to stand it."

As Anja topped up their glasses, Darcy thought about it. "I keep telling myself if I let them ruin this place for me, then they win. I worked hard to be here, and I'm not letting some creepy coward take that away from me."

"Well, as long as you're taking precautions. Being careful like the police advised."

Darcy smiled. "Yes, ma'am. I've even started researching CCTV. As much as I hate the idea. The thought of it makes me feel as if I'm in a prison rather than my home."

"I think it's smart, and you don't have to keep it forever, only until the creep is caught."

"True. Anyway, with the amount of time I've been spending at yours recently, I've not had much cause to worry out here on my own."

Anja looked a little sheepish. "I'm sorry about that. I know I've been dumping a lot on you recently."

Darcy waved her away. "Don't be daft. It's hardly been a struggle."

Anja raised her eyebrows at that. "Really?"

"Okay, you might have been hard work on one or two occasions."

"Cheeky..." Anja poked her in the side with a toe, and they both laughed. "Can we not talk about that tonight? I'm having too nice a time. Let's make this a Jason-free zone."

Darcy stretched out her arm and clinked her glass to Anja's. "Deal. Let's make it a stalker-free zone while we're at it."

They sat quiet again, sipping their wine. Darcy thought of Eilidh, wondered what she was doing with her Friday night since Darcy had cancelled their drink so last minute. Their conversations had never strayed to friends or family, and Darcy wondered if Eilidh had an Anja that she could spend a Friday night with, talking shite over cheap plonk.

She reached for the bottle and was surprised to find it empty.

"Are we mad if we open another bottle?"

"Never." Anja smiled. "In a minute though. It's too cold out there."

Darcy settled back and swirled her hands through the water. "It's starting to cool. I suggest rock, paper, and scissors for who has to put another log on the fire and get more wine."

"I think you'll find I'm the guest here, Darcy Rose Harris. I'm not moving from this spot."

She said it in her stern work voice, the one she reserved for when she had to actually act as Darcy's senior in front of the bosses, and the use of her full name always told Darcy she meant business.

"What? That's not fair!" Darcy flicked water her way. "I think you long ago stopped being a guest here."

"Still." Anja splashed water back at her and proffered her empty glass. "In that case I'm pulling rank."

"Fine." Darcy snatched it from her and plonked it on the side next to her own. "I'm not ready yet though. Let me psych myself up to it."

Anja splashed her again and whooped in victory. "Knew you couldn't say no to me."

"Only because you used your Bridget voice."

"My Bridget voice?"

"Aye, that's what Joe and I call it. When you're attempting to be authoritative and all Lead Engineer-y with us around the bosses. We play along for your benefit because we figure it would be better to have you rather than anyone else get Bridget's job when she moves up."

"Pfft…unlikely. Plus, who says I'd want to be the boss? The way I'm going with all the time off, they'll not be offering me Team Leader anytime soon."

"Nonsense. It's not as if you're off every other week with a 'cold'."

"Bridget wasn't mad at me being a no show today, then?"

"Naw, she was surprisingly supportive. I reckon there's an ugly ex lurking somewhere in her past that's making her uncharacteristically charitable. Remember how she was all cryptic in Amsterdam? Unfortunately, it did mean I had to put up with Joe on my own again though."

"What's the little sod done now?"

Wine had always made Darcy brave. Or was it daft? She chuckled conspiratorially and eyed Anja before blurting. "He thinks you fancy me. Or I fancy you. I can't remember which way round it was today. He's been at me for ages about it."

Anja's hands stopped swirling in the water. "Really? What gave him that idea?"

Darcy waved her off, suddenly regretting bringing it up. Why had she brought it up? "Ah, you know what he's like, him and his wife jokes. Then I cancelled my date with Eilidh today to see you, but no matter. He's probably jealous, that's all, and trying to stir up some shit."

"Hmm…probably."

Darcy had expected indignation and denial mixed with a number of expletives aimed at Joe. Instead, Anja twisted her empty glass on the ledge and remained quiet. It put Darcy on edge. Where was her inappropriate joke that would help Darcy disregard what Joe had said? The longer Anja didn't say anything else, the faster Darcy's heart raced, until she could stand it no longer.

"I'll go get that bottle."

She moved to stand, to get out and away from Anja's silence, but a hand grasped hers and pulled her back down in to the water. "Wait."

The intensity of Anja's gaze bore in to Darcy. The hand gripped tighter, pulling her closer. Still she didn't say anything. Goosebumps prickled on Darcy's neck, and she made to move away. "What's wrong…?"

Anja's lips were only cold on Darcy's for a moment before they pressed harder and the intensity of the kiss warmed them both. Wet fingers slipped around Darcy's neck, bringing their bodies together, and Darcy gave in to it. Anja was kissing her. Her best friend. In her hot tub. And Darcy was kissing her back.

Why was she kissing her back?

The butterflies felt wrong. An uneasy feeling washed over her, and she pulled away. Breathless and wide-eyed, she pressed a hand to Anja's chest and separated them fully. "What the hell?"

Anja's gaze mirrored her own, as if as surprised as Darcy about what they had done. "I'm sorry, Darcy. I thought…"

She trailed away, shaking her head, moving back into her seat away from Darcy.

"What? Where on earth did that come from? I told Joe he was talking shit today. Was I wrong?" Although Darcy had indulged a few fantasies lately, the reality felt wrong. She cursed herself for being so foolish as to think otherwise and for believing that their friendship might automatically translate into something more, rather than consider that they were friends for a reason.

She had been unprepared for the worst.

The worst being that she wouldn't feel the same and it would ruin everything.

Anja visibly swallowed and looked everywhere except at Darcy.

"Well?" Darcy prodded. "Say something."

"Yes," she whispered. "You were wrong."

Darcy sank back in to her own seat, the words punching space between them. "But…what? And how? Why?"

Anja stayed quiet. Her breathing heavy, she scrubbed her hands over her face and held them there, as if hiding from Darcy.

"Talk to me, Anja, because I'm freaking the fuck out over here."

"I don't know. Okay?" Her voice took on a panicked note. "I don't know when it happened. Or how. But it feels as if I've been hiding it for so long, and I don't want to hide it anymore. I'm sick of hiding."

The warm water was doing nothing to rid Darcy of the chill that prickled her skin and she began to shake. Was that shock? This wasn't new for Anja as Darcy had wondered. She thought back over the past two years, when they had become closest. The times Anja had been there, to reassure her, to protect and look after her. To sleep in her bed and wrap her arms around her when she got scared in the night. She'd allowed her in based on friendship, and now she couldn't help but wonder if every moment had had an ulterior motive or an excuse to be close to her?

"How long have you been hiding it? And what about Jason? You're married, for Christ's sake, Anja. All the tears over him cheating and then suddenly you're kissing me and telling me this? What am I? A rebound?"

"Never. Don't ever think that. He doesn't matter to me, Darcy. Not the way you do. We're connected in so many ways. Ways you don't even know."

Darcy blew out a breath. She couldn't even begin to fathom the situation, to figure out exactly what Anja was saying and what it meant for them. "I'm not even sure where to start. I mean, were you faking it? Being upset about him?"

"No," Anja cried. "It's not like that." She smacked the water in frustration, and Darcy pressed herself back further to the edge. "This isn't how it was meant to go. I knew it was too soon."

Darcy watched her climb out and pull on her robe.

"Can we go inside and talk, please? I feel ridiculous doing this out here."

Darcy didn't say anything. She still felt cold and knew it wasn't the snowy weather. Anja started towards the cabin, and Darcy had no choice but to follow. Once inside, she stalked to the fire and added a couple of logs, then rubbed her arms and willed the warmth back in to her limbs.

Anja stood with her at the fireside and moved to take her hand, but Darcy quickly pulled away.

"Don't. I need you to not touch me right now. It's too confusing." Darcy's heart thudded, and she felt Anja's stare but couldn't bring herself to meet it. "I feel as if I'm questioning every single moment of us now. It's always just been you and I, best friends, secure and safe." She finally raised her gaze to Anja's. "Special."

There was real sorrow etched across Anja's face, and it hurt Darcy to see. She wanted nothing more than to reach out and smooth it away, but this time she couldn't. This time it wasn't for her to make it all better.

"Exactly," Anja whispered. "I thought we were special. In fact, I know we're special. I guess I hoped that meant you might feel the same way. I kept looking for signs, and recently, I don't know? It felt as if there was something more there. Then we had such a wonderful time in Amsterdam, and it really clicked for me. I knew I had to tell you soon."

Darcy took a deep breath. She had no idea how to make this better but knew honesty was the only way forward. Anja was out on a limb, and it was only right that Darcy be upfront about her own thoughts and feelings.

"I'll admit I did consider it for a moment. I won't lie, I've wondered about us a few times. Questioned if my own feelings were more. And you're right, Amsterdam was wonderful, in fact at one point I thought you were going to kiss me. Then I told myself I was being an idiot."

"When?" Anja's voice was still barely a whisper.

"When did I think you were going to kiss me? In the hotel corridor."

Anja nodded gently. "I almost did. For a second, I thought you wanted me to, but I couldn't be sure." She sat on the arm of the sofa with her hands clasped in her lap and stared at the roaring flames. "Why did you never bring it up? Tell me you'd thought about us in that way?"

Darcy perched on the other arm, maintaining her distance. "I guess I never wanted to risk finding out I was wrong in case it broke us. Plus, you were married. Then in Amsterdam I wondered if it was because we'd been living in each other's pockets lately. If it was a way for you to forget Jason. I could never be used, Anja, especially not by you."

Anja's voice rose in exasperation. "I told you it's not like that, Darcy. I would never treat you that way, please believe me. This goes way beyond Jason. It has for a long time."

Darcy blew out a breath and looked to the ceiling, taking a moment in the hope of calming the thundering in her chest. Her legs trembled a little as the adrenalin of the hot tub moment faded. She slid off the arm to sit fully on the sofa and slouched down in to it. "I don't know what else to say right now. What this means for us?"

Anja tentatively did the same and moved a little closer to her on the sofa. "Then let me explain, Darcy, please."

Darcy wasn't sure she was ready to hear it yet. She felt bewildered and wounded by Anja's admission.

She thought of Eilidh and shook her head. Had Anja been manipulating her this whole time? Were her harsh words for Eilidh, for Amy, for all the others because she harboured her own feelings for Darcy?

She had been there for Anja through the entire Jason saga, and now Anja was telling her he didn't matter. Had all those tears and tantrums been faked?

Her imagination made a leap she was unprepared for, and she hoped badly that it was untrue. Had Anja used the Jason situation to get her to cancel her date with Eilidh and spend the night with her instead? Anja was yet to be clear on how Jason fitted in to this whole revelation of hers.

She was afraid to know but had to ask again.

"Was it all a lie, you being upset about Jason? If you're telling me he doesn't matter, then what have the past few weeks been all about? Was it a way to spend time with me? Or was it an excuse to make me cancel with Eilidh? I need the truth, Anja. It's the only way we're going to be able to deal with this."

"Fuck." Anja pulled at her hair.

"Are you kidding me? It was?" Darcy couldn't keep the incredulity from her voice. "That was all for show? To somehow suck me in and guilt me into being with you? Do you realise how fucked up that is, Anja?"

"No. That's not how it was. You have to believe me. It wasn't meant to go this way. Please understand, Darcy. I could feel us becoming closer, but I wasn't ready to tell you and I knew with Jason still around we had no chance of becoming more. You would never even consider the possibility of us."

There were so many questions and scenarios causing chaos in Darcy's mind, and so far, none showed Anja to be the person she thought she knew. The friend she loved and adored and trusted. "Did he even cheat?"

Anja hung her head, wordlessly answering Darcy's question.

"Oh, Anja. Tell me you didn't kick him out because of me? Tell me you didn't end your marriage of six years because of some crush on me?"

Anja's head snapped up again. "It's not a crush. Don't reduce it to something so easily dismissed. This is very real for me, Darcy, whether you feel it or not. I think deep down you do."

"You're wrong. This has never been more for me, Anja. Despite a few idle wonderings in the early days, then Joe messing with my head. Even if it were, how could it be anything more now with the lies you've told?"

"I only ever lied for you." Anja shifted in closer.

"Don't." Darcy held up a hand and moved back. "Don't you dare say it was for me. Can't you see how wrong you've got this?"

"Yes," Anja thumped the sofa in frustration. "I know I've gone about it all wrong, but once I'd told the lie about Jason, that was it, I had to see it through or risk losing you. I got impatient, okay? I knew you would never look at me how I wanted if Jason was still around. I thought if we spent more time together you would finally see me and know the truth. That I could be more than your friend. That I was the person you had been looking for all along. I thought if I kissed you it would all fall into place for both of us."

"What did you say?" Darcy's blood turned to ice, and the damp hair on her neck bristled.

Anja looked confused. "I wanted us to be more than friends."

"No, not that." Darcy jumped up and rushed past her to the bedroom. She yanked open the bottom drawer of her dresser and grabbed an envelope. She stormed back to a perplexed Anja and pulled a card from the envelope, one she'd kept from before the police had become involved.

She slammed it against Anja's chest. "Did you write that?"

Anja took the card but didn't look at it. Instead, she kept her gaze fixed on Darcy. "Darcy, please. Don't do this."

"Answer the fucking question, Anja. Did you write that?"

Anja finally glanced down at the card. "What is it?"

"Don't play games. You know what the hell it is. Read it." Darcy backed away from her so-called friend. "I said read it."

"Darcy, you have to understand…"

"Read the card, Anja."

Anja began to cry. She slowly turned the card over and sucked in a shaky breath. "*One day you'll see me. One day you'll know the truth.*"

It was whispered, but the words had the same impact as the first and every other time Darcy had read them.

"Tell me you didn't write that." Darcy choked back her own sobs as the pieces fell in to place. "Please tell me you didn't write that, Anja. Tell me it isn't you who's been torturing me all this time."

Darcy watched as the card fell from Anja's hand and tears streamed down her face. Her voice remained low, tinged with resignation. "I'm so sorry. But you don't know the whole story."

Darcy's legs gave a little then. She held onto the back of the sofa for support. Anja got up and moved towards her, hand outstretched, but Darcy knocked it away. "Get away from me," she screamed. "Don't fucking touch me!"

"Darcy, please. I'm so sorry. I love you. I need you to know the whole story."

"Love? Are you fucking kidding me? You don't know the meaning of the word. I need you to get out of my house."

"Not until I explain. You need to let me tell you everything. Why I'm here and how this happened. Then I know you'll understand."

"Explain what? That you're a lying manipulative bitch? If this is love to you, then you are seriously fucked up, Anja." Darcy stood up straighter and swiped at her tears before pointing towards the door. "Now get out. Before I call the police and tell them everything."

Anja moved towards her again, and Darcy flinched. She was suddenly very afraid of her so-called friend. She tried to put the sofa between them, but Anja was quick, grabbing her by the wrists and pulling her closer. "I need you to listen. It'll make sense if you'll allow me to explain. Please, Darcy, I'm begging you. Five minutes. That's all I'm asking."

Darcy twisted to get out of her grasp. "I don't want to hear another fucking word. How can I believe anything you have to tell me?" She managed to release her hand and shoved Anja with enough force to send her tumbling to the floor.

On her knees, she grabbed for Darcy again and gripped on to her robe. "Please, give me one chance to make it right and then I'll go."

Darcy shrugged her off and bolted for the door. She stuffed her feet in to her boots and relieved her keys from their hook. Anja stayed on her knees, and Darcy turned to face her, taking in the beautiful face stained with tears and anguish. It did nothing to thaw the ice that had set in Darcy's heart. "If you won't leave, then I will. I can't bear the sight of you."

She threw open the door and headed for her car. Anja's sobs followed along with the soft crunch of snow under bare feet. Darcy didn't look back. Once in the car, she thumped the button to lock the doors, then screamed through the window, "You need to leave me alone. If you're here when I get back, Anja, I'm calling the police."

She knew she shouldn't drive. There'd been so much wine. She also knew she couldn't stand another second of listening to Anja's pleading. As she drove down the track, she risked one last glance back in the rear-view mirror. Anja had fallen to a heap in the snow, sobbing into her hands.

When the world went to shit around her, this would normally be when Darcy would rush to Anja's to seek solace. Sorrow washed over her as she realised she had no idea where else to go.

Chapter 19

ANJA SCREAMED OUT INTO THE empty night as she watched Darcy's car lights disappear down the track.

How could she have been so stupid and weak? She had caved into months of pent-up feelings and fucked everything up. This wasn't how it was meant to go; the plan was for Darcy to come to her. But in that moment, Darcy had looked so beautiful, and the opening had been there. She'd been powerless to resist.

She scooped a handful of snow and threw it pointlessly towards the retreating car. Then the panic began to set in. Was Darcy going to tell everyone? Would she phone the police? What was stopping her?

Anja needed to try and speak to her, reason with her, calm her down and make her understand. Plus, she was drunk; they both were. Darcy shouldn't be driving. That thought didn't stop her from running back towards the cabin and grabbing her own bag and keys.

If she could follow her, make sure she wasn't headed for the nearest police station, then at least Anja would know she had time. Once Darcy calmed down, had space to think, maybe she would give Anja the chance to tell her story. Maybe she would have the opportunity to tell Darcy how it had all begun, how her feelings had turned from anger and hatred to love.

She slammed the car door and smacked the steering wheel a few times in frustration, with herself, with the whole situation. After weeks of emotional turmoil, ridding herself of Jason and the baggage he'd hung around her neck, she'd been so close. She could feel it. Darcy had begun to see her as something more, something real. She had more or less admitted as much. Had disclosed the fantasies, however fleeting, about whether they could be more. It was the shock of Anja's sudden kiss, that was all. She would come around eventually if only Anja could let her in on the heartbreak she had suffered, then her actions would make sense. As misguided as they had been, she was sure they could be rationalised and understood.

Sure, there was still the complication of Eilidh, but it wouldn't take much to derail that. Delete a few more texts, side-track Darcy with the guilt of friendship, and she was sure the other woman would soon run out of patience. Anja had done it before and was confident this woman was no different from the rest.

Once Darcy knew the whole story, knew what Anja had sacrificed and forgiven her for, she would realise Anja was someone who truly loved her. Someone who would do anything for her. In time, there would be forgiveness on both sides, and they would be able to move forward, to make it work. Anja knew it was meant to work; Darcy would see that eventually.

In the meantime, she needed to know that Darcy was okay and wasn't about to do something that could wreck it all before it had begun. Darcy didn't have her phone or her bag; where would she go? Who would she run to? Anja knew her mum was on the other side of the world. She had a few friends from the sailing club and hiking, but would she turn up on their doorstep in her robe this late at night? She didn't think so.

Who did that leave? Colleagues? She pictured Darcy showing up at Bridget's or Joe's. Did she even know where they lived? Would she run to Eilidh? A woman she may have been speaking to for weeks over text but who she had only actually met once? It didn't seem likely.

The roads were quiet, and Anja pushed her speed. She knew the twists and turns by heart having made the journey hundreds of times. Instinct made her take the right turn towards Inverness; there was no way Darcy would take the left. It followed the south shore of Loch Ness, deserted at this time of night with only a few tiny villages interspersing the long, dark winding roads. Anja was sure she would head for bright lights and perceived safety.

Red lights shone ahead, and Anja squinted, trying to make out the model of the car. It wasn't her. She gunned the engine and rode the car's bumper until a short straight appeared and she could overtake. Another set of lights dipped out of view over the brow of a hill, and she pressed her foot to the floor to catch them.

It was her.

Anja hung back a little but flashed her lights, willing Darcy to slow down. The roads were slick, and neither of them was in a fit state to drive. Hedgerows and trees flew by either side, making her head spin and her stomach lurch. They were already going too fast, but Darcy still increased her speed. Anja tried her lights again, keeping a distance but unwilling to give up.

"Shit." Her back end skidded out a little, and she turned into it while easing back on the accelerator. Darcy's lights disappeared around a corner, her car unaffected by the ice. "Fuck, Darcy, you need to slow down."

Anja tried a different tactic. She dropped back a turn and tried to keep a little distance. If she disappeared from Darcy's rearview, maybe it would make her think she had given up and she would calm down. Drive at a more sensible speed, or even pull over.

She crested the brow of a hill and began a descent that would take them to the edge of the city. The lights were bright in the distance, and Anja felt a little relief that Darcy would at least be forced to slow down. Between roundabouts and traffic lights, Anja could keep tracking her without the fear of icy roads.

She saw a flash of red through the trees at a corner below, before it disappeared around the next one. Anja's speedometer read sixty-five miles per hour, already too quick; she could only guess how fast Darcy was going.

The descent levelled out to an open straight, bringing them only a mile or two from town. She felt her wheels slide again, enough to cause a leap of panic. As she corrected, the red lights ahead caught her eye, swayed violently one way, then the other.

"Fuck, no."

She watched as Darcy's car fishtailed wildly. Anja began to quickly gain on it, so she slammed on her own brakes. There was nothing she could do to stop it. When Darcy's car hit the grass verge, she clamped her eyes shut as the unthinkable was set in motion.

Chapter 20

EXHAUSTED FROM A LACK OF sleep, Eilidh's legs refused to run. She kept moving anyway, one foot in front of the other, in an attempt to walk the claustrophobia off.

Claire had been gone for almost three weeks, and the house was still adjusting. Eilidh was still adjusting. Despite the sparseness now that it had been purged of Claire's belongings, when sat alone with only her thoughts for company, it suffocated her. The lack of colour and energy was now more apparent not only in her house, but in her life in general.

The doctors told her there would be days like this. Highs and lows. Uncontrollable but able to control her. She knew the exercises, knew the right pills to take; it was a matter of waiting it out and keeping busy until then.

Gratitude got her through most days. Through the therapy, the pain, the anxiety, and the trauma of what she'd been through. Most days. The days when she woke up in the morning and smiled because there had been a time when the doctors thought she would never wake up again.

She'd make a fresh pot of coffee and take a minute to stand over it to inhale the beautiful aroma. She'd savour a cup before languishing in a shower. Alone. Where the powerful stream of water would make her groan in appreciation, and her toothbrush was the best invention in the world after finally getting rid of terrible hospital breath.

But still there was the odd day where no matter how good the coffee, how hot the shower, or how minty fresh her breath was, she still needed a sign that the whole world wasn't shite.

Today was one of those days. She had gone from the high of a great first couple of weeks back at work and making plans with Darcy, to the low of Darcy cancelling their date at the last minute. The weekend stretched before her with nothing in it but to wallow in self-pity. Books couldn't hold her attention, TV offered no respite, and there was only so much social-media scrolling she could take. Even Sam couldn't save her tonight; his date was still on.

She'd tried the exercises, taken the pills, tried to wait it out. She'd cleaned and organised and changed bed sheets, moved pictures around, and thrown away trinkets that were meaningless now Claire was gone. She'd scrubbed and brushed and wiped and polished. She had half-heartedly replied to texts from friends who were long overdue her attention.

Yes, she was okay. No, she wasn't surprised about Claire leaving. Yes, they would make plans to catch up soon. She had even called her mum for a rare blether about nothing and everything, forcing her to make half-hearted promises to visit. But the anxiety still simmered under the surface, continued to pick at her fears and stop her cold with an irrational dread that wouldn't shift.

So now she wandered the darkened streets looking for kindness and light. For a sign, a conversation, a moment that would ease the panic and let her know it would be okay. If only it were that easy. The brashness of a Friday night in town came at her from every angle. Everything wrong jumped out at her. It made her flinch and cringe and want to cower away. The parent swearing full volume at their crying child. The teenager dropping litter in the street. The group of drunken men, rambling and swearing. The graffiti and the boarded-up shops. The strangers bashing shoulders because neither were willing to relent in their chosen path. The music blaring from an open flat window. The dog incessantly barking.

It was all too much.

The world started to spin around her, and the urge to flee took over. Her legs broke their sedate pace, finally giving in to what she needed. To run. To hide. To get away. She followed the river and headed out of town, towards the quiet. To the lanes beyond the houses, to the fields and the moonlit sky. Most of all, towards the blessed calm.

Her trainers broke through the dirty slush gathered at the edge of the lane. Each icy puddle she thumped through slapped her legs with cold until they were numb. They moved of their own accord, keeping rhythm with her breathing, propelling her further in to the darkness of the countryside.

She had no idea how far she'd come, was unaware of when the landscape had changed into one that was now unrecognisable. A car came around the corner, and she hopped on to the verge for safety. It didn't stop her being splattered with the filthy remains of the last snowfall. She tried to catch a glimpse of a familiar landmark in its headlights, but nothing stood out.

Finally coming to rest, she breathed out heavy clouds of air. The frost was biting, and her clothes were soaked. Her shoulder ached in a way it hadn't for weeks; she rolled it, trying to loosen off the throbbing clench of muscle around the joint. If the running had helped take her a step forward mentally, it'd taken her two steps back physically.

She spun around on the spot, trying to place where she was while waiting for another car to pass and light her way. Why the fuck hadn't she taken her phone? She turned to head back in the direction she had come; there was bound to be a village or brown tourist sign. This was Inverness— there were brown signs everywhere.

A screech in the distance snapped her head back around. She heard the gunning of an engine and the unmistakable sound of cars speeding. It was distant but approaching fast. She leapt on to the verge again and craned her neck to see past the hedgerows. If it was bloody boy racers out there, in the sludge and ice, buggered if they'd have consideration for an idiot jogger in the middle of nowhere.

She saw the headlights veer around one bend and head towards the one she stood a few feet ahead of. It showed no signs of slowing. The second car was a corner or two behind but gaining.

Eilidh braced herself for the car to turn and spray her head to toe on its way past. She had all her favourite swearwords ready to cuss its retreating bumper.

But it didn't turn.

The lights veered, left, right, left again. Tires squealed, Eilidh screamed, and the car straightened but too late to take the corner. It kept its line and ploughed over the verge, touching down at an angle.

Everything slowed as the dark mass began to rotate, once, twice, three times. It smashed into the frozen earth of the field, the grinding crunch of glass and metal cutting through the frosty night.

Eilidh winced and slammed her eyes shut, not daring to look again until she heard the ominous thump of the car finally coming to rest.

Chapter 21

ANJA MAINTAINED CONTROL AS HER car skidded to a stop. Her head slammed back against the headrest, and the seatbelt caught her as she flung forward again. As her head snapped back up, the shadow of Darcy's car disappeared over the verge. She saw the rear lights flash high in the air, streaking through the darkness as the car catapulted itself into a spin.

"Darcy," she screamed before she yanked off her belt and tumbled out of her own car. "Fuck. Oh fuck." The urge to run to Darcy, to help her, to save her, gripped her heart in a vice, but the fear that sat solid in the pit of her stomach held her back. She spun around, looking for other cars in the distance, for a sign anyone else was around.

A dark shadow darted over the verge, and Anja's headlights caught the reflective strips of a running top. "Oh shit."

"Help," the shadow screamed in her direction, and Anja froze. She ducked back into her car, where she slammed and locked the doors. She gripped the wheel in an attempt to ground herself while her mind spun. Her love for Darcy battled with self-preservation, threatening to render her immobile and fucked either way.

Darcy needs you, Anja. She's fucking crashed her car and she needs you right now.

But what if they say it's my fault? What if she tells the police everything? Says I chased her and caused the crash?

You're meant to love her and would do anything for her. Fuck everything else; you need to help.

She hit her forehead a few times with the palm of her hand.

Think. Think. Think.

Anja restarted the engine and rolled closer to the verge, lowering her window. "Is she okay?" she called out to the runner, now crouched by the driver side window. "Have you phoned for an ambulance?"

A torrent of swearing came back. "Who's there? Get your arse down here, I need your help. Please. I think she's really hurt."

Anja thought she might vomit. With the state the car was in, she could only imagine what it had done to Darcy. Her Darcy.

"Hello?" the voice called out again. "Did you hear me?"

She swallowed back the bile. "I'll call an ambulance."

There is someone with her. They will help and then an ambulance will come. Darcy will be okay. She has to be okay.

But Anja had to get out of there.

She made the call, leaving only the location and a hoarse plea for them to hurry. With one last glance towards the shadow of the stranger, she made a U-turn. She had to get back to the cabin and remove all trace that she was there that night. No one could know. Her whole life was over if Darcy told anyone.

In her rearview mirror, she watched as smoke began to plume from the car. She prayed the stranger had gotten Darcy out, that she'd be okay, and this whole night could be forgotten between them.

"She'll be okay. She'll be okay." Anja kept the mantra going as she raced around the cabin. She replaced her robe with clothes and hung it back in place. She cleared wine glasses and bottles, left the fire to dwindle, and binned the remnants of their dinner. Tears coursed over her cheeks the entire time, and she had to constantly gulp the panic down.

"She'll be okay. She'll be okay."

She surveyed the cabin one last time, satisfied every trace of their evening had been removed. Darcy had been surprised, that was all. They'd only ever been friends, so of course it would have been a bit of a shock, but Anja knew the feelings weren't one-sided. Darcy felt something, of that Anja was certain. She was just afraid of admitting it.

Anja would take care of her and prove to Darcy that she was worth it.

One day, Darcy would see her. One day, she would know the whole truth.

Chapter 22

A BURST OF WHITE EXPLODED in front of Darcy, crushing her chest and battering her face. It combined with the tooth-cringing groan of metal on metal and the musical shatter of glass. Pressure built rapidly in her head; it felt close to implosion, as her body strained against gravity.

The blood, cloying and sticky, attracted her hair and smothered her face. Her eyes wouldn't open. Her legs wouldn't move. Her mouth failed to form anything coherent, only panicked bursts of screaming.

While every sense was assaulted with chaos, the stranger's voice drifted through and offered her something to grasp on to, something real to believe in, as everything else around her twisted in confusion. It was a tether to the world that was attempting to destroy her.

It was muffled at first, and the initial few words were expletives. "Shit, shit, fuck." Followed by reassurances Darcy was sure were meant for both of them. "It'll be okay. Help is coming. You're going to be okay."

She became aware of banging near her head, but when she tried to turn towards it, her body refused to comply. The stranger's voice cut through again, and Darcy grabbed it, focusing on something she could make sense of while all around the fear closed in. "I'm going to smash the window. If you can hear me, cover your face."

She wished she could.

Eilidh's instinct screamed at her to get the woman out of there, and for a second time she cursed not bringing her phone. She craned her neck.

Where the fuck had the other car gone? What were her chances of help anytime soon?

The woman hung limp, upside down, the seatbelt straining against her neck and torso. She was almost ghostly, wrapped all in white, and Eilidh couldn't tell if she was awake. The roof was semi-caved, the windscreen a spider web of cracked glass, as was the window Eilidh peered through.

She scrabbled around in ice and dirt, feeling for something big and strong enough to do what she needed. Her hand finally wrapped around a good-sized rock, and she gripped it tight.

"I'm going to smash the window," she shouted. "If you can hear me, try to cover your face."

Eilidh paused, waiting for the woman to move. When she didn't, Eilidh took a breath, drew her arm back, and swung the rock against the window with everything she had. It didn't budge. She tried again. Three times, four. It finally relented, and her arm shot through the shattered pieces with the rock. She gasped as the glass tore at her arm, but the pain was quickly forgotten when she heard a groan escape the injured woman.

She used the rock to bash away the remaining shards, then leaned through the gap and pressed her fingers to the woman's neck. It was slippery with blood, but she managed to hold still long enough to feel it—the faint pulse of life. The woman was still with her. Barely.

Sharp sprinkles pricked Darcy's raw flesh, telling her the stranger had done as they'd said. She could feel movement, feel the stranger close to her. But the pain tore through her until blissfully the world went dark.

She wasn't sure for how long, only that the stranger was once again shouting. This time, the words were confusing and didn't seem meant for her.

How many people are out there?

The original voice became soft, muttering, "Fuck. Fuck. Fuck," on repeat. Then it was comforting, despite the quiver, despite the obvious fear. "Okay, I'm going to get you out of there. Then we'll decide what to do. All right?"

The stranger didn't wait for a reply.

They pressed up tight against her and began to fumble around, looking for something. "I'm so sorry if this hurts. I'm so sorry. But I need to unclip this to get you the right way up and out of this car."

Darcy tried to prepare herself for whatever might happen next. It seemed an age. The cursing was in full flow, laced with a note of panic. Without warning, her body was mercifully released, her head striking something solid as it crumpled. She tried to cry out, but the smoke had taken over and choked the screams in her throat.

The woman's face was a mask of blood, and her body weight combined with the cave in the roof pressed her chin against her chest. Eilidh could make out a dark patch blooming across her torso that seemed to be growing. She pulled aside the robe as best she could, but there was no injury that she could make out.

Then blood dripped on to the back of her hand, and she traced the source to a steady flow that was seeping from one of the woman's legs. It was jammed above her, twisted at an awkward angle. Her arms were flopped either side of her head, and her left wrist looked all kinds of wrong.

Eilidh didn't know what the fuck to do.

Right, what are my choices?

Try and move her or run for help.

There didn't seem to be a right answer. She wondered again where the fuck the other car had gone.

"Is she okay?" a voice called out from the road.

It made her jump, and she split her head against the sharp edge of the window frame.

"Who's there?" she yelled back. "Get your arse down here, I need your help. Please. I think she's really hurt."

Eilidh waited for a response but all she could hear was the idling of the other cars engine.

"Hello?" she called out again. "Did you hear me?"

"I'll call an ambulance," the voice finally replied.

Eilidh heard the engine rev and saw a flash of headlights as the car pulled away. "What the..."

The injured woman groaned, pulling Eilidh's attention back to the situation. She had a decision to make and needed to make it fast. "Fuck. Fuck. Fuck. Okay, I'm going to get you out of there. Then we'll decide what to do. All right?"

The woman groaned again, but Eilidh was sure she hadn't understood a word. She reached through the window, fumbling to find the seatbelt socket. "I'm so sorry if this hurts. I'm so sorry. But I need to unclip this to get you the right way up and out of this car."

When she got no response, Eilidh angled more of her body inside and braced her other arm and shoulder under the woman's torso in an effort to control her fall once the seatbelt released. She took a breath and pressed.

Nothing.

The belt stayed snapped in to place. She tried again, then yanked the clip with everything she had. It still didn't give.

Then she smelt it. Smoke.

"Oh shit. That can't be good." She squeezed her eyes closed and offered up a silent prayer.

Unclip this fricking belt and help me get her out of here.

She jammed her thumb against the button again, it popped, and the woman slumped on top of her. The smoke was stronger, filling her nostrils and choking her throat. Eilidh gradually pulled herself from under the woman's body and tried to ease her around so she lay sideways along what was the roof of the car.

"Oh my God." She surveyed the mess of the woman's leg, one foot clearly snapped in the wrong direction and a bone protruding from her shin, the source of all the blood. "This is going to be painful, but we need to get you away from the car."

Careful of her mangled wrist, Eilidh hooked both hands under the woman's arms and tugged. She braced her feet against the window frame initially, making slow but steady progress.

"C'mon, sweetheart. We can do this. We're getting you out of here. It's going to be okay."

So much smoke. And heat. And pain.

Firm hands hooked under Darcy's arms, and the blood rushed the other way as her limp form untangled and her legs flopped uselessly to the side. That's when the numbness started. When the cold began to take over.

"Oh my God." Even the terror in the stranger's voice could only evoke a groan from her. Another type of fear kicked in knowing she was completely at the stranger's mercy. Anxiety, futile and infuriating. Darcy wanted to help, but not an inch of her body would comply.

"This is going to be painful, but we need to get you away from the car." She knew she was moving. Start, stop. Start, stop.

The stranger was crying. Tears that seemed born of frustration, rather than fear, and Darcy wished she could return the favour. To tell them it was going to be okay too.

The air became thicker, oppressive. Was it the blood or smoke that stopped her lungs from filling? She couldn't tell. Only that heat scorched her face and the stranger's tugs had become more aggressive and urgent. She could hear the laboured breathing of her saviour and wanted to tell them, *Leave me, it's too late, my body has deserted me. Whatever this is? Wherever we are? Save yourself.*

Eilidh's eyes stung with tears. Was it fear, frustration, or the smoke that was becoming ever thicker? She needed a little distance from the car that seemed ready to blow. Then she could reassess, try to make her comfortable, and run for help if the ambulance showed no sign of appearing.

The woman wasn't heavy, but the frozen ground proved her nemesis, her trainers offering little resistance on the icy grass and slowing her progress. The smoke billowed dark against the twilight, and flames had fully caught hold, licking the sides of the bonnet.

As they grew, Eilidh glanced down at the woman's face. In the fire's glow, she tried to see if the movement was getting any response, but all she could make out was a grotesque mask of blood and bruising. Both eyes were shut, bulging and swollen. Her hair was thick with deep red clots and plastered her cheeks, sticking to what seemed to be a hundred minute cuts that peppered her skin. Eilidh looked away, afraid it was already too late.

"We can do this. We're going to be okay. Help is coming." She repeated the mantra, for herself, for the broken woman she held in her arms, and for whoever might be listening. They needed help, fast.

Eilidh dug her heels in again, bracing the woman's weight between her legs, adjusting her grip, and tugging her another foot from the car. The flames now roared in her ears, her breathing laboured; she choked and tried to spit away the acrid taste of smoke in her mouth.

A flash of blue cut across the horizon, and then she heard it. The blissful sound of a siren in the distance. She rose to her knees, leant down over the woman, and spoke close to her ear. "Help's here. It's coming, sweetheart. Hold on for me. It's…"

The explosion tore across them both. The heat seared their faces and pressed them tight to the ground. Pain split through Eilidh's head and shoulder, but only for a moment, before her body released her from the trauma and the night became darker.

Chapter 23

DARCY TRIED TELLING HER EYES to open, but they refused to comply. She could sense movement all around, raised voices, mechanical beeps, and the rhythmic beat of heavy wheels turning underneath her. Hospital. She must be in hospital. The woman had been right: help had come.

A fog sat heavy on her, pressing down and stifling any movement she attempted. Why wouldn't her eyes open? Why couldn't she get her hand to her face? She knew it was bad, knew there was pain underneath the fog, knew her body wasn't as it should be.

An argument cut through the battle to open her eyes. "Miss, are you family?"

"No, I'm not family. But can I please stay with her?"

"I'm sorry, you can't come any further. Besides, you need to get yourself checked out. You're bleeding. Follow my colleague and they'll take you to another room."

"But I was there. I got her out before it blew. I was with her in the ambulance. Please, I need to know she's going to be okay."

Blew? Before what blew? Darcy recognised the voice. It had been with her. It had saved her. She wanted to scream for them to let the voice stay, let it hold her hand and tell her it would be okay again. Would she feel it if someone held her hand?

"I'm sorry, Miss. Go and get yourself checked out and leave your details at the desk. If it's okay with the family, we'll call and update you, and I'm sure the police will want to talk to you at some point."

"I'm not going anywhere until I know she's okay."

"I'm sorry, Miss. I don't have time for this."

A bang, followed by a whoosh, and suddenly light attempted to penetrate the darkness. It blurred behind her lids, but the only colour she saw was red. The fog pressed heavier, and the voice disappeared. Why couldn't they hear her calling out, telling them it was okay for the woman to stay?

All around her, people murmured instructions, talking in a language she didn't understand. The beeps, the rustle of plastic, the footsteps and words, all incessantly surrounded her. They were no comfort. She didn't know them, and no one was talking to her.

Oh God, oh fuck, she felt that. That was definitely her leg screaming out in pain. Why wasn't she screaming? A groan managed to escape lips she couldn't feel, breaking through the fog.

"She's waking up. Morphine, please. We need to stabilise her, then X-ray, CT, and call ahead to theatres. Quick as you can, people."

She heard mumbles of acknowledgement and a rustling noise near her head.

"Hello? Can you hear me? We're going to give you something to make you more comfortable.

No, no, no…no sedation. It was already too dark.

The blackness took her anyway.

Eilidh's chin dropped to her chest, and she jerked it back up yet again. The monotonous beat of the machines, combined with whatever the doctor had given her for pain, threatened to lull her to sleep every few minutes.

She sat up straighter in the high-back chair and reached for the water sat on the woman's side table. This was no time to sleep. She wanted to be awake when the woman eventually opened her eyes, wanted to make sure she would be okay.

After proving to them that Eilidh was in fact a colleague, who had passed through their accident and emergency doors herself, they allowed her to sit with the woman until family could be contacted and had arrived.

It had been over seventeen hours since Eilidh had woken up in the field with paramedics surrounding her. Her first thought had been, *Surely this time I'm not going to be so lucky?*

But she was.

Seventeen hours since she had chased the mangled woman through the accident and emergency unit, only to watch her be wheeled out of site, blocked by doors she wasn't allowed to pass.

Since then, her arm and head had been stitched, bandaged, and a box of pills placed in her hand. So many hours of pacing, of coffee, of arguing with harried staff that were stressed enough. Of pleading and worrying, wondering what was happening to the woman. Was she in surgery? Was she okay? Was she alive?

The police had loitered for a while. They'd spoken to Eilidh, but she wasn't sure how much help she'd been. It had all happened so fast. All she could do was relay vague details of the other car, and she hadn't even seen the woman driving it. It seemed the stranger in the bed was the only one who could give the police, and Eilidh, some answers.

Now nurses completed their rounds with a simple nod in Eilidh's direction. She tried to stay out of their way and not draw attention to her presence, in case someone decided she shouldn't be there after all.

She studied the woman lying prone on the bed, followed each tube that left her body, each wire that signalled her condition. Every inch of her seemed to be bruised, stitched, and swollen. Her face, upper torso, and limbs were swaddled in bandages and casts.

Eilidh sighed as yet another nurse entered the room. She looked Eilidh's way and raised an eyebrow.

"Well, aren't you a sight?"

Eilidh smirked. "I'm sure."

The nurse looked between Eilidh and her patient. "You know we're not expecting her to wake up anytime soon, so you should get yourself home. Get cleaned up, eat, sleep, then you can come back here fresh and ready to be of some real help."

Eilidh chewed her lip. She knew the nurse was right but hated the thought of no one being there and the woman possibly waking up on her own. The nurse seemed to read her mind.

"I'll call if she does wake up. But I'm telling you, the amount of drugs in her system, it'll be hours yet. So go on."

"I guess you're right." Eilidh stood and stretched out her back. "You promise you'll call?"

"Promise." The nurse offered her a sympathetic smile. "Now go take care of yourself for a while."

Eilidh blew out a steadying breath and nodded her agreement. "Thank you. I'll be back soon."

"You're welcome, my love. She'll be right here waiting."

The sound of her keys dropping in the bowl echoed down the hallway. Eilidh sighed at the silence that greeted her return home and wished for a pair of comforting arms to wrap around her. She shook herself; there was no time to be maudlin.

For the first time since leaving the hospital, she became acutely aware of the acrid scent of smoke that clung to her. She peered at her face in the mirror, pulled the bags down that hung under her eyes, and inspected their blood-shot tinge.

That's when she noticed her eyebrows and lashes were lightly singed. She ran a fingertip across the rough texture. The ends of the dark auburn hair that hung around her face were curled and discoloured.

She shrugged out of her torn and stained running jacket and let it drop to the floor. Her leggings, T-shirt, and sports bra followed before she kicked it all in to a pile to be thrown away later.

The nurses had given her soap and the privacy of the injured woman's bathroom to attempt to clean up her hands and face. The blood still clung under her fingernails, and her face stung, scorched by the fireball that had billowed above them.

She set the shower to lukewarm, wrapped a plastic bag around her bandaged arm, and finally stood under the blissful stream of water. The few stitches on her head smarted, but the need to at least rinse her hair outweighed the pain.

With her eyes closed, images from the past twenty-four hours ran incoherently through her mind. In no order, she went from lying on top of the prostrate woman to standing on the verge with the car speeding towards her. From her walk in to town to waking up to the flashing blue lights and everything else raced in between.

Memories of her own trauma not so long ago tried to take grip. The alleyway. The fear. The men shouting in her face while another lay helpless on the floor. The sickening sound of each brutal blow as they kicked him, before their violence was turned on to her.

The moment of weightlessness before her head struck the ground.

She quickly pushed the images away, determined to maintain her focus on the person she had helped. The one Eilidh realised she had actually managed to save.

She used one arm to soap, lather, and scrub. Then did it all again until every speck of blood was gone and only the scent of honey and almond was left. Warm towels awaited her aching body, and they almost made up for the lack of hug she craved.

Her mind went back to the woman she had pulled from the car. Who was she? Did anybody miss her? And why had she been travelling with such urgency? Where had she been rushing to in her dressing gown of all things?

The memory of a voice shouting out to Eilidh resurfaced. There'd been someone else there. Someone who had called the police, then left. Was it the other driver, the person speeding behind her mystery woman? Had she somehow been involved? After speaking to the police, the questions kept mounting, demanding attention.

Eilidh checked her phone. There was no call from the hospital, only a text from Sam asking if she'd rescheduled with Darcy and wanting the gossip. She smiled to herself, grateful for her persistent friend and his positive advice. No doubt he had his own Friday-night tale to tell.

She tapped a short apology and promised to see him again soon. There would be a whole lot more than Darcy to talk about, but she couldn't go to him with only half the story. Right now, she somehow knew the woman needed her, and leaving her in the hospital felt like the beginning. First, she'd heed the nurse's orders, but tomorrow her mission was to find out who the woman was.

Chapter 24

EILIDH FOUND THE WOMAN AS she had left her the day before. It'd been almost thirty-six hours, and still no one had shown up to claim her. She took a seat and pulled it in closer to the bed, wrapping her fingers around the hand not encased in plaster. A doctor she didn't recognise smiled when she entered and picked up her chart.

"Morning, I'm Dr Jackman." She reached across the bed and shook Eilidh's hand.

"Nice to meet you. Eilidh Grey."

The doctor turned her attention back to the chart. "So, how's our patient this morning?" It was rhetorical, and Eilidh stayed quiet while the doctor scanned the various numbers and notes, occasionally glancing at the monitors. When she didn't offer any further information, Eilidh couldn't hold back her questions.

"Any idea when she's going to wake up?"

Dr Jackman shook her head. "I really couldn't say. But with this type of trauma, I wouldn't be surprised if it's another day or two."

"Oh." Eilidh couldn't cover her disappointment. "But her brain function is okay? There's not going to be permanent damage? And you've controlled the internal bleeding?"

"Yes, the scans are promising. There's some swelling on the brain, but we're keeping an eye on it." She looked at her watch. "You're here very early."

Eilidh nodded. "I couldn't sleep and felt useless at home. Although I feel just as useless sat here."

The doctor perched on the edge of the bed. "Listen, holding her hand, talking to her, that's not useless. We still know very little about what a patient can hear or feel when they're unconscious, but you being here will mean something to her."

"You think so?"

"I know so." Dr Jackman smiled again, and Eilidh felt a little reassured.

"Okay. Talk to her. I can do that. Although..." Eilidh studied what was visible of the woman's face: Bandages wrapped her head and looped under her chin, and gauze covered a sizable portion of one cheek. A few butterfly stitches crossed her nose, the white stark against the black and purple of her eyes. "I don't even know her name."

Dr Jackman looked rightly confused, and Eilidh mentally kicked herself. "Wait, what? I assumed you were a relative." She was on her feet again, edging towards the door. "You shouldn't be in here."

Eilidh stood as well, fumbling in her pocket. "No, no. Let me explain." She crossed the room and handed over a plastic ID badge as the doctor opened the door. "I'm a physio here, look. The nurses said it was okay."

"Okay to sit with a stranger?" Dr Jackman pointed through the door towards the corridor. "You need to leave. Only the patient's family is permitted on this unit."

"I pulled her out." Eilidh couldn't help her voice raising an octave. The thought of being kicked out had momentarily panicked her. "I'm the one who pulled her out of the car."

The doctor dropped her hand. "That was you?"

"Yes." Eilidh breathed a sigh of relief at the doctor's softened tone. "They told me I could stay until they could get hold of her family."

"I see. Well..." The doctor held her hands up apologetically. "I'm very sorry, Miss Grey. You wouldn't believe some of the characters we get roaming around this place."

Eilidh pointed to the card still in the doctor's hand. "I know. I work here, remember?"

"Oh. Of course." She handed the card back and closed the door again. She gestured towards the seat and Eilidh sat back at the woman's side. "Please. Let's try this again."

"Sorry. I didn't mean to worry you there."

Dr Jackman waved it off. "So you're the mystery heroine we've all been talking about?"

If her face didn't already feel raw with what looked like a bad case of sunburn, Eilidh was pretty sure it still would have been red. "I guess. It was no big deal."

"No big deal? From what the paramedics said to the A&E staff, if you hadn't acted as you did, our patient here would be lying somewhere very different right now."

Eilidh ducked her head in acknowledgement. The thought had occurred to her in the twilight hours when sleep had been elusive, but she had quickly pushed it away. It didn't bear thinking about. "Scary thought."

"Indeed," Dr Jackman agreed.

"Still no name, then?" Eilidh studied the woman's face, wondering not for the first time who she was.

"Not yet that I'm aware of. When I saw you, I assumed it had come in, but the early shift hadn't updated her records yet. Our only form of identifying her is through the DVLA. The Fire Service called in with the car number plate to the police and they'll get in touch with her details and the next of kin. We should get a name soon."

"Seems strange that no one is missing her."

Dr Jackman offered a sad smile. "Well, for now she has you, and I'm sure whoever she is, she's going to be very happy to meet you when she wakes up."

Chapter 25

THE WORDS IN THE EMAIL had blurred long ago. Anja stared dazedly at her screen, lost in a cauldron of panic, paranoia, and fear that threatened to bubble over at any moment. All day, it had been torture to pretend everything was normal.

She wondered for the thousandth time how she had reached this point. It had all started so innocently. A morbid curiosity had taken hold of her and nagged until she'd agreed to satisfy it. She had simply decided to find out a little more about Darcy: where she was now, what she was doing. Was she happy? Was she in love?

She hadn't expected the thrill that came with every new piece of information about Darcy that was revealed to her. She held the information close, peeling back the layers slowly and deliberately, taking her time and treasuring each discovery. She consumed every detail with relish and imagined herself there, alongside Darcy, experiencing life with her.

The more she learned of Darcy's life, the similarities of their chosen careers, the easier it was to insert herself in to it. To pretend and to hope. That it had all been a bad dream and he had actually taken Anja with him. That she had been part of that family.

But it was a fantasy. The voice told her so.

The more she tried to ignore it, the louder it became. It taunted her, reminded her of the truth, and turned a wonderful possibility into a relentless quest for revenge.

Anja eventually understood it, and she started listening carefully.

While she'd lost herself for a moment in the illusion of Darcy, her mother's voice, strong and steady, brought her back to reality.

Darcy was the reason Anja's father had left.

Darcy was the reason Anja's mother was dead.

Anja's goal became clear. Her mother's voice drove her on, persistent and unrepentant in its need for vengeance. Her father had chosen Darcy and her homewrecker mother over them. She deserved to suffer, and deep in her core, Anja believed she couldn't rest until Darcy had everything stripped away from her, in the same way she had.

Darcy had lived the life that was rightfully Anja's. That had belonged to her.

She had to lose it all, and Anja had to be the one to take it away. Anja wanted to be there, up close and personal when it all fell apart. She didn't want to witness it from the side lines—she needed to be close enough to touch her pain. To live and breathe it. To let it cleanse and wash away her own with the knowledge that Anja was the one causing it.

Only then would her mother be avenged and the voice appeased. She longed for the quiet, for the day when her mother told her it was enough and left her be.

That day had yet to come. Instead, the voice mocked and laughed at her weakness because she had dared to let feelings for Darcy cloud the mission. It was a betrayal her mother would never let go of, and the voice told her so over and over again.

It was right. She was pathetic. She had fallen for Darcy before she even knew it was happening. Now she felt Darcy's pain as keenly as her own, and she longed to take it away, not cause it. It terrified her, yet she was powerless to stop it. As the months had gone by and the love gained strength, she had begun to see another way. A way to finally be happy. To make those early exploratory fantasies come true. Oh, the irony that it was Darcy who had offered her that golden chance.

She tracked the movements of colleagues as they passed by and questioned every glance her way. Did they know? Could they tell something was wrong? Were they wondering where Darcy was? She chastised herself as the constant loop continued.

They don't know anything. Stop being a fucking coward. Don't blow it now.
"Shit. What's up with the boss?"

Joe's voice snapped her back in to focus, and she peered towards Bridget's office. She was on the phone and looked upset, forehead in hand

and brow furrowed. Anja watched as she reached for a tissue and dabbed delicately under each eye. She nodded a few times, and Anja strained to try and follow her lips to get a clue to what she was saying.

Then she was hanging up and heading for her office door. Anja quickly diverted her attention back to her screen.

"Anja. Can you come in here, please?"

She caught Joe's look of question and offered a faint shrug before pasting a neutral expression on her face and heading Bridget's way. She looked flustered and close to tears, which was as un-Bridget as Anja had ever seen.

"Take a seat."

Until that moment, Anja hadn't allowed herself to consider that Darcy might not have gotten out of the car. Might not have survived. Her body trembled, and she struggled with the little will left in her to fight it.

Fucking pull it together, Olsen.

Anja did as instructed and sat to attention in front of Bridget's desk.

Darcy survived. She had to. There was someone with her.

Or was this it? Was this the moment her whole world would implode? She gritted her teeth and braced herself for the onslaught, for the judgement, the shame, the scorn.

Darcy's woken up and told them everything. No doubt the police are on their way and it's Bridget's job to keep me here until they arrive.

It's all over.

They know who I am.

They know why I picked Darcy.

"Anja? Anja?"

Bridget's raised voice cut through the internal assault.

"Sorry. What's up?" Anja smoothed her skirt and clasped her hands together. It was happening whether she was ready for it or not.

"That was Darcy's mum, Liz, on the phone. From Australia. Listen…"

Anja gulped in a breath. To hear Darcy's mum's name would normally evoke rage within her, but right now she was filled only with dread.

"There's been an accident. A terrible accident. Involving Darcy."

Anja said nothing. She stared at Bridget and willed her to continue. To put her out of her misery and tell her everything she knew. Everything

Darcy knew. She wanted to scream for her to hurry up, to spit it the fuck out and stop trying to spare her feelings.

"What? What happened…?" She heard the rattle in her voice. Good, that was normal in this kind of situation.

Bridget fidgeted with a pen, clearly not comfortable being the one to break the news. "There was a car crash on Friday night. She's in the hospital, broken and bruised from what I've been told, but the doctors say she'll be okay. She had a lucky escape. They're still waiting for her to wake up."

She hasn't woken up.

Anja felt the tension physically release in her stomach and chest. An unexpected sob tried to break lose, and she muffled it with a hand, sinking back in to the chair. "Fuck."

"Yes, I know." Bridget agreed with her sentiments, unaware the reasons for the expletive were twofold. "But as I said, she's going to be all right eventually. She'll need your help."

"I can't believe this." Anja searched for all the right responses. The questions someone who was only finding out would ask. "Where? Did they say what happened? How did she crash? I was wondering why I hadn't heard from her."

Bridget rose and poured a glass of water, handed it to Anja, and perched on the edge of her desk. "All I know is it was somewhere between her house and town. Liz says the police mentioned ice, but they will also want to talk to Darcy when she's able. Apparently, there's a suspicion that she was drinking."

"Drinking?" *That's it, Anja, act outraged. Darcy would never drink and drive. Be as shocked as Bridget.* "No way. Darcy would never do that."

Bridget held up her hands as if she wasn't about to argue with that. "I'm only telling you what her mum said. There's no use worrying about it right now. What Darcy needs is someone with her."

"I can go." Anja was on her feet, practically throwing the water back down on to the desk. If and when Darcy woke up, Anja would be there. She would be the first to hear whatever dangerous words tumbled from Darcy's lips. "Can I go?"

"Of course you can. That's one of the reasons I'm telling you. As I'm sure you know, Darcy's mum is in Australia, and what with the situation with her little sister, she won't be able to travel over straight away. If at all."

Little sister.

Anja felt her face scrunch in confusion. "Her little sister? What situation?"

"Oh. Sorry, I assumed given how close you are and the way Liz spoke that you knew?"

"Well, obviously I don't." Anja did her best to curb the well of anger that threatened to rise. Darcy had a sister? Why had she never mentioned her? Although she had rarely talked about her family, only disclosing that her mum had stayed in Australia when she had returned to Scotland for university. It seemed odd that she would never acknowledge a sibling.

"She has Rett syndrome. It affects her both mentally and physically and her mum cares for her full-time. That's why getting away will be difficult. She said Darcy speaks so fondly of you as her best friend and so she asked for you to be with her, until she can figure out what to do. She didn't know who else to call. She feels so guilty about it, but I reassured her as best I could."

Anja's mind raced with the new information; she had thought she knew it all, through both her own research and from what Darcy had shared over the years. Why hadn't she told Anja, and how old was this sister? Had she come before or after her bastard father's betrayal?

"Why did her mum call you?"

"Purely because she didn't have your number but knew the company Darcy worked for. She was so upset I said I'd speak to you for her."

"She did the right thing. I'll take care of everything."

Bridget reached out and squeezed her arm, an unusually personal gesture. "I know you will. Darcy's one of the good ones, but I'm sure I don't have to tell you that. Take some time and take good care of her. Stay in touch with Liz and keep me updated, yeah?"

"Can you call her mum back for me now? Tell her it'll be okay, and she shouldn't feel guilty. She already has one child to care for."

"Of course. Now go."

A little dazed, Anja wandered back to her desk, her brain whirring a million miles an hour and heart beating the same. She could figure this out and be there for Darcy. Turn it around.

It wasn't over yet.

Chapter 26

ALL DAY AND WELL INTO the evening, Eilidh kept thinking on Dr Jackman's words.

When she wakes up.

She hadn't thought that far ahead and now wondered what would happen when that occurred. Should she stay, or would it be confusing for the woman to find a stranger there when she eventually opened her eyes? What about when her family finally showed up? There'd be no reason for Eilidh to hang around.

The thought of leaving the woman pulled at her insides. Would her family keep Eilidh updated? Would she be allowed to visit? There was a long road to recovery ahead of her that Eilidh understood. She'd been there—was, in some ways, still there.

Could she help, or was it purely selfish reasons that kept Eilidh at the bedside? Her own redemption after her past attempt and failure at being the heroine? Was she looking for plaudits and gratitude? A chance to do it right this time?

No.

She knew why she was there. It was so the woman would know that someone was with her. That she wasn't alone and someone cared. That someone had sat and pleaded for her to wake up and to live. Eilidh would be that person and sit at her bedside however long it took.

She loosely held the woman's hand. It was cold and pallid; she willed it to move, to flinch. Even for one finger to twitch. Her gaze fell on the battered face again, and she wondered what it looked like under all the gauze and stitches. What colour were her eyes? Did she have dimples when she smiled? Her hair was a deep russet brown, and Eilidh imagined her eyes would match.

What did she do for a living? Was there a boyfriend, a husband, a wife? Someone frantic with worry, wondering why their partner hadn't come home. Were there children or pets waiting to be fed, questioning where their mother was? A boss, angry that she hadn't turned up for work?

The sound of the door opening broke through her ruminations.

"Oh, hi." A blonde woman looked from Eilidh to the patient before turning her attention back to Eilidh again. She seemed flustered and a little bewildered to find Eilidh there. "Who are you?"

Eilidh stood and extended a hand. "Eilidh Grey. I'm the person who witnessed the accident. I've been keeping her company."

The woman shook her hand lightly and held her gaze. "You're the one that got her out of the car?"

"Aye..." Before Eilidh could say another word, she was being pulled into a fierce embrace.

"Oh my God. Thank you so much. I can't tell you... If we'd lost her..." She broke the contact and held Eilidh at arm's length. "I don't know what I would have done if I'd lost her."

Eilidh stepped back from the hug, unprepared for the show of emotion and suddenly embarrassed. "No problem. You know, anyone would have done the same."

"Nonsense." The blonde squeezed her upper arm. "They told me the car burned to a shell. If it hadn't been for you...well..." She wiped at some tears and looked over to the bed before echoing Dr Jackman. "It doesn't bear to think where Darcy would be now."

Eilidh nodded, unwilling to think about it either. "Wait? Her name's Darcy? And you're her..."

"Sister. Anja."

"Right. Okay." Eilidh looked between the sisters. Darcy. She finally had a name. Anja's accent had thrown her a bit: for some reason, she had assumed Darcy would be Scottish.

She watched as Anja took her place in the chair at Darcy's bedside, stroking the few strands of hair that poked through bandages before taking her hand. She felt awkward and unnecessary now that her family had arrived. "Well, I guess I'll leave you to it."

Anja glanced up at her as if she'd already forgotten Eilidh was in the room. "Yes. I'm here now." She smiled towards Darcy before leaning down to kiss the back of her hand. "And we don't want to take up anymore of your time."

"Oh, it was no trouble." Eilidh backed towards the door. She was reluctant to leave but had clearly been given her marching orders.

"That's kind of you to say, and thank you again. It was a miracle that you were there."

Eilidh stalled suddenly as the woman's name properly registered. It wasn't exactly common. "Wait. Darcy? Is her name Darcy Harris?"

She watched Anja's hands stop their stroking, and when her gaze fell back on Eilidh, it was loaded with suspicion. "How did you know that?"

If the situation hadn't been so awful, Eilidh thought she might have laughed. Instead, she studied the woman in the bed, searching for a clue that might have told her who she was before now. It wasn't there. But then they had only met briefly in person that one time on the bridge.

She shook her head slowly in disbelief. "We've met before. We were meant to go on a date Friday night. I was out running because she cancelled." She felt a little embarrassed admitting the last part.

"Wow." Anja sat back in her chair, arms crossed, appraising Eilidh. "So you're her."

"I assume from that, Darcy's mentioned me?"

"Maybe once or twice." Anja continued to stare. "Of all the people in Inverness, there you were, to save the day."

Her tone jarred Eilidh a little, lacking in its earlier gratitude and becoming almost accusatory.

"Seems so. That's kind of thrown me a little, I have to say. I didn't recognise her."

"Why would you? You've only known her five minutes."

"True. Although I thought she was Scottish, but you have an accent I don't recognise."

Anja sighed loudly. "I'm Norwegian. I had to tell them she was my sister so they would allow me in. I'm her best friend, and her mother asked me to take care of her. Is that all right with you?"

Eilidh shifted awkwardly on the spot, unsure why Anja had become so hostile but without a comeback or question to call her on it. "Uh, sorry. I didn't mean anything by it." Her gaze flicked back to Darcy. She was even more reluctant to leave now but still felt decidedly unwelcome. "I guess I'll get going, then."

Anja's attention was refocused on Darcy, and Eilidh had clearly been dismissed. She toed the ground, torn between leaving and asking to stay a little longer, despite the uncomfortable quiet. It hadn't occurred to her that she might not have the opportunity to say good-bye properly, but then what was there to say? *Nice to meet you? Hope you wake up soon?*

"Can I leave you my number?"

"Pardon?" Anja eyed her in confusion.

"My number. For when she wakes up. I'd really like to know how she's getting on, you know. Or maybe she'll want to contact me?"

"I assume she already has your number?"

"Aye, but you don't. I'd really appreciate it if you could let me know she's all right. You'll tell her I was here, won't you?"

"Right, well. Okay. Fine." Anja rummaged in her bag. She produced a phone and looked at Eilidh expectantly.

Eilidh reeled off her number as requested before giving Darcy one final glance. "Take care, Darcy."

If Anja heard, she didn't acknowledge Eilidh's parting words, and Eilidh slipped quietly from the room.

Chapter 27

The feel of Darcy's hand in hers did little to soothe Anja's fears. She held it tentatively, cautious, caught in the dichotomy of wishing with all her heart that Darcy would wake up, yet petrified of what she would say if she did.

She whispered reassuring promises, hoping they would somehow take seed and Darcy would open her eyes knowing it was all because Anja loved her. She pleaded for forgiveness, begged for a second chance. Told her she would prove her worth, make up for everything, and finally open herself up with the truth. Darcy needed the truth.

The shock and reality of the crash had unravelled her. Had taken any last doubt about her feelings and burned them in the flames of Darcy's ravaged car. Why hadn't she been brave enough to take the chance and talk to her sooner? Tell her story and hope Darcy would see past it to the possibilities. The hope to be found in being together.

It wasn't as if she hadn't tried, but every time, the words had lodged in her throat. The anger had still stunted her capacity to reveal it all, to loosen her grip on the secrets she had held fiercely for so long. Instead, she'd sent more gifts, tokens of everything she wanted but couldn't say. She'd actively pursued her changing feelings and tried to understand them. To pinpoint the moment when searing hate and overpowering anger had begun to turn to love.

As always, her mother's voice took hold and attempted to overpower the warmness that being by Darcy's side brought her.

This isn't why you tracked Darcy down. You're meant to make her pay. Make her feel as you felt when you were deserted and crushed all those years ago. She had everything you should've had. Or have you forgotten?

Anja hadn't forgotten. She never would. But the darkness no longer needed to reign; Darcy had shown her that. All her games, her interference in Darcy's life—the fake dates, the late night calls—they'd stop. She'd seen her error now. The cry tugging on her heart was no longer for revenge.

Now it was telling her they could be their own family, in a way Anja had never imagined. They could be happy together, build a home together; it could be everything Anja had lost and more.

When Darcy awoke, Anja would be there. She would tend to every need and whim until Darcy was healthy again and would make her see how wonderful life could be so long as they stuck together.

She lightly pressed her lips to Darcy's cheek and laid her head close on the pillow.

"I'm here, sweetheart," she murmured. "I won't ever leave you."

Chapter 28

SHE WAS AWARE OF THE light first, and her eyes rebelled against it. Each sense caught up with the other, slow but heightened, as if she were trudging through quicksand and could feel every grain rubbing against her skin.

She heard the sound of her eyelashes brushing together as she finally opened her lids, blinking against the raw whiteness that surrounded her. The tip of her tongue found a crack in her lip as it searched for moisture, and heavy blankets weighed on her legs. Why couldn't she move her legs? A hand, another hand, was in hers. It gripped tighter, and she focussed on each finger to return the embrace.

Then the hand let go. *No. Don't let go.*

The moment of reassurance disappeared before a voice was close to her ear, a voice she knew and loved. "It's okay, Darcy. Take your time. You're going to be okay."

Anja.

She wanted to reply, to cry, and to scream out as pain vibrated through one of her legs, but her lids drooped and she felt the blackness pull at her again. She fought it, clawed at the air, searching for the hand to hold on to again.

"What? Where…" The words shredded her throat.

"Shush, sweetheart. Here, try some of this…"

A straw parted her lips, and she sucked gratefully, the cool water offering life to her voice. "Anja…"

"I'm here, Darcy. I'm not going anywhere. Sleep now. There's time for talking later."

"Th...thank you. Don't. Go."

Darcy felt a warm hand stroke her arm, and a sigh of relief escaped. It didn't matter what or where: She knew she was safe because Anja was with her. She could rest easy.

A rush of relief swept through Anja's chest as she took a moment and stepped out of Darcy's room. The doctor was checking her over, encouraged that her patient had woken, even if only for a short time.

She doesn't remember.

At least she didn't seem to right now.

She hadn't screamed for Anja to get away from her. She was happy to have her there, reassured by Anja's presence. She had asked her not to leave.

Who knew how much of her memory was gone or for how long? Was it only the crash that had disappeared, or was it more? Anja couldn't just sit around hoping that the events of that night were lost to Darcy forever. She knew a trauma could blur the memories around and leading up to it, block out the pain and fear so Darcy wouldn't have to relive it over and over. She also knew that at any moment those memories could resurface.

Could Anja do anything to stop it? Could she lead Darcy's memory on a different path?

It might be possible if she could keep her story straight. Plant the facts so that Darcy would believe the version Anja wanted her to, then maybe she never had to know the truth about what had really happened. If Anja had the answers to make sense of it all, Darcy might stop asking questions. She might be relieved not to remember, and if it worked, Anja would have her second chance.

She had to try, to be brave and think of the payoff. A few more lies to satisfy Darcy's curiosity, to put more time between them and that awful night. Surely the more time that passed, the less likely Darcy was to remember?

The matter of Eilidh kept threatening to poke a hole in her plans. She needed to keep them apart, at least in the beginning. If Darcy remembered about their cancelled date and the reason why, then a whole other story would need to be told.

Or maybe it was wise to preempt that? Admit she had been at the cabin that night with Darcy but claim she'd left early. She could say Jason had called and wouldn't stop until she saw him. Maybe Darcy had encouraged her to go and hear him out, so she'd left Darcy and knew nothing of what happened next. She would claim to have no idea why Darcy got in the car...despite being drunk. It was surely safer to leave her wondering than taking the chance that Darcy would find out from Eilidh that Anja had been at the cabin. That she was the reason Darcy had cancelled the date. It would avoid Anja having to explain away another string of lies.

The Jason problem would remain, and she wondered if she could continue the façade that he actually existed. Could she explain his disappearance away? Anja could erase him in her mind as easily as she had drawn him, but he was very real to Darcy. She wondered if it served anyone for Darcy to find out otherwise.

Yes. She would continue to use Jason as she had all this time. He was an easy cover, already primed to be wholly dismissed from her life as a liar and a cheat. There was no need to add another dimension to her story. Their shared history was going to be difficult enough to fathom.

For now, she'd take care of Darcy, make her realise how much she needed Anja's help and support to recover, show her the value in their bond.

Then she'd tell her the truth, on Anja's terms.

However perverse the circumstances, the universe had offered Anja an opportunity to make it right. No matter what it took, this time she would.

Chapter 29

Every day for a week, Anja had been living on the brink. A ball of fear grew in her chest, threatening to burst every time Darcy asked a question about that night.

"Let me get this right. You were there, but left early?" She was propped up by a number of pillows, brighter and more alert than she had been since first waking. The bruising had started to turn shades of yellow and green that Anja found painful to look at. Darcy's beautiful face was ravaged and torn…because of her.

"Aye. We've been over this a hundred times already." Anja wheeled the lunch tray across the room, closer to the bed where Darcy could reach it.

"I know and I'm sorry. The police have put the fear in me though. I can't understand what would have possessed me or what could have happened to make me get in that car pissed."

"You might never understand. I think you need to consider that and stop torturing yourself."

"Easier said than done. Do you think it was because of Eilidh?"

"Eilidh?" Anja's eyebrow's furrowed. She hadn't anticipated this train of thought. "Why would it be because of her?"

"Oh, I don't know. I'm throwing anything out there right now. Maybe when you left I got a bit tipsy, took an attack of the loneliness, and decided to go and meet her after all?"

"In your dressing gown? Sexy." Anja winked. "I've seen you stupid drunk, my love, but I'm not sure I've ever seen you drunk enough to be that stupid."

"Ha. Ha." Darcy was droll. "Maybe I thought the bikini underneath might do the trick."

Anja remembered the bikini and the body it had scarcely hid.

Yes. It would've done the trick.

She perched on the edge of the bed and poured some grey-looking tea into cups for them both. "This is all speculation and maybes. Personally, I think you simply ran out of wine and decided to go get some more."

"Fuck off. You said it yourself, even I'm not that daft. Plus, I had plenty of other booze in the house."

Anja shrugged. "It's no worse than some of your theories."

"Well, it's better than the alternative."

"Don't go there again." Anja sighed. "It'll do you no good."

"What if they were there? The police are always talking about escalation—maybe it happened that night. If I was outside in the hot tub... alone, vulnerable, primed for stalkery advances."

"Again with the maybes. You don't even know if you were in the hot tub. You need to stop stressing and focus on getting better, Darcy. Nothing else matters right now."

Darcy thumped her hand into the mattress in frustration, forgetting the cast that held her wrist together. "For fucking fuck... Ow."

Anja wished she could bear some of the pain or take it away completely. She reached for Darcy's good hand and squeezed. "See what happens when you let yourself get all worked up? I told you, now isn't the time. We'll figure it out when you're better."

"Fine." Darcy half-heartedly yanked her hand away in a mock grump. "Whatever you say, boss."

"Good. And yes, until you're better, I am the boss. Now eat."

She watched Darcy remove the plastic cloche on what would be another depressing lunch, and they simultaneously wrinkled their noses.

"Please can you find me something better than this? I'd kill for a cheeseburger."

Anja laughed and peered under the pudding lid at something white and pureed. "What is that?"

"Exactly." Darcy pushed the tray away. "Save me from further suffering."

Anja stood and reached for her bag and coat. "Okay, but if I get caught the blame is all yours."

"Or you could not get caught."

Anja chuckled and shrugged on the heavy coat. "It's a good job I love you."

"Aw, you big softie. Come here." Darcy reached out both arms, and Anja complied. She allowed herself to be pulled into the hug, to press her lips to Darcy's hair and savour the moment of togetherness. A moment where everything was the same as before the accident. Unexpected tears slipped free, and she quickly wiped them away before releasing Darcy.

"Hey, you okay?" Darcy had caught her, and more tears threatened seeing the softness in her gaze.

"I'm fine. I'm being silly. I'm just so happy you're all right. You know?"

Darcy brushed a thumb across the dampness on her cheek. "I know, sweetheart. And I'm happy to have you here with me."

They smiled and held each other's gaze a moment before Anja sucked in a breath and stood again. "Anyway, one cheeseburger coming up."

Darcy groaned in anticipation. "This is why I love you too. Say you'll marry me."

Anja laughed and planted a quick peck on her forehead. "Tonight, I'll go to the cabin as well. Grab those sloth pyjamas and some more of your toiletries."

"And my phone?"

So far, Anja had managed to keep Darcy from it, prolonging the moment she would have to tell her about Eilidh's involvement in saving her from the crash. She knew Darcy's full attention would be lost then, and Anja would have to start managing their contact.

"You sure you want it? I'm not sure Facebook is going to help you heal."

Darcy poked her tongue out. "No, but it might help with some of the bloody boredom. Plus, it means I can call my mum when I feel like it, not only when you're here."

It rankled a little that Darcy still hadn't explicitly told her why her mum was unable to travel. She'd made vague excuses about money and work and reassured Anja that it was fine. She was a big girl and on the mend; she didn't need her mum there. So the sister question still nagged at Anja: her age, and more importantly, her parentage.

"Of course. I'll grab it. Anything else, Your Majesty?"

"Oh, I like that. Yes, you can keep calling me that. Chips. Don't forget chips. And a milkshake." She reached for her neck and forced a cough. "For my poor scorched throat."

Anja rolled her eyes, offered a shoddy salute, and headed for the door. The cheeseburger and chips would be a minor respite from all the wonder and maybes. She needed something more to help Darcy settle on the one logical explanation for that night on her own terms.

That her stalker had shown up and she had fled.

It was the truth.

Just not the whole truth.

Anja knew exactly how to do it. A small, simple gesture that she was sure would work. A test of sorts. Either it would reinforce the theory or spark something in Darcy's subconscious and backfire spectacularly.

She hated having to revert to her stalker persona for help. Every part of her wanted to leave that behind and do better by Darcy. To be better for her. It was so easy to slip back in to and would serve her purpose well. She swore to herself it would be the last time.

For now, it was a risk she had to take to release herself from the misery of wondering, waiting, afraid of the moment when it would all end.

"Cash or card?" The florist smiled Anja's way as she put the finishing touches to the impressive basket. It overflowed with flowers and fruit, a box of chocolates, and a "get well soon" teddy bear.

"Cash." Anja perused the message card options. Why were they always so impersonal and uninspiring, and why would you choose a card with a picture of flowers on it to go with a bouquet of actual flowers? It made no sense.

She withdrew a prewritten card from her bag, envelope firmly sealed, and handed it to the florist with the cash. It was elegant, traditional, and beautiful in an understated way—much the same as Darcy.

The florist tucked it safely in to the basket. "And we're done."

Anja surveyed the creation, delighted. "It looks amazing."

"Thanks. You must really like this person, the amount of gifts you send."

Anja shrugged coyly. "What can I say? I'm in love."

Chapter 30

PAIN THROBBED FROM THE TIPS of her toes to the tips of her fingers. Darcy glanced at the morphine button and considered it for a moment. She hated the murky place it took her, too much like those awful first moments when she'd woken up in the hospital bed. She decided against it; at least the pain reminded her she was still here. Still alive.

Anja's departure left an uneasy feeling in her stomach. The room felt smaller, and loneliness enveloped her. It left her mind only one place to wander, despite her friend chastising that she should be focusing it on getting better.

How could she?

The events of that night tormented her. There was no respite. When her eyes closed, a blurred vision of terror invaded her dreams, shredded and torn. It offered no answers. Instead, it taunted and wrung her insides out, wound her so tight she woke rigid and in agony.

What the hell had she been thinking getting in the car drunk? No matter the circumstances, there was no excuse for such reckless behaviour.

Unless those circumstances meant life or death.

Her train of thought came back to the stalker. Had they been there? If they had, what the fuck had happened that the only alternative was for her to flee in her dressing gown and speed towards town? Where had she been going? To Anja's, maybe? That seemed logical, because drunk or otherwise, she knew Anja's was the safest place she could think of.

The police suspected a combination of black ice, her speed, and lack of control due to the alcohol had caused the crash. She would have to answer for the latter at some point in the future, and the thought filled her with dread. She'd never been in trouble before, at least not this kind of trouble.

Although the stalker situation had been explained to the police as a potential motive for her carelessness, without proof it was merely conjecture. All they would concede was there had been another set of fresh skid marks on the road which could—emphasis on the could—suggest a chase. They had a witness too, who although unable to properly identify the other car or driver had indicated that another vehicle was speeding too. That maybe it was trying to catch Darcy.

This had piqued her interest more than a little, because she knew she hadn't been alone in the wreck. Well, she'd been alone in the car, but not afterwards. This mysterious witness had come to her rescue, freed her from the car, and no doubt saved her life. An unknown voice echoed in the back of her mind in the darkness of night. When the nightmares struck, it tried to offer her a thread of calm to clasp on to and told her she would be okay. She believed it. At first she'd wondered if she was imagining it, maybe making the voice up for comfort. Now she knew it had been her saviour.

The police wouldn't disclose her details, and all Anja knew was that a woman had been out jogging and come to her rescue. A healthcare assistant had told her that someone had sat with her through that first night, until her mother could be contacted, but then they had gone off shift and were unable to help with anything other than a rough description. She'd heard a rumour the person worked at the hospital, but with the way staff rotated, Darcy had been unable to confirm it.

It was difficult to stay positive, to not give in to feeling sorry for herself. The frustration of not knowing what had happened that night and why was enough to contend with. She refused to wallow on the injuries and discomfort. The injuries would heal, the pain would ease, but her memory may never be restored.

A nurse entered and offered her a cheerful smile. "Look at this." She carried a huge basket in her arms. "You're obviously very special to someone."

Darcy awkwardly pushed herself higher in the bed with her good arm and peered in to the basket as it was positioned on her bedside table.

Is it from my mum? Work, maybe? Or the guys at the sailing club?

The nurse plucked the card from within and handed it to her, then winked and headed for the door again. "Let me know when you open those chocolates. They look fancy."

Darcy's hands shook as she stared at the card that lay in them. She didn't need to open it: The picture would be the same. The message would be the same.

Still, she ripped open the envelope, and there it was—the sloth, the words. Only this time there was more.

One day you'll see me.
One day you'll know the truth.
Until then, feel better soon.
And know that I love you.

Love? Fucking love? If this was their idea of love, they could ram it up their arse. All the pent-up frustration tore through her, and she reached out unthinkingly, intent only on throwing the basket as far away from her as possible.

Her wrist screamed in agony along with the bruising that covered her chest and side. "Goddamn you," she yelled. Tears pricked her eyes, hot and infuriating. Where was the nurse? She needed the nurse. She stabbed the call button and then furiously screwed the card up in her good hand and threw it to the floor.

The look of alarm on the nurse's face when she returned did nothing to alleviate the anger. "Who delivered these? Did you see? Where did they come from?" she shouted through the tears, directing her rage at the wrong person but unable to curb it.

The nurse looked between Darcy and the basket, clearly confused and without an answer.

Darcy's fist wrapped around the bedsheets and twisted. There was no outlet for the well of fury that threatened to overflow. "I asked who sent them," she shouted. "Don't just stand there. Do something!"

The nurse hurried to her side, taking Darcy's frantic hand as she tried to turn herself away from the basket. To remove it from sight. She needed it away from her.

"Hey, stop that. You're going to hurt yourself more. Tell me what's happened." The nurse's voice was calm as she tried to sooth her. She stroked a cool palm up and down Darcy's arm and continued to grip her fingers.

"This." Darcy yanked her hand free and stabbed a finger in the direction of the basket. "This keeps happening. The stalker. Even in my hospital bed they won't leave me alone because they love me apparently. How is that love? Who the fuck are they? Please, take it away, I need it to be gone." The fight drained out of her, and she looked at the crumpled message on the floor, defeated. She nodded towards it. "The police will want to see the note."

Even if she was puzzled by Darcy's ramblings, the nurse remained professional, despite how awful Darcy was being. "Aye, of course, love. I'll put it in the relatives lounge, and I'll be sure to keep the note. First though, I need you to calm down and take some slow breaths. You can't be getting in a state like this."

Darcy did as instructed. The throbbing had taken over again, her leg vibrated hotly within its cast, and every inch of her skin itched with pain. She reached for the morphine button, unsure whether it was the hurt or the terror that made her want to give in to it. Either one seemed justified.

"That's it. No use trying to bear the pain when there's something that can help."

The nurse continued to rub her arm reassuringly as Darcy pressed the button. The warm fuzziness washed over her quickly, and her lids became heavy. "I'm sorry," she mumbled. With one last glance at the stalker's gift, she let the drugs do their job.

Chapter 31

IT WASN'T THAT SHE EXPECTED some grand gesture of gratitude, but a response to a text would have been welcome. Eilidh flopped back on her sofa and picked up the remote, then threw it down again without pressing a button.

Why was she wallowing? She had saved Darcy's life and could be proud of that. She didn't need Darcy or Anja to confirm that she'd done a good thing. That this time she'd gotten it right.

Deep down, Eilidh knew that it wasn't really about that.

It was about Darcy.

Maybe she should go back to the hospital? It had been a week now; surely Darcy would be feeling stronger and up to a visit? Every day at work had been torture, fighting the urge to get in the lift and press number eight, the floor Darcy was on.

Despite her part in it all, Eilidh didn't feel it was her place to be there uninvited. She was nothing more to Darcy than a few texts and a failed attempt at a date. The crash and her involvement didn't change that. Eilidh was still a stranger.

Then why can't I get her out of my head?

The questions continued to torture her day and night. What if Darcy had taken a turn? Maybe she wasn't okay after all. Perhaps chatting to the right nurse or doctor as a colleague would at least give her an inkling as to Darcy's health. Give her something to hold on to as a reason why she hadn't been in touch.

What was she thinking? As if finding out Darcy's condition was worse would help. Of course it wouldn't. Eilidh would be devastated to hear that after everything they'd been through that night, and she was sure Darcy was fine, though sorrowful and sore if her own experience was anything to go by. But fine.

Then why hasn't she been in touch?

She wondered fleetingly if Anja had told Darcy about her involvement. It was an explanation for the silence, but she saw no reason why Anja would withhold that information. If only Anja would get in touch with an update, it would go a long way to assuaging her restlessness. Eilidh understood the stress and anxiety she must be under, but a quick text took nothing. A simple "she's okay" would put her mind at ease, and it would cost Anja only seconds to send. So why hadn't she?

The snow had turned to rain, and it battered her living room window, in keeping with her mood. She threw a cushion at it, then another, as if some futile childish tantrum would help.

Beer. She needed beer, Sam, and rantings and ramblings without judgement. Unable to resist, she tapped off one final message to Darcy.

Are you all right? Be good to hear from you. E x

Then followed it with a begging note to Sam.

Sam, I need you. I need beer. The Castle in an hour? Help me. E x

The cabin stood in darkness with only the moonlight to cast shadows throughout the woodland and illuminate Anja's way. She sat in her car a moment and took a few breaths. Why was she being so ridiculous? Nervous about stepping inside?

You've been here a thousand times before; this time is no different to the others.

It was the second time she'd returned since that night, spurred on by Darcy's need to have her own things at the hospital. They offered a small measure of comfort that Anja couldn't deny her, and she knew she had to put her own irrational fear aside for Darcy's sake.

She gave herself a mental shake.

After everything, you're being fucking pathetic, Anja. Get the keys, get in the house, find Darcy's things, and get out. Simple.

As she stood at the bottom of the porch steps, she wished it were that easy.

It's only four steps up, then through the door. You know where everything is. Stick to business and don't get side-tracked.

It didn't take long to find the pyjamas and requested toiletries, nor the books Darcy had asked for, the fluffy socks, and her favourite hoodie. Anja moved around Darcy's bedroom as if it was her own. With the bag packed, she sat at the dressing table and unlocked Darcy's phone. Eilidh's name shone out; she'd sent three messages since Anja had last checked.

A tap on each revealed much the same theme.

Are you okay?

Can I come visit?

It would be good to hear from you.

Would she ever get the bloody hint? Anja held her finger on one and clicked to mark them all before pressing delete. She felt no guilt. It was for Darcy's own good. She didn't need distractions or more questions—she needed to forget about that night and focus on getting better. Eilidh would only add complications and interference.

If their paths were to cross again down the line, Anja had her cover story prepared. She'd lost Eilidh's number and didn't want to stress Darcy out with the weight of repaying Eilidh's bravery while she recovered. She'd claim that she would've told Darcy eventually.

Darcy might be a little peeved at first, but she'd understand. If she didn't, Anja had a backup plan. She'd plant the seed of doubt where Eilidh was concerned and make Darcy question her involvement. Was she really out jogging at that time of night? In the snow? Really? Was their first meeting really just a coincidence? Insert a little look of scepticism, perhaps a raised eyebrow, a sardonic smile. That's all it would take to get Darcy asking those questions, and maybe, just maybe, wondering if Eilidh was the driver that had left the other set of skid marks.

Misleading? Of course, but she wouldn't hesitate in offering it to Darcy as an explanation for that night. In fact, that doubt could well work to Anja's advantage. It was worth considering in any case, whether Darcy believed it or not. If she thought Anja saw it as a plausible possibility, her reticence to contact Eilidh would be explained away as over-protectiveness by her best friend, if nothing else.

The bottom line was Anja needed to put time and distance between Darcy, that night, and Eilidh. Any and every reminder was a potential spark to her memory, leaving Anja powerless to stop it coming to life. It was unthinkable that Darcy might someday remember the events leading up to the accident. Anja couldn't bear the thought…or the consequences.

She was doing the right thing keeping Eilidh away, although returning Darcy's phone to her was going to make that a lot more difficult. Could she pretend to forget it again? Say she dropped it?

No, too weak.

Maybe delete Eilidh's number? Although that wouldn't stop Eilidh from contacting Darcy, she'd demonstrated her persistence already. She could block Eilidh's number? That was an option, although it still left other routes of contact. There was nothing stopping her showing up at Darcy's hospital room.

What if she replied to Eilidh? As Darcy. It wouldn't be the first time. Put Eilidh's mind at rest and tell her she was fine but needed a little time and space to recover. She'd be in touch when she was ready. That would buy Anja some respite, but could she rely on Eilidh to accept it and not engage further?

It was a chance she decided to take.

> *Eilidh, sorry I haven't been in touch. I'm sure you understand. I owe you my life and someday I want to thank you in person. But for now I need time to recuperate with my family. I'll be in touch.*
> *D x*

There. It was apologetic without feeling the need to explain and showed gratitude and acknowledgement of what Eilidh had done. It also didn't invite any further conversation other than an acceptance of Darcy's wishes. Anja would wait until the morning to bring the phone to Darcy, which gave her long enough to deal with any texts that might come back.

Satisfied with her plan, she allowed herself to relax a little for the first time in days. She idly picked up a bottle of Darcy's perfume, a personal favourite of hers, and spritzed some on the cuff of her jumper. The scent further calmed her nerves and allowed the exhaustion she had been staving off to set in.

She kicked off her shoes and crawled on to the bed, pulling Darcy's favourite nap blanket with her. The pillow was nowhere near as good as the real thing, but she hugged it close and closed her eyes. Its scent was pure Darcy and reminded her of sunshine and summer holidays.

The perfume on her wrist combined with the soft fleece blanket on her cheek led her imagination to a shaded day bed for two by a private pool with a sea breeze rolling across their bikini-clad bodies. There was blue sky and the waft of sun cream, shared smiles, holding hands, and tropical cocktails.

With the dream fixed firmly in her mind, and hopes of one day making it a reality, Anja drifted to sleep.

Chapter 32

THE PUB AND BEER HAD done nothing for Eilidh but achieve drunkenness and the usual silliness that ensued when she and Sam were out together. Fortunately, she had at least managed to refrain from any regrettable drunk dials or messages.

When the message had come from Darcy asking for some time, she'd still been sober enough to reply coherently and thoughtfully. Despite the wish to scream at her phone and say it wasn't okay because the thought of more time without seeing Darcy made her feel awful.

But this wasn't about her. She knew that. Darcy deserved whatever she asked for, whatever she needed. Eilidh understood that, as hard as it was to push her own feelings aside until Darcy was ready.

Sam had suggested their tried and tested hangover cure for the following day, something she hadn't done since the alleyway incident that had left her with a dislocated shoulder amongst many other injuries.

"Sam, good to see you, pal." The sales guy at the water centre, Martin, engaged him in some kind of male greeting ritual, and Eilidh rolled her eyes. They'd flirted persistently for at least the last two years, and Eilidh wished they both get it over with and finally go out.

"What can I do for you today? The usual?" Martin included Eilidh in the question but clearly only had eyes for Sam.

"Aye, although we'll take a two-person kayak rather than solos." He nudged into Eilidh. "It's the first time this one's tested her shoulder since the injury."

Martin nodded knowingly, and Eilidh wondered exactly what Sam had told him. "Sensible. I'm sure you'll have no bother paddling the two of you back if she struggles."

Martin's attention was solely back on Sam, and Eilidh bit back the cheeky retort on the tip of her tongue. It was her that had gotten Sam into kayaking in the first place; she'd taught him everything he knew, and she could out-paddle him any day. Despite his bulging biceps, they were no match for her superior technique.

She made to wander away, but Sam reached out and tugged her back to the counter, throwing a protective arm around her shoulders. "My girl here can paddle better with one arm than I can with two. She'll be grand. Won't you, Grey?"

Martin stuttered a little. "I didn't mean it like that. I…"

Eilidh gave Sam a squeeze and put Martin out of his misery. "The two-man's still a good idea. I don't want to push it, and you're right, Martin, I'll feel safer with him sat behind me."

It took a lot for Eilidh to admit weakness, but she wasn't stupid. The loch was as dangerous as any sea and wouldn't think twice about sucking under anyone who disrespected or underestimated it. With its links to Loch Dochfour and the Caledonian Canal, it was classed as open water, and waves of over three meters high had been recorded off Dores Beach. At this time of year, seconds in the frigid water could be fatal.

Martin smiled and rang through the hire. He handed them a slip for the kayak and a couple of locker keys. "You thought about buying a new one yet, Eilidh?"

Eilidh looked across at the racks of kayaks, a cornucopia of colours and styles. Her last one had been sold on Claire's insistence; apparently it had taken up too much space, and what was the point of having one clutter up a bedroom when you could hire them? Well, Claire was gone now, and Eilidh could take up all the space she wanted.

"Maybe in time for summer."

She caught Sam's smile, her answer had clearly delighted him. From the despair of wondering if she would ever kayak again, to thinking about buying a new one, they both knew it was progress, and a flutter of happiness at the thought of getting back out on the water made her grin right back at him.

"Let's do this."

It was a different kind of quiet. Not the echoing loneliness of her house quiet, but the quiet that only the vast isolation of being out on the water could offer. Eilidh's breathing matched her rhythm, slow, steady, and calm. Peace seeped into her soul, and it felt like coming home.

Sam kept her pace, content for her to take the lead. He'd barely said two words since they'd launched, but she guessed he had sensed her need for it. She'd talk when she was ready, and they had an entire day of freedom on their hands which both seemed content to savour.

After leaving the beach near the Bona Lighthouse, the twenty-two miles of the great Loch Ness stretched before them. They followed the rugged north shore, the Clansman Harbour their aim and halfway point. This early in February it wouldn't be too busy, and it was a good place stop to and assess how Eilidh's shoulder was faring. With a south-westerly wind against them on the outward leg, the return journey would be easier if her arm began to flag.

She'd paddled seas, rivers, and lochs across the world, but Loch Ness would always be close to her heart. It was her territory, where she'd learned and practiced her skills. That in itself gave her the confidence to be out on a cold, still February morning, with her best friend in the seat behind her.

"Only another mile or so," Sam called.

Eilidh pulled her paddle up across her lap and gave him a thumbs up. Her shoulder needed to rest a moment, and they slowed down as Sam worked for the both of them. She closed her eyes and tuned in to the loch's natural symphony. Water lapped harmlessly at the side of the kayak, birds larked about their daily business, and both jostled with the hum of a distant motorboat and the repetitive rub of Sam's arms against his life jacket as he stroked their way to shore. Her shoulder felt loose enough and there was no indication she was struggling with it, but taking regular short breaks was still a good idea, and Sam was happy to keep them moving.

They approached the harbour, and it seemed their timing was perfect; a sightseeing cruise was just departing, meaning the place would be less busy. Safely on the beach, they secured their paddles and retrieved Eilidh's waterproof bag.

A short track led through some trees, taking them back from the water to a favourite picnic bench. As hoped, there was no competition for it; any tourists hanging around were no doubt cosy in the local restaurant or coffee shop.

"How's the shoulder?" Sam shrugged out of his life jacket and into the lightweight goose-feather jacket Eilidh passed him. They both sported dry suits, but when not moving, the added layer was necessary.

"It feels good." She zipped up her own jacket and rolled the recovering joint to demonstrate. "No tightness or pain. You did a good job, Tommo."

He smiled and gave her a wee shove. "Well, if I can't fix my best friend…"

"You're a brilliant physio, pal. Your patients are lucky to have you. As am I." She shoved him back as he reached to unpack their lunch from the bag.

"Yeah, yeah. Let's get to the important stuff. What's in the flask?"

"Hot chocolate. Of course."

"Mm…" Sam's eyes lit up as he unscrewed the cap and poured them both a cup. "And egg sandwiches? My favourite. I'm feeling well and truly loved today."

Eilidh shrugged. "I felt in the mood to spoil you. This was a good idea, by the way."

He huddled in close to her on the bench for warmth and wolfed a triangle of sandwich in one go. "I have them sometimes, and I knew you were ready for it."

"Ew, gross." Egg had flown from his mouth across the table, but he showed no remorse. Instead, he grinned at her with mayonnaise mouth. "You're disgusting."

He washed it down with some water and laughed. "Why, thank you."

They finished the sandwiches in silence, and Eilidh stared along the coast to the distant ruins of Urquhart Castle. It bore down over the loch, close to the shore, glowing in the sun against azure sky. Maybe next time they'd make it that far, but she didn't want to push her luck today.

"You ready to talk about it." Sam gave her a nudge and stayed comfortingly close, both hands wrapped around his hot chocolate. He didn't look at her, instead taking in the view himself.

She knew he was trying to be light about it and there was no pressure to talk, but he was right there beside her if she wanted to.

"I guess. You're going to think I'm being ridiculous though."

"Probably, but tell me anyway."

Eilidh took a sip of her own drink and thought about Darcy. "I guess in the cold light of day and without five beers in my belly, I'm feeling a little less dramatic about the Darcy situation. It's still getting to me though. Not being able to see her."

"I get that. It must be frustrating."

"That's exactly what it is. As I said last night, I'm not expecting some special place in her life; all I'm asking for is one visit. I know what she said in her text last night, but I still have this need for a real update. I want to see her in the flesh and know that she's genuinely doing all right."

"We could check the patient system."

"Sam." She slapped his arm, and hot chocolate slopped over his hand. "You know we can't do that. Not when I know the person and have no medical reason for it."

"Oi." He flicked off the sticky liquid and wiped the rest on Eilidh's sleeve. "Okay, I could check the system. I don't know her."

"Stop it." She threw him a stern look and pulled her arm away. "That's not how I want to do things."

"Fine, fine." He looked unfazed by her scolding.

"Promise me you won't look up her record."

"I said fine, didn't I?"

"Promise."

He held a hand up. "I solemnly swear."

"Good. You can have more hot chocolate for that." She topped up their cups and began tidying everything else away."

"I guess until she says different, you're going to have to respect her wishes and give her some space. What else can you do?"

"I know. It's not the physical stuff I'm so worried about, it's the psychological. It's…" She sighed. "I just need to see her face. To look her in the eyes and ask how she is."

"Have you thought that maybe she doesn't want you to see her that way?"

"How'd you mean?"

"Well, think about it. You told me what a mess she was. The cuts, the stitches, the broken bones, the bruises. You didn't even recognise her.

Maybe if she wants to date you, she doesn't want you to see her looking all broken and torn?"

"What? No, that doesn't make sense. Besides, that's so superficial, and she must know I've already seen her? Anja would have told her I was there."

"Hmm...true. Then I would remind you what you were like after the accident. Your opposition to visitors."

"It wasn't an accident," she reminded him. "I was attacked."

"Sorry, of course. I only meant how you struggled with people seeing you so broken. I know you thought it made you look weak, and it made you feel incredibly vulnerable. People only wanted to be there for you, but you couldn't stand them seeing you that way. It was too much for you."

She was pensive a moment. Some of what he said was true, but it wasn't the whole story. She didn't want to see anyone because she was too busy allowing the guilt to swallow her up. She'd survived, and she couldn't understand why. Couldn't figure out who or what it was that had decided between one person's life and another person's death.

For so long, she had been ashamed for being the one who lived.

"If I'm honest, it was more about hiding from what had happened. From having to explain to people why I did it and how I ended up in that hospital bed. How it was my own stupid fault for getting involved in the situation and for thinking I could stop it when I should have just ran the same as Claire."

"Hey, how many fucking times, Grey." Sam was on his feet. Indignant. "It wasn't your fault. You did nothing wrong. You can't honestly believe that still?"

"Calm down." She tugged at his cuff and pulled him back on to the bench. "I meant that's how I felt back then. With the rawness of it all. I know better now."

"Good. Well, maybe Darcy's just feeling a little bit the same, then? She got in that car smashed and then drove it off the road, putting herself, then you, in danger. She might be afraid that you'll blame her for that. That you'll be angry at her or think less of her for making such a reckless decision."

Eilidh shook her head. "No, that can't be it. My texts have been nothing but supportive. There's no reason for her to think I'm mad at her."

"Still. Even if she isn't worried about you, you can bet she's facing a whole load of shite from her family and the police. Remember what it was like for you? All the police interviews and constant questions from every direction. Give her a chance to catch her breath, yeah? I'm sure she'll be in touch when she's ready."

"You're right. It's only been a week, and who knows what kind of state she's in emotionally? I'm being a bit of a selfish brat, aren't I?"

"Nah. If I'd saved someone from a burning car, I'd be expecting a fucking parade. You're worried, that's all."

Eilidh couldn't help but laugh. "The visual of you on a parade float has cheered me right up."

He winked. "Always happy to help."

"I think I'll send one last message. Tell her again that I understand but let her know I'm here when she's ready. To give her a little more reassurance. Then I'll leave it."

"I think that's for the best. You need to stop torturing yourself with other people's problems, Grey. It's been less than a month since Claire left—how about you focus on yourself for a while?"

Eilidh gulped back the last of her chocolate. Sam was right, as hard as it was to admit. It had only taken a few hours on the loch, a place she always found solace, to realise she hadn't been good to herself lately. "One message, then I'll start worrying about myself."

"Deal. And what was it you were drunkenly getting all philosophical about last night? About the world conspiring to bring you together again?"

"Hey, no fair. You know the rule. Drunken laments are never to be brought up when sober."

He threw her a wicked grin. "All I'm saying is, if you believe it was fate that brought you back together, then I'm sure it will again."

She swiped at the back of his head. "Sarcastic shitebag. Just you wait and see. Darcy and I will meet again."

Chapter 33

DARCY PULLED THE BLANKET TO her chin and closed her eyes. She tried to pretend she was actually on her sofa, cosy under the fluffy fleece, fire and TV on low, drifting away to nap land…

A rattling trolley rumbled past her closed door and might as well have crashed right into the daydream. Then the woman in the next room called out for a nurse. Again. It was all Darcy could do not to shout out herself and remind the woman of the handy button they had for just such a purpose.

She sighed and gave up on the fantasy nap.

Anja had dropped by with a bag full of home comforts, and after seeing what the hospital was offering for dinner, she had quickly been charged with another food run. Darcy suddenly remembered her phone and threw her hands up to praise whoever for the small mercy of a distraction.

There were get-well messages from colleagues and friends that made her smile. In particular from Joe, who had kept a running commentary of gossip coming from the office and even Bridget's messages were surprisingly warm. There was an actual kiss on the end of one of them. There were thoughts and prayers posted on her timeline from friends far and wide, and as was the Scottish way, plenty of inappropriate GIFs on messenger taking the piss out of the whole ordeal.

Eilidh's name in the message list stopped her scrolling. The last text from her had been received the night before the accident, a reply to Darcy's cancellation of their date. She wondered if Eilidh had thought about her since then. It was unlikely given Eilidh hadn't been back in touch. The ball had been left in Darcy's court, so maybe it was up to her to restart the conversation.

She looked down at her broken form in the bed and smirked to herself. She was hardly in the position to be dating right now, but it was encouraging that she was thinking about it. Her foul hospital mood hadn't killed the romantic in her.

Who knew how long the road to recovery would be, and it seemed a shame to cut off all contact. By the time she was able, Eilidh might have long forgotten her, which would be extremely disappointing. There'd been such promise in their exchanges, and Eilidh had definitely, really, without a doubt, existed.

As if by Darcy's shear will in wondering, a text buzzed through with Eilidh's name attached. Momentarily stunned, she dropped the phone in her lap before instantly grabbing it again, eager to read the message.

She read and reread, confused by its content. For a moment, she wondered if the text was meant for her.

> I know I said last night that I understood, but it makes me want to see you no less. I can't stop thinking and wondering how you're doing. Would be good to see your face, if only for a few minutes. Tell me to bugger off if you want. E x

If it was meant for Darcy, it sounded as if Eilidh knew she was in hospital and had been in touch already but told not to visit. But who? And why?

Anja.

She was the only person with access to Darcy's phone. She would have needed her password to unlock it, but then she must have seen Darcy tap it in a hundred times, and perhaps she'd simply been fielding messages on her behalf. Protective as always; Darcy couldn't fault her for that. Although maybe she'd gone too far this time? Darcy would speak to her about that later, but right now, Eilidh's text called for a response.

> Would you believe me if I said I was just thinking about you? D x

Darcy stared at the screen, willing a reply. Blue ticks appeared, and the app showed Eilidh was online and typing.

> I would be surprised but it makes me happy that you were. How are you? Does your reply mean I can come visit you in the hospital? x

Darcy paused a minute. So Eilidh did know she was in hospital. Was it a good idea for her to visit, and why would she be so keen? It felt a little above and beyond for someone who had met her once.

How do you know I'm in hospital? And I'd say yes, but I look a state and it's not exactly how I envisaged our first date x

Now I'm confused? How strong are the drugs they've got you on? I'm betting you look more alive than a week ago. We can call this an interlude if you want, until you're feeling up to taking me out on that date x

A week ago? Had Eilidh been to visit already? Why would Anja not tell her that? Bluntness was required because Darcy needed straight answers.

A week ago? You've been here already? Eilidh I'm sorry, I don't know what's going on? Can you please explain why/when you were here? Questioning my sanity right now x

The blue ticks appeared but then Eilidh disappeared offline. *What the...?*

Darcy was about to send another message when the phone began to vibrate and Eilidh's name appeared on the incoming call. It made Darcy suddenly nervous to talk to her, but the need for answers overrode the butterflies, and she swiped the green circle.

"Hey," she answered.

"Hey, yourself. I hope you don't mind me calling?"

Eilidh sounded a little nervous herself which warmed Darcy and made her feel oddly pleased. "No, it's fine. I'm hoping you can fill me in on what's been going on?"

"From your message it sounds as if we both need a little of that. What exactly do you remember about the accident?"

"The accident? So you do know about that? And the fact I'm in the hospital?"

There was a moment of quiet, and Darcy was sure she heard Eilidh cuss.

"Erm...yeah. Listen, can I come see you now? I'd rather not do this on the phone."

"No. I mean, yes. You can come visit, but please, Eilidh. Tell me what's going on?

She heard Eilidh release a long breath.

"I was there, Darcy. When you crashed. I saw it. I was the one who pulled you out of the car."

The phone dropped in to Darcy's lap for a second time. Eilidh had been there? Eilidh had *saved* her? She was the mysterious woman the staff and Anja claimed to have no knowledge of.

Anja had lied to her face. Why on earth would she keep something so massive from Darcy?

"Hello. Darcy are you there?" Eilidh's voice rang out from the phone, and Darcy reached for it with a shaking hand.

"I'm here." Her voice came out in a whisper, and she cleared her throat. It burned with the threat of tears. A mixture of gratitude and anger swelled in her chest. "Eilidh, wow. I don't know what to say. You saved my life."

Eilidh chuckled. "Well, you know. I really wanted that date."

Her joke sucked the anger away in an instant, and Darcy laughed with her. "Idiot."

"I've been told that many times. I mean, surely only an idiot would run towards a burning car?"

Darcy smiled. If that's how Eilidh wanted to play it, she was happy to oblige. "Clearly. How about we call you a brave idiot?"

"If we must. I've made peace with plain idiot though."

"Not one for praise and plaudits, I assume?"

Eilidh laughed. "Is it that obvious? I much prefer self-deprecating humour and avoid scary thoughts at every opportunity."

"Okay, I can do that. You should see my face, by the way. It's a full on Picasso of prime colours."

"Oh, I've seen it. It looked like that Picasso had been torn up and stitched back together with a knitting needle. Yet here I am, still calling."

"It's confirmed, then."

"What is?"

"You're just a plain idiot."

"Why, thank you."

Darcy felt lighter than she had since waking up. A small part of the puzzle had been solved. It gave her hope that she would find the rest of the pieces, which she could one day use to complete the whole picture of what had happened that night. Still, once the laughter calmed, Darcy couldn't help but ask a question nagging at the back of her mind.

"Why didn't you tell anyone it was you? Leave your name? Come back to visit? The police wouldn't disclose any personal information about you, and it's been torturing me all week not knowing who saved me."

"That's why I'm confused. I stayed with you until your family were contacted. Then your best friend showed up—Annie, was it?"

"Anja." *So, she'd met Eilidh and not said a word about it.*

"Aye, that was it. She said she was your sister at first which I believed because until then I had no idea who you were; that Picasso face was unrecognisable. When she said your name was Darcy, it still took me a minute before I realised it was you. Then she confessed she'd lied about the sister thing because she was afraid they wouldn't let her in otherwise. I gave her my number, asked her to update me, and left. She didn't tell you any of this?"

"No." Darcy was back to anger. "She didn't. I'm sorry about that. I'd have been in touch sooner if I'd known."

"Hey, I'm sure she had her reasons. She was so scared and upset seeing you all torn up. We're talking now. That's what matters."

"True. She still has some explaining to do though."

"Maybe you can give me an idea of when that explaining will happen, so I can avoid it?"

Darcy couldn't help the laugh. "Probably best. I'll talk to her tonight. Are you free tomorrow?"

"I'm working, but free at lunchtime. Is that all right with you?"

"Perfect. Can I make a cheeky request of my brave idiot?"

"Sure. What can I do?"

"Bring food. Proper food. And real coffee, not the shite they serve in the canteen here."

Eilidh chuckled. "No problem. So long as it's not a date, because that would be very sad."

"Definitely not a date. This is the interlude, remember? Oh, and try not to drop the coffee."

Eilidh's laughter rang in her ears, long after she'd hung up.

Chapter 34

ANJA RETURNED, ARMS LADEN WITH bags full of heavenly scented food.

"You, my friend, are in for a treat. I stopped by that noodle and sushi bar you love and have one of everything from the wee-plates-of-joy menu."

Darcy watched as she pulled over the bed tray and started unpacking the small parcels of favourites. Despite the alluring smells and the rumbling of her tummy, Darcy knew she wouldn't enjoy it until she had some answers.

"Stop that a minute and sit down."

Anja paused, holding a foil box in mid-air. "What's up with you? I thought you'd be beside yourself when I showed up with this lot."

"I am beside myself. With anger. I need you to sit down so we can attempt to talk about it rationally before I blow my lid."

Anja's eyes widened, and Darcy understood why. She couldn't think of a single occasion when she had raised her voice at her friend or spoken with any hint of rage, which was why she was trying her best to maintain a calm approach.

Anja sat as instructed, and Darcy shifted to look at her. "Why didn't you tell me about Eilidh?"

"Eilidh?" Anja looked confused. "That girl you met on the bridge?"

"Yes, Anja. That girl I met on the bridge." She spoke through gritted teeth. "The girl who saved my life."

Anja breathed out a resigned sigh. "She messaged you."

"And a good job she did." Darcy felt her voice rise in pitch. It seemed Anja knew exactly what she'd done.

"I can explain, sweetheart." Anja reached for her hand, but Darcy pulled away.

"You bloody better."

She stood then and moved towards the window, running a hand through her hair. It was an action Darcy had seen a number of times when she was annoyed or irritable and needed a moment to compose herself.

She finally turned but kept her distance. "Please believe me when I say I did it for you."

"How am I to believe you when you've been lying to me this whole time?"

"It was for your own good, Darcy, because I know you."

"What's that supposed to mean? Why do I feel as if you're in the wrong but I'm the one about to be attacked?"

Anja came back to her side then. "You're not. I promise. I've been sick all week keeping this to myself, but you need to trust me, Darcy. I didn't do it lightly. I thought if you knew about Eilidh, you would get all worked up and worried. About whether she was okay and how you'd ever repay her. You'd shift the focus from yourself and getting better to her. I didn't think that'd be good for you. I didn't want you worrying. All I wanted was for you to rest and concentrate on yourself."

Tears leaked free, and Darcy hated seeing them stain a trail down her friend's lovely face, hated being the cause of them. But Anja's explanation wasn't good enough. She was holding back. Darcy wasn't getting the whole story.

Still, she couldn't help but reach out and offer Anja her hand. Anja gripped it tightly and sank on to the edge of the bed close to her. "Do you understand? Do you see why I didn't tell you?"

"To a point. You're right, I would've worried. But it's not good enough, Anja. She saved my life. Like actually pulled me from a burning car saved my life. That's huge. Were you ever going to tell me?"

"You think I don't know that? And of course, I would have told you eventually."

"You're still not telling me everything. I can tell. No more lies, Anja. What else are you keeping from me?"

Anja hung her head and brushed tears from her cheeks. When she met Darcy's gaze again her face was the picture of sorrow. "When I first saw you lying in this bed, Darcy, I was terrified. I thought I was going to lose you and from that moment, all I wanted was to protect you from everyone and everything. To keep you safe because I'd failed you once already and I wasn't going to do it again."

"Failed me?" Darcy felt herself soften towards her friend. She seemed so fragile and raw, Anja hadn't opened up this way throughout the Jason saga. "You didn't fail me. You didn't cause the accident."

"I should have been there to stop you getting in that car. If I hadn't been so wrapped up in myself, I wouldn't have left you that night, and you'd have had me to protect you."

Darcy shook her head and squeezed Anja's hand tighter, pulled her closer. The remaining rage had dwindled to mild annoyance. It hadn't occurred to her that her friend might be carrying some guilt over that night. "How can you think that? This whole thing is the result of a long chain of decisions outside both of our control, and we don't even know the whole story. Why I got in that car? Who else was there on the road? This is bigger than you leaving the cabin that night."

Anja smiled through the tears and pressed her forehead to Darcy's. "It's good to hear you say that, but it might be a while before I believe it. I keep thinking, what if?"

Darcy brushed a thumb under both Anja's eyes. "Believe it. It's the truth. This isn't on you, An. To have you here in my corner is what's getting me through this. But I need you to be honest with me. If I'm ever going to find out what happened, you can't hide things from me, okay? I won't fall to pieces."

Anja pressed a tender kiss to Darcy's injured cheek. "Okay. Although it wasn't only you I wanted to keep it from."

Darcy sat back and shuffled over a little, inviting Anja to sit back with her on the bed. "What do you mean? Who else?"

Anja slipped off her shoes and jacket and climbed up on the bed beside Darcy. After tucking a pillow behind her, she wheeled the tray of food towards them. "The police, Darcy. She was the only other witness that we're aware of. I couldn't be sure what she'd say, and I thought if she told them you were driving too fast, or erratic, or…that there was no other car out there… Well, I was afraid it might not help your case. It's too late now though; as you know they already talked to her the night of the accident."

Darcy pondered that a moment as she pulled the lid from a container of tempura prawns. "I know that, and I plan on talking to her myself. She might have remembered more since then about what happened. Something about the other car or driver? Any little detail could help."

Anja shifted beside her and cleared her throat. It was an awkward tic she had when she knew Darcy wasn't going to be happy with what she had to say. It normally occurred at work when Anja actually had to act like a boss and make Darcy work late or do something tedious. "I'm going to throw this out there, and you're not going to hate me for it or get annoyed. All right?"

"All right." Darcy dunked a dumpling in sweet-chilli sauce and popped it in her mouth.

"What if...what if Eilidh was the driver of the other car?"

Darcy choked a little on the dumpling and gratefully accepted the napkin Anja offered. "What? Are you serious?"

"Very." Anja nodded. "I mean, who goes running at that time of night along a dark lane in the middle of nowhere? Who goes running in the snow at six o'clock in the morning on a Saturday? When you just so happened to first meet her."

"Someone who enjoys running when it's quiet? Or has a job to go to afterwards?"

"Maybe. Or maybe Eilidh came to the cabin and you caught her there? Maybe she was the other driver and was chasing you, trying to stop you from telling anyone. Then when you crashed she conveniently became your heroine?"

"Anja, that's pretty farfetched."

Anja shrugged. "It's possible. We know nothing about this stalker of yours, Darcy. For all we know—"

"If she was the driver, what did she do with her car?"

"What?"

"The police said Eilidh came to the hospital with me that night?"

Anja nodded, her face scrunched in deep thought.

"Then where was her car when the police arrived at the scene? They said the road was deserted and only the wreckage of mine was left there."

"Okay." Anja nodded. "Fair point. I hadn't considered that, but what if she was in the car with you?" Anja shrugged as if it was feasible. "You were driving somewhere and that's when you realised who she was?"

Darcy sighed. "So, you and I were at my house, eating, drinking, chatting. You decide to go and see Jason when the cheating prick won't leave you alone, and Eilidh turns up?" She shook her head. "She doesn't know where I live."

"Your stalker does."

"If Eilidh were my stalker and turned up at my house randomly—without invitation—do you seriously think I'd get in my car with her? While I was drunk? In my dressing gown?"

"Maybe. If she forced you. If she had a weapon or a plausible enough reason. Perhaps you thought crashing was your only way out of it."

"I don't know, Anja." Darcy shook her head as she went over the myriad of possibilities. "As far as I know, she wasn't injured. If Eilidh had been in the car with me, then it's a miracle she got out."

None of the various theories made complete sense and came with a host of other questions, but they were enough to give Darcy pause. She had to consider every eventuality, no matter how unsavoury.

"She did take a few knocks. I saw her, remember? I know it all sounds outrageous, but then nothing about this has been normal, has it?"

"You're right and I'm hearing what you're saying. I guess everyone really is a suspect. She's coming to visit tomorrow."

Anja blew out an exasperated breath but didn't protest. "Just keep in mind what I've said. Okay? Keep your eyes open and your wits about you."

It was sound advice. Apart from keeping Eilidh from her, Anja had been amazing since the accident, and even that deception seemed only to have been done out of love and protectiveness. She couldn't stay mad at her for it.

"Noted. I'll be careful. So long as you promise me there's nothing else you're keeping from me."

Anja slung and arm across Darcy's shoulders and squeezed her close. "Promise."

Chapter 35

A TENTATIVE KNOCK CAME AT the door, and Darcy called for the person to come in. No one else ever knocked, and she was right in thinking it was Eilidh.

"Hey." Eilidh took a few steps inside and closed the door.

Darcy smiled. "Hey." She was surprised to see Eilidh in a hospital uniform: navy pressed chinos, fancy-looking trainers, and a pale blue polo shirt with "Physiotherapist" embroidered across the breast. A bandage was wrapped around her forearm, and Darcy wondered if she had suffered any other injuries from that night.

She was taller than Darcy remembered, and her thick dark hair was no longer hidden under a hat but instead pulled in to a tidy ponytail. The beetroot hue Darcy had witnessed on the bridge was gone, but her cheeks still held a tinge of pink.

Eilidh's gaze flitted around the room before it fell back on Darcy. "Is it me or does this feel a little weird?"

"It's not just you." Darcy shifted in the bed, trying to prop herself higher.

"Here. Let me help you with that." Eilidh moved to her bedside and adjusted the pillows behind her, giving Darcy a moment to study her face up close. A small white scar split her left eyebrow, and a smattering of freckles crossed her nose and forehead.

"How's that?"

She stepped back, and Darcy nodded. "Great. Thank you."

Eilidh smiled and took a seat. "I imagine you have a lot of questions."

Darcy tore her gaze from Eilidh's lips and met her eyes. The sight of her, the proximity, had momentarily stunned her. After all their failed attempts to meet again, she was finally here, and Darcy choked on all the words she wanted to say.

Instead, she cried. Great, wracking sobs tore through her body, and there was nothing she could do to stop them. Every injury ached with each shudder, but she didn't care: something about Eilidh's presence had undone her.

Arms wrapped around her and the mattress dipped as Eilidh, still a stranger in so many ways, held her close and whispered words of comfort. Darcy wasn't sure how long they sat that way or how long she cried. Every fibre of her being felt drained of energy as the last tears dried and Eilidh offered her another tissue.

When the moment had passed, neither seemed to know what to say. Eilidh returned to the chair and sat quietly, giving her time to find some measure of composure.

"Thank you," Darcy whispered.

Eilidh reached and took her hand again. "Any time."

"Seems I'm the idiot this time." Darcy smirked.

"Eh, not so fast. That's a title I'm wielding with pride right now. There's no way you've earned it yet."

Darcy couldn't help but laugh. She kept her gaze fixed on Eilidh, searched her face while she tried to find the words. How did you thank someone for saving your life? How did you repay them?

"I'm not sure about the protocol for when someone has saved your life."

Eilidh's head ducked a little then, and she broke the stare. "Well, you know, my friend Sam suggested a parade, but…I'll settle for a thank you."

"A parade, huh? I mean, I could make some calls, see if my balloon guy is free."

Eilidh relaxed back in to the chair and laughed with her. "Aye, okay, today you're the idiot."

Darcy gestured to the uniform. "You work here?"

"For my sins. Going on twelve years now."

"Wow. So all this time you've been here and I didn't know."

"Aye, and I'd be lying if I said it hasn't been difficult not to come and see you. Did Anja tell you why she didn't say anything to you about me?"

"She did. I guess she knows me too well and knew I'd worry about you. Stress myself over how to repay you when she wanted me to focus on getting better."

Eilidh's eyebrows knitted in a frown. "Darcy, you've nothing to repay. And I'm fine. Look." She stood and spun around on the spot. "Practically good as new." She lightly touched her bandaged arm. "There'll be barely a trace left of this, and even the sunburn's already faded."

"Sunburn?"

Eilidh chuckled. "That's what I called the scorching my face got when the car blew."

"Oh." It dawned on Darcy then, how much more Eilidh knew about that night than her, how many questions she might be able to answer.

As if reading her mind, Eilidh took her hand again. "I know you have questions and I'm here to answer them all. But first..." She moved to the door and opened it, disappearing for a moment before entering the room again pushing a wheelchair. "I'm going to get you out of here for a while."

Darcy couldn't hide her surprise. "Are you serious? Am I allowed? Where are we going?"

Eilidh secured the chair next to the bed. "Yes, I'm serious. Yes, you're allowed, for a short time at least. We're going to get that food and coffee I promised."

Darcy couldn't get the blankets off herself quick enough. After more than a week of the same four walls, she was desperate for a change. Under Eilidh's instruction and with her help, Darcy manoeuvred safely into the wheelchair. She winced as Eilidh elevated her leg and wrapped a blanket over her knees.

"Obviously I won't be your official physio, but if you'll let me, I can be your unofficial one?"

"If it gets me out of this room, you can be whatever you want."

Eilidh laughed. "Careful. I could interpret that in so many ways."

Darcy raised her face to the low winter sun and thanked the weather gods it wasn't raining or snowing. After a couple of suspect sandwiches, they'd taken coffees to go, and Eilidh had pushed her slowly through the hospital gardens. Clear of the main building and the groups of staff and patients wrapped up to enjoy an unseasonal lunch outside, they had found a low wall for Eilidh to perch on while Darcy stayed in the chair.

"Why on earth were you even out there running at that time of night? That's what I keep asking myself."

Eilidh shrugged. "All sorts of reasons. Running is my refuge and escape all at the same time. I hadn't slept properly for days, I'd had a shitty downer of an afternoon, topped off when you had to cancel our date. So, I did what I always do. I ran."

Anja's accusations ran through her mind, and as much as she didn't want to believe them, she had promised caution. Despite how genuine Eilidh seemed, Darcy needed more if she were to put her mind at ease.

"And happened to be right where I crashed?" She knew her scepticism was thinly veiled and Eilidh clearly picked up on it.

"Why do I feel like I'm being accused of something here? Yes, it was unusual for me to head out that far from the city. Yes, I happened to be in the right place at the right time, and yes, it's a huge fucking coincidence that it was you in that car. But I've done nothing wrong, Darcy."

The emotion in her voice threatened to send Darcy over the edge again, and she was immediately sorry to have suspected Eilidh. Darcy reached for her hand and squeezed it in apology. "I know. I'm sorry. There's a lot more going on here, and I shouldn't be taking it out on you."

"Like what? You're making me feel like the accident was somehow my fault."

Darcy took a deep breath and wondered where to start. "I'm struggling to piece it all together. To figure out why I was even in the car or where I was going? Who was in the other car?"

"You remember the other car, then?"

Darcy's attention was piqued at that. "No. I told you, I remember nothing. The police said there was another set of skid marks, and a witness who'd seen another car and spoken to the driver. Which I now know is you."

Eilidh nodded.

"They wondered if someone else had happened upon the accident and freaked out, or if maybe I was being chased. Can you tell me what you saw?"

"I'm afraid I haven't remembered anything else since that night, but I can tell you what I told the police."

"Please, if that's okay? I'd really like to hear it from you."

"Okay, well, it was dark, so I couldn't make out the model or the person inside the car. I remember hearing the screech as it stopped, but I was already running away from the road towards your car and didn't pay much attention to it. I know it was a woman driver. She called out to me while I was seeing to you, and I figured she'd seen what had happened and stopped to help. I wasn't sure I'd be able to get you out of the car. You were upside down and held in place by the seatbelt. I thought between the two of us, we'd stand a better chance. So, anyway, I yelled up at her to call for help and then get her arse down there. I was still struggling with the seatbelt when she told me she'd called an ambulance, then I heard an engine rev as she drove away."

"You're sure it was a woman?"

"Definitely. I didn't get a look at her, but her voice was high and shaky. As I said, I was focused on getting you out of there and she was up above the verge, a fair bit away."

"I can't believe she left you there alone and didn't even try to help."

Eilidh shrugged as if it didn't surprise her. "You'll be surprised what people will stand by and let happen. When fear kicks in, most take the flight option. We all react differently in a crisis and not always how we like to imagine we would."

"Aye. I guess. Lucky me that you aren't most people."

"Yip, you got the idiot." Eilidh smiled wryly, and then a thought seemed to occur to her. "Wait a minute, why would the police think you were being chased?"

Darcy blew out a long breath. Should she tell Eilidh? Perhaps if she were blunt and up front, Eilidh's reaction would tell her something. If she had something to hide, it might show. "I have a stalker."

"A stalker? Bloody hell, I didn't expect that."

Eilidh seemed genuinely surprised, but then maybe she had preempted that Darcy would tell her about the stalker and was prepared to react accordingly. Anyone hiding that kind of secret would have to be a good actress. Darcy studied her a moment: her face was etched with concern and a worry in her eyes that Darcy thought impossible to fake. She heard Anja's voice in her head, advising caution.

Was she really questioning the woman who had saved her life? All Anja's crazy theories had riled and twisted her into a distrustful mess. Darcy decided to give her the benefit of the doubt. She wouldn't dismiss the theory completely, but the possibility of more answers was too tempting to risk. Despite the misgivings Anja had voiced, Darcy's gut told her Eilidh was an innocent part of the puzzle. "Me neither."

"I imagine not. Is that why you got in the car? Why you were driving so fast? Did something happen? Were you trying to get away from them?"

Darcy threw up her hands in frustration. "Those are exactly the questions that are torturing me. Things have been escalating lately. They've left gifts at my house as well as work, getting braver, as the police would say. I think maybe they were at my house; it's the only thing that makes sense to me. I can't think of any other plausible reason why I would get in the car drunk."

"So you were drunk. I wondered whether that was true."

Darcy was sure she looked remorseful. She certainly felt it. "Unfortunately, yes. Which I'll have to answer for and why I know I'd never have gotten in that car of my own accord. I had to have been afraid or in danger, or both. I had to be."

If she said it enough times, maybe it would be true, because the thought of getting in the car in that state, for no good reason, was truly unimaginable to her. To be that stupid… Although the alternative was hardly palatable, at least it didn't call into question her own character and judgement.

"Shit."

"Exactly. Now you see why it's so important to find that other car."

"Aye, I'm so sorry I can't remember more." Eilidh knelt down at her side. "I'll do all I can to help you. Okay?"

Darcy nodded. "Thank you. I'm so happy you're here. Despite everything, it's great to see you again."

The warmth of Eilidh's smile was nearly enough to dispel any lingering fears Darcy had about her reasons for being out there that night. To shoot down any further suspicion Anja might direct her way. Almost.

Too much had happened, the stakes were just too high, and until Darcy had the answers she craved, she doubted anyone could evade the wariness that had set in. But for now, her heart told her to believe Eilidh. To accept her help and see where it led.

"Actually, there is something I do remember." Darcy felt shy in admitting it, but she wanted to impress on Eilidh exactly what it had meant having her there that night. Not only pulling her from the car, but for staying by her side.

"Really? What's that?"

Darcy reached out and locked their fingers together. "Your voice. Telling me it would be okay."

She watched Eilidh's face soften and thought there was going to be more tears. Instead, Eilidh crouched by the wheelchair and pulled Darcy into a hug. They both clung on tight, neither in a hurry to break apart. "It will be," she whispered close to Darcy's ear.

"Here you are. I've been looking everywhere for you." Anja's harried voice broke through the moment, and Eilidh quickly moved away.

"Hey, Anja. Sorry, Eilidh managed to sneak me out for a while."

"So I see. You could have left a note or something. When I saw the empty bed... Well... You're here, and you're all right, I take it?"

Darcy glanced in Eilidh's direction. "I'm fine, sweetheart. Eilidh was filling me in on what she remembers from that night."

"Oh, really." Anja rounded on Eilidh. "No doubt that was an interesting story."

Darcy reached out and swatted her arm. "Stop it, you." She held Anja's warning glare and shook her head lightly. "Eilidh saved my life."

Her friend's hardened features relaxed a little at Darcy's words. "You're right. Eilidh, I'm sorry. It's been a hard time, as I'm sure you'll understand." Anja held out her hand towards Eilidh. "I know I've said it before, but thank you for what you did."

Eilidh shook the hand, and Darcy smiled, looking between the pair. "That's what I like to see."

Anja brought her attention back to Darcy. "You look exhausted. Have you been crying? We should get you back to rest."

"An, I'm fine." Darcy wasn't ready for her time with Eilidh to end. There was so much more to say.

Anja stood hands on hips, head tilted. "What did we talk about? About looking after yourself?"

"I know, but—"

"But what? It's freezing out here and that leg should be resting properly."

Darcy glanced at Eilidh who was studying a nearby rock rather intently, clearly unwilling to get involved.

"My leg feels fine right now, and surely fresh air can only be a good thing? Just a little longer, An. Please?"

Anja threw up a frustrated hand and glared towards Eilidh. "Fine. Whatever. Do what you like."

"Aw, don't be like that. This is the most human I've felt the whole time I've been stuck in here."

Anja crossed her arms defensively. "I'm not being like anything. If you want to stay, then stay. Who am I to tell you what to do?"

Eilidh stood suddenly and made a show of looking at her watch. "You should go back inside, Darcy. My lunch break is over anyway, and I promised I wouldn't have you out for too long." She turned her back on Anja and squeezed Darcy's shoulder affectionately. "Same time tomorrow?"

Darcy couldn't help but grin. "It's a non-date."

Eilidh winked and set off at a jog. Darcy watched her go a moment, and as if sensing her stare, Eilidh turned and offered a small wave. Then Anja was grabbing the wheelchair handles and jerking it around to head in the opposite direction.

"Hitting on you while you're sat injured in a wheelchair. Classy."

"Hey. I told you to stop it. She was being nice, that's all."

"Nice my arse. She's got her eye on you."

"I hope so." Darcy chuckled.

The chair stopped abruptly, and Anja rounded in front of it. "What did we talk about last night? About being careful around her until we know the full story?"

"I know and I am being careful. But I don't think it's her. I mean, why would she risk getting in touch again? If the stalker did come to the house to attack me, or tried something, then surely they wouldn't be stupid enough to stick around. How could they be sure I wouldn't remember?"

Anja's brow furrowed, and Darcy could see she was torn with the logic. "True, I suppose."

"And she seemed so genuine with all the questions she was asking. I honestly got no inkling that she knew any more than she was saying."

"Well, of course she'd be asking questions. To cover her tracks. You'd be surprised how easily some folk can lie."

It still didn't sit right with Darcy, but after everything, she knew it was irresponsible to disregard Anja's warnings completely. "I know. I promised I'd be careful, and I will. Stop worrying, okay?"

"Fine."

"Fine."

Anja resumed pushing the wheelchair, and both women were quiet. Darcy hated the unease that seemed to have settled around them since the accident. This wasn't how they worked, but something heavy seemed to sit on Anja's shoulders that she was clearly reluctant to share. It suddenly occurred to Darcy what it might be. In the aftermath of the accident, she had entirely forgotten the reason why Anja had left the cabin that night.

"Do you want to talk about Jason?"

She heard Anja sigh behind her, and it was a moment before she replied. "He's gone."

Darcy tried unsuccessfully to crane around to see her friend's face. "Where? What happened?"

"He told me he finally got a job onshore. In Norway of all places. He asked me to go with him, to start fresh back in my home country. He thought that would make me happy. I told him there was no hope for us, but he should take the job anyway. So he did."

"Wow. That's it, then. Definitely over?"

"Yep. The rest of his shit has been cleared out, there's some financial papers to sign, and then he'll be gone."

"What about the house?"

"That was mine before we got married, and he's agreed I can pay him a lump sum to walk away as part of the divorce settlement."

"Oh, Anja." She reached her good hand up behind her, and Anja clutched it for only a moment. Darcy was sure she heard a small sob but didn't try to turn around again. The way Anja spoke, so matter of fact about it all, she was clearly trying to hold it together right now. She was fighting against falling to pieces, and Darcy knew that was for her benefit, knew Anja would be angry at any encouragement from Darcy to let it happen.

"You okay?" Darcy had to ask.

165

"I will be. I've had my meltdown, and it's just formalities now. All that's important right now is getting you better."

Darcy tipped her head back for an upside-down view of her friend. "I can see right up your nose from this angle."

Anja laughed. Loudly. And Darcy couldn't help but join in.

She felt a kiss on the top of her head as the laughter faded. "I needed that."

"I think we both did," Darcy agreed.

"I'm afraid I have to go back to work tomorrow. Bridget can't give me anymore time off, and I figured it might be better to save my leave for when you get out of here."

Darcy might have been more upset if it weren't for the knowledge that Eilidh was close by and had promised more visits, but she sensed Anja was far from happy about it. "We knew good-boss Bridget would only last so long. It makes sense to save your leave, although I feel guilty that you're planning to spend it with a broken me."

"Don't be daft. I'm sure it'll be fun, and you can make it up to me with some sunshine once you're better. Plus I can still visit you here in the evenings. Bring you dinner."

"I love you." Darcy wasn't sure where it came from, but in that moment, she wanted Anja to know it.

There was quiet for a few seconds before a palm pressed against her cheek. "I love you too."

Chapter 36

EILIDH'S HEAD APPEARED AROUND THE door, and Darcy beamed. "I was wondering when you'd appear."

"Aye, sorry, got caught with a patient." She produced two half-decent-looking chicken-and-avocado-filled baguettes and a large packet of crisps from her backpack, before adding fresh juice and a bag of Haribo to the haul. Her visits to Darcy were rapidly becoming Eilidh's favourite part of the day, and she knew never to show up empty-handed.

"Are those the sour ones?" Darcy grabbed for them.

"Of course. The patient shop came up trumps today."

Darcy popped one in her mouth, and Eilidh laughed as her cheeks and lips puckered. "That's a beautiful look."

Darcy drew a circle in the air around her face. "Are you kidding? It's a right state."

"Well, you're not quite so peely wally, at least. I can see some natural colour past the bruises. Which are fading, by the way."

They ate lunch, played cards, and had a few laughs at Darcy's expense. Eilidh liked that she didn't feel the need to tread carefully around her or watch every word. She seemed to appreciate that Eilidh took the piss a little in an effort to lighten the mood.

"Any more dreams?" Eilidh asked.

"Bits here and there. I'm in and out of sleep a lot between the meds and nurses always checking in."

"Have you remembered anything new?"

Darcy picked up a card and discarded another. "Nope. It's the same few fragments going around in circles, and even then it's more feelings than visuals. The pain, the confusion, that sense of choking. Your voice."

Eilidh smiled at that. "Why is it that you keep dreaming of me, I wonder?"

"Because you're the heroine of the tale." Darcy returned her smile, but it didn't quite reach her eyes. Eilidh knew it was nothing to do with her; it was clear Darcy continued to struggle with the gaps in her memory. She wondered if Darcy would ever get past Eilidh's association with the accident.

"Do you think it will always be this way? That when you think of me you'll think of the accident? I feel as if maybe having me around isn't always a good thing, because I'm a reminder."

Darcy seemed taken aback and began to shake her head even before Eilidh had finished. "Don't be daft. I don't associate anything negative with you. What you did… I'll be forever grateful and indebted to you. I'll always know you saved my life. How can that be bad?"

"See, that's another worry I have. I don't want you to spend time with me because you feel you have to. I've been showing up here every day for a week—uninvited. You must be fed up with me by now."

"Nonsense. As if you need an invite. It's the highlight of my day." Darcy laid her cards on the table. "I win."

"Dammit." Eilidh half-heartedly threw hers down. "That puts you in the lead."

Darcy snickered. "Your deal."

"Do you mean that?" Eilidh felt shy in asking, and it wasn't like her to be so insecure. "About me visiting. It's not as if there's much competition."

"Don't let Anja hear you say that." Darcy chuckled. "But aye. Mostly because you bring me sweets and she refuses. She says I'm hopped up enough on the drugs and caffeine without adding sugar to the mix."

"She's probably right."

Darcy grabbed the bag of sweets. "Too late. You can't take them back."

"Wouldn't dare."

They were quiet a moment as Eilidh dealt the cards. Darcy sucked on a sweet and stared out of the window, seemingly lost in thought.

"One day." She brought her gaze back to Eilidh. "When people ask how we met, we'll conveniently forget my clumsiness on the bridge and tell them the heroic story of how you saved my life. It'll be a riveting tale, and you'll bask in the glory of it."

Eilidh grinned. She liked the sound of that. "One day?"

"Aye, well." Darcy fumbled a bit, and Eilidh stopped herself from laughing. "We're friends, aren't we? I'd quite like it if you stuck around."

"Ah, yes. Friends. The interlude. Can I ask how long you intend for that to last? Because 'one day' sounds very far in the future."

Darcy didn't look away. Her eyes crinkled at the sides as she grinned mischievously.

"We'll know," she said.

What she was trying to say made perfect sense to Eilidh. She nodded in agreement. "We'll know."

They mechanically picked up and put down cards until Eilidh won a game back, making them even. The hospital bustled around them, and the sun cast a warm beam through the window across Darcy's battered legs.

Eilidh broke the quiet. "There's something I wanted to suggest. When you're ready. It helped me a lot."

"Oh yeah?" Darcy pushed herself up higher in the bed, and Eilidh helped her adjust the support under her leg. "What's that?"

"Therapy."

Darcy began to object, but Eilidh cut her off. "I don't mean that kind of therapy. Although you might want to consider it. I'm talking about hypnotherapy. There's a great guy in Edinburgh who helps with your kind of memory loss."

Eilidh could tell Darcy was sceptical. "How?"

"He taps in to all the senses. For example, your sense of smell is one of the most powerful triggers of memory. So he'd take elements of your story and use sensory techniques while you're hypnotised. To try and find those memories for you."

"Like what? I barely know any of the story."

Eilidh searched for an example based on what she knew of that night. "I can help some with that. What about the smoke? When I think of that night, the smoke always comes to mind. But he can take it back further. What about something you ate or drank? Before you left the cabin? I think it's worth considering, anyway."

"I'd say that's the last thing she needs." They both turned to find Anja stood in the doorway. "Don't you think her mind has been messed with enough already?"

"I'm not suggesting she do it tomorrow, Anja," Eilidh countered. "Only that she keeps it in mind."

"Sounds ridiculous to me. What's he going to do, stick her head in a fire to remind her how it feels?"

Eilidh got to her feet. "Now that's ridiculous, and I think you're wrong to write it off so quickly."

"And I think you're wrong for even bringing it up right now. She's still in her hospital bed, for goodness' sake."

"She's an adult who can decide for herself."

"She's in the room," Darcy called out over them both. "And doesn't appreciate being talked about like she's not."

Eilidh glared at Anja a moment longer before bringing her attention back to Darcy. "You're right. I'm sorry."

"Me too," Anja mumbled.

"I understand you're both trying to look out for me, but I'm a grown woman. I can decide these things for myself. Maybe the memories are best forgotten, maybe not. Thanks for the suggestion, Eilidh." She looked between them both. "I'll make a decision when I'm ready."

Eilidh nodded her agreement along with Anja. They both stood awkward and quiet.

Darcy looked to Anja. "What are you doing here at this time of day, anyway?"

"Sorry, I didn't realise I was interrupting anything." She was curt and clearly unimpressed with Eilidh's presence. "I'll go."

"No." Darcy tried to stop her. "Stay, play a round with us." She gestured to the cards.

"It's fine." Anja was already heading for the door. "I'll see you tonight."

She shot one last glare in Eilidh's direction, then left.

"Sorry about her." Darcy voice was softer as she tried to chill the frostiness Anja had left in the room.

Eilidh waved her off. "No big deal. She's worried about you. She cares, that's all. I understand where she's coming from." She glanced at her watch. "Now c'mon. I've got ten minutes left of lunch to whoop your arse. It's your deal."

Chapter 37

IT WAS ANOTHER TWO WEEKS before the doctors would consider allowing Darcy to go home. They thought it was still a little soon, but both Anja and Eilidh fought her corner, assured them she would be taken care of, and offered solutions to every concern they raised.

The stitches had been removed and the layers of gauze gradually diminished, leaving only the yellow tinge of bruises and angry red lines that promised to fade. It would be another few weeks until both casts came off and the real physio could begin. Until then, Eilidh encouraged exercise in her bed, easy stretches, and short walks with the aid of one crutch.

Eilidh visited every day, bringing food, her favourite coffee, podcasts, and book recommendations to pass the time. They played card games and laughed a lot; her company was easy, and the time with her passed too quickly. Each day, Darcy's suspicions diminished, until she realised her trust and faith in Eilidh was wholehearted.

Her evenings were spent much the same, with Anja taking over entertainment duties. Her commitment to Darcy never wavered, and it amazed Darcy regularly how naturally Anja took care of her. How selfless she was when it came to ensuring Darcy was all right.

The only true dark spot was Darcy's memories continuing to evade her. She'd regained a few flashes here and there; Eilidh's voice had become clearer along with the feeling of something choking her, and the noise. The sound of glass shattering and the deafening blast from the explosion woke her in the night, sweating and panting.

Often, she'd wake startled and shouting to Anja curled against her, a protective arm holding her tight. She'd stroke Darcy's hair and utter calm words of reassurance, while other fragments of memory tugged and toyed with her. She knew at some point she'd been shouting, crying, and angry, but at what or who, she had no idea.

When the day came for her to be discharged, she didn't mind admitting to being a little scared. The hospital room had become a sanctuary of sorts—a place where real life didn't need to be acknowledged. She had Anja and Eilidh at her side, and her mum only a video call away. Colleagues and friends stopped by with gifts and kind words; doctors, nurses, and numerous hospital staff tended to her every need.

Once she left this place, she'd have to fully face up to what had happened. To the police and to herself. She'd have to return to a cabin that had once been her safe haven, but which now teased her with memories she might never reclaim.

"You ready to get out of here?" Anja appeared at the door with a wheelchair and a hospital porter in tow.

Darcy glanced around the room one final time as she pulled her coat on. Anja had loaded everything into the car already, and the room stood stark, waiting for its next patient. She was ready. She had to be. Life had to go on, and it wouldn't wait for her forever.

She hobbled towards the chair. "As I'll ever be."

The cabin held a cold chill that did nothing to allay Darcy's nerves.

Anja bustled about her, chatting, unpacking, and updating her on the new CCTV camera installed on the porch, the provisions stocked in the larder and fridge, and the replenished woodpile courtesy of the farmer.

Darcy eyed the tablet showing the CCTV images uneasily. It was a necessary evil right now, she guessed, but it didn't feel right within the rustic confines of her simple home.

Anja positioned Darcy on the sofa, propped her foot on a cushion, and wrapped a blanket around her shoulders. She then placed a cup of tea between icy fingers and set about lighting the fire.

"I've reset the bedroom heater timers, so it'll be toasty in there whenever you want to nap."

Darcy settled back and tried her best to relax. "Thank you. I don't know how I'd have managed without you."

Anja looked up from the stack of kindling she was building and smiled. "I don't want to hear you say that again. No thanks needed. That's what friends are for."

Darcy shook her head. "This is above and beyond friends, An. And I'll thank you as much as I want."

Anja put a match to the newspaper, and they both watched for those few uncertain moments when you weren't sure if it would take. Flames curled the paper and tentatively licked the wood before rising and taking hold. "You're a dab hand at that these days."

Darcy wasn't sure when the strange sense of foreboding would leave her, but the fire was a good start. Anja closed the wood burner's door and opened the vent a little, then sat back on the rug against the sofa. They both watched in silence for a while as the glass window filled with dancing flames.

"Is it weird to be home?"

Anja looked up at her from the floor, and Darcy nodded. "A little. But this helps. I'm glad you're with me."

"I'll have to go to work tomorrow, but I can come back in the evening. I'll stay here as long as you need me."

Darcy set her tea aside and laid a grateful hand on Anja's shoulder, squeezing it gently in thanks. "I wasn't sure what I expected. I thought maybe once I was home, it would all come flooding back, you know? Because this place was so familiar, I hoped it would tell me its secrets somehow."

"Was?"

"Is," Darcy corrected. "I know it well enough, but right now it doesn't feel quite like home."

"I get it. You've been gone a while, and the last time you were here, well, you don't remember it. I understand why that would be frustrating, but give yourself a chance."

Darcy looked around her, let her eyes settle on random objects. The torch by the door, her graduation picture with her mum on the mantel, her bag on the dining table, the radio surrounded by plants on the kitchen windowsill. All of it known to her but none of it telling the story she needed to hear.

Exhaustion washed over her, and she felt her body sink further in to the sofa. "You're right. For now, I think I need some sleep."

Anja hopped up from the floor. "Of course, sweetheart. Let me run through a few things first so I don't have to wake you in the morning, and then we'll get you to bed."

She crossed to the front door and a bag Eilidh had left for her. "Your physio friend gave me a few gadgets to help make you more comfortable."

"Why do you always call her that? Her name is Eilidh."

Anja shrugged. "Whatever." She produced a long metal stick with pincers at one end and a trigger at the other. "These tong thingy's are meant to help if you drop something, or if something is out of reach. I don't know what happens if you drop the tongs though, so I'd recommend not doing that." She laid them on the table and perused the rest of the bag. "There's a list of the exercises you can do whilst sitting, some strips of coloured elastic which I hope you know what to do with, oh, and a pack of cards."

That made Darcy smile, and she wondered when she would get to see Eilidh again. "What about medication?"

"Oh, yes." Anja unpacked a paper pharmacy bag. "I got a little day-by-day tray, and I'll write down what you need to take and when. Some of these are pretty strong, and we wouldn't want you accidentally overdosing."

Darcy manoeuvred herself to get up from the sofa. Anja moved to help, but she put up a hand to stop her. "I need to do this myself, otherwise I'll end up festering all day in one place when you're gone."

She used her good hand to push off, and despite a small wobble with only one stable leg to balance on, she managed okay. "See, I'm fine."

"You're stubborn," Anja countered.

"Independent," Darcy insisted.

"Okay, well, the sofa is one thing, but please don't be attempting something stupid such as the shower or bath without me."

Darcy laughed. "Can't wait to get me naked, eh?"

Normally, Anja would have had a cheeky comeback, something about Darcy's dreams or wishes, but instead she blushed.

"Anja Olsen, I do believe I've made you blush." She attempted a sexy strut towards the kitchen that was anything but, as the heel of her cast clunked clumsily on the wooden floor. "You finally realised what hot stuff I am?"

She could see Anja trying not to laugh, but she failed miserably. "You're ridiculous, and you wish. It's the fire that's put colour in my cheeks, not your so-called hot body."

"Hmm... I'm not so sure that's true, but I'll take your word for it."

Darcy reached the kitchen counter and held on tight with her functioning hand. The short walk across the room had been enough to tire her, and her leg throbbed mercilessly.

"Hey, you all right?" Anja moved to her side and put a protective arm around her.

"Aye. Fine. I need a minute, that's all." Darcy took a few breaths and stared out of the kitchen window in to the blackness where nothing stirred or broke the faint reflection of her and Anja that shone back. What had she expected? A pair of ghoulish eyes watching their every move?

A slice of neon yellow caught her attention—the canoe paddle she used to stir the hot tub water. The hot tub. A memory clawed at the back of her mind but wasn't quite able to hang on. "Were we in the hot tub together that night? I know I was in my dressing gown and bikini, but I just had this fleeting feeling that we'd gone in."

Anja's arm slipped from her waist, and she moved back to sorting medication. "No. We had a plan to go in. I told you that. You had the fire lit to heat the water, but Jason called before we had a chance. Maybe you went in alone?"

"Maybe." Darcy continued to stare in to the night. "I guess it's possible if someone came by and I was out there, the car would be a logical thing to go for? But then how did I get the keys?"

"Darcy, you need to stop torturing yourself with this. I'm sure you'll figure it out eventually, but trying too hard won't help. You need to concentrate on resting and getting better."

Darcy sighed in frustration. She knew Anja was right. "I know, and I'm actually exhausted. I'll never remember anything if I don't get some shut eye."

"Exactly." Anja closed the lid on the pill box and placed it on top of the notes she had written. "Bed time?"

Darcy nodded. "Bed time."

Chapter 38

EILIDH FELT LIGHT. SHE CHUCKLED thinking that was exactly the meaning of her name in Gaelic. It suited her today; for too long, her surname had been more appropriate.

First Aid Kit, a Swedish band, sang sweet melodies in her ears as she made her way along Inverness high street. Sam was waiting for her in one of their favourite cafés for lunch, desperate for a long overdue catch up on Eilidh's gossip.

He wrapped her in a huge hug which only added to her good mood, and he had taken the liberty of ordering her favourite—chai latte.

"You look well, my friend. It feels like I haven't seen you in ages." He took a sip of cappuccino, daubing chocolatey foam on his nose.

"I saw you at work yesterday." She swiped at his face with a napkin.

"Aye, but that's not the same. A minute here and there between patients isn't enough, and I seem to have lost my lunch buddy."

She had the grace to look sheepish. "I'm sorry, Tommo. I know I've been spending a lot of time with Darcy, but she's out now. So, you've got me back."

"Hmm… But for how long? I've seen the way you look at her, and the way she looks at you, I might add."

Eilidh squirmed. "Straight down to business, I see."

He pulled a face like there was any other way to go. "Sorry, should we talk about the weather a minute first, like proper Scots?"

She laughed and stirred the cinnamon topping into her milky drink. "I really like her."

"Well, aye, that's obvious. So what's been happening? Are you seeing her?"

"We're on an interlude."

"An interlude? I'm confused." He sank back in to his armchair and gestured for her to explain.

"I guess neither of us wants to rush anything. Right now, she's fragile and hurt."

"So are you."

"This is different. I want to be there for her as a friend first and foremost. She has a journey ahead of her that I'm all too familiar with, and I don't just mean the physical stuff."

"I get that. But if you're in to each other, why hold back? Perhaps a bit of romance is what you both need."

A waiter came by to take their food order, and Eilidh thought on his words. Why was she holding back? Was it because she still wasn't quite over Claire? Or was she afraid? That Darcy wasn't ready? That she wasn't ready? That if either of those worries were true, it would all fall apart before it had a chance to grow?

Sam nudged her knee. "Well? What's stopping you?"

"I'm worried it's too soon. For both of us. It's only been a couple of months since Claire left, and maybe being Darcy's friend is enough right now. Anything more always has the potential to go sour very quickly, and then where will we be? I'd hate it if that happened and it made things awkward. If I wasn't able to help her anymore."

Sam shook his head impatiently at her and tutted. "If I know you, you've concocted some romantic notion that now you've saved her life, you are forever beholden to protect her. Which is shite. She has plenty of other people to help her through this, I'm sure. Her family? And didn't you say her best friend is always around?"

"Her mum's in Australia, no dad. I know she has other friends, and aye, Anja is always around. It's just... Well, you'll think I'm being daft and overprotective, but there's something not quite right with her."

"I've always thought you were daft, but what d'ya mean?" Sam was forward in his seat again, intrigued.

"I don't know. It's like..." Eilidh thought how to verbalise the uneasy feeling she couldn't shake when Anja was around. "No one else can touch

Darcy. Anja always knows best, and she seems to go out of her way to get between us. I've caught her looking at me a few times, and it's not exactly been a look of appreciation, or fondness—considering I did save her best friend's life."

Sam stirred his coffee, and his eyes squinted in the way they did when he was trying to figure something out. "Maybe she's suspicious? Given the stalker situation Darcy has going on. You have kind of come out of nowhere. She might think you're the stalker."

Eilidh pondered that a moment. Despite how ridiculous it sounded, she could see why it might be true. "Aye, I guess. I hadn't really thought of it in that way."

"She might simply be worried for her friend. Or jealous. She wasn't there to do the saving, and so now she's being protective, that's all, what with Darcy being in such a vulnerable situation."

"That's true. I suppose I'll have to stick it out and hope she begins to trust me at some point."

"Give it time. She'll come around. All best friends are naturally suspicious of a new person in their pal's life. It's in the contract. Even when they don't have a stalker. In the meantime, however, I think you should take Darcy out."

"As in a date?"

"No. Take her to church." Sam rolled his eyes. "Of course I mean like a date. It doesn't have to be fancy or over planned. Keep it simple, keep the pressure off, and see what happens."

"Okay, I reckon I can manage that. I'll have a think about it and see how she's doing. She only got discharged yesterday, so I'll give it a wee while."

"There. You've got a plan. Then you'll be dating, and I'll be dating…" He trailed away and waited for her to catch up.

"Wait. What? Who are you dating? Number-seven girl again?"

"You need to stop calling her that."

"I will when I get to meet her."

"That's never happening. You know too many of my secrets."

Eilidh laughed. "'Tis true. I can be bribed though."

"I'll keep that in mind. But I wasn't talking about number-seven girl. I mean, Emma."

"Okay, I'm still confused, and I can tell you're bursting, so just bloody tell me."

"Martin."

"Martin? As in kayak-hire Martin?" She slapped his knee. "Finally."

"What do you mean, finally? Why aren't you surprised?"

"Oh please." Eilidh attempted to flutter her eyelashes. "What big biceps you have, Sam. I'm sure you're strong enough to look after Eilidh, Sam. Please notice me, Sam, and ask me out."

Sam shoved her playfully and couldn't hide his blush. "Okay, maybe he was a bit obvious, but I didn't think I was."

"There's only so long you can hold out before you give in to that kind of attention. I know you, Tommo."

He poked his tongue out. "I hate you."

"Nah, you don't. So you're dating them both, then? Or is Martin a hook-up? I know your track record with men."

Sam feigned a horrified expression. "Please, do you really think I would have waited this long if it was purely sex? Unlikely."

Eilidh chuckled. "Seven girl is a no go, then?"

"Well, I wouldn't say that. But I'd rather keep my options open, and it's early days with both."

"Do they know about each other?"

"Of course. What kind of person do you think I am? Emma has been quite honest that she's seeing other people as well. We're all adults, we're all dating, there's no marriage proposals on the table quite yet."

Eilidh curled up in to her chair and sat back slowly, shaking her head at her friend. "From fear of even talking to a girl to dating two people at once. If I had half your gall I'd be in a very different situation right now."

Smugness was written all over Sam's face; he couldn't hide it if he tried. "Which is why, my lovely, you need to start taking my advice."

Eilidh thought again about Darcy, about the possibility of taking her out somewhere. Not a date, just a day out with a friend who had the potential to be more. Up until that point, discounting the bridge and the accident, they had only spent time together in the hospital. A change of scenery might do them both some good and give them the opportunity to talk properly, to discover if any potential lay beyond the "interlude".

Eilidh truly hoped there did.

Anja pulled her hat down so it covered her blonde twist of hair and sat only a little above her eyes. She wrapped a thick scarf twice around her neck and tucked her chin and mouth behind it. Once her coat was on, she finally stood, careful to keep her back to the couple of high-back armchairs behind her.

She'd heard enough.

It hadn't been difficult to find out where Eilidh lived, and after that it was only a matter of waiting. She'd followed her in to town, kept her distance, and walked mostly on the opposite pavement, with an excuse at hand in case Eilidh recognised her.

Once or twice, she watched the woman smile to herself and wondered what had triggered it. Her lips sporadically moved with the lyrics in her ears, and occasionally she nodded at the odd person in the street. Friends? Exes? Acquaintances? Former patients?

Anja knew so little about her, but she planned on changing that.

With Eilidh distracted by her friend, it had been easy for Anja to slip in to the café unnoticed. To find a seat nearby, order a coffee, open a book, and settle in for the conversation. She had been disappointed Eilidh had only hugged the man. A large part of her hoped they were lovers, someone hidden from Darcy that Anja could expose.

It didn't take long for the conversation to turn to Darcy.

Anja sat a little straighter and tilted her head slightly; she could make out almost every word. As suspected, Eilidh had clearly fallen for Darcy, and Anja heard her plot and plan with her crass friend, deciding between them what might be best for Darcy. They didn't care about her, not in the way Anja did. All Eilidh clearly cared about was when she could jump in to bed with her.

The way Eilidh had spoken about Anja told her she had no clue what it meant to be someone's best friend. To be loyal. To care and worry for them and be there no matter what, through the good and the bad. Of course Anja was suspicious, even if she knew that Eilidh was obviously not the stalker. She was still a stranger worming her way in to Darcy's life and fucking with Anja's plans in the process.

As she left the café, Anja chanced one last glance back. Eilidh and Sam were laughing, not a care in the world. Resolved to take action, she headed back towards her car. She had Darcy to herself tonight and would find a way to plant a few more doubts.

Tomorrow, she'd send Eilidh a message.

Darcy wasn't, and never would be, Eilidh's.

Chapter 39

Darcy watched from the sofa as Anja chopped and stirred. It made her jealous how at ease she was in the kitchen, producing delicious food with seemingly little effort. At the same time, she was grateful for her friend's ability, because it was all for Darcy's benefit.

A tray of lasagne already sat cooling, waiting to be divided in to portions and frozen. On the hob, Darcy's favourite, chicken Rogan Josh bubbled away, while Anja chopped up the base ingredients for a hearty Scottish broth.

"How was work today? Any gossip?"

Anja's back stayed to her as she chopped. "Aye, fine. Bridget was asking after you and Joe was his usual annoying self."

Darcy chuckled. "Is it weird that I miss work already?"

Anja scraped her board of carrot, onion, and celery in to the pot. "Very weird. I only wish I could have more time off with you."

"I know. But you need to save days for our trip to the sun once I'm better."

She turned and smiled Darcy's way. "I truly can't wait for that."

The thought of sunshine on her face and sand between her toes, a cold drink in her hand, and the sea calling her to swim, lulled Darcy, and she allowed her mind to drift. Or was it the pills. Darcy had never taken such strong painkillers before, and they hit her in waves. It sometimes felt as if her head was wrapped with cotton wool.

"Darcy?" Anja was in front of her, clicking her fingers. "I said have you any other visitors due?"

Back in the room, Darcy took a moment to gather herself, then thought of Eilidh. "I hope so. Eilidh said she would be in touch about a visit."

"I see." Anja said no more and headed back towards the kitchen, but Darcy could sense the apprehension.

"I haven't forgotten your warning, you know. Although you shouldn't worry. It's not her."

Darcy watched as Anja added the last ingredients to the broth and covered it with a lid, before coming and perching on the arm of the sofa. "What exactly is going on with you two, anyway?"

"Hmm… That's a good question." Darcy had been asking herself the same thing. They had spent so much time together since the accident, but so far it had remained platonic, which was likely a good thing. I mean, what exactly did she think might happen in a hospital room?

Despite their vague conversation about friendship and the end of the "interlude", it had remained guarded on both sides, and so Darcy still couldn't help but wonder if Eilidh was actually interested.

Although there were the looks. The little touches that were tender and caring and would be barely noticeable if they didn't make Darcy's heart pump like a steam train.

Every. Single. Bloody. Time.

Darcy could see in Eilidh's eyes that there was more hiding there. There was a story to be told, feelings to be shared, but she didn't know what it was or what they were yet. There was likely a reason she was holding back, and maybe it wasn't for Darcy to push. Or she could find herself mixed up in something that wasn't meant to be.

Anja lifted the cushion Darcy's foot rested on and slipped underneath it, replacing the cushion with her thighs. She gently lay Darcy's leg back in place. "You like her?"

"Aye, I mean, she's great. We've become friends, and I enjoy spending time with her."

"But…" Anja's eyebrows rose expectantly.

"I'm wary, that's all. Eilidh's not long out of a relationship, and I don't want to be that girl who falls in love only to find out she's a rebound."

"Love?" There was clear shock in Anja's voice. "You hardly know the woman."

Darcy squirmed. Damn these pills. She hadn't meant to be so forthright and loose with her words. Those kind of thoughts were meant to be kept for the dead of night and her dreams.

"Love. Lust. Like. Who knows? All I'm saying is whatever it might be, it could be a mistake. I'm aware I hardly know her, but I know I want to change that."

"Okay." Anja clearly wasn't buying the backtrack. Her face had hardened, the easy smile replaced with a look of suspicion. "Two things. One, there's a big difference between all of those words you listed, and two, does it feel like she's on the rebound to you?"

Darcy thought for a moment. This was Anja. Best friend and keeper of secrets. The woman who had suffered with her through the bad days and been the instigator of so many good days.

"She feels different to me."

Darcy watched as Anja looked across to the living-room window and the mountain views beyond. She chewed her lip, a habit Darcy rarely witnessed; it normally signalled she was operating at peak stress levels. When she returned her gaze to Darcy's, the warmth and encouragement she usually found there was missing. "Then I guess you need to ask Eilidh if you feel different to her."

With that, she extricated herself none too gently from under Darcy's leg and headed back to the cooker. She kept her back to Darcy whilst tending the pots, her shoulders hunched.

Darcy stared after her in confusion. What was that all about?

That's what she wanted to ask, but something kept her quiet. She left Anja to have her moment. She understood all too well Anja's immediate mode of protection when it came to anyone new in Darcy's life, but this seemed different. Didn't she like Eilidh?

They'd only met briefly a few times, and Anja had hardly been warm and welcoming. But given Eilidh's heroine status in Darcy's life, she thought it wouldn't be long before Anja reined it in a little and gave her a chance.

Or perhaps that was it?

Maybe she was feeling threatened by this new woman in Darcy's life? For so long it had been the two of them. Sure, there had been Jason, and both had other friends and different interests, but at the end of the day, they always knew the other was there. If Anja was struggling with the possibility of Eilidh, Darcy understood that emotion needed to be respected. Anja was her best friend, and she rightly came first.

As she stood at the stove, Anja swallowed back tears. It took everything she had not to scream at Darcy.

Not her.

Pick me.

Why can't you see it?

It's meant to be me.

Instead, she stirred and tasted, seasoned and stirred some more.

Darcy had remained quiet, and Anja knew she'd sensed all was not right. Anja's reaction to their chat about Eilidh hadn't been typical, and Darcy had always been particularly sensitive to people's moods and emotions. That's what made it so fucking difficult to hide things from her. To lie to her.

Anja needed to get a hold of herself or she risked another fucking disaster the same as the hot-tub night.

"I thought we'd have some of the curry tonight?" she called over her shoulder.

Darcy's response was muted, mechanical, and Anja dared not look at her.

"Sure. Sounds good. I'll go wash up."

At the same time as the bathroom door clicked shut, Darcy's phone vibrated with a message. Anja glanced at it, only a foot away charging on the worktop. Her fingers itched to tap in the code and see who it was. She looked towards the bathroom door; the toilet hadn't flushed yet. Darcy was insisting she could manage herself despite it taking twice as long.

Unable to resist, she swiped the screen and tapped in the four-digit code. As she suspected, Eilidh's name shone out, and Anja no longer hesitated as she tapped the green box and the message opened.

Cabin fever set in yet? Fancy a day out? E x

Anja changed gears into Darcy mode without a second thought. The fear that Darcy might find out was long gone, and it was worth the risk to Anja if she was going to succeed in keeping Eilidh away.

Appreciate the offer but I'm exhausted and don't really feel up to it. D x

The toilet flushed, and she quickly deleted both texts. She was sure Eilidh would reply again, and there was little time. The tap was running in the bathroom, but still there was no response.

As the door opened and Darcy hobbled back down the hallway, Anja flicked the phone to silent and slipped it in to the waistband of her jeans, pulling her jumper down over it. She put aside their awkward exchange of a few minutes before and automatically crossed to help Darcy back to the sofa.

She wiggled her fingers in Darcy's direction and pulled a face. "I'll go de-garlic myself while the rice cooks."

Safely in the bathroom with the phone, she checked for a reply. Still nothing. She sat on the edge of the bath, foot tapping, and after a couple of minutes, she flushed the toilet, then turned on the tap. As she lathered her hands in soap, Eilidh finally replied.

I understand. Maybe in a few days if you're feeling better? E x

Relieved to have a way to end the exchange, Anja dried off her hands and sent a final message before deleting them both again.

Maybe. I'll let you know. D x

She checked her reflection in the mirror and gave it a few more moments just in case of a follow-up text.

It was a small intervention and felt short term. Futile. She knew it would never keep them apart indefinitely. Eventually, one would again text the other and despite some minor confusion, they were likely to resume where they left off. She could feel Darcy slipping away, along with the power to stop it happening.

She pasted on a smile before heading back to the kitchen and setting the phone back on the counter. She'd bought herself some time, at least.

All was not lost yet.

It couldn't be.

Chapter 40

AFTER ALMOST TWO WEEKS CONFINED to the cabin, Darcy was bouncing off the walls.

The days dragged on, long and dull, her pain a constant companion. The nights brought no relief, only terror and trembling. When the medication allowed her a few precious moments of quiet, the nightmares soon invaded. As her eyes closed and she finally drifted, the ugly, unknown sounds of that night tore through the quiet. Her body became a ragdoll, twisting itself into knots until the sound of her own violent breathing eventually roused her and saved her from the darkness.

The cabin was suffocating, the trees around it closing in; she needed to get out.

Her salvation came in the form of Eilidh. She hadn't heard from her since being discharged and assumed Eilidh was giving her some space to settle back home.

The amount of time Eilidh had spent with her at the hospital had gone above and beyond, but Darcy couldn't help but wonder if her silence meant that would be the end of it. She thought about texting her a number of times, before remembering the complete mess she was in both physically and emotionally and deciding against it. She wasn't exactly the epitome of good company, drugged up to the eyeballs and unable to walk more than a few metres at a time.

But Darcy could no longer deny one small fact that kept prodding her for action.

She really flipping missed Eilidh.

So she caved and sent her a text.

Please come and get me out of here? D x

The response was almost immediate, which made Darcy smile.

I thought you'd never ask. Day after tomorrow? E x

With a weekend shift looming, Eilidh insisted on spending her days off with Darcy, and Darcy had no intention of turning her down. It seemed both were happy to remain in the "interlude" period. Friends enjoying time together, getting to know one another without any pressure. There was no worrying what to wear or where to go; it was simple and relaxed and exactly what Darcy needed.

"Fancy a drive?" Eilidh stood on the porch, hands behind her back. She rocked excitedly on her heels like she had more than a drive in mind. It was odd to see her out of uniform. She wore blue skinny jeans tucked into sturdy-looking ankle boots, and a soft-looking teal V-neck jumper that set off her eyes. It was the first time Darcy had seen her hair down, and it suited her. It fell a little past her shoulders with a slight wave that curled the ends.

"I'm up for anything that means getting me out of here. Come in a minute while I grab my things."

Eilidh tentatively stepped inside and glanced around. "Wow. This place is gorgeous."

Darcy couldn't help but smile with pride. "It's small and simple, but that's how I prefer it. The most important thing is it's mine."

"Well, it turns out I'm a fan of small and simple." Eilidh strolled around the living space, stopping in front of the wood burner. "You can't beat a real fire."

Darcy pulled the sleeve of her coat tentatively over the wrist still trapped in a cast. "Definitely one of my favourite things."

Eilidh came to her side then and helped with the coat. "How do you feel about a trip out to the Black Isle? We can stop at the brewery, and I packed a picnic. The views up there are great on a day like this."

It sounded perfect, and Darcy told her so. "The blue sky's been calling me all morning, so sounds great to me."

They drove in relative quiet, the radio on low, and Darcy took a moment to savour the sun on her face. She closed her eyes and drifted a little, content to be out in the world and in Eilidh's company.

"Keep your eyes closed," Eilidh whispered.

Which of course made Darcy open them.

They were passing "the spot". The fence still hung mangled and limp where Darcy's car had ploughed through it, and she could see the gouged chunks of turf and glass fragments glinting in the sun.

"Or don't." Eilidh glanced her way, a wry smile on her face. "I thought it might upset you."

"It's a bit surreal, that's all. I guess because I remember so little. The damage that's left doesn't really tell the full story."

She caught Eilidh flick her gaze to the rearview mirror. "No, it doesn't."

Darcy reached to cover her hand, which sat idly on the gear stick. "Do you think about it a lot? That night?

"I try not to, but we don't always have control over these things."

Eilidh turned her hand and intertwined their fingers, an action that surprised Darcy in a wonderful belly-flop-moment kind of way. It took a second to refocus and rewind, remember what Eilidh had said, and respond accordingly.

"True. Until now I don't think I've fully considered how horrific it must have been for you." Darcy kept hold of her hand, enjoying the softness of their palms pressed together. She stroked her thumb over Eilidh's and turned a little in her seat, to take in her profile.

Eilidh glanced down at their hands and smiled, telling Darcy that she felt it too.

"I think it was pure adrenalin that got me through it. It was all action and not much thought. All I knew was I had to get you out of that car."

"You're a brave person, Eilidh Grey. Many people would have simply called 9-9-9 and stood by and watched. Some would have even run away." She snorted. "Some did."

"Brave or stupid." Eilidh turned and winked, deflecting them both away from imagining the worst.

"I choose brave." Darcy lifted their hands and planted a kiss on the back of Eilidh's.

The brewery was a favourite of Darcy's, and she groaned as the smell of hops drifted their way. "I'm not sure we thought this through. I can't drink on those bloody horse tranquilisers I'm on."

Eilidh got out of the car and wandered around to open Darcy's door. "And I can't drink while driving…" She trailed away sheepishly, unable to take the words back but obviously afraid she'd put a gigantic foot in her mouth.

"Don't panic. I know that's not a dig at me." Darcy reached up a hand from the passenger seat and allowed Eilidh to help her out. She held on to the door while Eilidh relieved the back seat of her crutch.

"We can at least have a few sniffs and sips to try the new stuff, and then stock up for when you're off the meds. It'll be motivation for getting better."

"Hmm… There's a good idea in there somewhere, but it's not helping, I'm afraid."

Eilidh hooked her arm through the one not holding the crutch for added support and started them towards the Brewhouse bar. "Don't be such a grump or I'll take you home."

Darcy savoured each tiny nip, and they acted like true craft-beer connoisseurs.

"Yes, I'd agree." Eilidh ran the glass under her nose again. "Definitely floral undertones with a subtle hint of peach."

Darcy laughed at her plumbed-up voice and swirled her own amber liquid before swallowing it back. "I'm getting the taste of summer in this one: straw, citrus, and mountain streams."

The woman behind the bar cracked up at that one. She didn't get many customers mid-week, in the cold early days of March, and they had the bar to themselves. They worked their way through all eight beers on offer, and after packing a dozen bottles each in the boot of the car, they left the woman still laughing.

Eilidh headed for the Cromarty Lighthouse and the stretch of parkland and beach that sat where the Firth met the North Sea. She unfolded a couple of camping chairs and draped a blanket over each. Once Darcy was seated, she produced a small pillow for under her heel and tucked the blanket around her shoulders.

"How's that?"

"Perfect." Darcy looked out across the expanse of water and felt peace for the first time in weeks. It had been months since she'd ventured on to the water. Her small sailboat was currently tucked away for winter, not that it was any good to her with two broken limbs. The thought of it was added motivation to be the model patient, and Eilidh assured her she would be back as captain by the end of spring.

"I've gone for old-school comfort food." Eilidh passed her a Tupperware box of cheese sandwiches and poured them both a cup of tomato soup.

"My mum used to make this for me when I was home sick from school. It always reminded me of winters on the island."

"The island?" Eilidh took a bite of her sandwich.

"Shetland. That's where I'm originally from. We moved to Australia when I was twelve, and I came back here to Scotland for university when I turned eighteen."

"Wow, you've been around, then. I did wonder about your odd accent."

"It's not odd." Darcy feigned insult. "It's unique."

Eilidh laughed. "Is that what your mum tells you?"

"Maybe."

"Why did you leave Shetland? I mean, I can think of a number of reasons why Australia would be more appealing."

"Cheeky. Shetland is beautiful, I'll have you know."

Eilidh faked a shiver. "But Australia is warm."

"There is that." Darcy sipped at her soup. It wasn't often she invited questions about her childhood, her family. She had become skilled at deflecting them. Too much tragedy had plagued her younger years, and it did no one any good to talk about it. But Eilidh's face held so much kindness and wonder. She wasn't being polite, and it wasn't idle chat; she really wanted to know about Darcy's past, and Darcy was inclined to tell her.

"My dad died when I was eight. Testicular cancer. He'd had the symptoms for a while but was too stubborn and embarrassed to get it checked out. If he had, it's likely he would have lived."

"I'm sorry, Darcy. That's awful."

"Aye. I don't remember much about him. He worked a lot, and I don't think he spent much time with me. A few years later my mum remarried a guy called Cameron. Initially he worked offshore on the rigs for a Norwegian company, then he got offered a job in Perth, Australia, so we moved. He always had me in the workshop with him, taking something apart and piecing it back together. Radios, toasters, basically any small appliance when I was younger. Then an old classic motorbike he spent all his spare time restoring. He was a good guy, mostly quiet but charismatic and charming when he wanted to be. He took care of us, and clearly loved my mum."

"*Was* a good guy?"

Darcy nodded forlornly. "He died in a helicopter crash going out to one of the rigs when I was fourteen. My sister was only two."

"You've got a sister?"

"Aye. She's twenty now. She has a condition called Rett syndrome, and my mum has to take care of her pretty much twenty-four-seven. Cam didn't leave us with much, and I guess after losing two husbands, Mum shut herself off. Her heart never really mended, and she made peace with her life as it is."

"Christ." Eilidh blew out a sorrowful sigh. "I think my heart just broke a little for your mum. And you."

It had been eighteen years, and Darcy had made attempts to make her peace with her childhood, but thinking of her mum alone still had the ability to tug at her emotions. Her half-sister's condition and prognosis just downright crushed her.

Olivia was amazing and Darcy loved her dearly, but growing up with a sibling that needed so much attention had played havoc with her teenage hormones and emotions. She had gone through a period of hating her sister and loathed herself for it now. Then the hate had turned to guilt, because Darcy would never know her suffering and couldn't do anything to change it.

That a tiny mutation in Olivia's genes could cause such devastation was hard to grasp. The condition caused regular seizures, heart and breathing issues, difficulty eating, and the past decade had curved her spine and put her in a wheelchair. The surgery to try and correct it was so expensive in Australia, but Darcy had been working on raising the funds.

Most people didn't even know she had a sister.

She had simply found it easier over the years to keep her family and their past locked away in her heart, for fear that talking too much about them would break it open and the sorrow would consume her.

"I guess we'd struggle to find anyone in the world whose heart isn't recovering from something or someone?"

"True." Eilidh propped her chin in her hands and studied Darcy for a moment. "I suppose all we can hope for is the opportunity to mend it."

"That seems to be the human way." Darcy chuckled. "Always searching for our next heartache."

"And here was me thinking you might be the fairy tale type? Have I got you wrong, Darcy Harris?"

"You haven't." Darcy dipped a sandwich in to her soup. "I think we need the heartache to appreciate the fairy tale."

"Hmm… You'll have to let me think on that one." Eilidh reached and wiped a splodge of tomato soup that had escaped the sandwich and landed on Darcy's chin. "You're beautiful when you eat."

Darcy felt her cheeks colour but honestly didn't care. A convivial warmth seemed to wrap around her when Eilidh was near, and there was never a hint of pretence between them.

The superficial nature of dating had always been something Darcy hated. It made her sad that the majority of people felt the need to present a false version of themselves, polished and scripted, so great was their fear that someone might not appreciate the real them.

Darcy figured if it started out that way, it would ultimately end in disappointment.

"I can honestly say no one has ever given me that compliment before."

Eilidh laughed. "Only you would take that as a compliment." She poured out the rest of the soup and pointedly dipped her own sandwich. "How did you end up back in Scotland?"

"Free university tuition. As I said, we didn't have much. It seemed stupid not to come home where it was free for me. So I did my master's in Glasgow, got an oil job in Aberdeen. I hated oil and gas so moved in to renewables. That's what took me to Inverness. I've been here almost five years now."

"Well, flipping heck." Eilidh finished off her soup and looked out across the firth, clearly digesting everything Darcy had said. "That's some story."

"Yeah. Probably why I don't tell it often. In fact, you're the first person I've told since moving to Inverness."

"Really?" Eilidh looked back at her. "Not even the charming Anja?"

Darcy felt her eyebrows furrow. "What is it with you two? Because that 'charming' was anything but sincere."

Eilidh waved her off. "Sorry, I didn't mean to be that way about her. It's obvious she isn't keen on me though and I'm not sure what I've done to make her so…"

"You haven't done anything," Darcy reassured her. "I think she's still spooked about the accident, and the whole stalker thing hasn't yet been resolved, and…"

"Wait." Eilidh shifted around to face Darcy fully, remembering Sam's theory. "She doesn't think I'm the stalker, does she?"

"Not anymore." Darcy smirked.

"Anymore? Are you serious? I pull you out of a burning car, and she thinks I'm the person that potentially put you there?"

"Hey." Darcy reached and rubbed Eilidh's forearm. "You've got nothing to explain. I said she used to. I'll admit for a second that I considered it. She made a good case. But now I know you, I've told her it can't possibly be true."

Eilidh still didn't look fully placated.

"The fact I told you about my family, about my sister, tells me I'm right. I don't trust many with that story. Not even Anja. She knows some, but not all of it."

"Why do you trust me?"

Darcy shrugged. "I can't explain it yet. It could be the pills, I suppose."

Eilidh shoved her playfully. "Bitch."

"Listen, next time you see Anja, can you please make an effort? For me? It would mean a lot if you two could get on."

"Fine. I'll do my best to be nice when I next see her and try not to accuse her of being your stalker."

"What?"

"I'm kidding." Eilidh chuckled. "But you see what I'm saying now? Anja being that freak should be as ridiculous to you as me being the stalker."

"Point taken. How about we talk about something else? Tell me about your family."

Eilidh sighed and reached back in to her bag. "We'll need chocolate doughnuts for this."

"Oh no, is it awful? It's okay, you don't have to talk to me about it."

"No, no. It's incredibly dull compared to yours, so I thought these would help make it more interesting."

Darcy laughed and took one of the chocolate-filled sugared doughnuts.

"In a nutshell, I'm Inverness born and bred. My mum and dad had me quite young, got married too young, settled down too young. So it didn't take long for it all to fall apart. I went back and forth between the two; they parted on reasonable terms and my dad got a place not far away. Then they both remarried, both had more kids, and I guess that left me feeling a little left out of it all. There's ten years between me and my next sibling, even more between me and the other two, so we've never really been close. I went to Edinburgh for uni, and when I came back, I realised I was fine on my own."

"Do you see much of them?" Darcy bit in to the doughnut and groaned as the chocolate and sugar hit her senses. "This is awesome, by the way."

Eilidh laughed and took a huge bite of her own. Her eyes widened, and they both nodded at each other in joint appreciation of the gooey treat.

"I visit on the appropriate holidays and stop by with gifts for birthdays and the odd family dinner. I mean, it's all perfectly civil and pleasant. I know they're both there for me if I need them, but I'm living my own life and so are they."

Darcy licked chocolate from her fingers. "That must be a little weird though? I'd give anything to have my mum and sister closer."

"Aw, sorry, Darcy. I didn't mean to be flippant about it. I love them both and know I'm lucky to have them. I guess I've just never really fit in with either of their new families."

"Don't be sorry. I'm happy you have them. My mum's still trying to make a visit work, but I'm not holding out any hope. I can tell she's terrified of leaving Olivia in full-time care, and now I'm out of hospital, there doesn't seem any point."

"How do you feel about that?"

Darcy shoved the rest of the doughnut in her mouth. It was too much and her cheeks bulged, but it was pure heaven.

Eilidh chuckled. "Is that your way of avoiding the question?"

"Maybe," Darcy mumbled through the crumbs, trying not to laugh. She felt sticky all over, but it had been worth it. She brushed remnants from her lap, and when she looked up, Eilidh was knelt in front of her.

"Here, you've got something." She indicated Darcy's chin.

"Again?" Darcy wiped at it. "Did I get it?"

"Almost," Eilidh whispered. "Let me."

Her hand moved to Darcy's cheek, and she felt a few grains of sugar be brushed away. The hand remained, and as Eilidh's thumb stroked across her jawline, Darcy felt her eyes flutter closed at the tender touch.

She took a shuddering breath and waited. Hoped.

When Eilidh's lips pressed to hers, it still took her by surprise. They were tentative at first, only lightly brushing against Darcy's. When they found no resistance, they became bolder, still moving slow, but sure. Eilidh's fingers found the back of her neck and caressed it gently, sending a tremor through Darcy's spine.

Excitable energy tingled in her belly and urged the kiss on. She wished they weren't sitting, wished Eilidh's body as well as her lips were flush to her own. As Darcy's mind ran away, a tiny groan slipped between their mouths. Then Eilidh's lips were gone.

Her forehead touched to Darcy's, and it was a moment before Darcy opened her eyes. When she did, Eilidh held her gaze intently, a small smile playing on lips that Darcy longed to kiss again.

"I guess the interlude is officially over, then?" she murmured against Eilidh's mouth.

They both grinned and moved apart a little. Eilidh smiled coyly and took Darcy's hand, keeping hold of it as she moved to sit back in her chair.

"When a girl you've waited weeks to kiss has chocolate on her lip, I'd say it's reasonable to call off any interlude."

Darcy found herself licking her lips, but no trace of chocolate remained. "Is that your excuse, or was there really chocolate?"

"I guess you'll never know." Eilidh squeezed Darcy's hand and looked back out to the water. "I missed you."

The three simple words conveyed so much and caused a swell of exhilaration in Darcy's chest. Was this really happening? Nervous anticipation coursed through her body as she took in Eilidh's profile and imagined the possibilities.

"I missed you too."

Chapter 41

EILIDH'S HEART THUDDED WHEN SHE spotted the ivory envelope tucked under her windscreen wiper. It was the second day in a row that one had greeted her. She had an idea of what it might say, but opened it anyway.

Stay away from her.

That was it. Four words.

They required no explanation: the message was clear. She knew enough about Darcy's stalker to know it was likely the same person, and the thought gave her a chill.

She balled the note up in her fist and scanned the hospital grounds. Were they watching her? How long ago had they left it? How had they found out where she worked?

It was a public place, and strangers dotted the carpark and entrance ways. There was no way of knowing who should or shouldn't be there, and no one seemed to be paying her any special attention.

What did she expect?

A cloaked figure in a hat and sunglasses staring at her from a darkened alley?

She knew how they'd escalated where Darcy was concerned, switching between thoughtful gifts and cruel pranks. Their intentions confusing and unfathomable. The message they were sending Eilidh was more obvious: stay away from Darcy or there would be trouble.

How far were they prepared to go to make that happen?

It was the question that had kept Eilidh awake the night before. With Darcy, there was clearly love, sordid and perverse, maybe, but without violence. In her case, their objective was less confusing, and it both scared and angered her in equal measure.

She wondered again whether to tell Darcy. Or the police.

Safe inside her car, she glanced down at the balled-up note, now residing in the passenger foot well.

No.

Darcy didn't need to know right now, and really, what could the police do with two identical vague notes? There was something wonderful growing between her and Darcy, and whether her crazy stalker approved or not, Eilidh was going nowhere.

Anja slouched down low in the driver seat and watched as Eilidh left the hospital.

Once again, she was quick to spot the note. She plucked it out with less curiosity than the day before, quickly reading the message before screwing the paper into a ball.

She scanned the carpark, turning on the spot. She wouldn't see Anja; too many cars and distance separated them. Anja knew it was a risk to hang around but couldn't resist observing her reaction.

Eilidh opened the car door and threw the note inside, her anger evident. It wasn't the reaction Anja had hoped for, but she was only beginning. Soon fear and paranoia would kick in, and the message would eventually be received. Anja would continue to do her best to keep them apart, until Eilidh decided for herself that seeing Darcy wasn't worth the hassle.

She told herself again that Eilidh was no more than an obstacle. All her life had been a series of obstacles, and she had overcome all of them in the end. What was one more? This one she guessed would be stubborn, wouldn't give up too easily, but then neither would Anja.

This was only the first step. She had an entire arsenal of tactics aimed at getting Eilidh to back off. It was a game Anja knew she would win.

She had wondered initially if Eilidh would tell Darcy about the notes, but quickly resolved that it wouldn't be an issue.

Perfect, brave Eilidh wouldn't want to worry her.

That suited Anja fine.

Chapter 42

DARCY SHOUTED A CHOICE STRING of expletives that came from both pain and frustration.

The cast was off both her leg and wrist, the former replaced with a supportive boot. It sat in a corner and taunted her as limbs became jelly and coordination abandoned her. Sam tried to coax her a few more steps, but she was done. It felt as though every inch of her skin prickled with cold sweat, and her entire body throbbed.

Everything felt hard, and it was difficult not to take it out on Sam.

"I said I've had e-fucking-nough. Okay?"

Sam held up his hands. "All right. Whatever you say, Darcy. It's your body."

She felt tears sting her eyes. After a couple of weeks of great progress, they were tears of frustration, and she was determined not to let them get the better of her.

"I'm sorry." With his help, she limped to a bench and gulped at some water. "I shouldn't take it out on you. You've been great."

Sam took a seat next to her and bumped her shoulder. "Trust me I've heard worse out of folk. You're doing amazing, truly. Stop being so hard on yourself."

"It's just...argh...so infuriating. Everything is so bloody slow."

"Is that such a bad thing? Maybe it needs to be slow. It's not only our bodies that have to heal after a trauma like you've been through."

She rolled her eyes at him. "What are you? Physio and psych all rolled in to one."

He laughed at that. "Cheeky bugger. How about physio and friend?"

And they were. Eilidh had introduced them and promised he would have her fighting fit again in no time. She was living proof of that. Since then, Sam had seemed to sense exactly what she needed and when. He knew when to be gentle the same as he knew when she needed him to shout in her ear. There was the professional side of him that never mentioned or talked about Eilidh with her, but also listened when she had an off day and only a rant would help.

She bumped his shoulder back. "Suppose."

He glanced at his watch. "That's us finished now, anyway. Why don't you try something simple, something you would normally do in the real world? I think the gym sometimes puts patients under pressure to push too hard. Go take a walk in the park and I guarantee you'll surprise yourself."

They both looked up at the mechanical whir of the gym doors opening, and Darcy smiled when Eilidh appeared.

"Excellent timing," called Sam. "This one needs to walk off some rage. I suggested the park, and you'll be the perfect chaperone, I imagine."

"Yuck. Don't say chaperone. Makes me sound like some spinster aunt."

He stood and poked at her cheek. "Well, these are getting a wee bit saggy."

Eilidh slapped his hand away and pushed him aside. "Let's ignore him." She held out an arm for Darcy. "You up for it?"

"Only if there's coffee involved."

"Done." Eilidh helped her with the boot and her coat, then packed Darcy's bag and slung it over a shoulder.

"See this?" Sam took Eilidh's arm and moved it comically in to random positions. "She can do this because of me. She can carry your bag because of me, and this is how she treats me." He pouted.

Eilidh ignored it. "Cheers, Tommo. See you tomorrow."

"Fine. Away with you both." He waved them off, and Eilidh guided Darcy to the door where her crutches stood propped to the side.

"You sure you're up for this?" she whispered. "He doesn't always know what's best."

Darcy transferred her weight on to the crutches and pointed one through the door. "Let's go."

They found coffee and the wall that had become all too familiar during Darcy's stay in hospital. When the weather permitted, Eilidh had wheeled her down there to share lunch and good-natured gossip about colleagues who wandered past. The difference this time was Darcy could now sit on the wall instead of a wheelchair, and Eilidh was holding her hand.

"Hi." She leant in and pressed a gentle kiss to Darcy's mouth.

"Hey," Darcy whispered, before going in for a second one, allowing it to linger.

It was all still so new, and tentative, and unknown. Darcy was enjoying every second.

"Tough session today?"

"Aye. It's so frustrating some days. Sam's been great though, I have to say."

"He really is. Don't tell him that too often though."

Darcy chuckled. "Oh, I won't." She took a sip of coffee and wondered again about Eilidh's own accident. She'd yet to tell her anything in detail, and although curious, Darcy was afraid to pry. She knew how difficult it was to think about the night of her own horror story, despite only recollecting a few details. Maybe Eilidh didn't want to remember it. Although maybe they could help each other if they talked.

"You know, if you want to talk about your accident, I wouldn't mind. It might in some way help both of us."

Eilidh studied her over her cup as she took a sip, then another. "It might. Or it could add a whole heap of heavy shite to an already-laden-with-shite situation."

"You think of us as a shite situation?" Darcy tried to hide the smirk.

"No, no." Eilidh slapped a hand over her mouth. "I so didn't mean it that way. I meant your situation is shite. No. Wait. The fact you can't remember yours and the stalker and... Please stop me before I've dug my own grave."

Darcy laughed then. "I knew what you meant. However eloquently you put it. But it's okay, really." She leaned in again with a kiss she hoped conveyed reassurance. "You can trust me with this," she whispered.

Eilidh took her hand again and spent a moment studying their entwined fingers. Darcy sipped her coffee and waited. When Eilidh looked back up to meet her gaze, her eyes glistened with unshed tears. "It wasn't an accident. I was attacked."

"Oh my God, that's awful. What happened?" Darcy shuffled in closer and gripped her hand tighter.

Eilidh took a deep breath that seemed to push back the tears. "It was the night Claire and I first broke up. It was civil then, a joint decision. Anyway, we'd left the restaurant and decided to walk a while before getting a taxi. We were both a little sad, you know, our last night out as a couple."

All Darcy could do was nod encouragingly. She almost told Eilidh to stop; the thought of what she might be about to hear frightened her. The thought of someone hurting Eilidh was unthinkable.

"We cut down an alleyway. One we've walked a hundred times before. There was a group of guys at one end, laughing and shouting. Claire tried to get me to turn back, but I realised there was someone lying on the ground."

"And you couldn't turn back." Instinct and everything she already knew about Eilidh told Darcy she was not the kind of person to turn back.

"Exactly. I called out and ran towards them in the hope they'd scare off. I was wrong."

The tears broke free then, and they broke Darcy's heart. She didn't say anything; instead, she held Eilidh's hand fast and let her cry.

Eilidh took a breath and blew it out long and slow. "Claire was shouting for me to come back, but I saw one of them kick the person on the ground and I knew I had to stop it. As I got closer it was obvious it was a homeless person. I could see their makeshift bed in a doorway."

She spoke through the tears, but Darcy could hear the anger that simmered underneath. "One of the guys stepped in front of me, told me to turn around and mind my own business. I tried to push past him. I remember yelling and swearing at the other guy to stop kicking. Then I was falling. The guy had punched me, I hit my head on the ground, then everything blurred. I'm pretty sure he kicked me. My shoulder was in agony where I'd fallen awkwardly, Claire was screaming, they were laughing, and then it all went black."

"Bloody hell, Eilidh. That must have been terrifying."

"It happened so fast I don't think it had time to register. When I look back it's scarier—what I remember of it, anyway."

"So there's things you don't remember as well?"

"Aye. Claire witnessed it all, but even her memory was vague. It was all over in a minute or two and she was in shock."

"I bet." Darcy was at a loss and wondered how she would have reacted in the same situation. Would she have been Eilidh, running to help and putting herself at risk? Or Claire, screaming in retreat? "What happened afterwards? Did they catch the guys? Was the homeless person all right?"

Darcy saw Eilidh visibly swallow. Her head dropped, she set her coffee aside, and fidgeted with Darcy's fingers. "He died."

"Fuck. Eilidh, I'm so sorry."

"I tried to be the hero and he still died."

"That wasn't your fault. You did everything you could."

"Did I? What if my intervention only antagonised them more? What if I'd done as Claire said—called the police and let them deal with it?"

"You can't torture yourself like that because it will never change anything. You did what you thought was right at the time, and no one can blame you for the actions of those animals. You've suffered enough."

"I'm still alive though. He isn't. My shoulder was dislocated and a few ribs were broken which punctured a lung, but none of that compares to what that man went through before he died. Claire said they kept kicking. They only stopped and ran away once they heard the sirens. She'd run back out of the alley and called the police."

"She left you?"

"She had no choice. Don't think badly of her for that. I did at first, but what else was she supposed to do?"

"I guess. Is that why you stayed together? Until you were better."

"At first. I think part of her blamed me because she told me not to get involved. It was my fault she was put through this horrific experience, and it left her cold towards me. Another part of her felt guilty, I think, that she couldn't help. That she could only stand by and watch it happen. So she stuck around until I was better, and then I told her she could leave."

"Christ, Eilidh. That's so messed up."

"I told you it was heavy shite."

Darcy couldn't help her smile and was relieved when Eilidh returned it.

"Did they ever catch the guys?"

"Fortunately, yes. An appeal was put out. There was some CCTV images from earlier in the evening and from street cameras. People came forward with information, and they were rounded up. I managed to identify the one who had punched me initially, but they couldn't tell who had delivered the fatal blow to the homeless man. They've all been charged with various offences and held in custody. Now we're just waiting for a court date."

Darcy wrapped her arms around Eilidh and held her tight. "You really are a brave idiot."

Eilidh chuckled in to her neck. She pulled away a little but still held tight to Darcy's waist, her features turned fierce and determined. "And I'm thankful for that, because it meant I got to save you."

She kissed Darcy with an urgency that hadn't been there before. When their tongues connected, Darcy allowed any last shred of doubt about Eilidh's intentions slip away. A small groan hummed in her throat, and she felt her breath escape. On the brink of losing herself entirely to it, Eilidh suddenly pulled away.

"Sorry. I just realised we're sat in a hospital garden with any number of my colleagues around to witness this."

Darcy laughed and looked around guiltily. "Take me home?"

"Of course."

Eilidh hopped off the wall and stood in front of Darcy. Darcy held her hands out for support getting down, but instead Eilidh manoeuvred between her legs and looped her arms back around Darcy's waist. "I want you to trust me when I say that you will find the light again, even in your darkest hour. When it's the middle of the night and you're in pain, but you couldn't sleep anyway because your mind is racing with the terror of what you've been through, remember us here and now. Remember me telling you that you will find the light again."

Darcy ran her fingers through Eilidh's hair, then clasped her face in her hands. She had described so many of Darcy's nights since the accident, when everything swirled in a pit of desperation and darkness and Darcy felt as if she would drown in it. She had tried to explain it to Anja, on the nights she awoke and Anja was there at her side, trying to comfort her, asking to understand what was going on in Darcy's head. But it was impossible. The words would never form, and so she would simply pull Anja's arms around her in the hope they would bring the calm she needed. Almost every night, the horror was repeated.

Now as she looked in to Eilidh's eyes, she believed for the first time that the sun would rise again and sweep the night away. "You found it, then?"

Eilidh looked away a moment, out across the expanse of grassland and trees.

"Aye." She matched Darcy's own teary smile. "It came back the moment I saved you."

Darcy pulled her closer and lay her head on Eilidh's shoulder. "Thank you."

Chapter 43

So much for her surprise.

Anja watched as Eilidh led Darcy from the hospital entrance. They headed towards the surrounding gardens, Darcy on crutches and two steaming cups clutched in Eilidh's hands.

She had intended to swing by and surprise Darcy. Pick her up and take her home to a fresh-cooked dinner, rather than another painful and expensive taxi to go with whatever was left in the freezer.

Her notes clearly weren't getting the message across to Eilidh, and she felt the rage build every time one of them laughed. They might as well have been laughing in her face. This wasn't how it was meant to be. What was it going to take to get that interfering bitch to stay away from Darcy?

She found a seat in a bus shelter with a view of where they sat. Other folk milled around, providing some cover. She watched as they held hands.

Then the worst happened.

They kissed.

"Are you fucking kidding me?" she muttered.

Her handbag held an opportunity to interrupt them. She produced a new pre-pay phone and quickly started it up. There were only two numbers saved in it. She selected one and tapped off a brief text.

I see you.

Then she waited.

There was no reaction. Either Eilidh's phone was on silent or she was ignoring it. Frustration curdled with fury; their conversation seemed so earnest. They still held hands, and was...was Eilidh crying?

Good.

Although normally you would only cry in front of someone you trusted, someone you cared about, someone you didn't mind seeing you at your most vulnerable.

She sent another text.

Every time you see her you are tempting fate.

Was that the point Darcy and Eilidh had reached? Where they confided the worst?

Since the night at the cabin when Anja had intercepted the texts, Darcy had been tight lipped where Eilidh was concerned. Anja knew they'd still been spending time together but had wondered if the initial spark had fizzled. Otherwise why wasn't Darcy gushing about it to her? Why would she hide it?

They hugged for what felt like forever. It was physically painful for Anja to watch.

She sent another text.

This will only get worse for you.

It was as if Anja had started at the finish line. She'd known the outcome of her plan all those years ago, knew exactly how she wanted Darcy to feel, what she wanted her to believe. How she had hoped to force her world to crumble the same as Anja's had.

Yet it seemed the race still had to be run. Only now she was pitched against Eilidh to win Darcy's love, and every step was heavy, laden with regret over how it had all begun.

Could she try telling Darcy how she felt again? Do it different this time, not simply swoop in with a kiss? She remembered the look on Darcy's face that night, the shock and confusion.

The aftermath.

Would it go any different? Would Darcy feel something more than that night after all the support Anja had given, the care, the love? Would Darcy consider them a possibility? Would she be prepared to give it a chance?

They now held each other tight, heads close together. Anja could only imagine the words being exchanged, and she was sure she would hate every one of them. She turned away as they kissed again. It was unbearable, like a hot poker lodged in her chest.

She sent another text.

Is she really worth it?

These days, Anja didn't know who she had become or who she wanted to be. The voice she'd given her mother, the one who sought revenge, was fading. There was nothing to guide her anymore, only instinct and the will to get what she wanted.

Chapter 44

DARCY WAS GETTING USED TO manoeuvring around the cabin with one crutch and had become relatively self-sufficient. Her wrist still ached if she overdid it, but there was a vast improvement in the short time the cast had been off.

She hopped from freezer to stove, fridge to larder, and continued to wave Eilidh away every time she tried to help.

"If you really want a job, that beer we bought is in a storage cupboard outside and should be cold."

"Oh, I like that plan. Is it all right for you to drink?"

"Aye, I'm pretty much off the pills. I'm sure I can share one or two."

"I'm driving, so that'll be my limit anyway." Eilidh disappeared through the front door, and Darcy continued her salad prep. The lasagne was warming in the oven and the table was laid; she couldn't remember the last time she had cooked for anyone but Anja.

A little guilt crept in then. *Anja.*

She'd actively avoided talking about Eilidh with her since the night in the cabin when Anja had been uncharacteristically cold after Darcy had opened herself up about her feelings for Eilidh.

The food she was about to serve Eilidh had been cooked by Anja, her friend and protector, yet here Darcy was keeping secrets. It was unlike Darcy in so many ways, and she couldn't fathom what drove the urge to keep Eilidh away from her, at least in the short term.

Eilidh returned, popped the top off a bottle of Red Kite, and poured them both a glass. She held hers out for Darcy to clink and smiled. "Slàinte mhath!"

"Slàinte!" Darcy took a healthy gulp. "Damn, I've missed beer."

Eilidh carried their plates to the table and held out a chair for Darcy. "I genuinely don't think I could live without it."

Eilidh tucked straight in to the piping-hot lasagne. "I think I've just taken the skin off the roof of my mouth, but I don't care; this is bloody delicious."

Darcy squirmed. "Glad you like it. More beer?" She tried to deflect talk of the meal and topped up their glasses.

"Mm...yes, please." Eilidh took another bite of food and groaned. "Seriously, Darcy. This is amazing. What's your secret ingredient?"

Now Darcy was stuck. "Um...maybe it's the company. You're enjoying it so much because you're with me." She offered a cheesy grin and her lips.

Eilidh kissed them lightly and laughed. "Maybe you're right." She eyed another piece on her fork. "Although there's definitely something I can't put my finger on. Nutmeg? Is it nutmeg?"

"Okay, fine." Darcy let her own fork clatter to her plate. "I didn't make it. Anja did. All right? Now you know."

Eilidh lowered her own fork and stared at Darcy. "Why didn't you...?"

"What?" Darcy threw up a hand. "Would you not have eaten it if I'd told you before? There was a batch left in the freezer, and it's delicious as you have confirmed yourself, so don't give me that look."

Eilidh stared a moment longer then picked her fork back up. "Okay. It's fine. No complaints here." She began eating again without another word.

Once dinner was finished, they stoked the fire and turned the radio on low. Eilidh sat close to her on the sofa, and Darcy sank against her before propping her foot on an ottoman. The fresh wood crackled to life, and Darcy closed her eyes a moment, allowing the atmosphere to settle over her.

"I still can't believe you let me eat the enemy's food." Eilidh drew circles on Darcy's thigh and feigned upset.

"Oi. I thought there weren't going to be any complaints? I don't need that crap from you as well. I've had enough of it from Anja." She stilled Eilidh's hand as a hot tingle began to spread along her leg in a thoroughly distracting manner. She marvelled at the flood of anticipation that swelled within her and savoured each small touch Eilidh offered.

"Sorry." Eilidh seemed contrite. "I'm mostly just miffed because now I have to admit she's a great cook. But I promise I'm going to make more of an effort when I see her again."

"Thank you." Darcy strained upwards and touched her lips to Eilidh's neck. When she shuddered, Darcy did her best to hide a smile. It seemed she had the ability to illicit the same response in Eilidh. "You got off on the wrong foot, that's all."

"Aye. I'm sure it'll be fine."

"I'm her favourite person, and I know she wants me to be happy. Give it a bit of time, and I'm sure you'll soon warm that cold Norwegian heart."

Eilidh laughed. "Challenge accepted." She sealed her promise with a languid kiss that Darcy let herself melt into. They both cursed as the moment was broken by Eilidh's phone, which had begun to buzz furiously from where she had plugged it in to charge.

"I was just thinking how peaceful it was up here."

Darcy quirked an eyebrow. "Not while you were kissing me, I hope."

Eilidh chuckled. "Oh no, although I couldn't possibly tell you what I was thinking, then."

"I wish you would." Darcy moved in to steal Eilidh's lips again when the phone let out another buzz.

Eilidh didn't moved and instead pulled Darcy closer. "I'm ignoring it. The outside world doesn't exist right now."

From the coffee table, Darcy's phone began to ring, and she was sure Eilidh actually growled. Darcy leaned forward, saw "withheld number" shining out, and swiped the red button to ignore.

Eilidh must have noticed her shift in demeanour. "How often do you get those kind of calls?"

Darcy shrugged. "It's no big deal. I haven't had any for a few weeks. In fact, there's been nothing for ages. Not since the gift basket. The police told me to ignore them and log them. So that's what I'll do."

"You never really told me when it all started?"

Darcy put a little space between them and fidgeted with the strings of her hoodie. "Must be, a year and a half now, maybe two. It feels longer."

"I bet. I can't believe the police haven't caught anyone yet."

"Aye." Darcy sighed. "There've been no outward threats to harm me. Nothing violent. Which I guess puts me low down on their priorities."

"But that's how these things always start, isn't it? I'm not trying to worry you, but you read about it all the time. An ex that can't let go or someone with an unrequited crush. Eventually they get frustrated and flip out."

"Trust me, I've read every story going on this stuff and none of it is pleasant. I keep waiting for that day when they turn up on the doorstep with worse intentions than gifts and trickery. I can only hope I'm prepared."

Eilidh's phone began to buzz again, and she threw it a dirty look. "Seriously. I don't think I've ever been this popular." She got up and crossed the room to pick it up, and Darcy watched her eyebrows furrow as she read the messages.

"What's wrong?"

Eilidh glanced up from the phone, and her features softened a little. "What? Oh, nothing to worry about. Problem patient update from Sam."

Darcy's phone rang again, and she huffed in frustration and anger.

"How about we turn them off?" She watched as Eilidh held her finger on the side of her phone and then showed her the blank screen. "See. Problem solved."

Darcy chewed her lip. Who voluntarily turned their phone off these days?

Eilidh laughed at her obvious reluctance. "The world won't end. I promise. But I bet you'll feel better. I'm here with you if anything happens. A few hours without won't hurt."

"What if Anja needs me?" As tempting as it was, Darcy still wasn't sure.

"Why would she need you?" Eilidh sat down again and reached for Darcy's phone. "Go on. Do it."

"I've been worried about her, that's all. She's been strange towards me this past couple of weeks or so, and I'm not sure why. It feels as if she's bottling something up. She's been unwaveringly positive and attentive, and although I love that, it feels sort of fake. It's not the real her. She's the friend who would normally tell me to put my big-girl pants on and get on with it."

Eilidh chuckled. "Sounds like something my mum would say." Darcy's phone rang again, and this time Eilidh did the honours. "What's she got to bottle up, anyway?"

Darcy wondered a moment if she should tell Eilidh, then decided it wasn't exactly a state secret. It might also help to explain why Anja wasn't being particularly accommodating where Eilidh was concerned.

"She split up with her husband. Not long before the accident. He cheated on her, and since then all her focus and worry has been on me and she's stopped talking about it. I know he's left the country, gone for good, and I keep waiting for her to react. But there's nothing."

Eilidh draped an arm around Darcy and drew her closer. "Wow, that sucks. I imagine it was frightening for her. After losing her husband, she almost lost her best friend. Maybe this is her way of coping? She's concentrating on you because you're something she can help fix."

"Aye. Maybe. I'm sure we'll talk about it at some point, but I hope it's soon. I want the real Anja back. I miss her."

"She'll talk soon. I'm sure of it. I have to say though, I wouldn't have guessed that Anja was married to a guy."

Darcy shifted to face her. "Really? Why?"

Eilidh squirmed a little and couldn't quite catch Darcy's eye. "It's nothing, really. Obviously I don't know her, or your relationship, but something made me think she was maybe an ex? Or at the very least it was complicated."

Darcy found herself laughing at that thought, but something stirred inside her stomach, an uncomfortable feeling that made her tense. Why had Eilidh's observation made her react that way? "No. Definitely not. We always have and always will be friends and nothing more."

"Well, in that case." Eilidh picked up Darcy's phone again. "I'm sure she'll understand if your phone is off for one evening. If anything is really wrong and she can't get hold of you, I'm sure she'll come out here."

Darcy knew she was talking sense. A few hours of quality time in front of the fire with Eilidh seemed too good to be interrupted with a reminder of that night. Of the ghost that refused to show itself. She held down the power button and tossed the phone on to the armchair out of sight.

Anja crouched down and leaned back against her usual tree. It was high enough in the thick woodland that she was hidden from view, but it put her almost level with the cabin and its rear windows. When it was dark and the lights were on inside the cabin, she knew she couldn't be seen.

She seethed inside. Eilidh had been there more than two hours.

Her mind reeled with every imaginable scenario that could be playing out inside. She'd watched them cook, sit down to dinner, laughing and drinking. Eilidh had sat in her seat and drank from the fancy beer glass she'd bought Darcy.

Now they had moved out of view, and Anja couldn't be sure where they had gone.

The sofa?

The rug in front of the fire?

The goddamn bedroom?

She hit dial on Darcy's number again, not expecting her to answer but at least hoping it would intrude on whatever was going on in there. It didn't feel enough of a distraction, and her imagination raced with alternatives, something that wouldn't expose her prematurely.

A recorded voice in her ear told her Darcy's phone had been switched off. "What the fuck?" That never happened. She'd been a fidgety mess the three days it had been in the shop having the screen fixed.

They had to be in the bedroom.

The way they'd looked at each other earlier that day. The tears. The hugs. The kissing. She pressed her fingertips to her eyes as images of Darcy and Eilidh kissing progressed to worse.

Sex.

Eilidh's naked body snaking along Darcy's, her lips on places they had no right to be.

It was too much.

She thumped the ground and dug her nails in to the sodden earth, squeezing handfuls of it in an attempt to temper the eruption that threatened to blow.

Was Darcy in bed with her right now? What reason would she have not to be? She didn't know how Anja felt, but Eilidh had made her own feelings painfully clear.

All her plans to take care of Darcy, to make her realise how good they were together, had been royally fucked up by Eilidh. Why the hell couldn't she stay away and leave them alone? Take heed of her warnings and disappear from both of their lives.

Every which way Anja turned, Eilidh was there obstructing her. Taunting her. She felt Darcy slipping through her fingers and knew she was almost lost.

Her hand moved through the soil and found a rock. She let her fingers wrap around it.

She wouldn't allow it. Wouldn't allow Eilidh to get her claws in to Darcy any further. She was vulnerable, and between the injuries and the pills, she couldn't know what or who she wanted.

Anja stood tall. Resolute. With the rock held fast in her hands, she marched towards the cabin, unsure what she was going to do, but knowing she needed to do something. Only a few feet from the front steps, out of range of the camera, she stopped. A decision held tight in her hand.

She raised her arm and threw with every ounce of strength she had.

Chapter 45

Both women flinched, and Eilidh shot up from the sofa. The unmistakeable sound of glass shattering echoed outside the cabin. Eilidh saw the terror flash in Darcy's eyes and reached to place a calming hand on her arm. "Wait right here."

She tiptoed to the kitchen and flicked off the radio. "Stay still a moment and listen."

After a few seconds, all Eilidh could hear was her heartbeat thumping in her ears. "Do you have a weapon? A torch?"

Darcy nodded, eyes still wide. "There's a bat in the bedroom," she whispered. "Torch by the front door." She pointed in its direction. "But you shouldn't go out there. I'll call the police."

"It's okay. I want you to stay here and keep low behind the sofa. Get your phone switched on." Eilidh ducked down and moved quickly towards the bedroom. The bat stood propped in a corner near the bed. The anger at knowing why Darcy needed to keep such a thing handy replaced the fear. She headed back to the living room, adrenalin motivating every step, and slipped her shoes on.

Darcy hobbled to her side and grabbed a crutch and the tablet. They quickly scanned the small area that the CCTV covered but couldn't see movement or anything unusual around the steps or porch. "Seriously, you don't need to go out there."

"I'll be fine." Eilidh unhooked the torch and flicked it on.

"Then I'm coming with you. I'm not hiding from this anymore."

Eilidh took a moment before nodding. "Fair enough. Stay as low as you can and keep quiet. Move slowly."

They headed outside together. Darcy wielded the crutch like a weapon, limping but unwavering. Eilidh caught hold of her hand as they ducked behind the porch fencing. She scanned the woods and track with the torch, but nothing caught their attention. She brought the beam closer, swept it across Darcy's shed, then her car.

Eilidh's windscreen was a mesh of tiny pieces, apart from where a large hole gaped at the driver's side.

There was no sign of anyone, and despite the windscreen, she felt some relief seep in. "Flyaway branch, maybe?" She kept the light on the car as they approached.

Both spotted the rock on the driver's seat at the same time.

"Runaway stalker, more like." Darcy threw the crutch to the ground and scrubbed her face with her hands. She'd turned a pasty shade of white, and Eilidh could see the tremble in her movements.

"C'mon." She picked up the crutch and wrapped an arm around Darcy's waist before guiding her back towards the cabin.

Once safely inside, Darcy retrieved her phone. "There's more missed calls from an unknown number. I'll need to call the police."

Eilidh was at the fridge. She relieved it of another beer and raised it in Darcy's direction. "Do you mind?"

"Go ahead. You can't drive anywhere tonight with your car in that state. I'll make up the spare room."

Eilidh smiled gratefully and took a few gulps of beer while listening to Darcy on the phone. It was obvious she'd been through the routine many times before, and that realisation depressed the hell out of Eilidh. She considered whether to tell Darcy about the notes and calls but was quick to discard the idea. She was already so wired and worried, and Eilidh hated the thought of adding to her stress.

Or would it be worse if she hid it and Darcy found out at a later date?

Who knew what lengths this person would go to in order to keep them apart? Their objective seemed clear. The thought they'd been so close to the cabin and had probably been watching them made Eilidh shudder.

She was shaken more than she wanted to admit. It was another message for sure. Jealousy could be a destructive emotion, and it oozed from the stalker's every action. Darcy had said there'd yet to be violence against her that she knew of, but the night of her accident was still so unknown, and the crash had been rather fucking violent.

It also didn't mean there wouldn't be aggression against Eilidh. It might only be a smashed window now, but who knew what they were willing to do, to get their message across?

Darcy hung up and threw her phone impatiently on to the sofa. "Fat load of good they were. They've given me a crime reference and will come out to take a look as soon as they can."

Eilidh moved across the room and wrapped her arms around Darcy's shoulders. "We'll figure this out." She held her at arm's length. "Promise."

"I'm not sure how. Between the police, me, and Anja, we haven't the faintest idea who's doing this or why."

"They'll slip up at some point. They have to. And when it happens we'll be ready." She stepped back towards the kitchen and reached once again for her beer, then offered it to Darcy. She realised it was no good hiding the fact that Eilidh had the stalker's attention. The only way they were going to get through this was together, and that could never happen with lies.

"Have some of this." She headed back towards the sofa. "We need to talk."

Chapter 46

DARCY SEETHED AS EILIDH RELAYED everything she had been subjected to that past month.

"I could cope with the notes and texts, the late night silent calls. Yes, they had a clear message, but I kept telling myself they would never follow through with the threats. But now..." Eilidh gestured in the general direction of her car. "Now I'm a little worried and really fucking creeped out. I thought it was time to tell you."

Darcy winced as she hobbled the few feet back and forth in front of the fire. She couldn't sit still. *How dare they suck Eilidh into their twisted fantasy?*

"It's good that you did. I understand why you kept it from me, but it's gone too far now. Who the hell do they think they are? Interfering in my life like this. In yours."

A wreath.

They laid a fucking wreath on Eilidh's doorstep.

"We have to take all this to the police as well." Darcy stopped a moment and met Eilidh's worried look. "Have you kept everything?"

Eilidh shook her head. "I'm sorry, Darcy. I have the texts, and the Facebook messages, but anything else I needed out of my sight. They went straight in the bin."

Darcy began pacing again. "It's all right. We know how careful they are, although the messages on Facebook might lead somewhere. I doubt the account is still active, but surely now there are actual threats the police have to take it more seriously? Look into it further? Surely they'll believe it's the same person?"

Eilidh stood and caught her by the shoulders. "This isn't your fault, Darcy."

Darcy felt herself deflate, and the anger slowly seeped away as Eilidh drew her in to a warm embrace. Between physio, a lack of sleep, and the general battering her mind and body had taken the past few months, she didn't have the energy levels to maintain any prolonged period of outrage. Most days Darcy felt wilted, cast in shadow, but Eilidh's arms wrapped around her were like sunlight. They revitalised her with a flush of longing and excitement, as well as reassurance.

"I know." Darcy spoke in to her neck. "I hate this so much. That you're going through this because some psycho thinks I belong to them. I wish it would end."

"Me too, sweetheart." Eilidh squeezed her extra tight a moment before letting go. Her fingers trailed down the back of Darcy's arms and grazed her wrists before interlocking with Darcy's. "I don't think we're solving the mystery tonight though. Why don't we get some sleep?"

They'd reached this point of the evening a number of times before. It was when Eilidh normally went home, when the air would become heavy with all the things they both longed to do and say. Declarations that couldn't be taken back without damage and actions that Darcy ached for but knew would change everything.

Darcy never wanted her to leave, but something always caught hold of the words in her throat, stuffed them back inside her head. Eilidh would linger a moment, as if waiting for Darcy to ask her to stay, before smiling and leaving her with one last kiss goodnight.

It was always going to be up to Darcy.

"Sleep. Sure. The guest room is this way." Darcy kept hold of Eilidh's hand as she walked slightly ahead down the corridor. Her heart thundered in her chest as she led Eilidh towards the bedrooms. Turn right and show Eilidh to the guest room as promised, or turn left and... Her boot caught on the rug, and she fumbled forward a little at the thought of what might happen if she turned left.

"You okay?"

Eilidh held onto her from behind as she steadied herself. Darcy felt the heat radiate from Eilidh's body, her hands firm and sure on Darcy's waist.

"Yeah," she whispered as she pressed back lightly against Eilidh.

She heard Eilidh's breath hitch, felt her lips move close to Darcy's ear before she planted a shiver-inducing kiss behind it. One hand slid from Darcy's waist to brush across her stomach, and Darcy felt herself melt in to it. She was sinking into warm honey, the world muffling around her, where only the circle she possessed within Eilidh's arms mattered.

"Stay with me tonight." Her decision wasn't born from longing, wasn't her body's cravings speaking for her. She was ready. Darcy had wanted Eilidh from that first morning on the bridge. The random, astonishing, and terrifying ways in which the world had brought them together to this point had given her the final push she needed that night. Nobody was going to dictate Darcy's feelings, her life, or who she spent time with. The stalker had done her a favour.

"Are you sure?" Eilidh's hands had stilled.

She spoke into Darcy's hair, and Darcy heard the tremor in her voice. The slight uncertainty. The worry that question induced because what if Darcy wasn't sure? What if she changed her mind? Darcy loved her for asking, for giving her that one final chance, for giving her the power to decide.

She couldn't even contemplate parting with someone who had become so precious to her, in a thousand unique and wonderful ways. She wanted Eilidh to know that, to be free to feel it as well. Eilidh should no longer have to doubt and wonder what this was for Darcy.

She turned inside Eilidh's embrace, looped her arms around her neck, and twisted her hands into Eilidh's hair. She brought her lips close enough to Eilidh's for their breath to mingle. "I'm certain."

Eilidh kissed the words from her lips, and together they fell against the bedroom door. Darcy fumbled to get it open, and they both stumbled into the dark room. Darcy's body cried out, vibrating with delicious energy and desperate to satisfy the anticipation that had built within her for weeks.

But she could still sense Eilidh's tentativeness; she seemed unsure as her hands cautiously explored. Darcy cupped Eilidh's face and brought their eyes level. "It's okay, sweetheart. You won't hurt me," she whispered.

Eilidh lightly traced her collarbone with a fingertip, skimming one of the many deep red lines that still marred Darcy's skin. "Are you sure?"

Darcy pressed a firm kiss to her lips before trailing more along her jaw and nipping her earlobe. "Positive," she breathed as Eilidh shuddered satisfyingly. "Stop worrying."

Eilidh's lips became fierce then and she took control, backing them towards the bed whilst simultaneously pulling Darcy's top over her head. The cool air made her skin pimple momentarily before Eilidh's warmth covered her.

As her layers were stripped away, Darcy felt anything but exposed.

Hot breath, urgent tongues, and every brush of skin caused a ripple of reaction that spurred Darcy forward. It urged her to reach deep for Eilidh and learn all the parts of her that she craved to know.

Eilidh's skin was soft, supple, and fluid beneath her fingertips, and oh-so warm to her lips. Darcy was lost and found in her arms as she kissed and nibbled Eilidh's neck, smiling when the nip of her teeth at Eilidh's earlobe drew a delicious moan from her lips. The muscles in her back tensed like corded rope beneath Darcy's hands as she rose up enough to press herself against a need deeper than Darcy had ever felt before.

She felt her heart and soul piece back together as every question between them, every need, and every desire was asked and unequivocally answered. In Eilidh's embrace, she was strong, despite feeling every emotion, every thought, and every insecurity laid bare for her. In Eilidh's eyes she saw desire, she saw want, need, lust... But more than that she saw genuine caring that verged on adoration, and it was that look that undid her more than anything else.

Every kiss was a promise made between them. Promises Darcy hoped they spent a very, very long time living up to.

Again and again, they gave in to it, to each other.

Until a blissful, dreamless sleep descended upon their tangled limbs.

Chapter 47

AFTER A RESTLESS NIGHT, ANJA tore off the bed covers and stomped down to the kitchen. She was still annoyed with herself for being so reckless the night before, for giving in to the frustration and tempting fate. After all this time, she couldn't believe she had let her temper get the better of her judgment and put herself at risk of being caught.

As coffee brewed, she thought about the current situation with Darcy. About the Eilidh issue and the obvious fact that no matter what she had tried, Eilidh clearly wasn't going anywhere of her own accord.

She needed another plan.

Her rash action the night before had only done more damage. It had forced Eilidh to stay the night, and Anja had no question about where she'd spent it. The thought brought another surge of anger that she swallowed back and forced herself to breathe through.

She needed a day with Darcy.

Just the two of them. No interruptions. No Eilidh.

Anja needed to know how far things had gone with Eilidh. Not about the sex, or hopefully lack of it. It was about how Darcy felt. *How far gone is she emotionally when it comes to Eilidh?*

As she sipped her coffee, Anja considered a scenario that had looped on repeat through the night that had a variety of outcomes. If her stalker persona couldn't force Eilidh to back down, maybe it was time to be brave and fight for Darcy as Anja.

She thought again about telling Darcy how she felt. Well, not fully. A declaration of love might overwhelm her, scare her away. But if Anja told her she'd been having some kind of feelings other than friendship, something confusing and unexpected, it would surely be enough to at least get Darcy thinking.

Anja knew her friend would be understanding of that, wouldn't run or recoil. Even if outwardly she denied feeling anything similar, it would give her pause. Anja was certain of that.

It needed to happen soon, before she was in too deep with Eilidh and any declaration from Anja would seem like sabotage. It would be too difficult for Darcy to consider.

An idea came to mind. When she thought about everything Darcy loved, the boat was an obvious first choice. They'd enjoyed many amazing days on the water together, and Darcy would be reminded of that when Anja made her confession.

She would be in a happy place, comfortable, somewhere she felt in charge. The cabin was too risky; Anja was afraid it might invoke memories of her first clumsy attempt at honesty and the whole thing would fall to shit.

Yes, the boat could work. She knew Darcy would be missing it and would be aching to get out there again. Between them, they would manage fine. Darcy would not only be in her element, but when the moment came, she'd be unable to run away from it this time.

It also meant Anja couldn't do the same.

Anja reached for her phone. It was time. She couldn't hide forever, from her feelings nor what they might mean for her relationship with Darcy. The uncertainty of everything and jealousy over Eilidh was threatening to consume her.

She had to tell Darcy or risk losing her forever.

Darcy luxuriated in the satisfaction of a full-body stretch. Even her leg couldn't detract from her smile, and her wrist had more than managed. She imagined hinting to Sam about the extra physio session it had enjoyed and chuckled to herself.

Her phone buzzed, and she groaned but reached for it anyway. To her surprise, it was Anja, with an interesting proposition that got Darcy thinking.

Eilidh wafted in to the room carrying plates of sausage, eggs, black pudding, and toast. "Breakfast is served." She propped the tray on a pillow in the middle of the bed and climbed back under the covers close to Darcy.

"Thank you." Darcy leaned in and kissed her. "No fair. You've brushed your teeth."

Eilidh laughed and kissed her again. "What do you want to do today?" She stabbed at a sausage and looked at Darcy expectantly. "Your wish is my command."

"Well…" Darcy looked at her mischievously. "After our, erm, workout last night—which was incredible, by the way." She couldn't help but kiss Eilidh's smile. "I've realised how much I miss being active. I'm itching to get out of the gym and try this leg out doing something normal like Sam suggested. Something other than a walk."

"Such as? Why do I feel like you already have a plan?"

Darcy was relieved that the physiotherapist in Eilidh wasn't immediately protesting. "I miss my boat."

"You have a boat?" Eilidh's eyebrows peaked in curiosity. "I knew you sailed, but I didn't know you actually owned a boat."

"Part of one," Darcy corrected. "A few of us at the club went in on it a few years ago and either sail together or get to take it out on a rota. It's nothing fancy."

"You want to take it out?" Eilidh seemed keen and eager. "You know I love the water."

Darcy couldn't hide her delight. "I was worried you'd think it was a bad idea."

"Not at all. You know yourself what you feel capable of, and who better to supervise on your first outing without the boot than your own personal physio?"

"You sure? I don't want you to feel as if you have to say yes."

"Very sure. Anything to keep that grin on your face."

Darcy did a happy jiggle. "We'll play it safe. Attach the outboard in case we're struggling. I don't care as long as I'm on the water."

Eilidh nodded. "I know some basics, and I'm happy to take instruction from my captain." Eilidh saluted, and if it weren't for the tray of breakfast, Darcy would have pounced. Instead, she pulled Eilidh towards her by the scruff of her shirt and let her lips tell Eilidh exactly what it meant to her.

"I also have another idea, but I'm not sure how happy you're going to be about this one." Darcy was coy, reluctant to spoil the mood and their morning.

"You want to invite Anja?" Eilidh lay back against the pillows, cup of tea in hand. She seemed a little wary, as if Darcy was going to have to convince her it would be a good idea.

"Aye. I think this would be a good opportunity for the two of you to spend time together, get used to one another. You never know, you might even start to like each other."

Eilidh blew out a long breath. "Fine. But only because I really like you."

Chapter 48

Darcy's nerves were jangling. She hadn't sailed since the autumn, and despite her experience, the thought of being on the water while not one hundred percent unnerved her, even though she knew it was safe. Anja was a skilled sailor, and the boat was manageable for her with Eilidh's assistance.

"You're nervous. I can tell." Anja was prepping the boat while Darcy looked on. She eyed Darcy suspiciously. "This is second nature to you, Darcy. It'll be fine. And I'm here."

As another car pulled in to the club, Darcy realised it might not only be the sailing that had her worried. "I know. And you'll have some extra help." She looked as Eilidh climbed out of a rental car, and Anja followed her gaze.

"Are you serious? Why didn't you tell me she was coming?"

Darcy shrugged. She wasn't sure why she'd left it to the last minute. It had crossed her mind if she told Anja she might not have turned up. "I wasn't sure you'd be up for it."

Anja sighed. "So much for getting you to myself for a day," she muttered.

"I know. I'm selfish and I'm sorry. But I hate that you don't get on with Eilidh. I thought this was a good opportunity to change that. Plus after what happened last night with her car, I didn't want to just ditch her today. It was pretty scary, An."

Anja's focus was on a stubborn knot, but Darcy could tell she was quietly annoyed. "I suppose. Did you call the police?"

"Aye, they came out this morning to take a look. We went through the usual motions, although they seemed to take it more serious. Now there's been actual threats."

"Are you sure it's the stalker? I mean, how well do you really know her? She could have her own enemies."

Darcy stood hands on hips and gave her a look that conveyed exactly what she thought of that theory. "Anja, c'mon."

"Okay." She held up a hand in defeat. "I'm just saying."

"Well, don't.

"Does this mean you're getting serious, then? I can't help but notice you haven't talked about her much to me." Anja climbed down from the boat, and they both watched as Eilidh unpacked her gear from the boot.

Darcy couldn't hide her grin. "Maybe. It got very serious last night, that's for sure."

Anja rounded her stare on Darcy. "I really don't need to hear about that."

It was said with a level of harshness in her tone that Darcy wasn't used to, and she couldn't place the reasoning behind it. It irked her that Anja showed no shred of happiness that she'd found something great to hold on to, given everything she had been through. Everything she was still going through.

"You could sound a little more pleased for me. I know you have your issues, but I'm happy, Anja. This could really be something. And if you really want to know, your attitude is exactly why I haven't talked about her."

Anja sighed. "Does she even sail?"

"Don't be snarky. But no, not really. Although I'm sure she can help out."

"Well, that's great." Anja threw her hands up before heading to climb back aboard. "I'll just ferry you two around. What a romantic time it'll be for you both."

"Hey, don't be that way, An. Why're you making this so hard? We'll muck in together and you know it'll be fine. Please be nice. For me." She put on her best begging face and saw Anja's soften.

"All right, you can quit it with that face. So long as she doesn't get in my way."

Darcy headed across the carpark towards Eilidh. Trussed up in a wetsuit and life jacket, she looked ridiculously cute and also a little nervous. Any guilt over Anja's displeasure disappeared at the sight of her.

Eilidh greeted her with a quick peck and then eyed the boat and Anja warily. "How did she take the news that I'm crashing your mate date?"

"Don't worry about her," Darcy reassured. She took Eilidh's hand and led her to the boat. "I think a day on the water is something we all need. Let's make it a good one, yeah?" Her question was aimed at them both.

"Aye."

"Yeah."

Both women agreed sheepishly.

"Today's about you," Anja said. "We're going to get you back out there and blow away some cobwebs."

Darcy smiled at her gratefully. "Sounds good. We almost ready?"

"Yip. Go grab the cool box and I'll give Eilidh a few pointers before we launch."

From the vantage point of the car, Darcy watched as Anja gesticulated and demonstrated some of the basics for Eilidh. She was excited now to be heading out on the water again with her best friend and, dare she say, her girlfriend? It felt surreal to have reached this point after the trauma and subsequent difficulties since the accident.

She felt her worries melt away and set her shoulders. To have these two amazing women in her life filled her with hope and gratitude, a sense of optimism for the future. Stalker be damned; they weren't going to take this away from her. She refused to allow them any measure of control over her life.

As the wind whipped her hair across her face, Darcy grinned and threw her hands in the air. Eilidh and Anja laughed at her exuberance, but she didn't care. There was nowhere else she would have rather been in that moment.

Eilidh had proven a handy captain's mate, which Anja had admitted to Darcy quietly, and with obvious reluctance. They tacked through the Moray Firth with ease, swapping places regularly so Eilidh could learn to both steer and control the sails. Eilidh was a quick study and clearly comfortably on the water. Although modest herself, Sam had once told Darcy she was an expert kayaker and could read the conditions well.

The walls of Fort George rose in the distance as they approached Chanonry Point. Darcy's attention was caught by movement in the water, and she called out to Eilidh and Anja excitedly.

"Dolphins!"

Anja was straight in to action. She commanded Eilidh's attention and called, "Ready about." They tacked to close reach, and Anja luffed the sail fully, slowing them down and bringing them closer to shore. The bottle-nosed dolphins frolicked close by, as if putting on a show. It was a well-known spot for catching sight of them, and the three women grinned at each other and watched in awe. They eventually left the coast and followed in the wake of a trawler, no doubt after some easy lunch.

"Am I doing all right?" Eilidh flopped down next to Darcy and slung an arm around her shoulder. Darcy caught Anja side-eying them and tried to ignore it.

"You're doing great. Although the test will be mastering the gybe on the way back. That can get tricky if you're not quick enough."

"Don't panic me." Eilidh's eyes widened. "I was thinking I'd got it sussed."

Darcy chuckled. "Long way to go yet, I'm afraid. But you have a great teacher." She raised her voice for Anja to hear. If she did, she didn't acknowledge the compliment.

"Is she always this bloody hard work?" Eilidh muttered close to Darcy's ear.

Darcy nudged in to her. "Give her a break. She wasn't expecting you, and we've not exactly spent a lot of time only the two of us lately. It was naughty of me to invite you without asking."

"Still, we're here now. I'd have thought she'd have loosened up a little."

"That's not about you," Darcy reassured. "You can't arse about on the water, as I'm sure you know. She'll be worrying about something happening and ruining this for me. Don't be so hard on her."

"Okay, sorry." Eilidh held up her hands in surrender. "You know her best."

"I do, and she's amazing. So please, keep making the effort and I promise she'll come around."

Eilidh saluted her before planting a kiss on her cheek. "Yes, ma'am. I better return to my post."

As they took the stern through the eye of the wind, Anja took control of the tiller and was patient as she taught Eilidh to gybe. Firm in her commands and assured in her manoeuvres. Eilidh kept looking back at Darcy, full of smiles and clearly enjoying herself.

Darcy closed her eyes and tipped her head to the sun. The wind rolled over her face, invigorating and revitalising. The water lapped satisfyingly around her, and she heard Eilidh laugh. She didn't look, for fear of breaking whatever small moment Eilidh and Anja might be enjoying. Instead, she kept her eyes closed and allowed her body to relax and sway with the movement of the boat.

She heard Anja call, "Boom coming across." It was followed by a thud and a yelp that brought Darcy rapidly back to attention. She caught a flash of red as Eilidh sprawled sideways and the boom swiped her into the frigid water with a sickening slap.

Darcy was instantly on her feet and yelling Eilidh's name. She watched as a small wave ducked Eilidh under the surface for a moment, but the buoyancy of her life vest brought her quickly back up spluttering water. "Relax and stay calm," Darcy shouted as the boat moved away from her. "We'll come back around for you."

She saw Eilidh raise a thumb in the air but could tell by her expression she was unimpressed with the situation. Whilst Darcy fretted and kept her gaze pinned on Eilidh, she took control of the tiller as Anja trimmed the sails and they turned in to beam reach. The beam reach-gybe was the simplest manoeuvre to get them back to Eilidh, and Darcy was in autopilot as she willed them back to her as quickly as possible. It didn't matter that the water was relatively calm, that they had her in sight: every worst-case scenario still spun on an out-of-control wheel through Darcy's mind.

"How the hell did this happen?" she yelled.

Anja shrugged. "She's an amateur. She wasn't ready."

They gybed and headed back on the reciprocal course. They swapped positions, and Darcy braced herself on the port side as Anja eased them towards Eilidh. She was skilled and accurate and brought the boat alongside Eilidh with ease. Darcy caught hold of her lifejacket, and Anja joined her in pulling Eilidh back aboard.

"Are you all right?" Darcy flipped a seat cushion and dug inside the small storage space for a blanket. She wrapped it around Eilidh's shoulders and rubbed vigorously, holding Eilidh close.

"Aye. I'll live. That water is bloody Baltic though." She clutched at the blanket and shivered furiously. "What on earth happened?" Her question was directed at Anja who once again shrugged.

"You called ready, so I gybed. You weren't quick enough when the boom came across."

"I didn't call ready."

Anja looked at her with furrowed eyebrows. "If you hadn't, I wouldn't have started the manoeuvre. You definitely replied."

"I asked you to wait, because I wasn't ready." She spoke angrily through chattering teeth.

"Ah, sorry about that. All I must have heard in the wind was the word ready." Anja moved to the stern and made to drop the outboard. "Probably quicker getting you back to shore with the engine."

Darcy guided Eilidh on to a seat and kept her tucked under an arm. "Not far and we'll get you warmed up."

"She did that on purpose," Eilidh mumbled.

"What?" Darcy couldn't be sure she had heard Eilidh right.

Eilidh looked towards Anja, then back at Darcy. She held Darcy's gaze a moment, sorrow in her eyes. "Never mind."

Darcy didn't want to believe what Eilidh had said. No matter how reluctant Anja seemed to be to welcome Eilidh, there was no way she would be so reckless or intentionally put a person's life at risk. Anja would never be capable of that; it didn't make sense with everything Darcy knew about her.

The day which had started with such promise ended abruptly back in the car park. As Anja took down sails and secured the boat, Eilidh headed straight for her car. She angrily stripped off her wetsuit whilst Darcy looked on, unsure what to say.

"You don't really think she would put you in danger on purpose, do you?"

Eilidh yanked a jumper over her head and threw a glance in Anja's direction. "I really don't know what to think."

"C'mon, Eilidh. She'd never do that. I know her." Darcy pleaded for Eilidh to trust her, but it seemed to be falling on deaf ears.

"Do you?" Eilidh slammed the boot shut and pushed past her to the driver's door. "Because I haven't seen a single moment of this wonderful person you profess her to be."

Darcy caught her arm. "Wait. Don't leave here mad with me."

Eilidh sighed heavily. "I'm not mad at you, Darcy. I just don't want to be around the two of you right now. You need to talk to her."

"What about? I not going to accuse my best friend of knocking you overboard, if that's what you're thinking."

Eilidh shook her head and smiled sadly. "Maybe if you two could see past each other for even a second, you'd be able to see what I see. You and Anja are not just friends, Darcy." She stepped in to Darcy's space and left the faintest of kisses on her cheek before murmuring in her ear, "Unfortunately for me, only Anja's realised that."

Before Darcy could protest or respond, Eilidh had started the car and was gone. Darcy stood rooted to the spot, Eilidh's parting words echoing in her mind. She turned and studied Anja as she focused on releasing the sails. *Are we more than friends?*

It wasn't the first time Darcy had considered the question, only before it had been Joe that had planted it. Daft, immature, wind-up merchant Joe. This time it was Eilidh, someone close to her, someone special. Eilidh who had something to lose if the answer was yes.

Since the accident, she hadn't considered it again. The status quo had resumed, but with the added element of Eilidh, who she knew she was falling for. Everything up to and including their night together had felt so wonderful. So perfectly right in every way.

So why was she even entertaining Eilidh's statement? Why hadn't she dismissed it immediately and chased Eilidh down, told her she was the one Darcy wanted?

Anja looked up and smiled her way, and Darcy automatically returned it. Her heart thumped, and she pressed a hand against her chest, willing it to stop. It beat faster at the thought Eilidh might be right.

Fuck.

They really needed to talk.

Chapter 49

THEY SAT IN THE FRONT of Anja's car with a view of the Moray Firth before them. Anja offered her another sandwich, but Darcy shook her head.

"It was an accident, you know," Anja reiterated.

"I believe you." Darcy sighed. She couldn't meet Anja's eyes. Eilidh's words continued to tumble around in her head but wouldn't quite fall in to place. "I'm not worried about that. She'll be fine."

"What are you worried about, then?" Anja packed the last of the food away and turned towards her. "I know that look. It's not a good look."

Darcy couldn't help but smile because Anja was right. She knew all of Darcy's looks, how her mind operated, the right thing to do and say at the right time. She knew Darcy inside and out, and Darcy was the same when it came to her. They were bonded in so many ways, it was frightening to imagine losing her. Was this something she could lose Anja over?

"Eilidh said something before she left that got me thinking and I'm really not sure what the hell to do or say about it." She turned to look at Anja then, in some vague hope that Anja could actually read her mind and she wouldn't have to say the words.

She simply reached for one of Darcy's hands and held it tight. "You can talk to me about anything, you know that."

"I could say the same to you, but it seems it's one thing knowing it and another thing acting on it."

Anja looked rightly confused. "Darcy, I've no clue what you're on about. So spit it out."

Darcy took a breath and let the words fall out in a rush. "Eilidh thinks we're more than friends, but says we haven't realised it yet."

She felt Anja's grip tighten a moment, but she didn't say anything. Instead, she looked back out to sea, and Darcy watched as she took what seemed to be a few steadying breaths. Darcy could tell she was shaken by the words, and that unnerved her more. She had expected Anja to laugh or dismiss Eilidh's theory as daft and tell her not to worry.

"Anja. Talk to me. Because now you have that look."

She met Darcy's gaze. "I've very much realised it."

Darcy didn't know what to say. It seemed absurd, yet deep down a small part of her wasn't surprised. There'd been so many signs that had made her wonder, but something had always helped her shrug them off, refuse to acknowledge it.

"You like me?" Her tone was incredulous. It still made no sense. She was going to need Anja to spell it all out exactly to avoid any danger of misunderstanding. "As more than a friend?"

Anja hung her head. She let go of Darcy's hand and twisted her fingers together, clenching until the knuckles went white. "Don't be mad at me."

"Mad?" Darcy shook her head. "Why would I be mad? I'm confused, and I won't lie, really fucking shocked. But also strangely not shocked. Either way, I'm not mad." She heard a small laugh escape Anja and realised it had broken through tears. Darcy tapped her finger under Anja's chin and forced her to look up. "Talk to me."

Anja wiped at her eyes and took a steadying breath. Darcy offered her hand again, and although tentative, Anja took it.

"I wasn't sure how to talk to you about it. I've been afraid you'd think it was some kind of rebound thing after Jason. But it's not, Darcy. I promise."

"Okay." Darcy nodded. She was determined to hold it together and wasn't sure what else to say. The last thing she wanted was to freak out and scare Anja into silence again. This didn't have to be a wedge between them. "What is it, then?"

Anja rubbed her thumb over Darcy's, and Darcy stared at it, at how naturally tactile they were. She didn't pull away, didn't shrink at the contact. It was reassuring, exactly how Anja had always been. Did it mean more to Anja than that?

"It's as if I've always seen you in this one particular way, and I knew what our relationship was, who we were to each other. Then things began to change, and it became something more for me. I've only really been able to admit it to myself recently. Since Jason left and gave me the space to consider it properly."

"What things changed to make it more?" Maybe if Darcy knew what it was for Anja, she could hold it up against herself. Figure out if she was in complete and utter denial about her own feelings as Eilidh seemed to think.

"It was small stuff at first. I'd catch myself daydreaming about you and realise I couldn't wait to see you again. When you walked in to the office in the morning, I would feel this lift that was, like, mental as well as physical. Every time I saw I had a message from you, I'd get excited. I realised having you near me automatically made me feel amazing."

Darcy thought about that because seeing Anja walk through the door was always a cause for smiling, and it was true that a message from her always perked Darcy up. "I do that too. When you arrive after me. I guess I notice if you haven't texted or called in a while and I'm always a bit miserable the days you're not in the office. It feels as if all is not what it should be, but I don't know if that means any more than friendship, Anja."

"I know and I understand that. So often I've wished for you to feel the same. That it would eventually click, and you'd see me differently. Lately I've found myself making excuses to stand or sit close to you. To hug you. To touch you. Even though I would have done those things without even thinking in the past because they were natural. Then I was suddenly hyperaware of every movement I made around you, and that made me feel awful because you were unaware of what it did to me. I felt as if I was betraying our friendship somehow."

Darcy considered all the times when she would be upset by the stalker and Anja would stay over. The weeks after she'd kicked Jason out when they would fall asleep in each other's arms, comforted and safe. "It didn't feel that way to me. No matter what was going on inside your head, your heart, those moments would've been the same. They would've still happened because that's us, Anja. That's our friendship. You shouldn't feel bad about that."

"Friendship." The disappointment in Anja's voice as she uttered the word kicked Darcy in the gut. The thought that this wonderful relationship she'd been part of was suddenly no longer enough for Anja frightened her. There was no going back from this. What if they couldn't figure out a way forward?

One thing was clear. Nothing would ever be the same.

"I don't know what to say, Anja. I never expected this. I'll admit, in the early days I wondered about us sometimes, but there was Jason and it all seemed ridiculous. So I let it go."

"You did?" Anja looked genuinely surprised.

"Aye. I mean, look at you." Darcy smiled and cupped her cheek. "You're crazy intelligent and beautiful. You have the ability to charm honey from the bees one minute, then sting like one the next. You're so many things I was looking for in a girlfriend; instead, I found this amazing friend."

"I missed my chance, then?"

Darcy pulled a tissue from the glovebox as Anja's tears started again. "Honestly, sweetheart. I don't know." Darcy sighed. It was so much to take in. She felt in shock and heart sorry. She was unsure how to respond to Anja as the sinking feeling settled in that any fantasy she'd had about Anja in the past wasn't buried, it was gone. The space was now taken up wholly by Eilidh. Last night—before that, if she were honest with her self—Eilidh had touched her. Not just physically, but emotionally, and no matter how hard she thought about it, she could not picture anyone else in her place.

Not that she'd say that to Anja. Not now. That would be too cruel, and she loved her friend far too much to rub salt into the wounds she'd already inflicted.

"I'm sorry, An."

"Don't." In the blink of an eye, Anja seemed to collapse in on herself, crumpled like a piece of paper. Darcy wanted to hug her, to take away the hurt, but this time she couldn't. She suspected it would only hurt her more. She looked away and blinked tears from her eyes. God, she was sorry. She wished she'd never asked the bloody question.

"Come on, I'll take you home."

Darcy turned, and it was as though the wounded Anja had never been there. The walls had come up, and now Anja sat upright, her mouth set in a firm line. Darcy could only nod. She didn't know what else to say; she was too stunned to find words.

When they reached the cabin, Anja turned to her again, intensity in her stare. "All I ask, Darcy, is that you think about it. I know it might be weird because your idea of us as friends has never been challenged. But I want you to challenge it and consider it, because we work, Darcy. We really do. I'm prepared to take that further and risk it all, for the possibility of something truly wonderful."

Darcy swallowed back a lump in her throat. She couldn't refuse. She loved this woman and would do anything to avoid hurting her further. She already knew what the outcome would be, but she owed this to Anja. Owed her the time and the head space.

If only to consider how she would break her heart.

How she was going to avoid losing her forever.

She nodded. "I will."

Eilidh didn't go home. She drove around aimlessly, annoyed with herself for leaving Darcy that way, particularly after what had happened the night before. She hated the thought of Darcy being out at the cabin alone.

She'd also played right into Anja's hands and given her the opportunity to turn Darcy's head in another direction. As frustrating and scary as that was, she knew the conversation had to happen. Anja's obvious feelings lingered over them like a grey cloud, and Eilidh couldn't stand the anticipation of waiting for it to rain. For Anja to wash away what had been developing between her and Darcy.

Or would it?

Eilidh hadn't imagined their night together. Hadn't invented every touch or look from Darcy that made her heart swell and flutter. It wasn't one-sided.

So why wasn't she fighting? Was she really going to give up on something with such promise, something so astonishing in its ability to completely undo her? The stalker hadn't managed to put her off, so why should Anja? But could she really challenge someone who had been so important and present in Darcy's life for so long?

Damn right she could.

Darcy at least needed all the facts, and Eilidh needed to stop being such a fucking coward.

She pulled over and reached for her phone, tapping out a text to Darcy, telling her she was coming over to talk. She turned her car in the direction of the cabin. Now wasn't the time to run away. It was the time to speak to Darcy like an adult and make it clear exactly how she felt.

Chapter 50

DARCY HAD DITCHED THE CRUTCH and limped from one room to another, unable to sit still. She tidied some things away, washed dishes, and ordered a stack of books on a shelf. Anything to avoid thinking about everything Anja had said.

But it needled and demanded to be considered no matter how reluctant she was to go there. Anja had opened the box, and now Darcy was trapped inside. She finally grabbed a beer from the fridge and her cosiest hat and coat and moved to the porch.

She lit the chiminea in the corner and swung idly in the chair Anja had helped her hang the summer before, sipping rhythmically from her bottle as the fire warmed her feet.

Anja has feelings for me.

How many times in their early days had she wondered if that were true? Hoped it were true? Now it had spun her around and left her feeling unwell.

She hadn't tried to contact Eilidh and didn't think it was fair to until her mind had cleared and she was certain she was all in. That's what Eilidh deserved.

The crunch of gravel drew her attention to the lane, and a tingle of pleasure ran through her when she glimpsed Eilidh's car. She watched from the swing as Eilidh parked, noted the serious expression on her face as she looked towards the front door before spotting Darcy on the porch. She looked annoyed, and Darcy braced herself, unsure if she could cope with both the women in her life turning everything upside down in the same day.

"Hey," Darcy croaked.

"Hey." Eilidh sauntered up the steps and leaned against the porch fence. "You didn't reply to my text, but I came anyway. I thought we should talk."

"Sorry. My phone's inside." Darcy nodded in the direction of the door. "You want to grab a beer and join me out here?"

With a beer in hand, Eilidh came back outside but sat in a chair opposite rather than next to Darcy on the swing. That stung a little, but then Eilidh couldn't know how Darcy's conversation had gone with Anja.

"I'm sorry for showing up without calling or hearing back from you." Eilidh broke the awkward silence.

"Don't be." Darcy tried a reassuring smile. "I'm glad you're here."

"Really? Did you talk to Anja?"

Eilidh seemed almost afraid to ask and it choked Darcy that she was in that situation. "I did. We talked after you left, and you were right."

She watched as Eilidh heaved a breath and tears welled in her eyes. "You do have feelings for her, then? As more than a friend?"

Darcy only hesitated a moment, but it was long enough. The bottle was thumped down on the porch, and Eilidh was on her feet. "I knew it. I knew there was something holding you back. All those times I texted and called, left messages asking to see you only for you not to respond or fob me off. Or leave me hanging for so long I ended up chasing once again."

She paced the length of the porch, and Darcy tried to interrupt. Her words weren't making sense.

"Wait." Eilidh held up a palm in her direction. "I don't want excuses. I just want to know why? Why would you string me along like this? One minute you're there, you're present and warm and kind and affectionate. You act as if you wouldn't be anywhere else but with me. And last night... Well... But then you make excuses, or outright ignore me, and I'm left feeling like total shit."

"What? I haven't..."

"You have, Darcy. It's always been on your terms. When you're ready, when you have the time. The worst thing is I let you get away with it and I hate myself for that. I keep coming running, keep glossing over your behaviour because despite it all..." Her shoulders dropped, and she blew out a sigh. "I'm falling hopelessly in love with you."

Darcy sat dumbstruck, attempting to fathom everything Eilidh had said but finding herself stuck on the last sentence. "You're what?"

That moment. Those words. They answered all Darcy's questions.

It was Eilidh she wanted to be with. Eilidh who made her feel the way she'd always imagined she should. Eilidh who made her jump with every brush of skin, and Eilidh who had made her dream again of the future she had always hoped for.

"I'm falling in love with you," Eilidh said it again, and Darcy believed it.

Darcy wanted to go to her, wanted to wrap her arms around Eilidh and hold her until she trusted that Darcy felt the same. But her other words came flooding back, and they hurt. "Eilidh, I—I don't know what you're talking about. The texts? The calls? Always doing the running? That's how I've felt."

"You? There's not a time I haven't answered the phone to you or replied to your messages."

"Are you kidding me? You disappear all the time. I feel like if I didn't finally cave and message you, we'd never see each other again. I figured with Claire and everything you've been through, you needed time. I've been choking on questions, trying to be sensitive and not push." Eilidh was shaking her head and it annoyed Darcy. "Don't do that. Don't dismiss me. Admit it."

"Admit what? When have I ignored you?"

"I can think of at least two times."

"Twice? Are you kidding me, Darcy? First of all, that's crap. I would never leave you hanging the way you have me. And secondly, twice doesn't even touch the way you've been. All for it one minute then cagey the next. Look."

She pulled out her phone and crossed to kneel in front of Darcy. "Right here."

Eilidh began to recite a conversation to Darcy. The words were unfamiliar, and Darcy felt a rush of cold dread move through her body, from her scalp to her heart. "Hang on, stop. Stop talking." She tried to cut Eilidh off as she continued to reel off times Darcy hadn't responded or had coldly dismissed plans and offers of company, but Eilidh kept going.

"Eilidh, stop!" She grabbed for Eilidh's phone. "I didn't write those."

Darcy watched as confusion clouded Eilidh's features. "What?"

"Those texts. I didn't write them. Eilidh, I swear. That's not me."

They were quiet as Darcy's mind swirled uncontrollably, trying to settle on an answer to how this had happened. The when? The what? Who?

She saw recognition in Eilidh's eyes, knew she had caught up. She believed Darcy. "I'm such an idiot."

"Seems we both are." Darcy reached and pulled her on to the swing beside her. They sat close and stared out in to the woodland, searching for a solution as to how the deception had been achieved.

When it hit Darcy, it felt as if lead were being poured over her body. Her limbs became immobilised with dread, and she wasn't sure whether to cry or throw up. She knew when this had happened before but didn't want to believe it. "Oh my fucking God."

"What?" Eilidh turned to meet her widened eyes. "Darcy, talk to me. You're shaking."

"It can't be. Tell me it can't be. She wouldn't."

"Who wouldn't? Darcy you're not making sense."

"Anja." The name almost stuck in her throat but she forced it out in to the open.

"Anja? You think she had something to do with this?"

The memories came back in a rush. They knocked her back in to a cushion, and Eilidh's hand gripped her arm. "Darcy, what's wrong?"

Eilidh's voice faded to the background, and suddenly Darcy was in the hot tub, drinking cheap wine and laughing. Someone was with her. It was Anja. So Anja had got into the hot tub after all. Why would she lie about that?

Oh fuck. Anja's lips were on hers. She had kissed Anja in the hot tub. Or had Anja kissed Darcy? Then Darcy was pushing her away, and they were both crying. Shouting. She could see Anja kneeling in the snow. Then headlights in her rearview mirror, and she was crying again. All the while Anja's voice pounding over and over in her ears: "I love you."

"All this time," she whispered. "It's been her." Darcy tried piecing it all together, but the picture still wasn't whole. "That night. She told me that night."

"Shit, shit, shit." Eilidh's swearing brought her back to the porch. "Are you sure? What do you remember?"

"Enough." Darcy broke down in tears. "I remember enough."

Chapter 51

THE SILENCE WAS TORTURE. ANJA couldn't bear it.

She rechecked her phone, but still nothing from Darcy. What had she expected? It had only been a few hours, and she'd left Darcy with a heap of confessions to digest. The longer it was, the less likely Anja knew that she'd hear what she wanted, and that thought shredded her insides.

A weight bore down on her, one she had yet to unload and share with Darcy.

Her true identity.

It had seemed too much in the moment. The night of the accident had sat in the fore of her mind, urging her not to go too far, not to blow it again. It told her if Darcy felt the same, then she would understand the rest. She would have to.

Darcy would never know she was the stalker.

That needed to be buried deep, nailed shut in a box never to resurface. Their shared history, Anja's origins, and their familial ties were one thing. But Anja's journey to this point had to remain hers alone.

Her mother's voice chided her.

"How could you allow this to happen? How could you fall in love with her?"

Anja pleaded with her to stop.

"I'm so sorry, Mum. Please understand? I couldn't help it."

But as always, she was relentless.

"You're nothing but a failure. I knew you wouldn't be strong enough for this. I knew you would let me down."

Anja held back her tears. She wouldn't give her mother any more of them.

"What else can I do? I've given you years of my life. I tried my best. But this isn't the way. You have to let go. You have to let me go."

"So that's it. No one will pay for my death? You can forget about me that easily?"

Forget? How could Anja ever forget? About her sorry excuse for a childhood and the path towards death that her mother had chosen. She saw that now. It hadn't been anyone else's decision but her own.

She shook the voice off. It wouldn't control her anymore. She didn't need it, didn't want it. This was a chance for her life to finally be her own, lived on her terms with a semblance of happiness within reach.

What if Darcy says no?

Could she live with that? Watch Darcy as she fell in love with someone else? Fulfilled her dreams and ambitions with a stranger whilst Anja watched from the side-lines. She knew nothing would be the same, but what if it was worse? What if Darcy dropped out of her life completely? Left her job, moved away, broke all contact.

The thought was terrifying and left Anja numb.

She could never allow that to happen, wouldn't stand by and watch her dreams walk away.

Her phone beeped, and she flinched. Darcy's name shone out from a text, and her stomach churned with the possibility that it was good as well as the abject fear that it was bad. With a trembling hand, she tapped on the message.

Come to the cabin. We need to talk. D

Eilidh had begged Darcy to call the police, to leave it in their hands, but Darcy wasn't ready. She needed answers now, and they had to come direct from Anja or she wasn't sure she'd believe any of it.

As Anja's car pulled up by the cabin, panic threatened to get the better of her. Eilidh rubbed her back soothingly and laid a firm kiss on her cheek. "I'm right here if you need me. I won't interfere, but I'm here."

She moved to sit in the armchair, and Darcy smiled gratefully. "Thank you for staying."

A tentative tap came at the door, and that unsettled her even more. Anja never knocked.

"Come in," she called. Rooted to the spot, she leaned back against the sofa for support as Anja stepped inside. She hadn't been prepared for the moment she would stand in front of Darcy again. Bright and beautiful, almost every inch of her mind and soul had been known to Darcy, or so she had thought.

Anja glanced across the room, and confusion shrouded her features when she realised Eilidh was there. "I thought we were going to talk."

"We are." Darcy's voice shook, and she took a breath to steady it. "I wanted Eilidh here. This affects her too."

"It does?" Anja remained confused, and Darcy hated with every fibre what she was about to ask. If she was right, it would unravel everything Darcy thought she knew, about Anja, about herself. If she was wrong, it would be an unforgivable betrayal that she could accuse her friend of such a horrendous thing. But nothing else fitted with the memories from that night, and it was clear Anja had already been dishonest with her about what had happened.

"Are you the person who's been stalking me?" She hadn't meant to be so blunt, but what other way was there to ask such a question?

The colour drained from Anja's face, and she reached out for support. When nothing met her hand, she buckled and Darcy automatically went to her. She pulled a chair out from the dining table and eased her in to it. It took a moment to realise what Anja's reaction meant, and when that registered, Darcy flinched away as if scorched.

She felt sick. Bile rose in her throat, but she swallowed it back. She had to stay in one piece. Had to stay strong if only to get the answers she needed. She couldn't run away from this, and she wasn't going to let Anja run either.

"I need you to say it, Anja. Answer me. I can't believe it otherwise."

Anja looked up with tears swimming in her eyes. "Not until you hear me out. Not until I get to tell you the rest of the story."

Darcy held the gaze of the friend she loved. A woman who had stood by her in the darkest hours, had held her and reassured her. A woman who had brought so much joy and laughter to Darcy's life, had enhanced and lifted her higher.

Had that afforded her a chance to explain? To try and make Darcy understand how she had also been the cause of all those dark hours of despair and torment?

She dragged a chair out of reach of Anja, sat heavily, and clasped her hands tight together, focused on slowing her breathing. Her heartrate. As rage broiled deep in the core of her chest, she took a moment to steady herself before nodding that Anja should begin. Eilidh remained quiet in her peripheral vision, and Darcy knew she would be itching to scream and shout on Darcy's behalf. "I want everything, Anja. Leave nothing out."

She watched Anja take a shuddering breath. She looked toward the heavens for a moment before bringing her attention back to Darcy. When she began, her voice was low, resigned. "My mum liked a simple life."

Mention of Anja's mum threw Darcy. She had never talked about her more than to say that they weren't close and didn't really keep in contact.

"She was happy staying home, making it a place me and my father loved to come back to. We were her world, and she made sure we knew that every day. But it wasn't enough. Not for him, anyway."

Darcy wasn't sure why this was relevant but gave Anja the time. Allowed her to continue. Although not immediately apparent, Darcy thought it might help give her answers eventually.

"What happened?"

Anja smirked then. "Your family happened."

Darcy shook her head in confusion. "My family?"

"Yes. You and your mum." Anja was on her feet. Eilidh made to get up as well, but Darcy held a calming hand up and she stayed where she was. Darcy watched as Anja paced towards the kitchen and back again. Agitated. No longer able to look at Darcy.

"Anja, I don't understand? What do my mum and I have to do with your family?"

"You stole him away." Anja's voice rose, and she pointed an angry finger at Darcy. "Your mum with her looks and her grand ideas of moving abroad, exploring the world. And you, the perfect, ready-made daughter. It was so easy for him to swap one family for another. To leave us behind."

Darcy tried to connect the dots. Make sense of what Anja was saying. Had Anja's dad become Darcy's stepdad? Cameron? Was Anja his other family? She'd known a little about his past. That he'd been married before, but from what she had gleaned his ex was crazy and manipulative and wouldn't allow him to see his daughter. She'd turned her against him. So when the opportunity had come up to start again in Australia, they'd taken it.

"It wasn't that simple, Anja."

She stopped her pacing and turned her glare towards Darcy. "You knew about us?"

"No. I mean, yes. A little. But it was your mum that stopped him from seeing you. He wanted to, and I remember he would get upset if I asked about you. He wouldn't even say your name. I thought I might get a stepsister, someone to share things with. But he said it was dangerous for you at home, that your mum was manipulative and had threatened all sorts if he tried to keep in touch. So he had to accept that he might never see you again."

"That's a pathetic excuse and an outright lie. It was him who abandoned her. Us. Before he left, she was loving, and calm, and happy. It was him who manipulated her, destroyed her. He took away everything she held dear, as a mother and as a wife. I think he was actually glad when my mum found out about the affair; it gave the gutless bastard an out. It meant he didn't have to make a decision for himself."

"I can only tell you what he said to me, Anja. I know nothing more about it. But why didn't you tell me all this? When we first met? When you realised who I was? Why hide it from me? I could have helped, talked about it with you."

But Anja wasn't listening. Her anger was palpable. She was immersed in her story and wasn't coming back until it was told.

"He made my mum think the life she had with him was worthless. It ruined her, and she was never the same. He took her away from me as well. You all did. You left me with nothing. With no one."

There was venom in her words. Darcy had never experienced this side of her. It had clearly been hidden well over the years, and it made her ugly. Darcy couldn't reconcile the woman before her with the one she'd called her best friend. Her surface beauty no longer masked what clearly rotted inside of her.

"It wasn't my fault, Anja. Are you hearing me? I was a child. How could I have changed any of this?"

"Exactly. We were both children, but he picked you, Darcy. You. He deserted me and became your father instead. Do you have any idea how that feels? To know you're not enough for someone who is meant to love you unconditionally? To protect you from the world."

"Do you know what it was like growing up in that house? My mother became nothing more than a stain on it. Bitter and callous. She looked at me, and I knew she saw him. Saw something she hated. Until she stopped looking at me altogether. She left money on the kitchen table every Monday, for school supplies, food, clothes, but that's as far as her parenting went. No more exploring in the woods, foraging for dinner, picking flowers, laughing. Nothing. She would 'go for a walk' and not come back for days. I knew she was getting trashed in the local tavern and going home with any guy who gave her a second look. I heard how people talked about her. The town whore. If she were a guy, she would be celebrated, but that's not how the world works, is it? Imagine hearing the kids at school saying those things about your mother."

"Anja, I'm sorry." And Darcy was. She couldn't imagine such a loveless, lonely childhood. A well of guilt rose knowing she had Anja's dad there for her whilst Anja had suffered and went without. Still, the anger rose with it. That Anja blamed her. Darcy had been an innocent child in all of this.

"You're sorry? Oh, well, that makes it all fucking better. Tell me what was it like for you? Growing up with someone else's dad, knowing you'd taken him away from another child. Did you think about that? Did I ever cross your mind? Did you ever wonder how I was without my dad?"

Darcy was afraid to answer honestly but knew it was the only way. "No. I didn't. I guess after being told not to ask about you, because it upset him, I moved on and forgot."

Anja slumped back in the chair and laughed mirthlessly. "But you'd lost your own dad. That's right, isn't it? He died when you were young. Didn't it occur to you that there was another young girl out there feeling how you had then? Didn't it occur to your fucking tramp of a mother that she was breaking up another family?"

"Now wait a minute." Darcy was on her feet then. "You don't get to talk about my mother in that way. Families fall apart all the time, Anja, you're not unique. My mother did nothing wrong. She didn't ask him to fall in love with her. She didn't ask him to leave."

"That's lies. Don't be so bloody naïve, Darcy. Of course she wanted him to pick her. She loved him too and wanted him for herself."

"What happened to your mum?" It was the first Eilidh had spoken, and it broke the standoff that Darcy and Anja now found themselves in. They moved apart, back to their respective chairs.

Anja clutched her head in her hands and when she looked up her eyes were red rimmed with fresh tears. "Drink. Prescription drugs. You name it. Then one day she broke completely. I found her lying in the bath surrounded by her own vomit and empty booze bottles. She was so still. The water had barely a ripple. I remember how wrinkled her hands were, the blue of her lips. But it was her eyes, open and staring straight at me. Asking me why. I was sixteen."

She scrubbed at her face and then looked Darcy dead in the eye, dared her to look away. "There was a letter on the floor from his work. Informing her of his death and the benefit payable to her because of it. He hadn't changed it to your mum's name. That was the day she gave up, stopped asking herself if he was going to come home to her."

Darcy felt her own tears slip free as Anja buried her head in her arms and sobbed. She needed time to think. Everything she had known about Anja had been a lie, but she still loved her. She had seen the other side of her. Or had that been a pretence? Was this the real Anja? Bitter and twisted and filled with hatred. Anja wasn't even her real name: Cameron had called her Annika. Olsen must be fake as well, or else it was her mother's name.

Anja's story was shocking and tore at her heart, but it hadn't all been roses for Darcy and she refused to be blamed for Cameron's choices. For Anja's mum's choices. They weren't her doing, and Anja's blame was beyond misguided.

"How the fuck do you think my mum and I felt when he died?"

Anja's head rose. She seemed wary and didn't reply.

"We were left alone too. Along with a sister destined to depend on us forever. Your half-sister." It was the first time Darcy had ever mentioned her sister to Anja, but she showed no sign of surprise. "Did you know about her?"

Anja glanced towards Eilidh, then back at Darcy. "Bridget told me. She assumed I knew about her."

"So you know about her condition? What it takes to look after her? He left us on the other side of the world with barely a penny. I worked from when I was fourteen and Mum took every evening job going because that was when the carers came in and I could help them get Olivia to bed."

"Olivia," Anja murmured the name under her breath. "I never knew her name."

"Yes, Olivia. Our sister. Who relies on my mum for everything and is the reason they're still in Australia. The reason I came back here alone to study for free so I could send money back once I graduated."

"Oh, how noble. It changes nothing. Your mum getting knocked up with her was probably half the reason why my dad left."

Darcy shot out of her chair and unleashed a stinging slap across Anja's face. "How fucking dare you? She did nothing to cause this, and neither did I. The only people you should be blaming is your parents and yourself. You're the one that's twisted all of this, Anja. You're the one that's brought us to this point. What kind of sick game have you been playing?" She shoved both Anja's shoulders, pushed her upright, and forced her to look up. "I want my answer. I've heard enough of your bullshit. Are you my fucking stalker?"

Anja held a palm to her scorched cheek. Darcy saw her jaw muscles work as she clenched her teeth, but the slap seemed to have knocked the spite from her. Now only remorse swam in her eyes, and her expression was one Darcy recognised. One she would normally be doing anything to take away. Sorrow and pain.

"Yes," she whispered.

Chapter 52

Eilidh watched Darcy crumple to the floor as Anja finally admitted it. Until that moment, she had watched on patiently and quiet as promised.

She got to her feet. "Leave. Now."

Anja reached for Darcy, but Eilidh was between them before she had a chance to lay a hand on her.

"I said leave."

"It's not up to you." Anja was defiant. She tried to push past Eilidh to where Darcy sobbed on the floor, but Eilidh stood firm.

"Either you get out now, or I get the police to come and take you away for me."

That stopped her.

"You wouldn't. Darcy, tell her. Tell her I can stay. I want to figure this out with you. I need you to understand."

"Try me." Eilidh took a step in to her space. "The only reason I haven't already is because I care about Darcy and it should be on her terms. But I will if you push me."

"Care about her? I love her." Anja stood her ground. "You've been around five minutes. You don't know her. You don't know us."

"I know enough to laugh at what you call love. You think terrifying her was love? Tormenting her all this time? And now what? You tell her you love her, and she's meant to forgive all that?"

"Get out of my way, Eilidh. You don't speak for her."

"No, she doesn't." Darcy slowly rose to her feet. It was obvious to Eilidh she was in pain, physically and mentally. Eilidh watched her drag her injured leg, hold on to it as she attempted to stand tall. "But she's right. You need to get out of here before I do something I might regret."

Anja looked between them both, and Eilidh's stare never wavered. She braced herself for any sudden movements, any inkling that Anja wasn't going to go quietly. Instead, she kept her focus on Darcy, their gaze never breaking. "I know this started out all wrong. I know what I've done might be unforgiveable. But you have to believe me when I tell you how sorry I am. How much I regret every moment of pain I've caused you."

Darcy didn't respond. Eilidh held back the rage that wanted her to shove Anja to the door. That wanted to slap her as well and worse. She took a step, and Anja held up her hands.

"I'm going."

Quiet drifted over them once the sound of Anja's retreating car had disappeared. Eilidh turned to Darcy and shook her head. She was dumbfounded, unable to form anything coherent that might help.

"Fuck."

She watched Darcy slowly move to the sofa and joined her. She began to cry again and allowed Eilidh to hold her close. Great, wracking sobs tore through her, and she shook in Eilidh's arms. "How could she blame me? I was a kid. It wasn't my fault."

Eilidh knew she didn't want answers; she was simply trying to make sense of it.

"We should call the police, Darcy. They need to deal with this."

"No." She shook her head against Eilidh's chest. "I can't do that. Not yet."

"Are you serious?" Eilidh pulled away and held her by the shoulders. "After everything she's done, she doesn't deserve your compassion. Don't be fooled by her anymore."

"I'm exhausted. I need time to think about it all. She's not going anywhere."

Eilidh couldn't believe what she was hearing. After everything Anja had put her through, she still had a hold over Darcy. She still clouded her judgement and demanded understanding and kindness, and all the other things Darcy offered in the name of friendship.

"Are you sure about that? She could already be packing her bags."

"Well, at least then she'll be out of my life. She's been through so much; is sending her to prison really going to help?"

She was asking for Eilidh's support. For her to confirm that offering Anja some kind of leniency in the name of empathy was all right. That she wasn't being weak, unable to do the hard thing. Eilidh wanted to accept it, but a voice screamed that Anja should pay for all the hurt she had caused. No matter her motivation.

"What about what you've been through? After everything, are you really going to let her walk away? She needs help, Darcy. Who knows what she might do next? For both our safety, she needs to be handed over to the authorities. They'll get her the help she needs."

"And what if they don't? What if they lock her up and all she's left with is another thing to blame me for? Another way in which I've destroyed her life. Despite it all, I can't switch off how I feel about her. Don't you get that?"

"How you feel about her? Don't tell me... Darcy, do you love her? In *that* way?"

"No. I realised earlier that I never have, but I didn't know how to tell her." She reached to smooth the lines on Eilidh's brow and traced a finger down her cheek. "Tell her that I couldn't feel that way about her, because it's how I feel about you."

They were words Eilidh had longed to hear, and she hated that Anja had tinged them with sorrow and regret, but Darcy had still kept them only for her. That fact overrode the negativity and brought a sheepish smile to her face.

"You don't half-pick your moments."

Darcy returned her smile and leaned in to her again. Looping her arms around Eilidh's waist, she pulled her closer. "Is there ever a right time for these things? It seems the world isn't as perfect as I wished for."

Eilidh lay back on the sofa, shuffling Darcy with her so they lay intertwined, Darcy's head on her chest. However unrealistic Darcy's expectations of the world were, Eilidh loved her for her optimism. Her unwavering faith that it could all be wonderful if you tried hard enough and believed in it.

"We'll figure this out," she whispered into Darcy's hair. "Rest a while and then we'll make a plan to make it perfect again."

Chapter 53

Anja's tears had turned into something else. Fury burned in her throat as she watched Eilidh and Darcy embrace on the sofa. Watched that interfering bitch comfort Darcy. Who the hell did she think she was? Sat there in judgement of Anja, putting words into Darcy's mouth and forcing her to leave.

It was all over.

She knew that now.

Eilidh had won.

Night fell around her as a multitude of options circled her mind. She could run back to Norway. Or another country entirely? Maybe Darcy wouldn't call the police. Would stand up to Eilidh and allow her to leave.

The thought of never seeing Darcy again tore in to her gut.

What was the alternative? Stick around and hope that Darcy was able to continue as normal and forget all of it had happened? She laughed out loud into the damp air. There was no fucking way that was happening. At least not with Eilidh still around, whispering in Darcy's ear, driving her and Anja further apart.

She could stay in Inverness, quit her job, and keep some distance. Allow Darcy time to process it all, time to calm down, get over the initial anger and maybe see how Anja had been led down such a dirty path. Anja would agree to get help, to talk to a professional, to show Darcy that the side she loved was real. It existed. It hadn't all been a lie.

No matter what route she considered, one person was always a clear obstacle. The reason she was sitting cold and wet in the goddamn muddy woods on the outside, while that someone lay warm and cosy in Darcy's arms.

Eilidh.

Her smug face as Anja had left the cabin taunted her. She knew she had won. Had stolen Darcy from under Anja's nose without a second thought. The only thing Anja had left in the world now belonged to Eilidh, and it made no sense.

Why would Darcy pick her over me?

Even before Darcy had known the whole story, the stalking, the family shit, the lies—disregard all that and she had still fallen for Eilidh over Anja.

So what if she didn't call the police? So what if Anja stuck around? So what if Darcy eventually forgave her?

Anja would never have Darcy back.

Not as a friend.

Not as anything more.

Their world would never be the same, and Eilidh would always be a fucking part of it.

What did they say? *It was better to have loved and lost than never to have loved at all?* Could that be right? Was losing Darcy the only way for Anja to move on?

If she walked away, she would always know Darcy was out there.

With Eilidh.

Fucking Eilidh.

She'd ruined it all. Why the hell should she get to live out Anja's dream? Why did they get to be happy together? While Anja continued to suffer and tear herself apart over everything that had been done to her because of the choices others had made.

The rage she had tempered down as her love for Darcy had grown wrapped its ice-cold fingers around her heart once again. Her mother's voice chided her still.

Don't let them get away with it.

Time to finish what you started.

Chapter 54

THE SMOKE CLOYED IN DARCY'S throat, and she clawed at it, gasping for one clear breath. The blood coated her eyes and nostrils, as suffocating as the smoke. She tried to hold her breath a moment, to give herself time to figure out how to get out of the car, how to make her limbs work again.

Then someone was shaking her, calling her name. It was the voice. Her saviour.

"Darcy, wake up."

Her body shook again, and she tried to drag her eyelids open. *Wake up?* Was the accident only a terrible dream?

"Darcy," the voice shouted close to her again, and she felt her body being lifted upright.

She thought her eyes were open, but her vision was blurred; it stung. The smoke still sucked life from her lungs, and she coughed, bending double as it scorched her throat.

"What the fuck?"

"Quick. We need to get out of here, Darcy. The cabin's on fire."

It wasn't a dream. Darcy was wide awake as Eilidh's words hit her.

She scanned around, disoriented, and then remembered the sofa underneath. They were in the living room, had fallen asleep on it. "Eilidh, what's happening?"

Eilidh held her sleeve over her mouth and tugged at Darcy's for her to do the same. "I've no idea. All I know is we have to get out of here."

The smoke came at them in all directions; flames licked high at the door and front and side windows, the wood providing eager kindling. "The back bedroom," she shouted through heaving coughs. "The porch drops off to the burn. We can lower ourselves down to it."

Eilidh nodded and gripped her hand. "Stay close. Don't let go."

Darcy clung on, willing her bad leg to keep Eilidh's pace as she charged for the corridor that led to the bedrooms. The smoke dissipated a little but still hung heavy. Eilidh let go of her hand and tentatively tapped the door handle, feeling for heat. She nodded that it was safe, and they jumped back as she swung the door open. Blackness billowed from the room, and Darcy immediately caught sight of the flames rising outside the window.

Eilidh tugged her to it and cracked it open. They both pressed their mouths to the gap, but there was no relief to be found. "It's the porch that's on fire. We're surrounded."

They both ducked under the windowsill, close to the floor. Darcy was nearing panic; she felt it rise with every parched and painful breath. "It's too dangerous to try and jump it from here. The drop is too high."

Eilidh held her close, eyes screwed against the smoke. Darcy knew she was searching for an answer and wracked her brains for one of her own.

"The front door. It opens outwards, right?"

Darcy nodded. "We could make a run for it? The steps are right in front of the door."

Eilidh grabbed her hand and yanked her back towards the hallway. Her leg gave way and she stumbled, losing her grip on Eilidh. Strong arms hooked under hers and lifted her upright again before Eilidh tucked her head under one of Darcy's arms and offered more support. At the bathroom door, she repeated the same procedure as before, and they burst through into another room smouldering in flames. "Stand there."

Eilidh left her propped up against the tile while she saturated towels in water. She draped one around each of their shoulders before doing the same with two more. She lifted Darcy's arm again and retook her previous position. "Are your crutches by the front door?"

"Aye. But I'll be fine without them."

Eilidh started them back down the hallway into the living space, keeping them as low as possible. The front wall was blackening, and shards of glass lay scattered where the window had popped. The blaze rose within, reaching for the ceiling, the curtains, for anything that would feed its insatiable appetite.

She watched as Eilidh grabbed a crutch and angled it to push down the door handle from a distance. The door swung open, and flames immediately filled the space. She returned to Darcy and tented the towels over their heads. "When I say run, we go together. Block the pain, Darcy. Make that leg move. Get through the door and don't stop. Keep your face covered as much as you can."

Darcy squeezed her arm around Eilidh's waist and held her gaze a moment. "We can do this."

"Ready?" Eilidh set herself, taking much of Darcy's weight. "Run."

Darcy half-ran and was half-dragged, but she didn't stop. Pain tore up through her leg, and her lungs cried out as Eilidh led with her shoulder and they burst through the front door. The steps were invisible and came upon them fast. They crumpled together as gravity took them, a mass of limbs falling through the heat and acrid stench.

She heard Eilidh cry out before they landed with a heavy thud. Darcy gulped at the air, searching for relief. She felt around for Eilidh and found her lying nearby, eyes closed and still.

Darcy's leg protested as she shuffled across the ground, but concern for Eilidh pushed her through. "Eilidh, can you hear me?" She shook her shoulders and tapped lightly on her face. A groan came from her and then she was coughing, her eyes still closed as she heaved mighty breaths whilst clutching at Darcy's arms.

"It's okay. We're okay."

"My ankle." Eilidh choked out.

"Is it broke?" Darcy was afraid to look but forced herself. It seemed to be in the correct position, but that didn't mean damage hadn't been done.

"I'm not sure. Help me up."

Between Darcy's leg and Eilidh's ankle, they struggled but eventually made it upright. Darcy clung on to her, as she surveyed the blazing mass that had been her cabin. The night was broken by pops and crackles, as more windows gave way to the inferno and all Darcy's earthly belongings were consumed. It was oddly mesmerising, and despite the tears that streaked her face, Darcy couldn't look away.

"I'm so sorry, Darcy." Eilidh tucked her face in to Darcy's neck and drew her close. "I'm so sorry."

A wild scream cut through the moment of grief as Anja streaked from the depths of the woods, a log held high in her hands. It came down before either had a moment to grasp what was happening, crashing against Eilidh's arm as she raised it to protect them both.

Darcy fell to the ground as Anja raised her arm again, swinging the makeshift mallet against Eilidh's body.

From the ground, Darcy reached out and clutched Anja's legs, redirecting her attention from Eilidh. But Anja fought against it, and the blows continued to rain. Anja sat on top of Eilidh, the log discarded; she continued the assault with her fists.

Eilidh had stopped defending herself, her eyes closed again, her body limp.

Darcy rose to her knees and threw herself at Anja, tackling her from behind, hooking her arms around Anja's neck and dragging her away from Eilidh's battered body. Anja fought against her, and they rolled a few times, each vying to pin the other to the mud.

Darcy's wrist was her downfall. Anja straddled her and brought a stinging hand across her face. It made Darcy's ears ring, but she could still hear Anja's chastising words. "It was meant to be me. You were meant to pick me. This is all your fault."

Over and over, the words tumbled from her lips, dripping with scorn. "Anja, stop. Look at me. Look what you're doing." Darcy tried in vain to avoid each vicious swipe. She tried to meet Anja's eyes, but they were gone, glazed with cruelty. Her hands wrapped around Darcy's neck and squeezed. "No. An, no." Darcy's cries were stifled, and she clawed at Anja's fingers. "Please." Her body bucked as she tried to throw Anja off, but it only made her clutch harder.

Anja wasn't listening. "It was meant to be me. It was meant to be me." She spat the words through gritted teeth before raising Darcy's head by the neck and slamming it in to the ground. "It was meant to be..."

A dull thud broke the cycle, and Anja's eyes widened. Her grip released, and Darcy slapped her hands away as she fell sideways. In her vision, Anja was replaced by Eilidh, stood on one foot, her face bloodied and the log in her hands.

Darcy scrabbled fully away from Anja's crumpled body, and Eilidh threw the log aside in disgust. "Are you all right?" She reached for Darcy's hand and helped pull her up.

Darcy rubbed at her throat. "Fuck. Aye, I'm okay." She gripped on to Eilidh. "Do you think she's alive?"

They both stared down at Anja's still form as sirens rang blissfully in the distance. "I don't intend on checking."

The fire flared up through the roof of the cabin, and Darcy knew it was lost. All of it. She leaned in to Eilidh, and they propped each other up. "I can't watch anymore."

Eilidh tugged her away, and they retreated from both Anja's menace and the crumbling cabin. Through the pain, they made their way down the track as the glow of orange flames became blue flashing lights.

"You're safe," Eilidh murmured close to her ear. "We're safe."

Chapter 55

Darcy began to cry as soon as her mum's face appeared on the screen.

"Hey, sweetheart. What's wrong?" She reached out as if she could touch Darcy through the computer. "Are you in pain?"

Liz's tone was soothing, and Darcy would have given anything in that moment to feel her mum's arms wrap around her.

"Anja." She choked out. "Cameron's daughter. My stalker."

She watched her mum's eyebrows furrow in confusion. "Anja's your stalker? And what about Cameron? You're not making sense."

Darcy blew her nose and then gulped at some water, trying to find a measure of composure that would allow her to tell her mum everything that had happened.

She watched as Liz's eyes widened with every new revelation before she dissolved into tears as Darcy relayed the moment it had all come apart at the cabin and the weight of it sank in.

"I don't understand why on earth she decided to blame you. And the deception? Darcy, I'm so sorry, my love."

"It's not your fault, Mum. Don't ever think it's your fault."

"I know, but—"

"But nothing. Anja, or Annika, whatever her real name is, this is all on her. This isn't how she needed to do things no matter what ugliness happened in her past."

"I just can't believe it's been her all along. I can't believe I trusted her to take care of you when I couldn't be there after the accident. If I could get my hands on her..."

"I know, Mum. I feel so angry at everything as well. At the situation, at her, at myself. I can't believe I fell for it. She fooled me for so long and then tried to excuse it by saying she loved me."

Liz shook her head. "That's not love, sweetheart. That's a very broken person who never got the love and help they needed."

Darcy sighed and slumped back in her chair. "I can't help wondering what might have happened if Cameron had tried harder to see her. Does that make me a terrible person? I'm not blaming him, but maybe we did give up too easily? She could've been part of our family."

"Ah, hindsight is always what makes us feel guilty, Darcy." Liz sighed and scrubbed her face of fresh tears. "Cameron tried his best where that girl was concerned, but her mother was impossible. As far as he knew Annika was being taken care of. He sent money and presents, but with the threats her mother made, I guess it became easier for him to make peace with the fact that he wasn't going to see her again. So he focused on you and Olivia. I have every faith though that if he hadn't died, Cameron would have gone looking for her once she turned eighteen."

"Maybe. Although by then it still might have been too late."

Darcy wondered how long the "what ifs" and "buts" would plague her. She imagined they would never leave her and she would always carry a measure of guilt, despite so many of the events that lead to Anja's self-destruction being out of her control.

"I guess we'll never know." Liz took a steadying breath and moved closer to the screen. "What can I do to help, darling? And what about Eilidh? Is she okay? Is she with you?"

Darcy nodded and was surprised when a small smile came to her lips. "I'm staying with her for now. Until I can figure this whole mess out. She's been great through it all."

"She sounds pretty great to me. First saving your life and now this. It seems I have a lot to thank her for."

"Aye, one day, Mum. I hope you'll get to meet her."

"Why wait? You should come to visit and bring Eilidh with you. I'm betting a bit of quiet time by the pool is exactly what you both need right now. It would give us the chance to talk properly. I miss you, Darcy. Every day."

Liz visibly perked up at the suggestion, and a flutter of excitement and hope passed through Darcy at the thought of seeing her mum and Olivia.

She missed them too. It had been too long, and the opportunity to put some distance between herself and Anja was tempting.

"Really? I mean, it wouldn't be for a while yet. There's a lot to sort out at this end with the police, my court case, and the cabin."

She stifled another sob at the thought of her beautiful cabin razed to the ground. She knew the most important thing was that she and Eilidh had escaped alive, but seeing the charred ruins of her former safe haven had devastated her.

"Whenever you're ready, we'll be waiting for you, my love." Liz reached out towards her again. "Come be with your family, Darcy. Come to Australia."

Chapter 56

EILIDH PLONKED TWO MORE PINTS on the table in their usual corner of The Castle. She dropped heavily on to a chair and waited while Sam took a couple of hefty gulps and composed himself.

"I don't even know where to begin. This is so fucked up."

Eilidh took a healthy swig of her own drink. "Tell me about it. I think it'll be a long time before I can wrap my head around it all."

"Nae wonder." He squeezed her arm. "I've got like a hundred questions already."

"Imagine how Darcy feels."

Sam blew out a long breath. "Poor Darcy. After everything she's been through already. It's all so unfair."

"I know, mate. I'm so fucking angry and it's all I can do to hold it together. We're going to be picking up the pieces for a long time yet, but I guess all we can do is take it one day at a time."

"Aye, I get it. The anger, I mean. I'm raging for you both. I don't understand how someone could lie and twist things in their own mind like that for so long, yet seem so normal to everyone else."

"She fooled us all, Tommo. No one was immune to her bullshit."

"Where is she now, then?"

Eilidh shrugged. "Locked up, obviously, but we aren't sure where yet. She probably went to the hospital first. The police will want to interview us more, and my guess is there'll be a whole number of assessments done where Anja's concerned. I'm not sure prison is where she needs to be."

They were both quiet, and Eilidh sipped her pint as Sam continued to digest it all.

"So Anja and Darcy are stepsisters, then?"

"I suppose technically they are. Although they obviously didn't grow up together or really know anything about the other. They were so young when everything happened between Anja's dad and Darcy's mum. Darcy knew her as Annika then, and when they moved to Australia, she was told not to ask about her anymore."

"All this time it's been her. Torturing Darcy and threatening you."

"Yup." Eilidh shook her head in wonder. "After her mum died I guess it all just unravelled from there."

"Why Darcy though? Why not blame Liz? Or her dad?"

"Oh, I think she does. But she was curious about Darcy, I think because they were similar in age and in Anja's fucked-up view of the world, Darcy had replaced her. So she tracked her down and the obsession must have grown from there. From everything she said at the cabin that night, it's like all her anger and guilt was wrapped up in this little Darcy box and hurting her was the only way to make herself feel better."

"Until she fell in love with her."

Eilidh smirked. "If you can call it that. I don't think Anja truly knows how she feels about anything, never mind love. That's if she even feels at all."

"Wow." Sam sat back wide-eyed. "Is it wrong to sort of feel sorry for her?"

Eilidh shrugged. "I don't think so. I know that's what Darcy is struggling with right now. After everything she still feels bad about what Anja went through. I guess she thinks if she can put herself in Anja's shoes, she might understand how it escalated to all this and somehow figure out why it happened."

Sam shook his head in disbelief and blew out a long breath. "By the sound of it I'm not sure Anja could explain that, never mind Darcy trying to figure it out herself."

"I know. But it's a process. I've got to let her work through it in her own way and just be there for her."

Sam reached for her hand and squeezed. "Well, at least that's one good thing to have come out of it all."

"What?"

"It brought you both together. She's pretty great, Eilidh."

Eilidh smiled then at the thought that Darcy would be there when she got home that night.

"She really is."

He grinned. "You're smitten."

"A wee bit," she admitted, and clinked his glass.

He smiled, and Eilidh felt a moment of normalcy. It felt good just her and Sam in the pub, doing their usual thing by putting the world to rights over a few pints. She knew there would be more questions, she had a thousand of them herself, but for now she would savour every minute that Anja wasn't at the forefront of her mind.

"So when do you head off on your Australian adventure?"

"As soon as possible, and I can't fricking wait."

"I bet. You both deserve it. Although I'll miss you."

Eilidh scooped up their empty glasses and stood ready to head to the bar. She punched a meaty bicep playfully and kissed the top of his head. "I'll miss you too, Tommo."

Chapter 57

ANJA'S BODY FELT LEADEN AND useless. It refused do or say what she wanted whilst inside she screamed. She called for Darcy over and over, but no one was listening.

She blearily took in her surroundings. Two uniformed officers filled the small space, and she groaned as every awful moment from that night flooded her memory.

The throbbing in her head was relentless. It wouldn't give her space to think, and panic settled on her chest, robbing the breath from her lungs. She wanted Darcy, needed her there at her side to tell her it would all be okay, the same as Anja had done when the roles had been reversed.

You're never going to see her again.

Her mother's voice penetrated the fog, brutal and unflinching as always. She delighted in Anja's misery and failure.

All that time, all that work and planning, and you threw it all away for a daydream.

Shut up. Shut up. Shut up.

She screwed her eyes closed and focused on the pain, implored it to block the voice out. She needed to think, to figure out a way to make everything okay because the voice was right—that was the worst part—she had failed.

All because of Eilidh.

Eilidh had fucked everything up and stolen Anja's world away.

You can't blame her. You did this to yourself.

Anja refused to accept that. Yes, she had messed up in the end, but without Eilidh's interference, she knew it could have worked with Darcy. It would have. It was Eilidh who had pushed her to the edge, had forced her to let the voice take over and caused the chaos at the cabin.

The smell of smoke clung to her nostrils, and she longed to wash it away, along with the cruel events of that night. Anja had never meant to do any of it, but she had been powerless to stop it. She had lost herself to the voice for only a few moments, but it had been long enough.

Oh God, the cabin. Darcy's beautiful home reduced to ash because Anja had lost control. She had allowed her mother to consume her thoughts and actions, and then torn down everything that mattered to Darcy. Her home, their friendship, their love.

The thought of hurting Darcy in any way now ripped her apart. Anja needed to see her, to apologise, to beg and ask her what needed to be done to make it all right.

You'll never make this right.

Her limbs began to come back to life, and she writhed and twisted under the rough sheets, straining against them in an attempt to sit up. Her body bucked as she yanked and rattled her handcuffed wrists against the bars of the bed.

She pleaded with the police officers. "Please. I have to see Darcy. Let me out of here."

The one sat next to her stood and grabbed at her hands. He was firm and held them tight. "If you don't stop that I'll call the doctor and get him to knock you out again. Make this easier on yourself and behave."

"I have to see her. I need her." She saw pity in the officer's eyes and felt the fight desert her body. She relented and dropped back against the pillows with a heavy sigh. "You have to let me talk to her."

He sat down again and smirked. "The only person you'll be talking to is your solicitor and a detective. So calm yourself. Then this'll go a whole lot smoother for all of us."

Anja turned her attention to the officer stood at the door, but she avoided meeting Anja's sorrowful gaze. Instead, she pulled a vibrating phone from her pocket and spoke quietly in to it.

"Aye, she's awake. Seems okay, but I'll get the doctor in to take another look and report back." The officer nodded a few times and murmured her agreement to questions that Anja couldn't hear. She wished she knew what was being said about her. What her fate was.

It wasn't long before she found out.

She had a mild concussion, a couple of stitches and bruises, and was declared fit to be transported to the police station.

Where you belong.

She couldn't argue with the voice. As the car sped towards impending incarceration, her heart thumped and she swallowed back tears. How had she ended up here?

She leant her head against the car window and let the tears fall. She cried for her mother, for herself, for everything she had done to Darcy, and for what she had lost.

You didn't lose her. You never had her.

"But I could have!" she screamed out in to the stuffy air and hit her head against the window, infuriated and frustrated. All she wanted was a minute of quiet. A minute to herself.

"Oi! Pipe down back there." The officer glared back at her, and she stared him down. She held his gaze as she bashed her head against the window once more. Then again. And again.

"She's fucking losing it. Put your foot down."

They know who you really are, Anja. Darcy knows, and soon the whole world will.

She raised the cuffs on her wrists to her forehead and thumped with everything she had. Every broken part of her poured out as she screamed and cried, clawing and battering the body that kept her prisoner. She felt dizzy and exhausted, could taste blood in her mouth, but she was unrelenting until the voice fell silent and quiet finally descended.

Her body was no longer her own.

Anja allowed it to be dragged and manipulated as the officers processed her through the station and cautiously led her towards a cell.

She registered the odd few words—"need a doctor", "fucking mental", "twenty-four-hour surveillance"—but she was beyond caring. They didn't understand. They never could.

I understood you but then you abandoned me. Tried to replace me with her. Now look where you are.

Any attempt to speak with her, any question asked, any order given, her response was the same.

"Darcy."

"Yes, yes. Darcy. Darcy. Darcy. We get it."

That's all she wanted. All she needed. The frustration of having Darcy kept from her was unbearable. She had suffered in the past, but not knowing when she might see Darcy again was a torture she had never before experienced, and it choked her.

She felt cold. They had given her something. There had been another doctor, a needle, and now gentle hands eased her down on to a hard bed. The light was so bright.

"Darcy."

Footsteps retreated away from her, and she tried to raise a hand to stop them. She didn't want to be alone.

"Darcy isn't coming, Anja." It was the female police officer. "You need to forget about her and think about yourself right now."

She's going to forget about you, Anja. I bet she's so happy to have you out of her life.

Anja turned towards the wall and wrapped her arms around herself, curling in to a tight ball. "You're wrong. She won't leave me here. I know she loves me."

She flinched as the cell door slammed shut and the voice began to laugh.

Chapter 58

Eilidh threw another T-shirt towards her case, and Darcy automatically picked it up and started folding it. "Do you really think it will do either of you any good?"

"I'm working on the basis that it can't do us any more harm." Darcy laid the T-shirt on a pile and caught the next one Eilidh threw. "How long do you think we're going for? That's fifteen T-shirts now, six vests, and twelve pairs of shorts."

Eilidh shrugged. "I like to pack for every eventuality. It's going to be scorching, so I figure I'll need to change lots."

"My mum has this crazy contraption called a washing machine, you know?" Darcy dropped the T-shirt and moved towards Eilidh, slipping her arms around her waist she distracted her from more clothes with her lips.

"Mm... I know what you're doing." Eilidh tried to pull away, but Darcy held on tight.

"Are you complaining?"

Eilidh grinned. "Not even a little." She nodded towards their cases, Darcy's starkly empty compared to hers. "I think you're taking the piss though with only five T-shirts. I don't want to spend this trip doing washing."

Darcy laughed and kissed her again. "Okay, if it makes you feel better, I'll throw a few more in. But anyway, it's you trying to distract me now. Back to Anja."

"Oh yes, Anja. How could I forget?" Eilidh rolled her eyes and continued trawling through her drawers. "You know I'll support whatever you decide, but I'm worried about you going there. I'm allowed to be worried."

"I know, sweetheart." Darcy plopped down on to the bed. "And I love you for worrying. But the doctor thinks it might help her, and I think it might help me too. Which will help us. I've spoken at length with my counsellor and she isn't opposed."

"Really?" Eilidh stopped mid-rummage. "Is she not concerned it might set you back? Who knows what mindset Anja will be in or what she might say. How she might react. Given everything the counsellor has talked to you about, how the mind of a stalker works, the manipulation, the lies, placing her guilt on to you..."

"Aye, I know all that and I'm prepared for it. I understand when she says she loves me that it isn't real. That it can't be. That doesn't make it any easier emotionally to ignore. To forget. Maybe this is another important step towards doing that?"

"Maybe." Eilidh sighed but didn't argue.

Darcy knew it was difficult for Eilidh to comprehend that despite it all, Darcy still held very real feelings for Anja. No matter how falsely constructed Anja's friendship and love had been, Darcy had invested so much in that friendship and still grieved its loss.

"All I know is it feels unfinished. That night is such a blur. The fire, the blood and smoke, Anja in the mud, thinking she was dead. Then she's being whisked away in the ambulance and the police are telling us they'll formally arrest her when she wakes up. That's the last time I saw her. Lying bloodied on the ground."

"After she'd tried to kill you. Let's not forget that part." Eilidh crossed the room and sat close to her, slipping a reassuring arm around Darcy's shoulders. "You shouldn't be feeling guilty about that. In the moment it was all about survival, and I was the one that hit her. You don't owe her anything. Most folk would be shocked you're even considering going to visit her. It's not as if we haven't had a whole heap of shite to deal with since then."

"I know, but that doesn't mean I forgot about her through it all."

"I'm not suggesting you did." Eilidh gestured towards the chaos at the end of the bed and the dressing table laden with holiday paraphernalia. "But look. It's all finally over. We're packing our bags for an epic and well-deserved trip to Australia. Your mum and Olivia are beside themselves with excitement, and we finally get to move on. Together."

"And you think visiting Anja will mess all that up?" Darcy knew part of what Eilidh was saying was right. She knew why she was cautious and afraid of the potential fallout if Darcy went to see Anja. After months of high stress and turmoil, it did feel like they were finally turning a corner and laying ghosts to rest. The time had come to focus on each other and live the life they both dreamed of.

But Darcy knew this was the final piece, and she couldn't head to the other side of the world without seeing Anja one last time. She needed to know what had been real between them, if any of it, and what had been a façade. The doctor had suggested the visit as a way to help Anja move on, but deep in her heart Darcy knew it would likely help them both.

Eilidh fiddled with the zip on a bag and sighed. "No. It's not that. I trust you and know you're not going into this lightly."

She looked at Darcy with such tenderness and concern that Darcy was ready to cave. She hated being the cause of any moment that made Eilidh feel terrible.

"Tell me not to go and I won't."

Eilidh laughed. "As if I could tell you to do anything. Besides, that's not how we work. I'm not going to stop you doing what you think is right. But I'm allowed to have reservations and I'm allowed to be worried about you."

Darcy turned towards her fully and took both her hands. "Okay, then, let's talk those worries out. I'm not going unless you're one hundred per cent on board."

Eilidh met Darcy's gaze and smiled. "It's just…do you know how lucky I feel to have you in my life? After everything. It's as if the tide has turned and it's all finally going my way. Those bastards that attacked me are in prison." She furrowed her eyebrows at Darcy and attempted a stern voice. "You, thankfully, are not."

"Phew." Darcy wiped invisible sweat from her brow. They both knew how lucky she had been to get off with only losing her license for a year, a fine, and a community order. The judge had thankfully taken in to account the mitigating circumstances of that night and Darcy's previously clean record.

"Now it's our time," Eilidh continued. "We get to be happy. I want us to be happy."

Darcy tugged her closer, and they both fell back on the bed where Darcy tucked herself under Eilidh's arm. "I am happy, my brave idiot." She prodded Eilidh's side. "But I still need to do this. You'll see. It'll all keep going our way, and I'll feel a lot better about how things were left with Anja. I'm sure of it."

Eilidh sighed dramatically but pulled Darcy in tighter. "Fine. But only because I love you."

Darcy chuckled and planted a kiss on her chin. "Does that mean you'll drive me there?"

Chapter 59

DARCY WAS NERVOUS. SHE STARED up at the reinforced windows and took a deep breath. Doubt gripped her stomach, and the urge to flee was powerful. Eilidh had tried to make her reconsider one last time, had pleaded with her to wait until after their holiday, but she couldn't. She had to see Anja.

After Anja's arrest, all contact with Darcy had inevitably stopped. Darcy had been reassured any mail would be intercepted and there would be no more phone calls. The silence had come with a sense of relief but also depression. The contact had stopped because her best friend was in prison.

A little of what had occurred had been reported in the news. The fire at the cabin had drawn attention, and predictably more details of the case had gotten out. A female stalker was a rare occurrence, and the level and length of deception seemed to have captured a number of journalist's attention.

Then Anja had gone on hunger strike.

It made the headlines after three weeks when she was hospitalised. Her demands had been relayed via a solicitor—she wanted to see Darcy.

Darcy had refused then. Eilidh's court case was in full swing, and she was Darcy's priority. There had been no question of Darcy abandoning her to satisfy another of Anja's twisted cries for attention.

Then Anja had attempted suicide.

Now the system had her housed in a secure mental-health facility, for a yet-to-be-determined amount of time. She was deemed unfit at present to stand trial for her crimes, and Darcy believed it was the correct place for her. Even after everything, all Darcy wanted was for Anja to get the help and support that had been missing from her life for so many years.

All that Darcy had confided in Eilidh was true. Until she saw Anja, she was unable to move on. To work on putting the pieces of her own life back together. Eilidh had stood solid at her side through it all, offering her everything and anything she needed. Yet Anja still created a wedge between them that Darcy knew Eilidh felt as keenly as she did.

It wasn't for lack of trying on Darcy's part. She wanted nothing more than to lock the Anja part of her life away. To stop asking questions and forget about her, the same as she had done as a child.

But look where that had gotten her. So the memories refused to fade.

No matter Eilidh's objections to Darcy visiting, they both knew it was the only way. It was born out of fear and protectiveness that Eilidh wanted her to stay as far away from Anja as possible. But in the dark of the night, when neither of them could sleep, she knew Eilidh understood Darcy's murmurings of unfinished business. Her sorrow at the loss of her friend. The tears of guilt Darcy had shed and the sick feeling that arose every so often, knowing that Anja resided in a facility she might never leave. Abandoned and alone once again.

It was those thoughts that pushed her on, through the front gate to security. Once processed, she was supplied with a photographic ID. It was strange, as if it told Darcy she belonged there when she would rather be anywhere else in the world.

Anja's doctor entered the reception to greet her and immediately recognised Darcy's trepidation. She placed a reassuring hand on her shoulder. "You're going to be fine. It's natural to be nervous, but if anything should happen there are panic buttons in the room and someone will be with you straight away. You'll have the room to yourselves. It'll be quiet, and you can take as long you need. All right?"

Darcy nodded. "I think so. I'm doing the right thing, aren't I?"

The doctor offered a non-committal smile. "If it feels right for you, then it is. I believe it will help Anja in the long run, but only time will tell. Are you ready?"

Darcy glanced back towards the exit. Beyond it the safety of Eilidh awaited her in the carpark. She wouldn't leave. Instead, she straightened her shoulders and took a galvanising breath before following the doctor towards the visitor's room.

Darcy fidgeted in her seat and sipped some water whilst waiting for the secure door to open. She was impatient to get it over with, yet afraid of the moment Anja appeared. It would be the first time Darcy had seen or spoken to her since Anja had ripped both their lives apart.

She sucked in a breath as the metal lock clunked and the door swung open. Anja was led in by a burly nurse and she instantly sought Darcy's eyes before smiling. He muttered something and she nodded, her gaze never leaving Darcy's, then he left and the door clanged ominously closed.

Anja had lost weight; her face was gaunt and her eyes sunken, but they'd not lost their steely hue. Her hair lacked its usual lustre, and the grey tracksuit she wore matched her pallor. The room settled around them, and Anja stood still, as if waiting for permission to approach.

"Come and sit down." Darcy's voice broke, and she took another measured breath, gritted her teeth. She would not cry. She would be strong. It was the mantra she had recited on a loop as Eilidh had driven her to the hospital.

Anja sat and broke her stare. She looked about the bright visitor's room and studied the view of the hills beyond the hospital grounds. "I haven't been in here before."

If Anja's lack of visitors were meant as a jab at Darcy's conscience, it worked. "How are you?" It seemed a hollow question and one she didn't expect Anja to answer truthfully.

Anja shrugged. "As you'd imagine. They treat me okay."

She seemed serene, almost ethereal in her demeanour, and Darcy wondered if that was the power of the medication and whether Anja could still feel anything.

"Good. I'm glad you're getting the help you need."

Anja's stare zeroed in on Darcy again, and Darcy felt herself shift under its intensity. "If thinking that makes you feel better, fine."

Darcy refused to be baited. She wasn't sure what she would find when face to face with Anja again, wasn't sure what she might say, but an argument was not what she wanted. There'd be no more accusations, no more blame, no ifs, buts, or maybes. It was about hard facts and the feelings that came with them.

Darcy was about to speak when Anja cut her off. "Are you still with *her*?" She bit out the last word, and Darcy felt herself shrink back a little. She knew the topic of Eilidh could be dangerous, but she refused to lie.

"Yes." She kept it simple. There was no need to elaborate, no need for Anja to know anything about her outside life. The doctor had warned her about giving Anja too much information or any kind of hope to cling on to. It would only feed her illness and set them back further in her treatment.

She watched as Anja slowly nodded as if confirming something to herself. She linked and twisted her fingers, picked at the cuticles, and said nothing more. Darcy questioned the merit in visiting when Anja was in such a fugue state, but the doctor had assured her that she would understand and remember it all.

"I came here to tell you something," she began, and Anja's head slowly rose to meet her gaze. "I won't be visiting you again. This is the first and last time."

Anja's eyes widened a little, and her mouth opened and closed. Then her arm was shooting across the table, clutching for Darcy's hand. "Don't say that, Darcy. I need you."

Darcy yanked her hands out of reach and sat back in the chair. "You don't need me, Anja. You need to focus on yourself. You need to get better."

"What I need is you. How many times do I have to say it? That's all I've ever wanted." Her tone was pleading, and it tugged at Darcy's vulnerability and pain. To see a person she'd loved reduced to someone who had to be medicated to get through each day.

"You'll never have me, Anja. You need to hear me when I say that. We're not connected. I'm not the person to make all this better. You are, Anja. Only you can make this better for yourself."

Darcy pushed her chair back. She'd said almost everything she needed and could only hope it would get through to Anja. She didn't think it likely, but at least in Darcy's own mind she'd been clear. She'd snuffed out any lingering fantasy Anja might have in order that she could hopefully begin to move on, to start over.

"Don't leave." Anja's voice was small, imploring. "This can't be the last time." She held Darcy's gaze again, and tears swam in her eyes. There was a look of inevitability in them, as if she knew her pleading was futile but had to try.

"It's for the best, Anja. Seeing me again is only going to keep hurting you, and I never wanted to hurt you."

"I did." The tears fell but Anja didn't look away. "For so long all I wanted was to hurt you. Until I fell in love with you. But by then it was too late. The damage was done and now I've lost you."

Darcy coughed as she tried to swallow her own tears, but it was impossible. When Anja reached for her hand again, she allowed her to take it. They sat that way for a few minutes, and Darcy knew that it was over.

They'd both reached the end.

This would be the last time they would see each other, despite Anja's protests. The relationship they'd shared hadn't been real. The love, the laughter, and the time invested had been for different reasons. Darcy knew that now but still allowed herself a few final moments to recognise the parts that had been real to her.

Darcy's feelings hadn't been imagined. Darcy hadn't lied. She knew her time with Anja would live on in them both forever, for very different reasons.

Anja's love wasn't real. It was obsession and compulsion spurred on by a fantasy. If Anja needed to cling onto that false happiness, that was her choice. Darcy would play no part in it anymore.

But she would offer Anja one last hope, a lifeline, a grain of potential that might help her be well again one day.

"I forgive you," Darcy whispered, before releasing Anja's hand and walking out the door.

Epilogue

DARCY WATCHED AS EILIDH MADE her way slowly through the water, guiding and supporting a laughing Olivia. She had experience of Olivia's condition, and they had spent hours every day of the holiday so far bonding in the pool.

"She's a rare find, Darcy."

A hand squeezed Darcy's shoulder, and she smiled as her mum lowered herself on to a nearby deckchair.

"Aye, she really is. Olivia loves her already."

"And what about you?"

Darcy offered her a wry smile. "Are you kidding? How could I not?"

Liz handed her a cold beer, and they both sighed simultaneously with content. After over a week in Australia, Darcy was finally beginning to relax.

"I can tell you her regular hydrotherapy sessions are nowhere near as fun as this."

Darcy laughed. "Yeah, I'm wondering where this fun Eilidh was when I was grunting my way through physiotherapy."

"I still can't believe everything you've been through, my love. I'm so sorry I wasn't there for you."

Liz reached out a hand, and Darcy took it. She held it tight and reassured her mum not for the first time, and likely not the last. "None of this was your fault, Mum. You've nothing to be sorry for."

"I still should have been there." She wore sunglasses, but Darcy knew fresh tears were hidden behind them. She heard the break in her voice.

Darcy looked away, back to Olivia now screeching and splashing for all she was worth as Eilidh good-naturedly played along. "You were where you were needed most, Mum. Here, with Olivia. I understand. You know I do."

Liz gave her hand a last squeeze before clearing her throat and taking a few deep breaths.

"I still can't believe I talked to her and didn't realise anything was wrong. She was so calm, Darcy. So reassuring. She made me feel better about not being there for you. Said all the right things and she was so friendly. And it was all an act. She gave nothing away that she knew who I was. Who her father was. How can someone be that way? Be so natural at lying and pretending?"

Darcy sighed. She'd asked herself all the same questions. "I can only think it's years of practice. She had to lie to herself, over and over, to get through those miserable times with her mother, and then cope with her death. She had to tell herself something to make it matter. She created a delusion, an alternative version of events that justified what she was doing, and once she had fixated on me, that was it for her until the end."

"It's frightening how easily the mind can trick a person, isn't it?"

"Terrifying."

They were quiet a moment, watching as Eilidh expertly used the hoist and a number of techniques to safely help Olivia from the water into her chair before wrapping her in multiple towels and pushing her towards them.

"That's it. She's exhausted me again." Eilidh reached for Darcy's beer and gave her a wink before taking a long drink.

Liz stood and crouched by Olivia, stroking a palm over her face. She offered her hands, and Olivia began rubbing them. "Time for a nap and a snack, sweetheart." She kissed the top of Olivia's head and took the chair from Eilidh. "I'll leave you girls to it."

Eilidh took her place in the deckchair and reached in to the cool box for two fresh beers, then passed one to Darcy.

"I saw you both talking. Looked serious. Is Liz all right?"

Darcy nodded and grabbed on to the hand Eilidh offered. She tugged at it until Eilidh got the signal and scooted over on to Darcy's deckchair. "She'll be fine. The guilt is tearing her up right now, so I just keep having to reassure her."

"And what about you?" Eilidh scooped her close and peppered her hair with kisses.

"I'm getting there, and this is definitely helping." She directed Eilidh's mouth to her own and sank into the luxury of a leisurely kiss.

They parted, breathless, foreheads pressed together. "I wish we could stay longer," Darcy whispered. "There's a lot of healing to do, and it feels like we should all be together for it."

Eilidh smiled and laid another gentle kiss on her mouth. "You know, I told Sam once that I thought the world had conspired to bring us together again. That it was meant to be me who saved you from that car."

"You did?"

"Aye. And I wholeheartedly believe it. If this is where you need to be, Darcy, then this is where we stay. Besides, I think I could get used to all this sunshine and pool time. I'm having a cold beer at two o'clock, and the woman I love is in my arms. We'll make it work, Darcy. Together."

Darcy was speechless. All she could do was hug Eilidh close and press kisses to her face as happy tears ran down her cheeks.

She believed it too.

About Wendy Hudson

Originally from Northern Ireland, Wendy is an Army kid with a book full of old addresses and an indecipherable accent to match. As a child she was always glued to a book, even building a reading den in the attic to get peace from her numerous younger siblings.

Now settled in Scotland, Wendy loves to explore the country that inspired her writing in between travelling to as many new countries as the calendar will allow. Summers are all about camping, hiking, sailing, and music festivals. Followed by a winter of avoiding the gym, skiing, football, and not dancing at gigs.

She's always enjoyed writing and turning thirty was the catalyst for finally getting stuck in to her debut novel, *Four Steps*.

CONNECT WITH WENDY
Website: www.wendyhudsonauthor.com
Facebook: www.facebook.com/wendyhudsonauthor
Twitter: @whudsonauthor

.

Other Books from Ylva Publishing

www.ylva-publishing.com

Mine to Keep
Wendy Hudson

ISBN: 978-3-95533-882-4
Length: 291 pages (77,000 words)

Plagued by childhood nightmares since losing her mother, Erin embarks on a journey to rural Scotland, hoping to trace her father and put the darkness to rest. When she meets Abigail, they quickly become search partners and together pick apart fact from folklore. Erin takes sanctuary within Abigail's castle walls as her nightmares start to close in. Can she defeat them and learn to live again?

A Curious Woman
Jess Lea

ISBN: 978-3-96324-160-4
Length: 283 pages (100,000 words)

Bess has moved to a coastal town where she has a job at a hip gallery, some territorial chickens, and a lot of self-help books. She's also at war with Margaret, who runs the local museum with an iron fist. When they're both implicated in a senseless murder, can they work together to expose the truth?

A funny, fabulous, cozy mystery filled with quirkiness and a sweet serve of lesbian romance.

Payback
Charlotte Mills

ISBN: 978-3-96324-125-3
Length: 219 pages (76,000 words)

Det. Constable Kate Wolfe is sent to a small backwater, but before she can settle in, something catastrophic happens. There's an arson attack, a dead body, and a missing man to investigate. Not to mention the new boss to stare down. But her growing attraction to Det. Chief Inspector Helen Taylor is the least of her problems when a dumped vehicle in a lake changes their lives forever.

A thrilling lesbian mystery about trying to right a past wrong…despite the consequences.

A Heist Story
Ellen Simpson

ISBN: 978-3-95533-958-6
Length: 315 pages (113,000 words)

Life gets weird for Marcey Daniels when an art thief dies and leaves her a curious and much sought-after book. Suddenly a determined Interpol agent named Wei is sniffing around, along with the mysterious, flirtatious criminal, Kat. Everyone has their own agenda in this intricate suspense thriller. As the double-crosses pile up, can Marcey unpick the trap within the puzzle?

Credits
Edited by Andrea Bramhall and Amanda Jean
Cover Design and Print Layout by Streetlight Graphics

Printed in Great Britain
by Amazon